OPEN
PLAY

ALSO BY JN WELSH

Back on Top Series by JN Welsh and Carina Press

In Tune

In Rhythm

In Harmony

Holiday Novellas

Pining Over You

Gigolo All the Way

Sea Breeze Seduction Series

Before We Say Goodbye

OPEN *PLAY*

JN WELSH

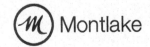 Montlake

Text copyright © 2022 by Jennifer Welsh
All rights reserved.

Published by Montlake, Seattle

www.apub.com

Amazon, the Amazon logo, and Montlake are trademarks of Amazon.com, Inc., or its affiliates.

ISBN-13: 9781542034777
ISBN-10: 1542034779

Cover design by Hang Le

Cover photo © The Cover Lab

Printed in the United States of America

To all the globe-trotters and wanderlusters. May your desire and love for exploring the world never dull.

Chapter One

Ayanna Crawford had stretched her last hamstring and bent her last kneecap for the next ten days. In less than twenty-four hours, she'd be nestled in a business-class seat beside her best friend, Charlotte, on her way to Ireland for a four-day stay. The short girls' trip to Ireland and much-needed break would round out Ayanna's heavy travel schedule, which had included Nashville, Pittsburgh, Ecuador, and Qatar, before the physiotherapy convention in Liverpool. She loved visiting new places, but with her recent itinerary, she'd been unable to see all the sights of the places she'd visited.

"You're all set, Vicki. I'll see you in two weeks for your follow-up." Ayanna watched her last client sit up from her reclined position on the massage table.

"Thanks, Dr. Crawford. I'm excited to get back on the court." Vicki Smith, celebrity basketball player in the WNBA, rolled her leggings down to the ankle.

Though Vicki didn't need assistance, Ayanna helped her off the table, feeling the pull of her oversize royal-blue Rafaela scrubs top and the grip of her conditioned thigh muscles as she used them to aid her client. "You're almost there. Let's see how things look when I see you next, but I'm very hopeful I'll be able to clear you for regular practice."

Vicki beamed. "That'd be great."

"I know you're anxious to be free from all the restrictions and to get out of this routine with me and your trainer." Ayanna held up a hand and soothed in a deeper, professional tone, "I just want to be a tiny bit cautious." Vicki's drive to return to the court was admirable, but seeing it all go down the drain due to not adhering to the routine wasn't what Ayanna wished for her.

"I'll take it. I'm already coming back almost two months sooner."

"Six weeks," Ayanna clarified.

Vicki smirked. "Okay, six weeks."

"I just want to be precise so that any information shared is accurate and that I'm not giving my future clients unreasonable expectations." Ayanna casually slipped her hands in her pockets and fiddled with her ID and office keys. The impressive timeline of this woman's healing had once again confirmed Ayanna's case findings, which gave her more fuel for her upcoming presentation.

"I get it, Dr. Crawford, but you gotta admit that my progress has been pretty remarkable. I don't know how to thank you for working with me."

"Working with you is reward enough." Ayanna shared the sentiment. "You were the one sweating through the process and the pain to get better." What good was her role as physical therapist and her exercises, stretches, and healing recommendations without great, hardworking patients?

"Yes, the pain was real those first few sessions . . ." Vicki let out a burst of air. She slid into her sneakers and grabbed her bag. "Well, good luck in Liverpool."

"Thank you." Ayanna needed all the luck she could get. She'd done many presentations, but this one had her nerves rattled, and she hadn't even boarded the plane yet. More and more people were learning about her research, and with each success story, the demand continued to grow. "Remember your routine. Don't be afraid to push a little bit more, but don't overdo it."

"Got it, Doc." Vicki thanked her again and left.

With the athlete's parting, Ayanna was free. Her files were packed for her meetings, and her presentation for the physiotherapy convention in Liverpool was on two flash drives as well as her laptop, her tablet, and her phone.

Charlotte, Ayanna's best friend since middle school, had come over the other night and helped her pack for their Ireland trip. According to Charlotte, Ayanna needed to "sluttify" her wardrobe, which Ayanna emphatically rejected. A normal exchange ever since puberty had taken hold of Charlotte and turned her into an even wilder child, in contrast to Ayanna's overly intellectual and sometimes overly mannered way of interacting and coping. Nonetheless, their trust of and loyalty to one another transcended their differences, and as such, Ayanna had allowed her friend to add a touch of sexiness to her buttoned-up girls' trip outfits. Given they'd be together, Ayanna was more open to gallivanting around Dublin with Charlotte's choices.

They'd both wanted to go ever since they'd watched *Leap Year*, a romantic comedy classic (in their expert opinion) about a woman trying to propose to her boyfriend on a day that only came once every four years. In fact, she and Charlotte had watched it again on Netflix when they'd been deciding on their itinerary. The main character of the movie was completely ridiculous, but it had given her and Charlotte some good laughs and haunted Ayanna's dreams with the country's gorgeous green landscapes and rolling hills.

A knock sounded on her office door, and Solomon, a therapist on her team, entered. "Hey, Ayanna."

"Hey, Solomon." His dark, nearly black, shaped-to-perfection Caesar haircut contrasted with his tan skin and white therapist coat. He was only slightly lighter than she was, and given their complementary temperaments, they were often mistaken for either relatives or a couple.

Solomon had offered to be the point person for Ayanna's conferences while her admin was out on maternity leave. This increased responsibility had revealed a new talent of Solomon's.

"I've connected with our partners in Europe to make sure they have everything they need, as well as all our patients who are attending to give live testimonials. Everyone has everything they need," he said.

"Flight arrangements?"

"Yes," said Solomon.

Ayanna lifted one brow. "Hotel stays and event transportation?"

"Everything's covered."

She shot off more questions as thoughts continued to surface. "And we responded to the dietary-information requests for dinner to the nutritionist? There's vegan, gluten-free, dairy-free, nut-free . . . ?"

"Yes, yes, and yes."

"Great." Ayanna nodded. "Do you need anything else from me? I sent an email earlier today, but you're the only one who's stopped by."

"Am I?" Solomon parked half of his rear on her desk. "That's surprising."

Ayanna looked down her nose at him. "You better not even imply that I'm unapproachable when I'm leaving the office for a bit."

"You said it, not me," he said.

She pouted.

"No, Ayanna. I don't need anything. I'm all set, and according to everyone, we're polished." Solomon placated her worries a tiny bit, but not by much.

"So they've talked to you?" she asked.

"Is that what I said?" Solomon avoided her eyes.

"Hmm." Ayanna wasn't such a hard-ass that her colleagues needed to hide from her, but she assumed they felt more comfortable connecting with Solomon. She had a tendency to be a little controlling when it came to these events. She wanted things to go well with no surprises. She hated surprises.

"Okay, well . . . I guess I'm headed out." She lingered.

"Need something?" Solomon raised a brow and asked.

Her fingers played with the tiny dark curls at the base of her neck as she scanned her office for wires to her electronics or documents she might have missed. She checked all the drawers. Locked. "I think I have everything."

Solomon crossed his arms. "You're going to do great."

She sighed and this time ran her hand over the short coils of her pixie cut. She'd been working with Solomon for almost five years, and he had been one of her biggest advocates when she'd first revealed her recent research findings on sport ACL injuries. Ayanna had often heard that no one made it to the top alone, and she'd experienced that first-hand with the dynamic people surrounding and supporting her, even though accepting help wasn't always easy. She worked her team hard but always made sure to show appreciation to those around her. However, when she gave a presentation, she stood alone on the stage, a feeling that she knew all too well and that was no less a part of her than the skin covering her body.

Her stomach contracted as if reacting to a drop of something sour. "It's the biggest talk I've done this year. The top researchers, physical therapists, and doctors will be there." She tapped her finger on her desk. Over the past few months, Ayanna had done talk after talk to health professionals, the crowds had begun to grow in attendance, and the locations had become more prestigious. With the recognition came more scrutiny and more nerves.

"You've had loads of practice with this talk. You're more than ready to face this crowd."

"I know, but—"

"Ayanna, you've graduated with a dual PhD from the top school for physical therapy and bioengineering in the country and did not one but *two* postgraduate residencies in orthopedic and sports PT. Not to mention your ridiculous patient schedule, all while researching and developing techniques to decrease recovery time." Solomon recited her qualifications, each one straightening the vertebrae along her spine.

She'd labored over her research. She needed an IV drip of fluids just thinking about the blood, sweat, and tears she'd poured into medical cases, diagrams, sketches, data, and test exercises. Her eye twitched as if recalling the massive amount of reading and analysis that rivaled her PhD studies.

After one of her clients, Oni Moore, had suffered a debilitating tibia fracture and anterior cruciate tear, Ayanna had taken the heartbreaking ordeal personally. With the short shelf life of sports careers, Ayanna wanted to make it possible for athletes—especially women, who were at a much higher risk for ACL tears—to come back from injury in record time and still thrive.

When she'd first tried to share her findings, colleagues had waved her off. She was Black, young, and female, but they didn't know her or her tenacity. She'd raised herself and her little sister, Jada, all while taking care of her mother, whose depression over her father's passing had rendered her unable to take care of herself, much less Ayanna and Jada. Still, Ayanna had overcome the odds, excelling in school to get the hell out of her house. She'd had her moments of doubt, but when pushed, she pushed back and hard. Now she was one of the youngest in the field and leading the way.

She nodded. "I got this."

"There's my girl." Solomon smiled and stood to move closer to her. "Go have some fun in Ireland, and I'll see you in Liverpool."

Ayanna hugged him and grabbed her stuff. "You know what? I'm just going to check in with everyone one more time. Just to make sure that they really don't need anything signed, or have an escalated issue, or need help with a patient, or . . ."

Solomon shook his head. "I'd expect nothing less."

"See you in Liverpool."

◆ ◆ ◆

Ayanna practiced her speech as she drew herself a bath. She had packed her suitcase down to the Q-tips in her toiletry bag, so tonight she intended to relax. Tomorrow morning she and Charlotte would share a car ride to the airport. A layover vacation wasn't Ayanna's regular protocol when traveling, especially before a big event like the Liverpool conference, but still, prevacation excitement tingled through her submerged limbs.

She finished her bath and dressed for bed in her favorite ivory, stretch-knit, bamboo pajama set. Spring was only a week away and had made a few brief appearances, yet the chill of winter still blew through New York. She poured a glass of wine and took the first few sips of the ruby-red liquid. By this time tomorrow, she and Charlotte would be having themselves a pint of Guinness in the place where it had originated.

Ireland's natural scenery and lively cities made it an idyllic getaway. She'd be able to visit some of the places from the movie, like the picturesque Dingle Peninsula, and a couple of others not from the movie that Ayanna had added to her and Charlotte's shared list after scrolling endlessly through blogs, pictures, and travel sites online. Bonus—Dublin, which would be their base for the trip, was a mere forty-six-minute flight from Liverpool and her conference.

She snuggled into her couch and tossed a throw over her bare feet, then pointed the remote control toward the TV and pressed the on button. The news plastered her screen, and within two minutes the anchor had blown through six horrifying stories. Ayanna flipped to the screen saver, and the beautiful Swiss Alps covered in snow floated onto her screen, followed by the Kwahu Plateau of Ghana. She called out, "Hey, Siri. Play Esperanza Spalding."

That's more like it. She was nestling into the plush cushioning of her textured, tan couch when her phone buzzed. Charlotte.

"Hey, girl." Ayanna turned down the music volume and put the phone on speaker.

"Hey." Charlotte's greeting lasted two seconds too long, and her tone didn't hold the same excitement it had over the weekend when she'd dug through Ayanna's closet and joyfully tossed complete outfits onto her bed.

Ayanna sat up, and her glass clinked as she set it down on the side table. "Everything okay?"

"So I, um . . . I have some news."

"What?"

"A work thing came up today, and I really tried to delegate, Yaya. Believe me, I really tried. But I have to go to Atlanta tomorrow." Charlotte rushed on, and Ayanna barely understood the words.

Ayanna couldn't believe the bomb her friend had just dropped. "Atlanta? Not Dublin? No . . . come on. We've had this scheduled for weeks."

"I know, girl." Charlotte's regret saturated those three little words. "But there's not much more I can do about it. I'm the boss, so it falls on me to fix things that go wrong." Charlotte owned an international apparel and footwear brand. Seam and Sole had doubled in size over the last two years and with that gained some influential clients and more brand recognition. If Charlotte said she needed to tend to an emergency, it probably involved a big-name company or client. That information, however, didn't stop Ayanna's chin from dipping to her chest.

All the planning and organizing had been for nothing. Charlotte ditching her for work threw a wrench into their fab plans. Ayanna reined in the feeling that she'd been left on a doorstep, swaddled in a basket with a note pinned to her blanket.

"Charlotte . . ." She didn't want to guilt-trip her friend or make her feel bad, but she still felt abandoned.

"But you're going to have such a great time," Charlotte continued. "I'm so jealous."

Ayanna's hands crowned her forehead, and she squeezed her temples to ease the tension. "What do you mean . . . great time? I can't go."

"Oh yes, you can. Everything's all booked. Changing your flight at the last minute is going to cost you mad bills, and the family at the Airbnb sounds really nice."

Charlotte could sell razor blades to hair if she wanted to, and she positioned the trip as a too-late-to-ditch opportunity. Plus, Charlotte knew Ayanna was a sucker for friendly families, especially given the complete breakdown and dysfunction of her own.

"I don't care about the money. I care that we're not doing this together. We were going to cancel the airplane movies and watch *The Fifth Element* together."

"Aww . . . and recite every word and annoy the other passengers. I'm going to miss watching the scenes with Tricky. He's so fine," Charlotte commented about the actor and musician.

"The tours and plans . . . we were going to have high tea and shit." Ayanna groaned.

"Yaya, I need you to go. You can't bail on this trip. Dublin calls. Plus, it's your civic duty to see the sights, meet the locals, drink as many pints as you can stomach, and perhaps also get laid for the both of us."

"Charlotte."

"Yaya."

Ayanna's hard sigh vibrated her lips. "This is awful."

"I thought we had our Big-Girl Drawers conversation over the weekend. Remember when you claimed your power and you were going to be less organized, predictable, and methodical? You were going to be spontaneous and open to your experiences."

"That was when I was going with you! It's easier to do that shit when your best friend is with you." Ayanna often traveled alone, but this girls' trip with Charlotte had taken forever to schedule. She'd finally started to embrace a more carefree attitude, but now the old familiar Ayanna reappeared.

"I haven't heard you whine this much since that one time I suggested we go hang gliding in Cali."

"More like forced." Ayanna's heart raced at the memory of flying over Lake Arrowhead.

"It was fun, wasn't it?"

"Sure, about three-quarters of the way through, and after I'd literally screamed myself hoarse." Everyone needed a friend like Charlotte. She pushed Ayanna's boundaries yet still gave her a safe place to land and express her emotions—good, bad, and ugly.

"See?" Charlotte sang. "Sometimes, you just need a little shove, boo. Like now."

Ayanna sighed. Running through their last adventure only intensified the gloom surrounding Charlotte's last-minute bail from the trip.

"I really wanted to go with you, Yaya, you know that, but go and live a little. You deserve it. You're always doing the right thing, double crossing your *t*'s and triple dotting your freakin' *i*'s. Go and let loose. Put professional Ayanna in a little beautiful black velvet-cushioned jewelry box—because you's a dime, girl—snap the box shut, and don't open that shit until you get to Liverpool. You need to go, put on those sexy clothes, and find yourself a few Irish boos to get your freak on with."

Ayanna's brows wrinkled. "What is with you, me, and sex all of a sudden?"

"Besides the fact that I know you're not getting any, which I find to be a travesty, it's the best way to kick up a little dust and reclaim your sexy."

Charlotte wouldn't be her best friend if she couldn't read her like her *Gray's Anatomy* book. They'd known each other since the know-it-all age of nine, after all. It wasn't until they were eleven, when Ayanna's father had passed away and the event had ripped her childhood to shreds, that Charlotte had taught Ayanna what true friendship meant.

"I know it's not your fault you can't go. I'm just really bummed."

"Same." Charlotte's voice held a solemn tone that mirrored Ayanna's. "So you'll go?"

"Yeah. I guess." The thrill and anticipation of the trip hadn't completely gone but rather dulled in comparison to the excitement Ayanna had experienced only minutes ago. She really didn't want to do this trip without Charlotte.

"Great," Charlotte yelped. "You're going to have beaucoup fun. I can't wait to hear about it while you're there and when you come back."

"Yay." Ayanna's enthusiasm didn't even hit one on any scale.

"Not the exhilaration I hoped for, but I'll take it."

Chapter Two

Ayanna stepped out of Dublin Airport after a smooth flight. The morning sun, partially hidden by clouds that threatened rain, had no impact on the chilling temperature. She tightened her fitted, fleece-lined parka as the frigid gale whipped her hard enough to knock her hood off. She hid behind her suitcase, to no avail. She gathered herself to find her car at the port information, which was easy enough, especially when she saw *Bowman/Crawford* on a whiteboard.

"Hello," she said and pointed to the name. "That's me."

"I'm to be expecting two of you," the man said, barely flinching at the aggressive winds.

"My companion had to cancel, so it's just me," she explained.

"All right, then. Welcome to Ireland, miss."

"Thank you." She gave a modest smile for fear the cold would freeze her gums. While her driver took care of her luggage, she bundled herself into the back seat and rubbed her hands to warm them.

"It's blustery out," she commented when he slid into the driver's seat on the right side.

"No worries. The wind'll die down by lunchtime. It changes as it pleases. Soon you'll have a fine fresh day," he said. His untamable hair, a by-product of the elements, matched the whiskers he grinned through. "First time to Ireland?"

"Yes. Unfortunately, I'm only here for a short while."

He stopped at a light and craned his neck. "I'll take you on a scenic route, but don't you worry. Everyone comes back to Ireland."

"Is that a fact?" she asked, certain it wasn't, but she liked the mysticism he tried to infuse into the country.

"It is, miss." He pointed out some of the parks and the Docklands as well as a few bars and colleges. They neared Sandymount.

"There's Shelbourne Park Greyhound Stadium, where they run the dogs," Dan, whose name she'd come to learn over their short trip, said.

"What's that?" Ayanna pointed at a looming glass stadium.

"Ah, that's Aviva Stadium, home of Ireland's national football team. Also rugby's played there."

"It's massive." Ayanna stared at the structure that rose above the town and the trees. "You literally can't miss it."

"Right you are, miss."

They finally arrived at a beautiful terra-cotta-colored brick home with a semidetached addition situated in the historic district in Sandymount. Irish ivy crept up to the roof and over the front doorway, and Ayanna felt like she'd stepped into another world. Smoke puffed out the chimney, and the smell of wood burning added to the charm of the house.

"Here we are, miss." Dan brought her luggage to the front door. He inhaled. "Ahh, the smell of Irish peat. Nothing like it."

She went to tip him.

"Already taken care of. Enjoy your stay, miss." Dan bowed as he nodded and backed toward his car.

Ayanna thanked him as he left. She pressed the bell, the ring loud enough to echo outside. The door opened, and a family of four presented itself to her.

"I'm Kathleen McKinley," the auburn-haired woman, holding a lovely carafe of lemonade, greeted. "And these are my boys, Lars and Connell." She introduced her sons, one of whom held a plate of cookies.

"Hello. I'm Ayanna," she returned.

"Greetings to you." Their warm welcome was just what she needed after such a long flight.

"My pleasure," Ayanna said. "H-how wonderful."

"I'm the husband, Paul," a man announced and ducked out from behind Kathleen and the boys to stand beside Ayanna. "Sorry, you're not allowed any of this. Especially not the biscuits."

"Pay him no mind, Ayanna. He's a jokester is all," Kathleen said. Her sons giggled.

Ayanna turned to face Paul, who winked, smiled, and tended to her luggage.

"Would you like a biscuit?" one of the boys asked.

"Why, yes, please." Ayanna plucked one of the small cookies off the plate and took a bite. The combination of sweet cranberry and lemon exploded in her mouth. "Mmm. These are delicious." She'd swear that was the best cookie she'd ever had in her life, or maybe she was just hungry.

"Follow us," one of the light-brown-haired boys said.

"Connell?" Ayanna asked the young boy, who couldn't have been more than six years old.

"Lars," the boy corrected.

"All righty, Lars. Lead the way." Ayanna followed him to the backyard with the family close behind her. The property was surrounded by a gallery of green trees, and though decorative landscaping lined the house and the addition, the flowers of spring were not yet blossoming.

"Here we are." Kathleen opened the door. She and Lars put their treats on the table.

Ayanna stepped into the two-bedroom apartment. The quaint space felt perfect. Ayanna ran her finger over the warm black steel of the modern wood-burning stove.

"Have you ever used a stove like this?" Paul asked.

"Not in a while, but I'm sure I can remember," Ayanna replied.

"I'll show you all the bells and whistles, which are few," Paul said and gave her the two-minute tutorial.

"Got it."

Charlotte had outdone herself in not only picking a place with amenities for the both of them but choosing one in an ideal location close enough to all the happenings in south Dublin.

"I'm taking the kids to the school, but it's a pleasure to meet you, Ayanna. Boys?" Paul urged his sons along. "Anything you need, just let us know." They said their farewells and departed.

Kathleen handed her the keys. "The fridge is stocked with a list of things Charlotte and I came up with. Coffee, some breakfast items, and a few snacks. She was adamant about not wasting time on food shopping so you both could enjoy your time here and eat out when you wanted."

Images of Charlotte bombarding Kathleen with a VIP list of requests plagued Ayanna. "I hope it wasn't any trouble."

"Not at all. It was good fun chatting with Charlotte. Me and my husband offer the service for our visitors." Kathleen moved an elbow-length auburn braid around her shoulder.

"Thank you. I'm sure it's all fine." Ayanna waved her hand to reference the kitchen nook with the red chair and small vase of delicately blooming yellow Irish Hope roses and other colorful wildflowers she couldn't name.

"I hope it's to your liking," Kathleen asked more than stated.

"It's such a sweet apartment. I really couldn't have asked for a more comfortable and charming place to stay." The attachment to the McKinleys' family home had a spacious living room. The morning sun blasted in through the large windows. Ayanna was grateful for the privacy the separate apartment provided. It would be beyond weird if she had to traipse through the house in her pj's.

"I'd hoped to meet your friend. She sounded absolutely lovely," Kathleen said.

"She said the same thing about you and your family. We're both sad she couldn't make the trip."

"Then we must make sure you have the best time here in Ireland." Kathleen moved toward the door. "Now that my husband and the boys are out, it'll be quiet for now if you want to sleep off the jet lag, but I know your stay here is short, so best be gettin' in your sights."

"Thank you, Mrs. McKinley. I appreciate it."

"Kathleen, please."

Ayanna nodded, and the woman departed to the main house. Left to her own devices, Ayanna strolled through the apartment to the bedroom, where she unpacked a few things. A nap sure did sound nice. She pulled up her phone to make sure she remained connected, given the cell phone provider changes. She typed in the free-Wi-Fi password on the fridge. Though the flight had been direct, she felt the travel in her bones and stretched. Messages came through, including one from Charlotte.

CB: WELCOME TO IRELAND, BITCH! DON'T GO TO SLEEP!

"Damn." Though Charlotte was surely asleep in America, Ayanna thought it best to heed her friend's words. Ayanna might have just arrived, but the countdown to leaving had begun the minute she'd touched down. She freshened up and made herself a coffee. She was thrilled to see a Nespresso machine, because it meant she wouldn't have to spend the next twenty minutes trying to figure out how to use another brand. She looked forward to a real Irish breakfast, but her body wanted sleep and her appetite was finicky. Also, Kathleen had already promised to cook the morning meal "right and proper with all the fixings" for Ayanna in the next day or two. If Ayanna wanted an authentic Irish breakfast, that would be her best opportunity. She opted for the fresh soda bread and jam conveniently located in a welcome basket on the kitchen table. Charlotte hadn't exaggerated. The family really did sprinkle charm over every aspect of the place.

When she'd finished her quick breakfast, she freshened up with a shower and change of clothes, called a taxi via the Mytaxi app, and then headed out to explore Dublin.

◆　◆　◆

Ayanna's jet lag nipped at her heels, but she edged ahead of it and rallied to her day-one itinerary. The taxi ride to her first stop, Glasnevin Cemetery, stimulated her more than the coffee had, with lively streets and speeding cars that kept her on the edge of her seat, given the surreal experience of driving on the left side of the road. Thrice, she grabbed hold of her imaginary steering wheel in desperate need for control. Once she relaxed, she took in the small cobblestone roads, charming, brightly colored buildings, and historical pubs. She hadn't even stepped onto the streets yet, and already the old and new clashed in a cultural vibe that surrounded her, even through the glass of the taxi. It didn't take her long to fall in love with the bay city.

She arrived at her destination early for her tour. She'd learned from a young age when traveling to Sint Maarten with her family to do as the natives did to blend in, read directions and instructions before asking questions, and recognize that she was a guest in another country and not entitled to anything. She did all of the above, got her ticket stamped, and soon followed her guide along with the other tourists.

Her black riding boots lightly thudded as she strolled through the curated, evergreen grounds of Glasnevin Cemetery. The sun came out, like Dan, her taxi driver, had promised, and its rays streamed through the huge gnarly trees to kiss the tombstones. She snapped pictures to capture the one image she could stare at for hours. She wouldn't compare it to the famous Woodlawn Cemetery in the Bronx or even Sleepy Hollow Cemetery. Glasnevin was as grand and beautiful as it was haunting and eerie. She listened to the tour director give information about the war and the famous people buried there, like suffragette Constance Georgine Markievicz, writer and painter Christy Brown, and Luke Kelly from the Dubliners, but really, she wished for quiet so she could more clearly hear the wind whistling through the headstones and around the grand monuments. Had she not been so enamored with the tour director's accent, she might have. Or maybe she was just tired.

She took a quick tour of the National Botanic Gardens for fear of missing something spectacular but found herself and a few others heading to the bus stop and hanging out as they waited for the Dublin tour buses.

She rode the Dublin hop-on-hop-off tour bus and hopped off when the Gothic architecture of Christ Church Cathedral drew her off. The grand and impressive structure, in the heart of Dublin's medieval district, framed its interior like artwork. If Charlotte were there, she'd convince the tour guide to forgo the demonstration and let her pull on the blue, velvety cushioned ropes and ring the bells. Ayanna giggled inside. She had a feeling all her trip highlights would have a moment when she wished Charlotte were here.

Outside, Ayanna walked the labyrinth, joining the fun of the stone maze that she witnessed a few young children enjoying. Back inside, she followed the row of pews to offer a donation and light a few candles for Charlotte and her coworkers, as well as for her mother and baby sister, Jada. *Lord knows the both of them need it.* Ayanna was thankful for the tour, but between the cemetery, the flying buttresses, and the heavenward pinnacles of the medieval-aesthetic cathedral, she was ready to rejoin the living.

Back on the bus she listened to the live guides and digital commentary as the vehicle made its way through each point of interest. She was so relaxed her lashes felt like ten-pound weights her lids tried to lift.

"Saint James's Gate, where you'll find the Guinness Storehouse . . ."

"This is my stop," she announced. Had she just realized her stop on the New York City Subway, the doors would have closed and the train would already be moving. Luckily for her, there were many tourists getting off at the popular stop.

She suspected her choice to take a tour of the Guinness Storehouse had something to do with the caffeine coursing through her system, persuading her that a tasting of alcoholic beverages equaled hydration. She didn't realize how many floors the facility had until her tour guide gave their group her welcome and introductory remarks.

"Seven floors?" *That's what you get for wanting to "experience it when I get there."* Ayanna hoped she had enough gas left in her tank to enjoy the various highlights in the impressive pint-shaped glass atrium.

She soldiered on through the tour, learning about the history, ingredients, and brewing processes. At the end of the tour she enjoyed a connoisseur session at a private bar for a tasting of the various varietals with about a dozen other tourists. She savored the first rich Dublin porter, but by the time she reached the fourth "foreign extra," her cheeks ached from the permanent smile on her face, and her blinking had slowed.

"I didn't even know they made this many." Ayanna chatted with one of the tourists as the guide readied to show them how to pour a perfect pint.

"Lucky thing we're not driving," the woman responded, her accent musical and light and unmistakably French.

Ayanna agreed as she blinked to clear her glazed eyes. She'd started to sweat in her multiple layers, so she stripped out of her parka and gray-and-white infinity scarf, resting both items on the back of her chair for the remainder of the tasting. Much better. Earlier, she'd been dressed perfectly for sightseeing. Now, with the libation in her veins, she stripped where she could.

Maybe she should stop drinking, or at least slow down until she got within the vicinity of her lodging. This wasn't her country or her town, and she needed to be alert enough to do things like read maps and signs and understand people.

"Water, please," she asked their guide.

She thought of visiting the Phoenix Park and its zoo, but even a buzzed overachiever, hot off a flight from the US, had her limits. Plus, the animals might freak her out in her mash-up of states. Instead, she opted to find a place where she could grab a bite to eat. And *maybe* get another drink.

Her final hop-off from the bus was back in Sandymount. Now on foot, she walked her booted feet over the stony streets. The energetic vibe of the town whirred with locals doing their daily routine in addition to loads of tourists who snapped photos of the looming Aviva Stadium. Soccer and rugby were the hot sports advertised throughout town on buses, billboards, and digital screens. Ayanna knew of them given the amount of athlete injuries included in her research. However, she neither watched for entertainment nor played either sport. Though her excitement for the stadium lacked luster, she appreciated the beautiful design and the modern yet fluid structure glistening in the sun. The beams warmed her skin, and she soaked in the rays, knowing cloudy days were in her imminent future.

As she continued down the cobblestone roads, she noted an old bakery. *Est. 1941*, Ayanna read and promised herself she'd stop in for some treats to bring back for the McKinleys. She peeked into the many bars lining the streets, a partying college student's spring break fantasy. Her own college days had been filled with books and the occasional party when Charlotte had come up to visit. Ayanna popped into a clothing store and picked out a funky, green, hand-knit, wool loop scarf with dark-brown buttons, for her bestie. Apparently, Ayanna's pastime preferences hadn't changed that much. She'd been shopping for others since she was eleven, and though it was no longer mandatory, it was still second nature.

Ayanna matched the material against her army-green skinny-jeans-covered legs and was trying on the scarf when a saleswoman approached her. "These are of wool from the Aran Islands." The woman showed her how the buttons fastened to make a neat wrap around her neck for a snug fit.

"Oh." Ayanna smiled at the woman.

"They're naturally water resistant because they keep their lanolin oil. Garments knit from this wool were popular among the seamen," she explained.

Ayanna nodded along. "That's great information. I wish that was on the tags where I shop. Most I get on a tag is cotton or polyester. Thank you."

"You're welcome." The woman's cheeks reddened, and she smiled at the compliment.

"They're very special. I'll take it." Charlotte would love it. An additional natural-colored one for herself made it to the checkout counter.

Ayanna's next order of business? Go to a real Irish pub and have a proper pint. It was on Charlotte's list, as was the Guinness Storehouse. Ayanna couldn't help but wonder if Charlotte's main goal for the trip was being drunk the majority of the time.

She found a few pubs named after the area and gravitated to a lively spot. The blue-and-white storefront reminiscent of Santorini lured her in. The hour was late enough in the afternoon and early enough in the day for her to enjoy another drink without feeling like a lush by her standards. Ayanna entered the place, and her stomach lurched at the fragrance of baking bread that cut through any smell of ales on tap. Loud shouts drew her attention to a group of too-handsome men cornered in a space by the bar. Other patrons watched a soccer match on high-perched plasma screens.

She might have been more interested if she weren't tired, hungry, and somewhere between decreasingly buzzed and fully sober. She needed to get food into herself, and soon. Ayanna slid onto a cushioned wooden stool at the bar, and a bartender approached. "What can I get ya?" he asked.

"Can I get an Irish pale ale, please?"

"American, eh?"

Ayanna touched her nose with one hand and pointed at him with the other. "What gave it away? The accent? No, let me guess . . . my order."

"The accent." He smiled. "And your order. Kinsale?"

"Uhhh . . ." Stumped. When had ordering a beer gotten this hard? "What's a Kinsale?"

"It's an Irish pale ale."

"Oh. Yeah, sure." She relaxed like she'd just completed a state exam.

The bartender slapped down a circular cardboard coaster embossed with the bar logo and dashed to get her drink.

"Don't go too far." She gave him a brilliant smile. "I got in this morning, and I'm starving. Can I order food with you?"

"Course." The bartender opened a leather menu and handed it to her.

"This won't take long." She scanned the menu while he pulled her pint. Pizza? That was all that was on the menu. She'd landed in an Irish pub that only served pizza? "Oh, come on," she muttered to herself, but hunger overruled. To make things interesting, she decided on a pizza with smoked chicken and fresh chilies. Ingredients she'd never had on a pie in New York.

"I'll have your pollo caldo."

"Good choice. Comin' up." For a weekday, the bar hopped, and Ayanna equated it to the beginning of happy hour as it filled up. Her bartender returned with a frosty glass.

"What brings you to Ireland?" His blond man bun and matching fluffy beard decorated a handsome, square face. He moved quickly, whether he was tossing coasters down for his patrons or asking her a question. He could have been from Brooklyn if not for the accent.

"Vacation."

"Welcome to our fair, beautiful, and green country."

"Thank you." She lifted her beer to him and sipped.

"Are you visiting alone or with friends?" His fingers hugged the bar rim.

Ayanna struggled with her answer. She'd toured the city solo, and no one but she needed to know that. Her bartender didn't give her any heebie-jeebies, and by how long it took her to answer, any lie would be detected. She blurted the truth. "Alone but staying with a wonderful family."

"There's lots to see and do here. You'll meet loads of people. We'll look after ya."

"Thanks. Anything you suggest I see while I'm here?" She had a list of things already scheduled, but if she had time to squeeze in anything else, she'd rather go with a local's recommendation.

He opened his mouth to speak.

She held up a finger. "Before you answer. Let me just inform you that I've already done a few stops on the big red tour bus."

"I can suggest a place," an energetic baritone floated from behind her.

Ayanna turned her head to lock eyes with one of the too-handsome men she had seen on her way in. Tall with an athletic build, the man parked himself between her and the stool next to hers before he addressed the bartender. "I got it, Liam."

Ayanna tilted her head to meet his light-brown eyes. He sported a five-o'clock shadow, and the messy dark hair on his head peeked out from beneath a heather-gray beanie. He peered down at her off-the-shoulder baby-powder-white knit sweater.

Liam nodded and tended to another patron.

"Thank you." Ayanna pulled her eyes away from him, her yellow-and-white-gold bracelet dangling as she slowly spun her beer glass to two o'clock. A warm, woodsy scent with hints of ginger awakened her like a shot of espresso.

"You're welcome." He set his glass down before holding his hand out to her. "Name's Eoghan."

"Ayanna." She grasped his large, strong hand, his skin slightly cool and damp from holding his pint.

Eoghan squeezed and continued to hold her fingers while a boyish smile splashed on his face, which tugged a similar reaction from her lips.

She extracted her hand from his grip. "So you have some suggestions for me or what?"

"Right." Redness kissed Eoghan's cheeks and made him even more attractive. "Well, deer's Christ Church Cathedral if you're da religious type, but really, the arch'tecture's pretty impressive. If you're wantin' to see da animals, head on over to Phoenix Park. You'll find the zoo here's a bit different from what you 'ave in America." He spoke with a fast and heavy accent.

"Hey, Eoghan? I know you are speaking English," she interrupted, "but would you mind slowing down a little for me?"

"Yeah, I talk a bit fast, even for me mates. I'll Americanize it for ye," he said.

"No, don't do that. I'm sure I'll get used to it," she pleaded. "Just a tiny bit slower, if you don't mind."

"Okay." He lightly pinched his lower lip with his index finger and thumb. "Then, of course, you have the Guinness Storehouse. It's for sure a tourist spot but worth visiting."

Ayanna had to concentrate on listening to the information, because the musical flow of his words delighted her. "So . . . obviously you missed the part where I explained to Liam here that I've been hopping on and off the big red bus with the Dublin pass all day. I'm looking for recommendations that are off the beaten path. I've seen the places you've mentioned so far."

"When did you arrive," he asked.

"This morning," she said.

His eyes popped out of his head. "You work fast."

Little did he know that was her MO. Still, she wanted to branch out for the times when she didn't necessarily want to follow her pre-planned itinerary. She wasn't going to be in Ireland for much longer and was curious about what else there might be to do. "What do you guys do here for fun?"

"Much of the same things you do in America, but there are many pints and matches in between."

Ayanna couldn't mistake the team loyalty that floated around the bar. "Is there a game today? I mean, match?"

"Rugby or football?" Eoghan asked.

Ayanna shrugged. "Uhh . . . let's go with football?"

"All right, then." He squinted at her uncertainty. "No, the football match is the day after next." Eoghan straightened and grew in height.

"And it's sold out too," Liam called from the other end of the bar.

Ayanna gave herself some credit for knowing that *football* meant soccer. "Seems like people are pretty fanatic about football."

He played with the rim of his beanie. "Yeah. Ever been to a match?"

"No. The opportunities to see soccer/football have gotten a lot better, but it's still not as popular in the US as it is here. Except for the women's team, of course." Ayanna sipped her beer.

"Shame," he said. "Well, do you like football, then?"

Ayanna thought about it. "I don't know, really. I've watched a little here and there. I wasn't bored, per se, but . . . you know, I understand it for the most part, but I don't seek it out. Do you play at all?"

Eoghan chuckled, as did a few people around them. "A bit."

Ayanna side-eyed the peanut gallery. "I know it's very popular in Europe."

"All over the world, actually. America is the exception, but like you said, it's changing with your national team, where the women dominate. You should see a match while you're here." Eoghan rested his elbows and forearms on the bar and spun his beer in place. "Would you like to go?"

A football match in Ireland? That had to be the soccer lover's dream. For her, though, it'd be something different to do and a story in her arsenal to share. "That would be cool, but if I heard Liam correctly, it's sold out."

"I can get an extra ticket," Eoghan declared.

"Really?"

"Yep."

Well, if he really could get an extra ticket . . . it could be fun.

"Are ya up for it, Ayanna?" Eoghan's good-looking charm cast a "he's not dangerous at all" spell, and he seemed to be well liked in the bar, but the truth was, she didn't know him.

"We just met," Ayanna said. "I don't know."

Eoghan stood close enough that she heard the sound of his fingernails scratching the stubble on his chin over the noise in the bar. "We've shared a pint, and I've been your trusted tourism guide. We're practically dating, so. At the very least we're friends. Ireland is known for its hospitality, you know." Eoghan nudged her with his body, and the connection made her sit up straight.

"Practically dating, huh?" Ayanna laughed. She had never been one to throw caution to the wind, but when she searched Eoghan's eyes, she felt as though she could trust him enough to at least attend a soccer game. Not to mention the hologram of miniature Charlotte on her shoulder hollering at her about Irish boos and once-in-a-lifetime opportunities.

When would she get a chance to see a soccer game in Ireland again? Plus, a stadium couldn't get more public. "Okay. Yes. I'll go to the game."

"Great. It's at Aviva Stadium. You can walk to it from here."

"Yeah, you can't miss it," Ayanna agreed. The huge stadium towered above the city.

They exchanged information, and Ayanna scrutinized what he'd written in the name field on her phone. "What's that, a code name?"

She showed him and spelled it out: "E-O-G-H-A-N. I don't even know how to pronounce that."

"That's my name. You've been pronouncing it just fine since we've met."

"Oh. I assumed it was spelled O-W-E-N?"

He shook his head. "That's sooooo American," he teased.

"Touché."

"Meet me here at around two," he instructed. "It's important you let me know what you're wearing. It'll be jammers on the day."

"Jammers?" Ayanna asked.

"Crowded," he clarified.

"Oh." Ayanna chuckled and logged the word in her growing Irish-slang file. "That stadium is gigantic. I can imagine thousands of people attend."

Eoghan smiled like he harbored a secret.

"What's that smile about?"

"Nothin'." He again played with his hat. "It'll be an experience. I promise you that."

"Hmmm. I'm trusting you. Don't let me down." Ayanna sipped her beer.

"I won't." His eyes rested on her lips.

His flirt game was tight. She had only known him for a nano-second, and yet here she was blushing, bashful. When her own eyes fluttered to flirt, she acknowledged how much she liked him already.

"Your order." A server presented her meal, shaking them from their playful yet unspoken exchange.

"Oh. Thank you," she said and focused on her food and the fragrant smell of the smoked chicken, mixed peppers, pancetta, cheese, and sauce. The pizza had her wishing she could transport to her lodging at the McKinleys', slip into her pajamas alone, and devour the hell out of that pizza. Instead she pinched the smallest slice and took a careful bite.

"Mmm," she moaned as the flavors exploded in her mouth. *Fuck it.* She took a healthier bite. "Please, Eoghan, help yourself."

"I just had a whole one. Enjoy." He patted his stomach and settled against the bar, which brought him closer to her.

"Oh, I will. It's so good." His body heat warmed her right side. The way he watched her gobble down her food made her pause and drink some beer.

"So, Ayanna, what part of America are you from?"

She dabbed a napkin at the corners of her mouth. "New York."

He arched a high brow at her plate. "And you're having pizza. Here?"

Her hands dropped to her lap. "I know, right? Thanks for judging me, but I get it."

The carefree way he shook his body sent a gentle breeze her way, and the hint of his fragrance tickled her nose.

"I was hungry, and this place looked really cute . . . the rest is history," she said. "Have you ever been to New York?" Ayanna waited for the normal love-or-hate responses about her city.

"Loads of times." He waved a hand as if he commuted there on a regular basis. "It's a great city. I'm to be there for a wedding this summer, but with work it's not likely."

"Oh, that's a shame," she briefly commented. "Well, I'm not in the city, exactly, but I'm not too far from it. Do you know the town of New Rochelle?"

"'Fraid not," Eoghan offered.

"It's a nice town. Most of Westchester County is pretty nice."

"I sort of know some other towns in Westchester but not many. What d'ya do there?" he asked.

"I'm a physical-rehabilitation therapist." Ayanna beamed. She loved her work, but in social settings like this she wished she could be more like Charlotte and just lie.

"Oh, you help people after injuries and surgeries, then?" he inquired.

"Yes." She shoved more pizza into her face. He didn't need to know that she specialized in knee injuries and worked with elite athletes or that those in her field labeled her as the woman with magic hands.

"That's grand," he said.

"Yeah, I love what I do." Ayanna restrained herself from blabbing about her job by mirroring the questioning. "And you, Eoghan? What do you do here in Dublin?"

Eoghan took a long sip of his pint. She didn't think she'd asked him a trick question, but it took him a long time to answer. "I'm involved in sports. I travel a bit with my work, and, um . . ."

An anomaly of a man, with light-gray eyes in stark contrast to the darkest and richest brown skin on a person she'd ever had the pleasure of laying her eyes on, rushed over to them. He gave Eoghan a hard slap on the shoulder. Eoghan elbowed the man in the ribs.

"C'mon, Eoghan. Time to go," the man said. Add another layer of confusion when the most Irish of accents came from his mouth. For Ayanna, experiencing this man obliterated one stereotype after another, and she loved each and every contradiction. He was, in a word, striking. "We have to be at the hotel."

"Is it time, then?" Eoghan addressed his friend, yet his eyes returned to her.

Ayanna enjoyed the interaction between them as she finished her pint. They shared the familiarity of longtime friends.

"Ayanna, this is Pippin. Pippin? Ayanna."

She reached for Pippin's hand. "Hello there, Pippin."

"Lovely to meet you, darlin'," he cooed, and Ayanna blushed at his obvious wink.

Eoghan gave Pippin a bit of a shove. "He's a full-on flirt. Ignore him."

Ayanna rubbernecked at Eoghan. "And you're not?"

"I'm more subtle than this one." Eoghan pointed sideways to Pippin, whose innocent smile stayed plastered on his face.

Ayanna giggled and couldn't help but enjoy their easy conversation. "Well, it looks like you have to head out."

Eoghan hesitated before departing and called to Liam. "Another for the lady. I'll cover her meal as well."

"Oh no, you don't have to do that. I've had a pint, and it was great. I don't need another."

"Don't ever go to an Irish pub for one pint." Eoghan turned his attention back to Liam. "She'll have another."

She cringed slightly at his assumption and fixed her mouth to complain. "I'll be too drunk to see myself back to where I'm staying."

"You'll be grand," he bellowed.

Once Liam set the fresh new pint before her, Eoghan clinked his empty glass with her full one. "Pleasure to meet you, Ayanna."

"You too, Eoghan." Ayanna refrained from hugging him and touched his tattooed forearm instead. "Thank you for your hospitality. It was a treat."

"Hospitality, is it?" Pippin's fists rested on his hips like a parent waiting to find out what else his kid had done wrong.

Eoghan ignored him. "I look forward to seeing you on match day."

"Match day? But—" Pippin started, but Eoghan silenced him by squeezing the trapezius muscle between Pippin's neck and shoulder, steering him away.

Ayanna might have thought more about Eoghan and Pippin's hasty exit, but she had a delicious pizza and frosty pint in front of her. If she had more questions for Eoghan, she'd have all of game day to ask him about them.

Chapter Three

Shane MacCallum changed the sheets on his bed. Something about the smell of fabric softener and the crisp snap of freshly washed bedclothes made him feel normal. Perhaps it was the years of living away from home to pursue his dreams that made him love this so. Either way, as he folded the ends, hospital-corner-style, and spread the duvet on the mattress, he knew he'd have a restful sleep.

He got himself a beer from the fridge and settled onto the couch for the evening. His friends had wanted him to go out on the lash and throw back a few beers, but he had to work. After all, he wasn't part of the team in the traditional sense anymore. He turned on the television to energize the quiet space and looked over his work schedule on his phone to prepare for the next day. Most of his appointments centered on the arrival of the new team doctor. As team liaison, he was tasked with orienting the man to their club and their facilities. Engrossed in the details of how he'd get through a week of practice, marketing, executive meetings, and managing his logistical staff regarding all the player requests and needs in addition to making the new doctor feel welcome, he assessed which responsibilities he could move or skip altogether. None.

Shane jumped off the couch when a knock sounded on his door. He squinted through the peephole and groaned when the morphed mugs of his best friends, Eoghan and Pippin, filled his vision.

"Fuck off. I'm not going out," Shane growled.

"We already went out. Open the door, you dolt," Eoghan grumbled.

Pippin started to bang on the door and sing his name. "Shaneyyy!"

"Why does every Irishman decide to sing when he's locked?" Shane opened the door, and his two inebriated friends, leaning against it, tumbled inside.

"You should have seen her." Eoghan grabbed his head, simultaneously sliding off his gray knit beanie.

"Who?" Shane smothered his face with his hand, not very interested in the answer.

"Eoghan met an American girl tonight." Pippin fluttered his eyebrows.

"She's fucking deadly, man." Eoghan bit down on his hat. "Delicious, golden-brown skin and smells like heaven."

"What else is new?" Shane asked. This American wasn't Eoghan's first pull.

"He invited her to the match." Pippin smirked.

"What?" Shane's eyes ping-ponged between the two men. He tried to keep up, but Eoghan and Pippin had obviously been drinking and skipped all details required for him to understand their tale. Whatever had happened had Eoghan in rare form. "Eejits. Stop. What are you going on about?"

Eoghan recounted the story of how he'd met a woman named Ayanna from New York at the Paddy Bath pub in Sandymount.

"Brilliant. Sounds monumental." Shane's voice tapered. "Why are you here?"

"Take all the air out of the bright, shiny balloon, yeah? Let me enjoy the moment." Eoghan sobered a bit. "You wouldn't come out with us, and you've been scarce now and for days. You all right, mate?"

Shane didn't need his friends checking up on him, but his behavior apparently gave them reason to worry. They used to have good fun together, but now all he did was work, which had made him a bit of a

Holy Joe in his friends' book. "Yeah. Things are just busy. I like it that way. Once things settle down, I'll go out and get locked with ya."

Pippin hit his arm. "We're still a team, right, mate? We still MAKin'."

Shane and Eoghan had met Pippin when they'd attended their first football academy, Glentoran, in Belfast. The three had become close and shared their dreams, disappointments, and successes as they'd striven to become professional players. The three of them had been teammates on the same club when they were younger and referred to themselves as MAKin' in relation to their football positions: midfielder, attacker, and keeper.

Shane nodded. "Yeah. We're MAKin'." They clasped hands, and Shane drew Pippin into a shoulder bump. He did the same to Eoghan.

Pippin had been loaned to a premier club in Barcelona and played for two years before being loaned to another elite club for half a season in England. Now that he was finally back home with the Rovers in Ireland, the trio was together again. They didn't know how long Pippin would stay, because he didn't think twice about going to where opportunities presented themselves. Despite the ruckus he was making at present, Shane was happy to have his friend back.

"So what's the story with this girl?" Shane asked against his better judgment.

Eoghan arched an eyebrow at him, and Shane knew all too well that a big ask headed his way. "I need you to take her to the match with you."

"Me?" Shane pointed to himself. "Why can't she go on her own?"

"She's a tourist, and I overheard that she's not here with anyone. I could get her a ticket and she can go alone, but where's the fun in going to a match by yourself?"

"I go alone," Shane highlighted. "Lots of people do."

"It's part of the experience I'm trying to create for this woman. C'mon. Give us some help."

"Why do I always get duped into your stupid antics?" Shane sighed, already aware of the answer. He didn't play anymore. "Fine."

Eoghan gave him the details on where to meet this Ayanna person. Eoghan grabbed two beers from the fridge, one for himself and the other for Pippin. "Be at the bar at half one, because it'll be jammers. She'll be there at the bar at two, and I don't want her to be waiting. She's expecting me, so you'll have to come up with a reason why I'm not there."

"The match isn't till four. This is elaborate." Shane swigged the beer he'd been nursing for the last hour.

"It'll be worth the look on her face." Pippin chuckled. "She hates football."

Eoghan threw his hat at Pippin. "She doesn't hate it. She just doesn't really watch."

Pippin ducked, a bright grin on his face. "You said she called it boring."

Shane rubbed his head. "Disaster."

"Don't worry about that part," Eoghan reassured him. "Just make me look good, Shane."

"I definitely will, yeah." He definitely wouldn't.

"I'm serious. This woman . . . she's . . . wow."

The alcohol had tranquilized Eoghan with Cupid's mischievous arrow, but Shane would help Eoghan out. "Don't worry. I'll do your deed."

"We'll leave you to your zen. Pippin?" Eoghan rested a hand on the doorknob.

"I haven't finished my beer," Pippin complained.

Eoghan darted back to Pippin and banged the bottom of his beer on the mouth of Pippin's open bottle. Foam erupted like a volcano from the top of Pippin's beer, and he hurried to drink the gushing liquid without spilling a drop. "There you go. Drink up." Eoghan laughed.

Shane chuckled at his friends. "Go home. Take the damn beer with you." He shoved them toward the door.

Pippin and Eoghan departed, and the energy in the room deflated, leaving Shane, once again, in peace. He'd been looking forward to the match worry-free. Just his luck he'd have to spend match day chaperoning a helpless American.

Chapter Four

Ayanna was thankful for Kathleen's suggestions. "Take a hooded jacket with you everywhere rather than lug around an umbrella," she'd said the day Ayanna had arrived. The spastic shift in weather had Ayanna basking in the bright sun and blue skies one minute and then running for cover from rain showers the next. The previous day she'd taken a one-day adventure to Northern Ireland. The weather turned south as their group hit Dunluce Castle, which added to the mysterious atmosphere of the ruins but had them rushing through and ducking the huge droplets. Being there threw her back in time, letting her imagine people on horseback galloping across the palace bridge. She wished they'd had much more time in the north—in fact, days there would have been great—but with her limited time, her itinerary with Charlotte had been organized to get as much as possible out of their quickly passing days. On their venture south the fine weather returned as they toured Belfast historical murals via black taxi. Their driver had told them of a time loaded with political and religious conflict known as the Troubles. She wasn't a history buff, but the mix and depth of the stories and the artistic and colorful murals were among the most memorable parts of her day.

Today, the sun shone, and the fresh but not-too-chilly day remained fine for an outdoor match. She wanted to arrive at the pub by two to meet up with Eoghan on time. Ayanna's already short curly hair didn't mind the rain, but the clothes Charlotte had packed had a way of turning transparent when wet. Ayanna had remedied that with a long-sleeved, fitted white thermal underneath.

The area around the pub crawled with people attending the match and brimmed with team spirit. Here she was, an American on a brief visit, with an opportunity to go. Luck had touched her on this one.

Though she was sure she would recognize Eoghan's tall, athletic figure and dark hair, she didn't see him in the crowd. The night before, she'd texted him what she'd be wearing—jeans, a yellow T-shirt, and a clear raincoat—so she would stand out . . . not that being Black didn't make her stand out enough. Dublin had its level of diversity, but even with color peppered into the salty majority, compared to New York? There was no comparison.

As she waited, a short man of advanced years tried to make his way through the crowd toward the pub. He moved slowly while others around him, some already quite sloshed, sang and carried on, tossing him about. The short, hunched man with his wool English driving cap held his own, but to watch this was more than Ayanna could bear.

She pushed her way through to the man and shielded him. She didn't take his arm because maybe he would appreciate being helped by or touched by a stranger, but maybe not. The older man might gnash his teeth and curse at her for assisting him, but she couldn't help doing what she viewed as the right thing. She'd heard worse from the mouths of her clients when she worked on their injuries and pushed them back to health. She armored her heart, one of the superpowers she'd developed since she was eleven, and decided not to take the possible rejection personally.

To her surprise, the man hooked his arm around hers and nodded his thanks before he plunged forward with her. They arrived at the pub entrance, where he let her arm go.

"Enjoy your pint." Ayanna smiled and began to walk away.

"Thank you, dear." He tipped his hat and went inside.

"You're welcome." She continued her search for Eoghan, but she couldn't find him on first glance. She feared she was about to be stood up internationally.

"Hi. Might you be Ayanna?" A freckled man too delicious to be walking around unattended approached her. He sported a gray hoodie that only emphasized the definition of his shoulders and arms. Wisps of red hair framed his face, matching his thick beard and mustache, and she drowned in his deep-sea-blue eyes.

After she recovered from the velvety bass of his voice, she gave him the New York sniff. "Uhh . . . who are you?" His muscular build showed athleticism, and his height was closer to Eoghan's than to hers. His nose slanted slightly to the left like it had been broken, his bottom lip was fuller than the top, and his mustache was half a shade lighter than his beard. Doing a mental shake, she thought, *If one could call a man imperfectly beautiful, that would certainly be one way to describe him.* Still, she wasn't about to confirm her identity to a stranger.

"You're beautiful," he said to her, and it took a moment before she realized he hadn't just read her internal thoughts.

Ayanna frowned at her own foolishness. "Sorry, do I know you?" Who the hell did she know in Ireland?

"He said you were, but you're right fit." He breathed deeply and visibly, appraising her with a glance up and down. Immediately, he pressed his lips together, and his skin colored as if someone had dabbed red paint on his face.

"Fit?" Ayanna exercised regularly, but she suspected he held a different definition of the word. Her hand snatched the air into a tight fist. "Who are you?" Neck action followed.

"Name's Shane. Eoghan's me mate. I'm to take you to the match."

Ayanna searched around for the Dublin Metropolitan Police in case this Shane person got wily. *And what am I going to say? That this colorful dude assaulted me with compliments?* She straightened, and her hands rested on her hips. "Well, where's Eoghan?"

"He's a bit tied up today and didn't want you to miss the start of the match, but we'll see him there." Shane's explanation didn't quite assure her. "We should get goin' before it's black."

"What? Black?" Ayanna tried to keep up with Shane, but she continued to ask for clarification, especially since she didn't know him.

"Right. American," Shane muttered. "We should go before it gets too crowded to move."

"I don't know you. I know Eoghan." As a matter of fact, she didn't really know Eoghan that well. She flattened her palm against her forehead. "What am I doing? This is how people end up kidnapped or locked up abroad. You know what? I think I'll forgo today's match and see if I can salvage my day of sightseeing."

"No, don't do that. Eoghan will explain himself later. Don't worry. You're safe with me." His freckled hand gently stroked his beard, and the motion disarmed her. "I'm not doing a good job here," he mumbled and rubbed his forehead.

"Not at all," Ayanna agreed.

Liam, the bartender from the pub, poked his head outside. "Shite, it's jammers." Then his eyes settled on the stranger. "Shane?"

Just when Ayanna thought Shane couldn't get any more attractive, he pulled off his hoodie for a brief moment to identify himself and revealed a man bun tied atop his head.

"Liam," Shane replied and saluted.

"What are you doing here? Shouldn't you be inside? You'll get clobbered if you stay here." Liam's harsh whisper added even more intrigue to their current plot. Then Liam did a double take at her and snapped his fingers. "Aya, right?"

"Close enough. Ayanna," she corrected.

"Why aren't you at the match? Eoghan forget about you?" Liam asked, his face contorted with disapproval.

"No. He sent this guy to get me." She pointed sideways to Shane.

"Oh, Red's all right. He's—"

"A friend of Eoghan's." Shane cut him off. "Give her the okay, would you, lad?"

"I think he just did," Ayanna said.

"Please come with me." Shane's sweet plea softened her like warm taffy.

"Your job on the line or what?" she asked.

"Sort of," he said.

This day would prove to be either an adventure or a very bad idea. Why hadn't Eoghan told her that he couldn't meet her and would be sending Shane? A simple text would have sufficed. She worried her lip. "And you say Eoghan's just tied up and will meet us there?"

"Scout's honor. I think that's what you say in America." Shane held up three fingers and smiled down at her, as did Liam.

"Your ass is on the line, Big Red. You, too, Mr. Bartender," she warned, and Liam held up his hands.

"I have to head back in. Come by the bar later, if you can," Liam invited them both before sliding back inside and hollering some undecipherable thing to the crowd inside. They all cheered.

Ayanna evaluated her two options. One, blow off this invite to the match altogether, return to her approved itinerary, and listen to Charlotte beat her up about this for the rest of their lives because this was a once-in-a-lifetime opportunity. Or two, take a chance, go with this dude, hope that both he and Eoghan are on the up and up, and potentially enjoy a premier football match in real life. Ayanna mulled it over and sighed.

"How 'bout it?" Shane asked.

For all her practicality, Ayanna hated nothing more than Charlotte pummeling her with would haves, could haves, and should haves. "All right. Let's do it."

"Yeah?"

"Yeah."

They were at a bar with people and also headed to a crowded stadium, not to mention that if this dude messed with her, she would straight fuck him up, but when in Ireland . . .

Shane moved quickly through the masses, and Ayanna's sensible footwear choice of olive-green-and-white Converse sneakers paid off, because she wouldn't have been able to keep up with him otherwise. To say the stadium was crowded was to say a book had pages. Ayanna suspected that no word for this type of crowd existed in the dictionary. Shane used the term *black* and Eoghan used the word *jammers*, but neither of those descriptions conveyed the feel of the stifling crowd trying to pack itself through the small entrances of the stadium.

"This way." Shane pulled her in the opposite direction of where people were funneling inside.

"Whoa!" Ayanna sidestepped fans and ran a bit to keep up with Shane. "Where are we going? The entrances are that way."

"Special entrance," he tossed back at her.

"Special?" she pressed, her breathing short.

"Yeah. We have good seats."

Soon they arrived at a covert entrance. Shane greeted a security guard by name and then showed the guard a pass. They proceeded through a series of security checks before gaining access to the stadium, all of the guards welcoming Shane.

"What are you, some kind of ambassador?" Her phone buzzed, and she pulled it out of her pocket to find a text from Eoghan.

Eoghan: Sorry, love. A bit tied up. My mate Shane'll take care of you. See you at the match!

It would have been nice had she gotten that message this morning or even half an hour ago. She showed the message to Shane.

"See?" Shane almost bowed.

He guided her down a few long corridors until they arrived at a sign that read **WEST END**. She continued to follow him to a store displaying jerseys and other memorabilia for fans.

"You can't wear that where we're sitting. They'll murder us," he said, eyeing her bright-yellow shirt and cardigan.

"Why?"

"Rival club colors. You'll have to put on a proper jersey."

"Um . . . okay. I certainly wouldn't want to get murdered on my first trip to Ireland." Ayanna started to grasp just how serious fans were about representing their soccer teams. The closest thing she'd ever experienced to this level of fandom was a Yankees-versus-Boston game at Yankee Stadium up high in the nosebleed seats, where die-hard, drunk fans went at it pretty hard core. "Any number or person you'd recommend?"

Shane smirked. "O'Farrell fer sure."

Ayanna shrugged. "Okay."

"Ron, gimme an O'Farrell traditional," Shane said to the clerk. "In a . . ." His eyes settled on Ayanna. "Your size?"

Impressed at his eye control, Ayanna gave him her shirt size. "Medium."

Shane unnecessarily relayed the information to Ron, an average-height clerk, who probably still attended secondary school.

"Friend of yours?" Ayanna jutted her head toward Ron.

"We're buds. Right, Ronnie?" Shane's voice boomed.

"Right for sure." Ron approached with the jersey and placed it on the counter.

Ayanna dug into the slots on her phone case for her credit card.

"We're good." Shane nodded at the clerk, who held up a hand before returning to his business.

"I can't leave without paying for this. It's a nice gesture—" Ayanna started, but Shane was already steering her out of the shop to another location. They'd only been inside for less than a half hour, and loud, cheering fans in green filled the walkways. They arrived at a stadium pub that whirred with the chatter of people, though it wasn't overly crowded. At the bar, Shane ordered a Murphy's stout. "And you, Ayanna? What're you drinkin'?"

"I'll have an ale," she called to the bartender. Her go-to response.

"Smithwick for the lady," Shane added.

Ayanna put the green-and-white jersey on over her yellow T-shirt. The fit was near perfect, with the exception of being snug around her breasts. "Is this your favorite player?" she asked.

Shane smoothed his beard like he'd done a few times since they'd met. "He's pretty good."

"Cool," she said. He obviously had a word-count limit for the day. The difference between him and Eoghan was becoming clearer the more time she spent with him. "So is Eoghan going to meet us here?"

"No, he'll meet us at our seats." He took a healthy sip.

"How long have you and Eoghan known each other?" A question she might have asked before she agreed to come to the stadium with Shane.

"Since we were wee ones kicking the ball around. Oh . . . 'bout age four."

The image of little Shane and Eoghan toddling about with a soccer ball too big for their tiny feet flashed in her mind.

"You've been friends a long time."

"Grew up playing football, fighting, and chasing girls with our friend Pippin," he said. "Eoghan's a good friend. Thick as thieves, us. Made it through a lot."

Her curiosity was piqued at the ambivalence in Shane's tone. Had he and Eoghan made it through good and bad times like her and Charlotte? She snuffed her nosiness and kept to small talk.

"I've met Pippin. He was at the bar when I met Eoghan." *Mr. MIA.* "Did you grow up here in Dublin?" She drank her ale and enjoyed the hoppy malt flavor.

"No. Midwest Ireland, in Limerick." He leaned on a bar, which brought him to eye level with her.

"I wanted to go there, but I don't think I'll have time this trip." She'd seen images of the countryside from north to south and east to west. Four days would give her the CliffsNotes tour, but she had a feeling she'd be back. "I've seen quite a bit already."

"So you're not here long." His eyes focused on her, trapping her in their depths.

She shook her head. "My plans got disrupted the moment I met this missing Irishman. I think you might know him."

Shane smirked. "He has a good reason for not being here."

"Yeah, yeah. So you keep telling me." She didn't mean to give him a hard time, but with Eoghan unavailable to explain himself, Shane was a good target for her not-so-subtle digs.

"Are you looking forward to the match, then?" Shane asked.

"Being able to add in a real football match is a treat. I'm not like these fans here, but this is an experience I can't get anywhere else. It'll be one for the highlight reel. With the crowd and all the security, it feels like a special game."

"It's a World Cup–qualifying match for Ireland. You'll be watching the national team play." He studied her response.

"Wow, are you serious? That *is* special."

Shane nodded, amusement in his eyes.

Even she knew what a big deal anything with *World Cup* attached to it had to be. Why hadn't Eoghan told her?

Shane brought the glass to his lips. She did the same. "Why are you here alone? Do you not like traveling with friends or your fella?"

She fumbled with her words for a bit at his abrupt change of subject. She didn't have to answer, but she wanted to, because Shane's questions harbored neither hostility nor accusations. "My best friend, Charlotte, and I planned to be here together, but she had a work emergency. I don't mind traveling alone."

"And your fella?"

"You mean a boyfriend?"

He nodded. "Your fella." The bass in his voice stripped her of the option of delivering any untruth.

"Oh. Well, I don't have one, or else I wouldn't go to a game with . . . you . . . Eoghan, I mean . . . I still might, but he'd probably be here with me or whatever, you know." She bit her tongue to cease her ramblings. For an instant she wondered who he asked the question for. "Do you have a girlfriend?" she blurted. She played it cool and refrained from slapping her hand over her mouth. What was her problem? He had her all chatty with a pretty thin filter, but the truth was, she wanted to know. Plus, it was only fair that she know his status, since she'd divulged hers, wasn't it?

"No." The corner of Shane's lip curled, and she squirmed under his azure gaze. He finished his stout and ordered a second. "Would you like another?"

"Sure," she said, realizing she'd almost finished hers as well. They weren't allowed to take drinks to their seats, and she didn't think she'd be able to drink all of it, but she needed more ale to make her forget the last part of their conversation and to quench the dryness in her mouth. "And a water, please."

Shane ordered for them, adding a basket of french fries that came with some dipping sauces. "Help yourself to some chips."

She loved all things potato, especially french fries. Her resistance was nonexistent, and the delicious smell of the hot, fried stuff commanded her hand to dive right into the basket. "What do you do here in Dublin, or are you just here to see the game—I mean, match?" Ayanna asked.

"It's fine if you call it a game. You're a foreigner. You'll be forgiven," he said. "I have my hand in a few things here and there, but I also work for one of the local teams, the Dublin Rovers."

"Oh yeah? What do you do?"

"Liaison of sorts." He regarded her snug-fitting jersey. "Are you comfortable?"

Ayanna drew a blank and tried to follow his change of subject. "With what?"

"Your jersey. If you need a larger size, Ronnie'll switch it out for ya."

"I think it's fine. It's just that it's over my other shirt. Why? Does it look crazy?" She'd just met him, but his opinion mattered.

"No. It looks good."

She relaxed but made a note to adjust her clothing in the bathroom. "Thanks."

"Even for an American non–football fan," he teased.

She folded her arms. "You know what—"

Shane's hearty laugh cut her off, and the sound opened her chest as if it had been filled with fresh, cool air. "We should head to our seats. The players will be on the field soon."

"Okay. Lead the way," she said. Her comfortableness with Shane grew by the minute, and curiosity tugged at her. She wanted to know more about him, but they had a game to watch.

Ayanna had never been to a stadium with better seats. She and Shane sat field level, right beside the action. With premium seating like this, they could have been press or celebrities. The enormous stadium with its beautiful oval cover and curving pattern of steel and glass conveyed an element of grandeur. The afternoon sun started to fade, and more clouds grayed the skies, but the bright stadium lights lit the field, adding even more majesty to the place. Horns blew and people cheered for their team and jeered the opposition, singing about their players and how undefeated they were. Ayanna could feel the deafening, crazed energy of the thousands of fans all around her. The violence of some of the taunts had her looking over her shoulder.

"They don't play around," she called to Shane.

"No." He drew her closer to holler in her ear, his touch warm even through her clothing. "We should be okay here, but you'll be wanting to stay a bit alert."

"Noted." She added hand gestures, which distracted her from the heat of his hand spreading up her arm.

A short ceremony of sorts began, and the players walked onto the field, each paired with a child. Her past client Oni Moore had explained it to her once as a way to keep youthful wonder part of the game. Ayanna always thought the gesture endearing. Fans cheered, cameras flashed from everywhere, and excitement built for the match.

"Ahh, Eoghan's here," Shane announced.

Right, Eoghan! "What?" Ayanna blushed as if caught in the act of cheating and peered down both sides of their aisle and behind her. "Where?"

"There." Shane pointed to Eoghan running across the field.

The fans cheered his name and sang. "O'Farrell. We have O'Farrell . . ."

"Holy shit." Ayanna realized whose jersey she wore. "He's a player?"

Chapter Five

Ayanna shoved Shane, and his body swayed. "You knew this whole time?"

"Surprise." He clapped as the players took the field. "It was Eoghan's idea," he said in his own defense.

Eoghan got closer, waved to her, and then gave a thumbs-up to Shane.

"You're in big trouble," she yelled to him but was positive he couldn't have heard a word.

Shane laughed. "I told you he was tied up."

"He said his job involved sports and that he traveled for work," Ayanna said. "Wow." She watched Eoghan's effortless moves on the field. He darted about, making small and quick shifts in direction with grace and athleticism.

Pippin also trotted onto the field in a black uniform, wearing a cross between gloves and mittens on his hands. As he jogged to his goalkeeper position at the net, he pointed at her and then slapped Eoghan's hand in a high five.

"Pip-Pip," a group of fans yelled.

"Hooray," much of the stadium responded. Back and forth they went.

Pippin jumped up and down with impressive air beneath his feet.

"Him too!" Her conversation with Eoghan and his interaction with Pippin now made perfect sense.

"Yep."

The match started, and Ayanna couldn't keep her eyes from tracking Eoghan on the field. The game's intensity stayed cranked to high the entire time with constant cheers from the fans.

"Go-go-go-go-go," Shane hollered as Eoghan dribbled the ball down the field. Ayanna giggled as Shane hunched like he was running on the green grass with the team. Eoghan kicked the ball, something happened because the referee blew a whistle, and the crowd cheered. Ayanna's theater clap wasn't quite in line with the excitement around her. Eoghan had played a role in the good play, and that was a good thing.

"Do you understand the game, Ayanna?" Shane asked.

"Kick the ball into the net. Cheer for the team in green." Though some of Ayanna's clients played soccer, her focus lay squarely on joint mobility and muscle stretching and strengthening. As the agile men ran on the field, hammering their lower limbs and overextending their flexibility, Ayanna saw ligament-tear and muscle-strain prospects. She bit her tongue to keep from blurting out diagnoses.

"Right." Shane stroked his beard. "To enjoy it, you'll have to know some of the rules."

Ayanna rubbed her hands together. She loved learning new things or more about a topic. "Okay, so what just happened?"

"Ireland got a penalty kick because a member of the opposing team touched the ball with his arm." Shane tapped his body from shoulder to fingertip to show her what constituted an "arm."

"So . . . an arm," she said in jest.

A smile broke across his face, and she stored the image to her hippocampus. "You're funny," he said.

"Am I?" She was hard pressed to believe that anyone would think she was funny, least of all her family or her friends.

"Funny for sure," he confirmed. "The player can only juggle the ball with the rest of his body, including his head."

"So someone from the other team broke that rule, and now the players are setting up for a penalty kick?" she asked.

"Exactly."

Ayanna found Eoghan in line as another player kicked the ball. They scored, and lots of running theatrics and knee slides across the grass commenced.

"Are they allowed to do that on the field? They don't get carded or flagged or whatever for that?" Ayanna asked.

"Eh-eh. Not a field. The pitch," Shane corrected.

"I've actually heard that one. My bad."

"The players are celebrating with the fans when they slide or dance or whatever absolutely ridiculous thing they do. It's grand," Shane explained before he continued his lesson with corner kicks and throw-ins when the ball went out of bounds, but Ayanna had questions.

"So the last person who touches the ball doesn't throw in the ball. It's the team who *doesn't*?"

Shane nodded.

"Interesting. Do players ever force a touch so their team isn't the last to touch?"

"Of course. It's not malicious as much as it is strategic."

"Hmm . . ."

"Halftime'll be coming up soon. Would you like anything else?" Shane pointed in a random direction.

"Nah. I want to know more about the game. Do you mind?" she asked. When Shane talked about soccer, his eyes lit up in a way that made him dangerously charming despite his previously economical communication.

"Be happy to." His chest puffed.

During halftime she and Shane had a lengthy discussion about offsides.

"It's not easy to follow. It's the most confusing and complicated element of the game. They don't even introduce it to young players."

"I get that it applies to the opposing team's side, which already seems unfair, but I still don't get it."

He explained it again. "The second to last defender standing offside is closer to the penalty area and can't be running toward the goal before the ball is touched to him. And remember, the rule doesn't apply to throw-ins, but rather as soon as the ball is in play, the rule is back in effect."

Ayanna smacked her forehead. "Still confusing as fuck, and I'm pretty smart. Must be an absolute delight for the referees and linesmen calling the game."

"You're using your words." Shane's pride beamed. "Honestly, it's hard for them to call offsides as well."

"Then why do they even have the rule?" She'd pull her hair out before the second half ended.

Shane's laughter rumbled even over the loud cheers of the fans. "It protects the integrity of the game by protecting the defenders and not giving attackers unfair advantage."

"English, please."

His chest rumbled. "Say Pippin and Eoghan are on different teams? It protects Pippin and doesn't give Eoghan an edge."

"Ahhh . . . that one was really good." She thought he'd make a good teacher or coach. She had all but forgotten about Eoghan and made up for it with strained vocal cords. "Come on, Ireland," she yelled. "Let's go, O'Farrell."

"We want them to win, but a draw isn't a bad thing. At least for Ireland. We're leading in ranking points."

"And here I thought all you had to do was kick a ball into a net." She appreciated the game a bit more.

"We'll make a true football fan out of you."

Later in the second half, Ireland ran down the length of the field, and players on the team passed the ball to Eoghan, who darted aggressively around his opponents. He kicked it to another teammate. Each pass got the team closer to the rival team's net. Several short bouts of wrestling feet with their challengers occurred before the ball was again with Ireland. Back and forth the plays went until a midfielder on the Irish team headbutted the ball into the net for the final goal. Ireland won, and the headbutting player slid through the grass down the field in celebration with the crowd. Eoghan hadn't scored the winning goal, but he'd participated in setting up the play.

She and Shane jumped up and hollered their heads off. They slapped each other's hands with high fives.

"Look at you there, happy and leaping about the place." Shane eyed her.

"That was freakin' awesome." She side hugged him, and all she felt was muscle from a tight set of abs. *Okay obliques.* "Thanks for the expert tutorial. I had a great time."

"Sure, it was great *craic*," he said.

"Now what does that mean? Crack? Spell it."

"No. *Craic*." He enunciated and then spelled it for her. "Good fun." She repeated the word exactly as he did. "Yes, it was."

They shared goofy smiles for a moment longer than she expected. She blamed the hints of blue shining behind rust-red, bushy lashes.

Shane broke eye contact first. "So . . . um . . . Eoghan will need to debrief with the team and get a meal after such an intense match. We'll have to wait a bit before I can take you to him."

"Oh, okay." She'd enjoyed the match so much that waiting for Eoghan was a minor concession.

"I can show you around the stadium if you like. It'll allow the crowd to thin out some before we go."

"That would be great."

When their section emptied, Shane gave her a mini tour. The stadium spanned several city blocks, and though they wouldn't be able to see it all, Shane showed her some of the highlights.

"There are sixty-nine pubs in here or something like that," he said. "Eoghan and I have shared a pint in each one."

"That's a lot of drinks and great conversations as well, I'm sure."

"We've gotten fairly ossified."

"Drunk?" Ayanna took a stab at understanding him.

Shane grinned at her like a teacher to his student. "Well done."

He took her to the top of the west end of the stadium to see the view, and Ayanna came to the conclusion that there wasn't a bad seat in the house. Even from the nosebleeds near the top, the view of the field was phenomenal.

She peered over the rows of seats. "This is really cool."

"I like it up here. It's my favorite place." Shane stared out into the distance.

"Why?" she asked. He gave her a quizzical look, and she clarified. "I mean, it's beautiful up here . . . I don't want to assume—"

Shane stretched his arms out over the back of her stadium seat, and he appeared massive in the smaller seat. "It's peaceful. I like hearing the faraway sounds of people and how music echoes. Mostly when the lights lower and the pitch is bright like this. It's dreamlike. I come here when I need to relax, think, or make big decisions."

She pictured him brooding over a problem here, and her heart warmed. "It's a great spot, Shane. I can see why it's special."

He'd drawn his eyes from the field to meet hers when she heard his phone buzz. Shane checked the notification. The corner of his mouth twitched enough for her to notice. "Eoghan's ready for you."

"Okay." Hesitant to leave the tranquil spot and the intimate conversation, she began to slide out of the aisle. She lost her footing over a bracket that secured the seat before her. She stumbled forward, losing her balance and on her way to toppling headfirst over the row of seats below her. "Whoa!" Visions of blunt-force trauma and a concussion danced in her head.

In a moment an arm hooked around her waist and hoisted her back up with little effort. Frightened at the thought of almost breaking her neck, Ayanna felt her breathing speed up as adrenaline flooded her system, making her light headed. White spots danced across her eyelids.

"Steady there. You're okay." Shane's soft assurance produced a heady effect, and she clutched his arms. He smelled like a combination of fried chips, cinnamon, and beer. She didn't know if she wanted to eat him, lick him, drink him, or all of the above.

She shook her head and blinked, her face inches away from his. She was out of any real danger, yet the pace of her breathing increased. Shane stroked her cheek and repeated, "You're okay."

Ayanna nodded, and the abyss of his blue orbs locked her in place. His eyes shimmered and evaluated her with low-lidded curiosity and something else she couldn't decipher until his face moved toward hers for a brief moment before he pulled back. He continued to hold her steady but at arm's length.

"Let's get you to Eoghan." Shane kept one hand on her waist to usher her out. Ayanna glanced down at his hand, then back up at him, but she didn't swat him away. He removed his hand, and the strange absence of his touch followed.

The silence on the elevator ride down to Eoghan was perfect for crickets. What had just happened? She'd come to match day for Eoghan. So why had she almost kissed Shane? Her brain fired off reasons, from their day together to his entrancing gaze, but she had more control than that. Didn't she? Ayanna longed to fill the tense, quiet air with something witty or funny, but her mind drew blanks. They had enjoyed a great match together, and he'd taught her so much about the game. Maybe she'd confused his obligation to a friend for something more.

When they got out of the elevator, Shane walked with speed to the garage.

Ayanna slid to a halt. "I thought you were taking me to Eoghan."

"I am." Shane about-faced when she didn't follow.

"Then why are we in a garage?"

Shane tossed the key fob from one hand to the other. "We're in the car park to get my car so I can drive you to the training facility. That's where Eoghan will be. It's dangerous for you to meet him here."

"Oh." *Yes, Eoghan. Focus on Eoghan.* Ayanna still didn't move. Shane had elicited some conflicting feelings in her, and she wasn't sure being in a car alone with him was the best idea.

"It's all right, Ayanna. I'm taking you to Eoghan. That's all."

She nodded and followed him to his car. A charcoal-colored Audi SUV.

"This is nice." Her small talk game wasn't quite on point, but she tried.

"It does the job." Shane focused on the roads, maneuvering the stick to change gears on the manual transmission as they went along.

With his eyes straight ahead, she took in his imperfect nose and thick, long lashes. She wondered if he could even see through those damn things.

"Through what?" he asked.

Fuck. She'd said that out loud? Was it the influence of the ales from earlier or the adrenaline that had caused her filter to flee? She cleared her throat. "Your lashes. They're long."

"I can see through them jus' fine. You're safe with me, Ayanna. I'll get you to Eoghan in one piece and as fast as I can." He appraised her quickly. His brows knit and his forehead creased.

"I'm not worried." She tried to keep her mind from speculating and scrutinizing every physical and verbal interaction between them. *Get your life together, sis. He didn't even kiss me.*

Disbelief saturated his grunt.

She kept her eyes ahead, taking in the twilight of the pending night. The brilliance of the city lights shone through the tinted car windows.

"There's Saint Stephen's Green. You can see the Shelbourne Hotel from here. If you have the time, you should go there for tea or dinner." He pointed to the window on her side.

The hotel glowed through the forested darkness of Saint Stephen's Green. Ayanna couldn't take her eyes away from the breathtaking, regal presence of the architecture.

"It's on my list. Charlotte and I were supposed to go together." Ayanna shrugged off the disappointment.

"Go on. Have a good look." The car slowed, and the majesty of the hotel commanded all her attention. She even snapped a picture of it with her phone. Once the building was out of view, the car sped up again.

"Thank you for slowing down."

Shane grunted his response.

Ten minutes later they were at the training camp. After security ID'd Shane and let them in, he parked the car in a spot labeled *MacCallum*. Some players were heading to their cars, while others congregated inside.

"There's Eoghan." Shane exited the car and pointed at the glass portion of the building, the players and team staff funneling through the halls. He jogged around and opened the door for her, and they entered the facility.

Ayanna felt like the smallest person in the place amid a sea of players. Eventually parents, significant others, and friends hovered in the area, waiting for their people. She and Shane waited only a few minutes before Eoghan strolled over to them.

"Hello there." Eoghan greeted them in a pressed, cream-colored shirt and brown slacks. "Sorry for the wait. I had to get something from my locker."

Ayanna's temperature shot up. "You asked me to a football match but seemed to leave out the part about you being a player. Very tricky," she scolded.

The glint in Eoghan's eyes showed pride in pulling off the ruse. "Did you enjoy the match?"

"Yes. It was great . . . what was the word, again . . . craic," she said. "You played well and you all won. Congrats!"

"Craic? Who taught you that?" Eoghan asked and glanced at Shane.

Ayanna winked at Shane.

Shane stifled a laugh while Eoghan's chuckle barely escaped his chest.

"Well . . . ," Eoghan said and eyed his buddy again.

"I'm going to head out," Shane said. "Ayanna, Eoghan will take you home. I leave you in good hands."

"Thanks for helping me pull this off." Eoghan clasped hands with Shane.

"You were right. She's deadly." Shane's gaze washed over her, and he might as well have painted her with a powder brush dipped in pink blush.

Ayanna didn't know if she was meant to hear, but she did, and with hands on hips she asked, "I'm what?"

Eoghan gave her a brilliant smile. "He means you're wonderful."

"Oh." She blushed, then muttered, "Thanks."

Shane chuckled and began his departure, and it hit her that she would never see this red-velvet cake of a man ever again. She rushed over to Shane. "I won't see you before I leave Ireland. Thank you for everything. You were very kind to me, and I had a great time with you." She wrapped her arms around him and squeezed him in a hug.

His body, stiff with surprise, relaxed, and he returned her embrace. "I had a good time with you as well, Ayanna."

Her heart stuttered at the tenderness in his words, whispered against her ear. She pulled away from him and stood by Eoghan's side. Shane left soon after, and Ayanna felt a pinch in her chest as she watched him go.

Eoghan touched her hand. "I'm no good to you tonight, Ayanna, but I wanted to see you home, if that's okay."

Did she feel comfortable having him take her home? Though she'd met him the other day, she'd spent most of game day with Shane. Eoghan played soccer, but that was all she knew—that and that he gave repetitive tourism advice.

Little Charlotte appeared on her shoulder again. *Let that boy take you home, girl. Just don't give him any. Yet.* The ghost of Charlotte's geeky laugh followed before the vision disappeared.

"Yeah, it's okay."

By the time they reached his white Tesla, he was holding her hand. He opened the door for her, and she slid into the sleek black-and-white interior of the minimalist yet also high-tech cabin. She'd never classify herself as a person turned on by a car, but between the blue-black night sky and city lights of Dublin in the distance, she acquired a new fetish. When Eoghan ducked in and gently fastened her seat belt with his too-handsome face inches from hers, she stopped breathing.

"It's tricky sometimes," he said, and she inhaled him, a combination of grass, cucumber, and a hint of cedar.

"Uh-huh." She rolled her tongue in her cheek and tried not to giggle at the move. He had to know that a seemingly new Tesla with a "tricky" seat belt buckle was far fetched, and when his face lingered close to hers, she knew for certain he'd slid into seduction mode. After he closed the door, she ran her hand over the dash and let the seat absorb her into a lavish cocoon.

Eoghan hopped in. "Ready?" he asked and tugged on her seat belt, his knuckles barely grazing midway between her neck and breasts.

She sucked in his fragrance as it filled the interior of the vehicle. She bit back the brimming smile threatening to overtake her face. "Yeah," she said, surprised by the seduction in her voice. The faint taste of the beer she'd had earlier lingered in her mouth, but a different kind of intoxication took over.

On the drive to her place in Sandymount, she worked on stabilizing her unpredictable emotions and recounted the fun she and Shane had had watching Eoghan. "It was a really thoughtful surprise. No one's ever done that for me," she said as they neared their destination.

"I'm glad I can send you back to America happy. But I hope our time is not yet up." Eoghan steered the car, but his eyes quickly fluttered over her. "And, um, nice jersey, by the way." His hands might as well have covered her like the shirt did.

"Thanks. It's an O'Farrell jersey. He played a great game today. In fact, I've been screaming his name for the past few hours."

Eoghan cleared his throat. "Are you flirting with me, Ayanna?"

"Am I?" She needed water to quench her thirst and cool her down.

"Oh yeah, you are."

"Teapot." She pointed at him, then at herself. "Kettle."

"You can't blame me. I've been wanting to see you again. Talk to you more." Eoghan stopped the car outside the driveway and twisted in his seat to face her. "If you're not busy tomorrow, I'd like to take you out."

"It's my last full day in Ireland. I'd planned to go visit Galway and the nearby towns." She had a list of places to see. If anything, she could save some of those trip items for when she and Charlotte could come back here together. Couldn't she?

"I promise to make up for anything you might miss. I have training in the morning for a few hours. Perhaps I can pick you up or meet you somewhere in the city? I'd like to show you around Dublin, and maybe we can work in some of your other locations."

Part of her wanted to decline, as she'd already given him the match today. However, the way his brown eyes warmed her and the lengths he'd gone to surprise her today replayed in her mind.

"I'll think about it and text you before you're done with training."

Eoghan sighed. "Of course, but I'm hoping you'll say yes."

"Thanks again for an exhilarating day." She went to kiss him on the cheek, but they bumped noses when Eoghan attempted to redirect his face and kiss her. She smacked his shoulder and quoted from one of her and Charlotte's favorite movies.

"What?" Eoghan said.

"It's from the movie *The Fifth Element*," she said.

Eoghan repeated the words. "What does it mean?"

"Never without my permission."

He patted his chest. "Sorry. I'll make sure to ask next time."

Ayanna smirked. "You seem sure there'll be a next time."

He licked his lower lip. "Pretty sure."

She pressed her lips together, but their corners curled upward without consent nonetheless. "Take care," she said before leaving to go inside. She started a fire for the chilling night and held two briquettes of Irish peat, one in each hand. She looked at one. "You gonna stick to the plan?" she asked one hand and then addressed the other. "Or live a little?" She shrugged and tossed both pieces of turf into the stove and let the smoke decide.

Chapter Six

Ayanna's smoke trick hadn't worked to help her make a decision about Eoghan, so she phoned a friend. Minutes later, after she'd explained her quandary, Charlotte yelled at her from another time zone. "Fuck the itinerary. This is a once-in-a-blue-moon-type situation. Do you realize the Dublin Rovers are a Premier League club? Sports elite. I literally want to strangle you through the phone." Charlotte took a breath.

"As opposed to . . ."

"Girl."

Ayanna could hear the whirring of Charlotte's Beamer tires and her personal anthem by Lizzo playing in the background. "Okay, okay."

"I'm kind of feeling the 'let me make him wait for my answer' vibe, but bitch, if you don't want to go for you, then please go as my representative."

Charlotte was turnt all the way up, and Ayanna couldn't help but laugh. "Fine. I'll go. He did promise to show me the sights."

"And I hope one of them is his luxury apartment, followed by his bedroom."

"Skank."

"And proud." Charlotte didn't miss a beat. "Did you have fun at the game? That was the stuff of romance movies. He did a lot to impress you."

"Like go to work?" Ayanna teased.

"Ha. Ha." Charlotte's smug response whipped Ayanna's cheeks like a physical smack. "What about his friend? He was sweet to keep you company."

Shane. It would be nice to see him again. A smile tugged at her mouth when she thought of their day together. She might not have appreciated him at first, but he'd turned out to be pretty cool. "Yeah," Ayanna said.

"Do you have time to hook up with him too?"

"Ew, Charlotte! They're friends."

"So?"

Ayanna puffed air through her nose. And that was Charlotte in a nutshell. She only saw opportunities, while so many red flags flapped around Ayanna that she couldn't even keep count.

"What if someone did that to us?"

"They have. In the same club with us literally standing next to each other," Charlotte said, reminding her about that one time . . .

"Shane taught me so much about the game, and we really had a lot of fun. He ordered fries, and you know those are like an aphrodisiac for me, girl, and—"

"You like him," Charlotte interrupted.

"What? No. I'm just telling you about the game." Ayanna's face felt like the sun was beaming down on her.

"No, you weren't. You were all Shane this and Shane that. Matter of fact, you've been that way since you got on the phone. You like him. I mean, he's not my choice for you with the footballer in the mix, but do you, girl."

"I don't know what you're talking about." Ayanna knew exactly what Charlotte was talking about, but what did it matter? How would she see him again? Ask Eoghan for his number? "I mean, he's cute and has nice abs, but . . ."

"See? Look, I don't care who you do, but do one of them."

"I can't with you."

"I just want you to be happy, Yaya. Physically, emotionally, spiritually, and yes . . . sexually too. Pick one and go play."

Ayanna's last boyfriend had been years ago, and it had been eight months and counting since she'd been with anyone. When her desires flared, she'd seek out someone to satiate her urges, but intimacy had taken fourth fiddle to work, research, and speaking engagements. While she placed pleasure in the back seat, love, on the other hand, she'd locked in the trunk of an abandoned car somewhere. The present, however, provided her an opportunity to enjoy herself, carefree.

"I hear you. I mean, this is the best place, right? No one knows me, and I'll be leaving soon."

"That's what I'm talking about. Go 'head with your empowered self."

Ayanna laughed and yawned simultaneously. "I'm hanging up. It's late here."

"Have fun, and don't let me down," Charlotte threatened more than wished her well.

"Bye." Ayanna hung up and readied herself for bed. She took inventory of her day and logged the goodness in her brain's "fun file." She rolled over and grabbed her phone and sent Eoghan a text.

Ayanna: Happy to hang out tomorrow.

She didn't expect Eoghan's immediate response, but just as she laid her phone on the night table, it vibrated an alert.

Eoghan: I'll pick you up at noon for lunch. Would like to take you out for dinner as well if you're game.

"Wow. Lunch and dinner, huh? I didn't realize we were trying to spend the whole day together," she said to herself out loud as she typed a more temperate response.

Ayanna: We'll see.

She had a date with Eoghan—most likely dinner, too, if all went well. Now if only her mind would stop flipping back and forth between brunet and redhead.

◆ ◆ ◆

Shane had had one job. Pick up the girl, take her to the stadium, and let Eoghan impress the American with his match-day shenanigans. Deliver the woman into his friend's arms and leave. That was it.

Then why had he almost kissed her? Why had it been so hard for him to leave her with Eoghan? And why the fuck did her lips and smooth, light-brown skin float through his head like an anchored boat? She wasn't remotely close to his type. He tended to go for long-dark-brown-haired green-eyed lasses with small, delightfully perky tits. Yet he still smiled at the thought of Ayanna's awful jokes, and his heart pounded against his rib cage at remembering her chest pulling against an O'Farrell jersey that he wished were his.

He parked his car and stopped at the lobby to get his mail. He hoped his quick pace would expel the pent-up energy circulating through him. What did it matter? Eoghan would bed her, and she'd be out of both their lives and on her way back to America in no time.

"Good evening, Mr. MacCallum."

"Aye, James."

"Great match today."

"Yes, it was," Shane returned.

"Think Ireland has a chance this year?"

"Ireland always has a chance," he responded. "Good rest to your evenin'."

He ducked into the elevator and rode up to his flat. One thing he still had left from his professional days was his Dockland apartment. He'd considered buying a home with a bit more property, but he had yet to decide if he wanted to remain in Dublin. The location worked for now with his job with the local Dublin Rovers, and he was satisfied with things for the time being.

His current mission, however? Get Ayanna out of his head, fast, and for a slew of reasons, including the top three: she was on a date with his best friend, he had a pact with said best friend about dating the same woman, and she lived in America. What good could come out of any interest in her?

"Blasted." The woman wouldn't dissolve from his mind. He settled onto his couch and turned on the TV. Highlights from the match he'd returned home from played on the news. The two announcers offered additional commentary on the success of the national team and the standings for the cup-qualifying groups.

Like Pippin and Eoghan, he'd played for the Dublin Rovers and the Ireland national team, including playing in the cup-qualifying rounds. Their success and any mention of either should leap to his primary focus, but Ayanna's smiling eyes sparkled at him as if she were in the apartment with him. He leaned forward, his eyes glued to the announcer on the screen.

"The Europa tournaments are coming on fast. If the Rovers maintain their place, then they'll secure their spot . . ."

She does smell like heaven, but in the springtime. "Like flowers," he mumbled. He shook his head and surrendered to the hold she had on his sense and senses.

". . . bringing home a World Cup title next year." He caught the end of the announcer's thought.

Since he and his friends were little ones, they'd dreamed of holding up various cup trophies for Ireland, especially the most coveted one. The dream, though no longer possible for Shane, was one he helped instill in players as a team liaison. He wanted to see Ireland win and celebrate with the players and coaches, but most of all with his friends. Despite all that had happened between him and Eoghan, they were still thick as thieves, just not as thick as they once had been.

He washed off the day, letting the jet pressure beat at the tension in his shoulders and softening muscles. Most would say he was still in good form, but during his days as a player, he'd been in machine shape. Back then, he'd been pursuing his passion and motivating his teammates to do the same. He dressed for bed and cracked open a beer he'd snagged from the fridge. He stretched his right leg and circled his ankle both ways. The injury ached from time to time, depending on the temperature, the humidity, and his activity. The leg that he'd once used to drive the ball into the net as one of the most sought-after midfielders to play the game.

Three years after he'd signed a five-year, multimillion-dollar deal, he'd suffered a career-ending injury. He guzzled his beer instead of reaching for the painkillers that rested on the night table by his bedside. Even now, he longed to be on the field, wished that things could have turned out differently, but after three years without playing, he did his best to stay connected to the game in any way possible.

He expelled the heftiness of the history. With so many overlapping tournaments, in addition to working with a new team physician, he had many long and exciting hours ahead of him. Tonight had been fun, watching a novice experience the game from such a close vantage point. When they'd jumped and cheered, it had made him remember to just be a fan again, not only a member of an organization.

Ayanna.

Why'd he bring her up again? Certain that the only way he'd get her out of his head was to go to sleep, he finished his beer and retired to bed. He didn't expect to dream about her.

Shane woke up grouchy and cursing a beautiful short-haired vixen for his lack of sleep. He met up with the kit man and some of the coaches regarding the team's upcoming match against Derry. He'd be away with Daniel Finnegan, their new head physician, though he'd much rather be watching the match from the sidelines if he could. Shane wasn't sure why he needed to chaperone Finnegan, but he suspected that as player liaison he could be helpful to the doctor. Part of injury prevention included a level of intuition about player needs like R & R or more physical conditioning. Evaluating player personalities and whether some players downplayed or exaggerated minor injuries also contributed. No matter the reason, he'd be accompanying Dr. Finnegan.

Shane texted Eoghan to find out about his evening with Ayanna, for no other reason than he wanted to know.

Shane: How was your date last night?

Eoghan: No date. I was knackered after the game.

Eoghan: Meeting up with her for lunch today and dinner tonight.

Shane's elation that Eoghan and Ayanna had had a short night quickly deflated.

Shane: The whole day?

Eoghan: And night if things go my way.

Eoghan: I'm dead for her, mate.

How many times had he heard that one? The phone creaked in his hand, and if Shane hadn't been convinced of it before, he was certain of it now. He wanted Ayanna too.

Shane: Grand.

Eoghan: Still thinking of where to take her for dinner.

Shane thought of his evening with Ayanna, and only one place came to mind that would make her happy.

Shane: You should take her to the Shelbourne.

Eoghan: Not trying to marry her.

Shane: She mentioned it at the game. Take her there.

Eoghan: Guess it'll do. Still training. Make us a reservation will ya?

The response shouldn't have pissed him off as much as it did. It had been years, but even though he and Eoghan had buried the hatchet, some of the comments, in this case texts, that Eoghan made ticked Shane off.

He typed and erased, typed and erased, sure that on the other end of the phone ellipses kept popping up in his and Eoghan's text exchange.

Shane: Sure. Okay. Have fun.

Shane thanked God for texting, because if Eoghan knew how he really felt about his date with Ayanna, he'd surely box him right in the face.

He packed for his trip and called the hotel to make reservations for Eoghan and Ayanna. He texted Eoghan the time, and then he focused on getting to the airport. Perhaps his travel to Liverpool would abolish any visual of her at Eoghan's flat and help erase the woman who trudged with heavy boots through his mind.

Chapter Seven

Early the next morning Ayanna sipped a cup of coffee and practiced discussing the case studies from her research until Kathleen invited her to breakfast. Kathleen had to get the boys to school but insisted on cooking a traditional Irish breakfast for Ayanna, complete with eggs, beans, blood sausage, and toast.

"We can't possibly send you back to America without you having a proper morning meal," Kathleen said when she fixed Ayanna a plate. The meal was more than she normally ate this early in the morning, but Ayanna's excitement to enjoy the meal had her gobbling forkfuls of the tasty breakfast. All it needed was french fries.

When Eoghan arrived to pick her up at the McKinleys', Ayanna was still stuffed and wished she'd worn leggings with an elastic waist instead of her skinny jeans. Though a driver manned the wheel, Eoghan hopped out and opened the car door for her. She took in his energetic form, from his loose-fitting T-shirt down to his snug jeans.

"Hey, didn't I see you yesterday at some soccer game?" she asked.

"It wasn't me," he teased back.

She slid into the car, and he followed.

"I'm all yours," she said.

"Are ye now?" He was even more handsome when his rascally smirk revealed he was up to no good.

"So where are we going?"

"Are you hungry?"

"Not at all." She explained Kathleen's massive breakfast.

"I also ate after training, but I could have another bite. It's a nice day. How about a walk in Saint Stephen's Green?"

Ayanna had seen the park during her travels but hadn't spent any time inside. "Great," she said. "Is it okay for you to be out in public? You have a driver."

"He's better at getting us out of a situation should a crowd form."

"Oh, okay. But you said that doesn't happen much, right?"

"Definitely."

She squinted at him. Eoghan wasn't her first high-profile rodeo. "Why don't I believe you?"

"Sometimes fans will give me a hard time about plays I could have done better or want a picture or autograph. They hover some, but they don't attack me often. The paparazzi are another story."

"Hmm." Her mouth twisted to one side.

"Let's be off," he said, and they were on their way.

Saint Stephen's Green reminded her of Central Park, only much smaller. Eoghan's driver let them out by one of the entrances. The delightful patch of green was in the densest part of Dublin. She would have loved fewer naked trees, but the green grass and early blooms of red tulips and yellow dandelions sprinkling the gardens still made their walk a bright point.

Eoghan grabbed a bite to eat at a little burrito place.

"Burritos? Seriously? I come all the way from the States and not only have pizza here but also burritos."

"Yeah, they're popular here. There are at least half a dozen places to get them just around the green alone," Eoghan stated. He stood at least six feet, and if his training resembled anything close to the cardio required in his games, then his body blew through calories. She was still stuffed from breakfast.

"Thank goodness I had a real Irish breakfast this morning."

"With all the blood sausage and such?" he asked.

"Yes, and it was very tasty but heavy."

"Good for you, Ayanna."

They strolled for a while until they were deep into the park. The mostly bare trees offered hints of the fast-approaching spring. Tiny buds were forming, and the branches housed songbirds chirping their presence. They found a bench, and though people watched them, Eoghan didn't seem to notice as much as she did. Maybe it was the nerves that had her partaking in Eoghan's burrito.

"I thought you were stuffed. I would have bought you whatever you wanted." He gave her half of a second burrito.

"I don't want that much." She nibbled at a small piece. "Never did I ever think I would be in Ireland eating a burrito with a professional soccer player."

"Never did I think I'd be eating a burrito with an American from New Rochelle." Their repartee and playfulness reminded her of Solomon at her medical institute. He and Ayanna often kept each other alert with bad jokes and wordplay.

"So how long have you been playing professionally?"

"Oh, about ten years now," he said. "I was selected for academy early on and then called up to play in the under-twenty league."

Ayanna had worked with athletes of all types in her career and had seen how playing at that level could take its toll on the body.

"Do you still love it as much as you did when you were younger?" Ayanna took another bite of her burrito.

"I love it still, but it's a bit different," he said. "I'm more focused on winning on a level that I could never comprehend as a boy."

"I get it." Ayanna had never dreamed she'd find a career she loved as much as rehabilitating people with injuries. On the flip side, she hadn't comprehended the hard work, long nights researching, and physical exertion of massaging, stretching, and flexing muscles and joints until she was knee deep in her career. "I've never played sports to that level. Maybe a little tennis and running, just to stay fit."

"Fit?" Eoghan smiled.

"What?"

"Well, when we say 'fit,' here it means good looking. You know, sexy like." Eoghan winked and took a swig of water.

Ayanna did the same and remembered Shane's first comments to her. "Oh." She blushed. She handed him the rest of her burrito, but he fumbled the pass, and the food fell to the ground. They both went for it, and she banged her head into his.

"Owwah!" She rubbed her forehead. "Your head is so freakin' hard!"

"Mine?" he laughed. The heel of his hand massaged his reddening skin. "Yours is harder than Drombeg stone."

"Whatever." She giggled despite the dull ache.

"Here, let me." He replaced her hand with his and thumbed slow circles over the sore spot.

Ayanna sobered from their collision and looked up into Eoghan's face, now inches away from hers. When his hand slid from her head to her cheek, she brought her hand to his but didn't move his hand away.

"I'm going to kiss you, Ayanna," he said.

"Okay," she whispered and waited.

"Are you going to say that thing to me again? About permission?" he whispered inches from her lips, his breath tickling the fine hairs there.

"Not this time."

His lips were soft and warm. They were both tentative for their first kiss, but soon Eoghan's lips separated hers, and she felt the gentle touch of his tongue against hers. He didn't rush, but his jagged breath, flowing into her mouth, signaled his deliberate pace. Their kiss wasn't unpleasant, but she awaited sparks that never came.

"Mmm." He pulled away from her. "You taste like a chicken burrito."

Ayanna couldn't help but laugh out loud. She then made a noise with her mouth as if she tasted something. "Kinda gross, but must say . . . you're pretty tasty yourself."

He grinned and tugged her to stand with him. "I thought I'd take you for a pint."

"Sounds good."

"In Kilkenny." His eyebrows fluttered.

"But that's more than an hour away."

"Right. We should leg it now."

◆ ◆ ◆

An hour and a half later they were having a pint in Kilkenny after Eoghan's driver cruised through the town.

"I grew up not too far from here. I was raised in Limerick," he explained before they landed at the Smithwick's brewery. They took the tour, and a few people spotted Eoghan, but like he'd assured her, they had a quick chat, got a photo or autograph, and then let him be.

"This country is seriously beautiful."

"Filmmakers love it. They filmed plenty of *Game of Thrones* here."

"My tour to Northern Ireland the day after we met did mention that quite a bit when we toured the Dark Hedges. I only wished we had more time there. We were up before the crack of dawn and got back pretty late."

"It's quite the journey. What'd you see up there?"

"We saw a few places. Excuse me while I completely mutilate the county names." She attempted to relay the places she'd seen.

"Ahh. County Antrim and Binevenagh."

She tried, getting tongue-tied in her attempt to sound fluent. "Yeah. That. I also walked Carrick-a-Rede Rope Bridge."

"Grand," he said. "Brave woman."

She sipped her beer and thought of his words. Growing up, she'd experienced much scarier situations than a suspended bridge between the mainland and the little island of Carrick-a-Rede. "Out of all the ales we tasted, I like this one the best. I think I had it at the stadium yesterday."

"It's one of Shane's favorites if he's not downing a stout, but for me, it'll do the job." Eoghan swigged from his glass.

"Shane," she repeated. She did recall him ordering the ale for her. Twice. Her mind shot back to him sharing another favorite of his up in the stands of Aviva, and she attributed the fluttering in her stomach to hunger or the beer.

"Yeah, me mate who took you to the match."

"Yes, I remember him." How could she forget? Before she'd gone to sleep, her mind had finally stopped flipping images of both Shane and Eoghan like a stuttering 8 mm film.

"We should head back to Dublin. Will you let me take you to dinner?"

She took pride in her decision-making capabilities, yet her mind was doing a number on her with Shane and Eoghan. The latter sat with her, took her around Ireland, and showed motivation to "move things along." Her past had taught her to take minimal chances and bet on a sure thing. "Yes."

"Great." He scanned her from her white linen button-down shirt to her high-waisted skinny jeans. "But you can't go dressed like that."

"Okay, then. I guess I'll change. Is there a specific attire I should keep in mind?"

"Wear what you like. You're in Ireland."

"But you just . . ."

He winked at her with a toothy smile.

"You know what? I'll follow my instincts on this one." Why she'd asked this tough soccer player what she should wear was beyond her.

Ayanna dodged her first bullet when she and Eoghan stopped at his apartment so he could change. He invited her up, but she waited in the car and mumbled something about having to make a nonexistent call. She lost her nerve. In the car she used the time to give herself a good talking to and recited, "What happens in Ireland stays in Ireland." It didn't inspire her to bolt up to Eoghan's apartment but instead loosened the reins on her control of the situation. With the driver in the front seat scrolling through his phone, she did the same and thumbed through her pictures from the trip.

Eoghan returned in record time with wet hair. He wore an off-white button-down shirt under a smart herringbone plaid tweed jacket, black trousers, and brown shoes.

"So I think I'll just do a quick change when we get to my Airbnb." She sniffled.

His chest rumbled. "Whatever you like."

She grinned. "Lookin' sharp, O'Farrell."

"Thanks," he replied, and they were on their way to the McKinleys' house.

He smelled like a nutmeg-spiced bouquet that had been sprayed with citrus fruits. The musk filled the car, and she sneezed.

"Are you allergic to me now?" he asked, staring at her.

"No." She sneezed again. "Your cologne is just a little strong." She sneezed a third time and rolled down her window.

"Are you going to be okay?" Eoghan asked.

The driver handed her a Kleenex, and she blew her nose. "I'm sure it'll be fine in a little bit." They drove to her house with Ayanna hanging close to the window and inhaling what fresher air she could get to settle her swelling nose.

On the ride over she dug deep inside herself. Though she didn't quite have a "love 'em and leave 'em" attitude like Charlotte, she never let herself get too attached when she dated. Despite her current drought, she'd have fun, and then it was back to the business of being a medical professional. That was her wheelhouse. So why did asking him inside feel so . . . off?

Eoghan touched her knee. They'd arrived.

"Do you want to come in?" Ayanna tested the question to see the results both from him and within herself.

"Yes."

Her internal reaction wasn't terrible, but she didn't do backflips either. They exited the car and started their walk to the house. Ayanna tried to avoid disturbing the family, but Kathleen's husband, Paul, was steadily sweeping the yard outside, and when he saw them, he immediately recognized Eoghan.

"'Tis O'Farrell at my house." Paul was awed.

Paul had used clearer English with her, but now in full fan mode, he rattled off his words. Ayanna laughed and gave up trying to understand. Paul called for his wife and two sons, Lars and Connell.

Ayanna felt strange introducing the McKinleys to someone they considered a celebrity, but she did. "I have to change. Maybe while I do that, you all can chat."

"It'd be a pleasure," Eoghan said.

Another bullet successfully dodged. Maybe she just needed more time with Eoghan. She was rusty, after all, and navigating a fling in another country and culture. *Just chill.*

Paul entertained Eoghan, and Ayanna relaxed.

She took a quick shower and swapped her jeans for a fitted black dress Charlotte had forced her to pack. When she'd completed the final touches to her makeup, she slipped on her wine-red ankle-strap stilettos with bows at the back. She slipped into her black hooded wrap coat and grabbed her purse before heading back out to reconnect with Eoghan.

Paul held a soccer ball in his hand and was showing Eoghan a stance or play while Kathleen took pictures and the kids watched with intrigue.

Both men straightened when she approached.

"You look lovely, Ayanna," Eoghan said.

"Yes, Ayanna. Very pretty," Kathleen said.

"Thank you." She stood and waited for a moment.

"Well, it's been a pleasure." Eoghan shook hands with everyone and then turned to her. "Ready?"

"Yes." They said their goodbyes to the family.

"Thank you for the treat, Ayanna. It was monumental." Paul beamed.

◆ ◆ ◆

Ayanna's eyes were wide with fascination and wonder as the doormen on each side of the grand turnstile entrance to the hotel greeted her and Eoghan. "Oh my God. You're taking me to the Shelbourne Hotel for dinner?" She stared up at Eoghan, who had just leveled up. "How did you know?"

"How'd I know what?"

"That I really wanted to visit the hotel and have tea or dinner here?"

He scratched his head. "Em . . . I didn't, but it's class, and I promised to show you the best parts of Dublin. You're happy, then?"

She put her arm around his waist and squeezed him. "I'm thrilled."

He hugged her shoulders, and his head pressed against hers briefly as they strolled through the lobby.

The chandelier above illuminated the space, giving the slightly tapered cylindrical white columns at the far end and intersecting gold accents on the ceiling a candlelight mood. She and Eoghan then passed some gray-marbled square pillars, the tops embellished with carved gold capitals that rested just below classic Corinthian-style entablatures. These grand structures stood like guards for royalty on both sides of the lobby. The arched entryway on either side of them led into various lounges and reception, but Eoghan led her with confidence toward the stairs at the far end.

They proceeded to their reservation in the Saddle Room, where a staff member took their coats. Ayanna slid into one of the gold-cushioned booths. "I'm about to have dinner in the freakin' Shelbourne," she muttered.

"Sorry?" Eoghan asked.

Ayanna waved him off. She'd been to nice places before, but this was special. Eoghan had pulled out all the stops for her. She might not be a full-time princess, but tonight, she felt like one.

"Good to see you again, Mr. O'Farrell. Great match the other day."

"Thank you, Tom."

Eoghan had obviously been here before, and Ayanna didn't let the fact that she might not be the first date he'd brought here ruin the experience.

"May I start you off with something from the bar or one of our bottles for the table?" Tom asked.

"Ayanna here is a visitor from America. Let's give her our best. We'll do the tasting menu with the wine pairings."

"A fine choice, sir." The waiter noted their order without pen or pad.

Ayanna had never let a man order a meal for her at a restaurant in all her adult life without her contribution. Obviously, this trip documented a string of firsts. However, her face must have revealed her inner thoughts, and Eoghan shifted in his seat and looked a little abashed.

"I hope you don't mind me ordering for you," he said. For someone who didn't know her, he read her well.

"I do mind," she blurted.

"Oh. I thought that even if you don't like everything on the menu, you can pick and choose what you like or just try a few things."

"I appreciate the thought, I really do, but if it's going into my body, I'd like to have the final say." She finessed her answer as best she could. His sweet gesture had made an impression, and she didn't want him to feel bad.

His feathers seemed a bit ruffled. "We can change the order if—"

"No worries. It's more for future reference." She smiled.

"Got it," Eoghan said.

She peered at the drink recommendations, and one stood out to her. "I would, however, like to enjoy a premeal drink. A Shelbourne Bramble, please," she said to their waiter, who grinned.

"Excellent selection, madame." He then left to tend to their order. A busser immediately followed to pour water for them.

"*The waiter* seems to know you. Do you eat here often?" Ayanna sipped from her glass.

"It's tradition for our team to stay here the night before the last home match of the season, so we're regulars."

"Oh. That must be amazing. I'm sure the rooms here are great."

"Yes. They pay close attention to detail, and the personal touches go a long way. Our team takes over an entire floor. It's quite an honor to stay here, and it's as much a treat for the staff as it is for us."

Her beverage arrived, and the darling little drink with a raspberry skewer on top made her smile. She tasted the gin-based cocktail, and a burst of berries exploded in her mouth as well as tang from the lemon. The sweetness from the simple syrup brought all the flavors together. "Mmm. This is fantastic."

"Yes, it's very nice. I've tried it."

"Want some?" she asked.

He scrunched his face. "I much rather my liquor straight."

"Okay, purist." She laughed, and he joined her.

Their starters were presented, and she enjoyed a goat cheese, tomato, and basil plate. The savory and tart notes brought out the light apple and citrus in the sauvignon blanc that had been paired with the course. She sampled the terrine, and though tasty, the celeriac rémoulade didn't do it for her. "I'll stick with this heavenly cheese."

Over dinner, she listened to Eoghan talk about football, and she chatted about her work, though she stayed mindful of not getting too deep about it. In less than twenty-four hours she'd be in the thick of work, and she wanted to have fun while the break lasted.

"How do you manage your time being on both a local team and a national team? That sounds like little sleep to me."

"I eat, drink, and breathe football. I get it from my father." He scratched his head and reddened. "If my mental is off, he has more than enough passion and toughness for both of us. He knows how to push me."

She watched him closely, expecting to see a kind of appreciation and love for his father, but instead hard intensity etched his features.

"He sounds like a supportive dad." She chose her words carefully, not knowing what response she'd get. In her experience, in most cases, having a dad was better than not having one.

"I guess you can call it that." His chuckle carried a bite she almost expected, and she wondered if they got along well.

She steered the subject away from what she personally knew, from having lost her father abruptly in a car accident at a young age, could bring up traumatic emotions. "It sounds like you work really hard, but you take time to enjoy your life, don't you?"

"Like now? Of course." His boyish smile returned. "I always find time for fun and pints, but the rest of the time I'm practicing, playing, or promoting the sport. During the off-season I get to relax. A little, anyway. I have to keep my figure." He smoothed his hand over his stomach.

She giggled. "Your figure is fine." She indulged in a quick perusal of his abs.

"Wait till you see it up close."

She patted her mouth with her napkin. "That impressive, huh?"

"You've no idea."

Damn if his confidence didn't hatch tiny butterflies in her tummy. "We'll see." Two drinks in, her tongue whipped up a few pretty nice comebacks.

The waiter returned and set their mains on the table, followed by a bunch of words that she disregarded because she was still caught up in Eoghan's abs.

"Do you prefer fish or chicken . . . umm . . . or beef?" Eoghan asked.

"I normally like to have beef when I dine out. Wagyu is my favorite." She tried the beef, and the seasoned, juicy meat melted in her mouth, but the fragrance of the fish blew her away.

"I don't care much for rosemary." Eoghan pointed to the green herbs and lemon decorating the seared plaice.

She forked tender filet into her mouth. "Oh yeah, I'll take this one." They switched plates, and she enjoyed the fish sauced with rosemary beurre blanc, but they went splitsies on the potato dumplings and white bean cassoulet. "Everything is ridiculously delicious."

"Next time, you're ordering." He dived into his food. They swapped drinks as well, as the pinot grigio paired well with the plaice, and the cabernet sauvignon went better with Eoghan's beef.

"Deal." The abstract, possibly future "next time" hung in the air.

While she enjoyed warm chocolate fondant topped with vanilla ice cream for dessert, Eoghan enjoyed a dry white port. The sugar and wine definitely affected her in a mirthful kind of way, and as she licked her spoon with all eyes on Eoghan, the knob on her seduction gauge also turned up. He reached across the table for her hand and intertwined his fingers with hers. "Are you having a nice time?"

She nodded as the cold ice cream slid down her throat. "A very nice night, and dinner was outstanding."

He squeezed her palm to his. "The night's not over yet."

The *more* that he implied thrilled her as well as woke her up. "I'm going to run to the ladies' room. I'll be back." She released his hand.

He tilted his head as his heavy study of her body drizzled over her like the misty rain of a "soft day." "Hurry back."

The bathroom was just as nice as everywhere else she'd been in the hotel. Modern fixtures, a porcelain sink, and gold accents created an upscale feel. She faced herself in the mirror for a good talking-to. "This is all set. You want this," she said as she searched for her lipstick to refresh the color that she'd eaten off during dinner.

Damn right you do, came Charlotte's nagging encouragement. Along with the liquid courage she'd had at dinner, her friend's words again gave her the boost she needed. "Let's go make some good, bad choices," Ayanna said to her reflection.

When she returned, Eoghan was sitting at the bar with another drink in his hand. She sat next to him and rested her knee against his.

"All good?" His hand caressed her leg and slid up to her waist, confirming that he planned to serve up a few bad ideas of his own to go with her bad choices.

"I should take you back to your flat, Ayanna," he whispered in her ear, "but I'd like to take you to mine instead. That all right with ya?"

"Yes." As soon as she said the word, Shane caressing his beard popped into her head. *Whaaat the . . . why now?* Her face ached from her creasing brow. Shane had been dashing in and out of her mind ever since he'd left her with Eoghan. If she said she hadn't been comparing her day with him to her day with Eoghan on a not-so-subconscious level, she'd be lying. Yet here with Eoghan was where she'd chosen to be.

"Are you sure, Ayanna? I don't want you to feel—"

"I am. I want to go with you, Eoghan." She offered him her mouth, and he pressed his wine-blushed lips against hers. She pushed her thoughts of Shane aside. She'd never see him again, and to give him so much importance was impractical and irrational, two characteristics that no one would ever attribute to her.

"Come," Eoghan said and got their coats.

They made their way to the car and slid into the back seat. Silent, tense touches under the cover of darkness made her breathless, in a game of follow-the-leader. First his hand glided up her thigh, tickling her skin, making her breathless. Then she widened her legs for his caress. He followed. She cupped his package, and though he hadn't fully hardened, there was no mistaking his arousal. With her heart racing, she stifled a moan into his shoulder. He responded, groaning his pleasure into her short curls.

"Feck, Ayanna. I'd ride you right here if you'd let me."

No translation needed. "I'd let you if we were alone," she whispered.

"Find your way, Garrett," he hurried on the driver.

She resisted the urge to kiss him. What they'd done in the back seat was already more than she'd ever imagined doing with an audience. On and on they played until they arrived at his apartment. Getting inside proved to be a challenge with their mobile make-out session and Eoghan's slower, less precise movements.

"Let me help you." Ayanna tried to grab hold of his keys.

He swatted her hand away. "Shoo, I've got it."

She laughed, and he brought a finger to his lips. "Shh," he snickered.

She covered her mouth with her hand to snuff an outburst.

Seconds after his key-holding hand circled the hole, it finally slipped in, and he unlocked the door.

Once inside, Ayanna sauntered through the luxuriously large and modern apartment with tentative steps. Eoghan illuminated the mostly white space. Much of the color accents were provided by the wood from the flooring and two tables—one for dining, with a green-plant centerpiece, and another attached diner-style to the kitchen, with a set of black chairs accompanying each one. An overstuffed gray couch decorated the living space, as did a modern chimney with a wood-burning stove at the base, and she hoped Eoghan didn't plan on lighting it, because neither one of them should be handling fire.

"I'm decently merry," he said to her.

"Yeah, you are," she said, proud of herself for even knowing what that meant without having to ask.

Eoghan stumbled over to her and pulled her in close. He buried his head in her neck and nuzzled. Ayanna laughed as she stroked his back.

He spun her and molded the front of his body against the back of hers, the weight of him heavy as he steered her to his bedroom. Eoghan flicked one of two light switches, and a lamp by the bedside glowed onto the charcoal duvet, white sheets, and pillows. Three skylights lined the slanted ceiling, framing the night like picture frames, and she couldn't help but wonder what it would be like to come while staring at the stars.

In an instant she fell face first onto the mattress with Eoghan flattened on top of her. "Eoghan!"

"Whoops," he said.

Her face was smushed into the plush duvet, and her body shook with muffled laughter. She wiggled onto her back, unable to stop her stomach from contracting in fits. "You're a mess."

"I'm sorry, Ayanna. I didn't mean to splatter you across my bedclothes," he slurred.

"So you want me to get off your bed?"

"No, darlin'. I . . ." His hands slid her dress up to her waist, exposing her legs and doing little to temper the heat on her skin or at her center. "I want you out of this."

"You first." She yanked his shirt out of his pants and made quick work of the first few buttons, allowing Eoghan to tug the shirt over his head and toss the garment. Ayanna ran her hand over his chiseled torso. The feel of his muscles against her palm was strong and supportive from the athletic movements he performed daily. "Oh man." She couldn't help evaluating him as a professional in perfect form to play.

"I told you you'd be impressed," he chided.

She opened her mouth to deliver a witty response, but Eoghan captured her mouth, reducing her reply to mumbles. His lashing tongue prompted her to tend to his belt. He released her lips and awkwardly stood at the edge of the bed. "Get you out," he said, referencing her dress, as he undid his belt and pants.

She bridged her hips to ease her dress to her lower back. Sitting up, she pulled the material over her head. "Better?" she asked, as she lay on the bed in her matching dark-chocolate-and-pink bra and panties.

Eoghan's eyes took in her near-naked body. "Definitely." He fumbled to quickly shed his clothes, then fell on top of her to deliver a sloppy kiss to her mouth and chin. He cradled her in his arm and flipped to his back, bringing her along to lie on top of him.

His palm cupped her jaw and his thumb delicately caressed her cheek, all while he stared at her with unfocused pupils. "I've wanted you, Ayanna, since that moment I saw you at the pub."

"I want you, too, Eoghan." This time when they kissed, she lost herself in the moment with him and forgot about her travel the next day, her speech, and her practical life.

Chapter Eight

Ayanna awakened to circles being drawn on her naked stomach. She squinted one eye open to see Eoghan with messed hair and that perfectly handsome face she'd never get used to. The pungent, sour smell of hangover morning breath emanating from his mouth was in stark contrast to his beauty.

"Morning." Mischief written all over his pretty face.

Reality settled over her like dust and moved her into action. Adventures in Ireland had come to an end the minute her eyes had fluttered open, and practical Ayanna peeked out of her box to remind her about her jam-packed itinerary, which started in—she glanced at Eoghan's radio clock on his night table—three hours.

She sat up and swiveled her legs over the side of the bed. She adjusted the bra and underwear she'd slept in before she located her dress and retrieved it. *Thank you, Lord, baby Jesus in heaven, for the small things. What a night!*

She quickly glanced at the Premier League footballer, then slid the dress over her head and stretched back into it. She couldn't have made this up if she'd tried.

"Where are you going? I thought that we could, em . . ." He gestured to the space next to him and rolled onto his stomach, his naked ass rounded to perfection under the sheets. He nestled his head into his pillow, and his bedroom eyes roved over her.

"Tempting, but I have to go. My flight is in a few hours." She plopped down on the bed next to him after donning last night's outfit and ran her fingers through his hair. "I had fun last night. Thank you for taking me around. We got . . . ossified?" Ayanna confirmed with him to see if she'd used the word in the right context.

Eoghan's chuckle vibrated the bed all the way to her rear end. "Not quite, but close . . . and *definitely* me more than you." He held her hand. "I should have been better to you, love."

"No worries. I had an amazing time with you." She kissed his cheek. "I have to go. I'll look for your games."

"I should walk you out." He made no real attempt to get out of bed.

"It's okay. I got it." She headed to the bedroom door. "Take care of yourself, okay?"

"I will. You too." He waved.

Ayanna left Eoghan's flat and welcomed the cooler morning air that filled her lungs. She took a cab back to her lodging and, on her way, itemized the things she needed to do before she had to get to the airport, like pack. Any other time her suitcase would have been ready and parked by the front door.

When she arrived at the McKinleys', a few parting gifts from the family awaited her on the kitchen table. An Avoca woven blanket and Irish sea salt were neatly placed in an Irish bridge tote.

"They remembered." Ayanna had asked Kathleen about the seasoning she'd used in the beans for the breakfast meal she'd made, which had been heavenly and perfectly seasoned.

"It's the Irish sea salt," Kathleen had revealed.

Ayanna cherished the gifts. The McKinleys' hospitality had made her stay in the country even better. She promised herself to send them some American novelties and gifts for the kids when she returned. However, she was sure the gifts would dull in comparison to the soccer superstar's visit.

Ayanna wouldn't see the family, who had plans for the day, but she left them a detailed note and promised to return one day.

She showered off her wild night and dressed in a fitted green ankle-length pantsuit and cream-colored blouse. She finished her outfit with rose-gold three-inch pumps. They were one of Charlotte's creations, with memory foam sneaker cushioning and more space for her toes. They were so comfortable Ayanna could sleep in them. No matter Ayanna's practicality in life, her sharp and sophisticated professional wardrobe even made Charlotte envious. Some might even call it adventurous. She wished she had the same bravery in her nonacademic, nonprofessional life on a regular basis. Here in Ireland and under her fairy slut-mother, Charlotte, she dared to be spontaneous and adventurous. To live in the moment and then bounce like she had this morning with Eoghan and like she did now as she wheeled her luggage to the waiting taxi.

Two hours later, she checked in and flew from Dublin Airport to Liverpool's John Lennon Airport. Having endured Eoghan's drunken snores for most of the night, Ayanna rested her eyes for the short flight after reviewing her notes for her presentation. When her lids closed, she remembered her time in Dublin.

Her family and coworkers depended on her practicality and her track record of doing the right thing, getting things done, and making the best decisions for optimal results. In her field, people looked up to her professionalism, so when she'd had the opportunity to gallivant around Dublin, she'd taken it and let loose. Her mind scanned the events, and she searched for her best memory. Her eyes flew open when it wasn't Eoghan's face that popped up into her mind but Shane's—at Aviva Stadium. She let the image of him resonate and wondered what it would have been like and what might have happened if she had let him kiss her up there in the stands.

The hotel hummed with guests she recognized, as well as camera-toting tourists dressed as the famous Beatle who'd helped put Liverpool on the map. She hadn't seen nor would she see much of the modern city. It had only a touch of the medieval excellence of Dublin, but as she dragged her luggage through the lobby, she still wished she had even a little time to see the city.

"Dr. Crawford," a man called to her as he rushed over, and Ayanna immediately turned on her heel.

"Hello," she greeted.

"I'm excited to hear your talk. I was wondering if I can get a little time with you to discuss a patient." He pushed his dark-rimmed glasses up to the bridge of his nose. "I know you're busy . . . have you just arrived?"

"Yes"—she indicated her luggage—"but I'll be happy to discuss further with you just as soon as I settle in. Do you have a card?" she asked.

"Absolutely." He pulled one out of the inside pocket of his suit and handed it to her.

"Great. We'll talk soon." She took it and excused herself to check in.

In her room she rehearsed her speech one final time, certain she'd dream about it even after her keynote that evening. She didn't get too comfortable, as her stay at the hotel only extended for two nights, with a schedule full of meetings and a workshop she'd conduct. After hanging a few items and retrieving her toiletries to freshen up after the flight, Ayanna plopped into a chair that hissed under her weight. She took a few deep, cleansing breaths to catch up with this new reality. She stared out the window at the expanse of historical Stanley Dock. The industrial views, a flashback to the past, meshed with the deluxe contemporary comforts of her room, and it took her a moment to fully step into what she had to do.

"People are relying on you. Show up," she said to the room.

The elevator ride down gave her a few last peaceful moments to fully transition back to Dr. Ayanna Crawford and break ties with her

Ireland-gallivanting alter ego. She strutted to the conference area, passing the bar and taking in the brick ceilings and archways that gave the place a loft-style feel. A few twists and turns later, she reached the conference room. The house was packed. The room hummed with bigwig investors, professional sports coaches, team doctors, and therapists from all over the world. She found her colleagues from her institute in New York, and relief melted the tension in her shoulders.

"I hope you got some rest in Ireland. This could be a tough crowd once questions start up," said Lenny, one of the therapist assistants from her institute.

"Eh." She flipped her hand a few times. She'd given talks before, but this was the biggest by far and saturated with skeptics and critics as well as those who hailed, praised, and promoted her work, all from the top medical institutions. She could feel the warmth and the chill from the men and women in the room. Perhaps she'd be able to convert the doubters and reinforce the supporters.

"You know this stuff, Ayanna. Hell, half of the therapies we use now you developed or improved. It's why they call you the miracle hands. Don't let the heavies in the room intimidate you," Solomon chimed in.

"You're right." Ayanna's chest inflated from the encouragement, but the stiffness in her neck and shoulders returned.

"Truthfully, Ayanna, I'd be scared shitless too!" Lenny patted her shoulder.

The crease in her brow deepened, and her head ached. "Not helpful."

"They're getting ready to start. Knock 'em dead," he said.

Ayanna side-eyed Lenny as someone from the convention staff ushered her to her seat in the front row. A few minutes later the program started, and soon the moderator welcomed Ayanna to the stage. She delivered her speech like she'd practiced and presented the case studies from the athletes and patients she worked with. Oohs and aahs floated during her explanations, and attendees scribbled furiously in their note-books and journals.

Once her presentation ended, she fielded questions from colleagues who not only wanted to get their hands on her research findings but also wanted to work with her at the institute or apply for residency spots.

Soon, the question-and-answer session came to a close, and Ayanna shook hands with people who thanked her for her research and presentation. Others wanted more of her time and information. The convention staff ushered her through a thicket of attendees and reminded those who approached her of their appointments with her over the next few days.

Ayanna spotted Dr. Daniel Finnegan, an Irish colleague who she'd worked with over the years when he'd visited their facility in New York. Daniel had been a supporter of her theories and always willing to help.

"Daniel." Ayanna shook his hand when he neared.

"Ayanna, always a pleasure to see you. Fantastic presentation. I didn't think the physios would let you off the stage." He gestured toward the podium. "It's good to see that some of the cases we tackled together were included in the study."

"Well," she said, patting his shoulder, "as I've told you often, I value your contributions."

"Thank you for the credit. Working with you is always a breath of fresh air. Creative and innovative," Daniel noted.

"Speaking of work, congratulations on your recent assignment. I hear that you've been hired as the lead physician for a sports team."

"Thank you." Daniel's pride splotched his cheeks.

"Look at you." She smiled. "I take it you're happy."

"Very."

"My travel schedule has me spinning in circles—I can't even remember what sport. What team hired you?"

Daniel chuckled and strolled with her away from the crowds. "You're lucky we're friends, or I might take it personally," he teased.

"I know. It's horrible." She shook her head. "Tell me all the details."

"I'm with a football team in Ireland. By 'football' I mean soccer."

"Yes, of course." Ayanna nodded.

"I didn't expect to land with a football team but thought I'd continue in a private practice or something similar. But when the Dublin Rovers got hold of my CV and offered me a very lucrative contract, I couldn't pass it up. I started with them, oh . . . about two weeks ago and have been getting myself oriented. This is exciting work. I'm sure I'll need your resources. ACL injuries are quite a common injury for football players."

The coincidence stopped Ayanna in her tracks, but she recovered to cheer for her colleague. "That's fantastic, Daniel. I know the team. I had the pleasure of seeing a game at Aviva Stadium a few days ago."

"Really?" His eyes widened. "Were you there on assignment?"

"No, just a layover for a quick trip of the country before coming here." She adjusted her note cards into a tidy stack and slipped it into her suit jacket pocket. "Had I known, I would have looked you up, and we could have had a coffee or shared a meal to catch up on all this."

"How are things in the New York office? Any way we can persuade you to this side of the world for a few years at least?"

Ayanna had been offered positions in other countries as well as in locations across the US, but she wasn't ready to leave New York. "Not at present, but you never know what the future holds."

Ayanna would have loved to travel the world more, but in addition to her allegiance to the institute, she had some familial responsibilities and was always needed to clean up their messes. Things had been quiet recently, and perhaps it might give her a chance to start thinking about possibilities for the future. She didn't hold her breath.

As the scheduled convention activities ended, Ayanna headed up to her hotel room.

"Do you have dinner plans for the night?" Daniel asked as they walked the perimeter of the conference room, inching their way toward the exit.

"I'm taking a few meetings, and then I have dinner with some of the organizers from tonight."

"Oh." His disappointment resonated.

Daniel was a lovely, quirky man, talented at what he did and passionate about the field. His intelligence and insights always challenged Ayanna when they worked together and were reminiscent of her intense years at Pitt.

"Would you like to join us, Daniel? It would give you an opportunity to network with some of the bigwigs. How about it?"

"Thank you, but I'm here with a colleague and wouldn't want to impose. I doubt it'd be appropriate to add us both to your party."

"It's okay. I'm sure they can accommodate two more." She snagged one of the staff and asked if they'd be able to help organize additional guests for her dinner.

"Of course, Dr. Crawford."

"See?" she said. "Having you there with some of the team will be like last spring."

"Then I'd be delighted to join."

Ayanna left the conference room with Daniel and felt eyes on her. She looked around until she located the source. A ginger-haired man whose blue eyes she would never forget stared back at her. She hadn't expected to see him in Liverpool, much less at the convention.

"Shane!" Daniel called to him. "Ayanna, this is the team liaison I mentioned. Shane MacCallum, I'd like you to meet my friend and colleague Dr. Ayanna Crawford."

Holy shit.

Ayanna somewhat relaxed when Shane followed her lead and pretended that they didn't know each other when Daniel introduced them. She'd left her adventures in Ireland behind with the intention of jumping solidly back into her real life. She hadn't expected one of those adventures to follow her to Liverpool or to inadvertently invite him to her keynote dinner table. All throughout dinner, her mind created question after question. Had he seen her keynote? If he'd seen her, why hadn't he said hello when she'd come offstage? Had he not seen her? Had he known who she was when he'd met her in Dublin? Had Eoghan?

During dinner Ayanna barely ate because her colleagues continued to flood her with questions. She tried to promote discussion so she could get in a few bites of her meal. Her brain began to fog from the constant firing and the work of conjuring answers. Shane's intense gaze didn't help.

Later, when the crowd dispersed, she walked to her room while some of her dinner associates went to the bar for more talk. She hadn't gotten a good understanding of the hotel and walked in a full circle, passing the bar not once but twice.

"Are you lost?" Shane's voice was as welcome a sound as it was nerve inspiring.

"No . . . I think I'm just turned around a bit." She peered at him, and he arched a brow. "Okay, yeah, I'm lost." She told him her hotel room's wing.

"I'll take you," he said, and she half thought he'd pull her along like he had at the stadium only days ago.

They walked side by side in silence for a minute before she spoke. "How have you been?" she asked.

"Do we know each other now, Dr. Crawford?"

The formality hit a nerve. "In my defense, I wasn't expecting to see you again. I think I panicked."

"Why would seeing me again cause you to panic?" he asked. The tailored dark-blue suit he wore accentuated his broad shoulders and trim waist, and she immediately thought he should be photographed.

She shrugged and pivoted. "Were you there for my speech?"

"I was," he answered.

"Well, why didn't you say hello?"

"You were swarmed by people. You mentioned your work, but this . . . you're famous."

"I'm not famous." She rejected the title for a lot of reasons, the first one being that she didn't want to be known. She wanted her work to be useful.

"Years of research, talks all over the world, a keynote speech at a world-famous conference. Ayanna . . ."

"When you say it like that, it sounds like I'm famous. My research is respected." She blushed. She loved that her work helped people, and the rest of it she took in stride.

"Call it whatever you want, but you're famous. Nothing wrong with that. It's a bit strange to see you up there like that instead of the American I taught football."

"Yeah. It's strange seeing you in a suit instead of in a sweater dragging me around the stadium." She smiled.

More silence followed. Then she added, "Daniel is an exceptional doctor. We've helped each other over the years. I value him as a trusted colleague and friend. The Rovers are lucky to have him."

"Is that why you pretended not to know me?" Shane sighed.

"No . . . I mean, yes . . . he doesn't need to know about Dublin."

"Which part? About me, or about Eoghan?"

"You?" The sole of her shoe slipped against the tiled floor, and she stumbled. His hand slipped to her waist to steady her but did less to help her recover than to make her hop slightly at the current flowing through her from his touch.

"We had fun, didn't we?" His voice was gooier than honey twirling on a dipper.

"Yes, but—"

"I should have kissed you," Shane shared. The impulse of his statement colored his upper cheeks.

Ayanna swallowed dryly. "What?" she croaked, needing to hear the words again to be sure her foggy mind hadn't made them up.

"At the stadium. I should have kissed you." Shane wasn't hiding his thoughts this time. They stopped in front of the lift to her room, and he squared to her. "Did you want me to?" He called for the elevator, yet his eyes pinpointed her mouth.

"I . . . well . . . I mean—" Under normal circumstances she'd come up with a defensive fib quicker than this, but the urgency in Shane's eyes quickened her pulse. All lies bounced. "Yes."

He raked a hand through his hair, slightly messing up the neat man bun, which only upped the sophistication factor. He diminished the space between them and cupped her face. His hand a mere degree cooler than her hot cheek. "I wanted to kiss you then, Ayanna, like I want to kiss you now," he said, inches from her mouth, and the heat of his words tattooed her lips.

"Shane." Her hands slipped around his waist, and she was glad for the vacant section of the hotel where they stood, because she wanted nothing to stop her from pressing her lips to his and feeling how divine it would be when he kissed her back. His soft lips against hers, his warm tongue playing in her mouth. She could almost feel him drawing her into the elevator and up to her room, where they would make out frantically, touching, licking, embracing. Their wild foreplay would only be the beginning. "Why didn't you?" she asked, teasingly close to him.

He withdrew his hand and stepped back as if waking up, while she still slept and dreamed about the kiss she still hoped they'd share.

"I was bringing you to Eoghan. What kind of friend would I be if I snogged his girl?"

"His girl? Eoghan and I met briefly at a bar, and he invited me to a match, where I spent most of the time with you." She pressed her lips together to prevent further admission. "I'm no one's girl."

"And yesterday? Last night with Eoghan?" he demanded as if entitled to an answer.

The heat of her blush stung her skin. She didn't know what details Eoghan had shared with him, but by the way Shane squinted through his lids, he seemed rooted in his opinion. The last thing she'd waste her time on was setting him straight. He'd already decided.

She lengthened the space between them further and crossed her arms over her chest. "Then it's a good thing you didn't kiss me, huh?" She evaluated his response.

He sucked in an openmouthed breath. "I guess you're right." She shivered through her jacket from the chill in his voice. "Have a safe trip home, Ayanna."

Four fucking days of behaving like Charlotte had gotten her into this mess. Thank goodness, tomorrow she'd leave it all behind. But why did she still feel so sad watching Shane walk away?

Again.

Chapter Nine

"Another," Shane hollered and kicked balls at Eoghan in rapid succession. Each one he launched faster and farther. He'd been back from Liverpool for weeks and approached his work both for the organization and for the players with newfound enthusiasm. Anything to stop playing alternate outcomes at the hotel with Ayanna. He'd almost kissed her and tasted how sweet he'd known she'd be. Now back in Dublin, he was running drills with Eoghan at the team's training facility before the rest of the team arrived.

Eoghan dribbled the ball across the field, rolling and tapping it with cleated feet. Shane propelled another ball. Then another. This was Eoghan's fault for meeting the American to begin with and sending Shane on a fool's errand. Eoghan chased down the balls, his footwork on point, and his jersey clung to his torso. They'd done these drills since they were boys in Limerick, playing on their first teams. Once they'd become professionals, they'd adopted and intensified the practice.

The Dublin Rovers had one more league match in their local team season before the Europa tournaments started. The players were thrilled they'd made it this year, but they wanted the championship. Their first obstacle would be Madrid. The competition season was upon them, but Shane's schedule had been jammed with demands from his needy clientele. Between housing appointments, sponsor calls, flight and hotel arrangement confirmations, management meetings, and the slew of texts from players, he barely had time to scratch his arse. For the first time in the past month, he thought about going out for a well-earned pint with his brothers.

He kicked a ball, and it hit Eoghan in the face.

"Fucker!"

"Focus," Shane sang. "Or you'll lose a tooth."

Eoghan ducked another ball careening toward him. "I think you just like throwing balls at me."

"Again. Use your whole body. Not just your feet," Shane shouted for the billionth time. As a former player, he knew Eoghan's body automatically responded, but the reminder always helped.

"Had I seen it, I would've," Eoghan snarled back.

"Let's see it, then." Shane kicked the ball high.

Eoghan jumped into a header and delivered the ball into the net.

"Better," Shane called.

"That was fucking great," Eoghan retorted.

"Quiet your ego." Shane booted a ball hard Eoghan's way, and pain radiated through his Achilles. The ball deadened against Eoghan's chest and slid down his body before he dribbled the ball toward the penalty area and kicked it into the net.

Shane missed the days when he could execute similar moves with ease. He rolled his right ankle and limped slightly as he approached Eoghan.

"Let's take a break." Eoghan jogged toward him.

Shane held up a hand to halt his advance. "No breaks. Again." He hurled more balls at Eoghan, this time using the arch of his foot instead of the top. Shane's injury had never quite healed right even after months of painful physical therapy. Some days were better and he forgot he had been injured, while other days, just walking the streets around Dublin drained his energy.

They went on like this for an hour before one of the field assistants arrived. The young man ran a lap and stretched quickly before running to where Shane was readying another set of drills for Eoghan.

"I got it, boss," the young man said and took over.

Shane wanted to complain but conceded to the pain. He longed to run with them like they had in the past, but his limitations were obvious. Shortly afterward, the coach and the rest of the team arrived.

"All right, I'll leave you to it," Shane said.

"You're comin' out with us to the bar? We're going on the lash in Sandymount."

"Not if I want to make it to the match. I'm meeting to check in with the team physician. It's been about a month, and he's been busy with Lloyd and Baka. The training wheels have come off, but technically he's still fairly new. I also need to get some work done."

Eoghan didn't relent. "We're sure to meet a spare arse or two."

Eoghan's mention of loose women grated on Shane's nerves. Eoghan had all but forgotten about the American who still haunted Shane's dreams every so often. According to the chatter amid the team, Eoghan had already found several replacements. Shane had sent an email to Ayanna's work address, which had been in the Liverpool conference literature, but she'd never responded. He didn't blame her but rather fate for not allowing him to meet her first.

"Have fun."

A whistle from one of the coaches cracked, but Eoghan continued to persist.

"C'mon, Freckles. It's been ages since you've come out."

"I went out last month."

"Like I mentioned. Ages." Eoghan scoffed. "What do they call it in America? Stick-in-the-jam."

"It's stick-in-the-mud, and it originated in England, eejit," Shane corrected.

"Right. C'mon, then."

"Pass." Shane slapped his back. "I'm off."

Eoghan flung his hand up at Shane's departing figure. "Oi! You're not waiting for Pippin?" Eoghan pointed to their friend, jogging onto the field with the rest of the keepers.

Shane had stayed for practice a few times over the past month, but each time the nostalgia surfaced like the thin foam on top of a perfectly pulled Smithwick ale. "I'll see him later." He limped toward the field exit.

"So you'll come out?" His friend sounded hopeful.

"Maybe." He'd say anything to get Eoghan off his back.

"Grand, we'll link up with you later, then?"

"Why not." Shane's response might have lacked excitement, but it also left too much of an opening for Eoghan, who'd surely rabbit on to Pippin about Shane's potential cameo at a team outing. As Shane limped off the field, he had a feeling he'd find himself on the south side of Dublin tonight.

◆　◆　◆

Shane moseyed into the Paddy Bath with seven of the Dublin Rover players. Maybe it was his lack of going out, or perhaps he'd gotten older and thus more cautious, but being out with several main players in their club didn't seem like the best idea.

"There they are. Ireland's finest," Liam called. "Cut off me legs. Shane's graced us with his presence this evening."

"Shut your bake, Liam," Shane returned, but he gave Liam a handshake and hug.

"Good to see you, man," Liam said.

Shane always appreciated Liam's hospitality and how easily he remembered all their orders. Pints of Murphy's, Kilkenny, and Bru House floated around, as well as pale ales, stouts, and Munich malts.

"Smithwick stout for Shane."

"Aww, laddie, you remembered," Shane teased.

Liam kissed his middle finger as he flipped him off, and Shane chuckled. It felt good to be out again.

"*Sláinte!*" they called with an easy toast, as many of the men had already gulped at their drinks.

Eoghan clinked glasses with him and guzzled his malt. "Ahh. That's easy drinking."

Pippin slapped Shane's back. "Drink up, Shaney. You have rounds to go."

Shane didn't doubt it. Now that he frequented the bars less, his friends would make sure he made up for lost time.

Naturally, the chatter among them slanted toward their sport, and Pippin talked about plays. "I think we need to restrategize. We're flat and tripping over our fucking feet after halftime. We need to sharpen things up."

Shane got a kick out of how Pippin always took a tactical approach to everything ever since their coach had sent the team to a military training facility. He'd taken on the new skills and philosophies as his own personal charge and reminded his fellow players to behave as one cohesive unit.

Pippin launched into his plans. "We have to use a different strategy on the field not only when on the attack but on defense as well. You know when Kirby kicked you in the last match on your wall pass?" he said. "We should have got the call. If ref's not going to call it, we have to make them pay, run them down, make them play our game."

"But the formations we've been using have won us matches. It's not a good enough reason for Boyle to make changes to our strategy now." Eoghan referenced their head coach.

"I dunno. We want to be sharp for the tournament. Better. They expect our formations now. They may not be able to fully get through them, but it's only a matter of time before they figure it out."

"Pipe down, Pippin," Lance, another midfielder on the team, howled. "We're trying to have a drink over here. We can talk strategy once we've had a pint or two."

Pippin flung the contents of a bowl of nuts at Lance. As a keeper on their team, Pippin was protective by nature but also tenacious, like Shane used to be.

"Oi, dick!" Lance called.

"I'm thinking about us as a team, idiot," Pippin ranted, then reached out for support. "You agree with me, don't you, Shane? You've seen the matches, and you've played with us."

All chatter quieted, and the heads of the men on the team turned to him. He wasn't a player anymore or a coach, but as a former leader on their team and now as team liaison, he had gained the trust of the players.

"Pippin's right, but so is Eoghan. Teams will always start anticipating your plays. Normally, gaffer changes it up, but he may be more focused on filling in the gaps for the players who are down right now. Maybe it's a good time for the captain to be more vocal with a few of you in agreement to make your case." Shane's eyes met squarely with Eoghan's.

Eoghan scratched his head. "All right, then. We'll have a chat tomorrow." As team captain, Eoghan rallied his teammates and fought for every win. That Pippin instead of Eoghan led the discussion gave Shane pause.

"Thanks, mate." Eoghan raised his glass to Shane.

He returned the gesture, leaned against the bar, and sipped his beer. Eoghan might not have been open to expressing his thoughts at present, but Shane knew his friend would blurt out his opinions eventually.

The team had made the Paddy Bath one of their randomly frequented spots. A match played on the screen: Gorica versus Napoli. The match was close, but the Croatian team led in goals two to one. If the Rovers won against Real Seville next week, they'd play the winner of the match they watched.

"Whatever happened with you and the American girl who you met here?" Liam called to Eoghan.

"Oh, Ayanna. She's gone back, but she ruined me. I wish you could have seen her that night we went out. All thanks to my bud here." Eoghan went on about the story of the match at Aviva.

Shane bristled.

"You all right, mate?" Pippin asked him.

"Yeah." Shane's shoulders felt like rubber bands wrapped too tightly around a pencil.

"And back at my place—" Eoghan bit his knuckle. "Fellas."

Shane's glass cracked in his hand with a loud pop. Beer and glass spilled all over the floor. A shard stuck in his hand and stung. "Fuck," he hissed and yanked the piece cleanly out of his palm. Ayanna had been gone a few weeks, and yet the thought of her with Eoghan still poked him like a pitchfork would a bear.

"You okay, Shane?" Liam threw a bar towel at him, and one of the staff tended to the spill.

"Yeah, just clumsy is all." Shane looked up to see Pippin's amused expression.

Eoghan chatted with some other members of the team.

"So . . ." Pippin slapped a hand on Shane's shoulder, and the contact pricked and heated the spot. "When did that happen?"

"What?" Shane tended to his hand.

"This thing with the American," Pippin asked more than stated.

"What thing?" He remained stupid to his friend's prying.

"This thing with herself and yourself," Pippin persisted.

"I don't know what you're talking about, but keep your voice down." Shane shrugged his hand off.

"You know how to hold a pint glass, Shaney."

"Fuck. Off."

"It's true, isn't it? You know what happened the last time you and Eoghan kept such secrets."

"I said fuck off, Pippin." Shane didn't need a review of his and Eoghan's altercation some years back, when they had been in love with the same woman. Eileen. The soap opera of events had caused a rift between them that had taken over a year to mend and resulted in a pact never to let that happen again.

"And that stupid pact you two have—"

"Will you stop?" Shane whispered. The bar walls were shrinking in on him. "There's nothing between me and Ayanna."

Pippin nodded. "That's why you're cracking glasses."

"She's back in the States and away from the both of us. What does it matter?" Shane asked.

"Good point, but it's clear that Eoghan has moved on." Pippin noted Eoghan chatting up another lass at the bar. "You, on the other hand, are bleeding all over Liam's lovely bar towel."

"Mary'll fix you up, Shane," Liam called to him and pointed to one of the barmaids heading to him with a first aid kit.

Luckily, no more glass was in his hand. Mary disinfected the wound with antiseptic that stung more than the beer had, and the scent burned his nostrils.

She slapped a bandage on. "You're all set. Don't break any more of my glasses, will ya."

"Will do, Mary," Shane promised.

"Good?" Pippin asked.

"Yeah."

"You know my saying, Shaney. Things have a strange way of happening. If this American is stuck in your mind, then . . ."

"Pipe down, Pippin," Shane warned.

"Rather I talk about Maeve's wedding?" Pippin asked.

Shane's first cousin on his father's side was getting married in New York, and Shane had been looking forward to it. He'd promised Maeve that he'd do whatever he had to in order to be present for the event and in the wedding party.

"Please don't. I'm still trying to sort out the details, and my folks are nuts about the possibility of me missing it for work."

"Sure Maeve's fuming her wig off about it. She sent me a hot email when I RSVP'd no, because if we don't advance, I'll be in Nigeria." Pippin bristled. "And Eoghan's trembling in his boots to send the same because he may need to train or play depending on how things go."

"Can't believe you all won't be there. It's Maeve's wedding. In New York. Going shouldn't be this difficult for us," Shane said. His cousin hadn't grown up in Ireland, but she visited as much as Shane did the Bronx. Annually. His friends were family, and as a family, they should be there for Maeve's nuptials.

"She planned it during a cup-qualifying year."

"Go on and tell her that," Shane said.

Pippin tapped his chin and looked up at the ceiling. "You know who is also in America?"

Shane lunged for Pippin, whose speed and agility won over his civilian body.

Eoghan moseyed over with the woman he'd been chatting with at the bar. "This is Channing."

"Pleasure," Shane said. The brunette, with eyes bluer than his, was all legs.

"Howdy, Chan," Pippin chimed in.

"It's Channing." The woman's disinterest in them reminded him of Eileen, who he'd thought only had eyes for him, but it was his status and celebrity that had really turned her on. He hadn't thought of his and Eoghan's ex-girlfriend in ages. Between hiding his feelings for Ayanna and quieting Pippin, Shane was mentally exhausted. The last thing he needed was to add Eileen to the list.

"Sorry. Channing," Pippin corrected, too sweetly for anyone to miss his inauthenticity.

"Glad you came out, Shane. Will chat, yeah? We're going to head out," Eoghan said.

Nothing new there. "Just make curfew and stay in town so you can make your flight." Mentioning curfew was Shane's way of reminding Eoghan of his suspension years ago when his ego and stupidity had cost him valuable playing time and a lot of money. Ever since, Eoghan had become notorious for getting distracted and chasing pretty lasses with flexible legs into other counties.

"Like I'd make that mistake twice." Eoghan groaned.

Shane and Pippin looked at each other. "You would," they said simultaneously.

"Gentlemen," Eoghan crooned.

Shane stared at his friend's departing figure, just as he slid his hand over Channing's arse. He could see Eoghan pulling the same moves on Ayanna. The brown enameled wood and low lighting in the bar camouflaged the heat that no doubt splotched Shane's face.

"Another, Liam." If he couldn't keep his thoughts of Ayanna at bay, then perhaps, with a little luck, he could drink the thoughts of her away.

Chapter Ten

Ayanna carried a few patient files in her arm and marched swiftly to her office. It had been about a month since she had gotten back from Liverpool, and the catch-up had just started to calm down. She'd been booked solid with educational and training engagements. She'd expected as much, especially after the reception her presentation had received at the conference. She hoped her research, along with some of the curriculum changes she'd suggested, would be helpful to her colleagues. What she hadn't anticipated was just how much people wanted to connect with her in person.

Back from maternity leave, her assistant, Chloe, fastened her dark-brown hair up into a bun with a pen and huffed. If Ayanna felt overwhelmed, then Chloe's experience was magnified by all the calls and emails requesting Ayanna's time.

"How are you doing?" Ayanna asked.

"Holding down the fort." Chloe gave a sheepish grin.

You're famous. Shane's words rang in her ears, and she cursed herself for conjuring him up. She'd finally stopped the fire of their last conversation from both arousing her and boiling her blood and allowed the regret to settle into a neat pile of ash.

"Do what you gotta do. The work will be here, so if you need to go pump or eat or just take a break, let one of the other admins know,"

Ayanna said. She appreciated Chloe's hard work but wanted to make sure she took care of herself.

"Thanks. Oh, and the exercises you gave me are helping. I do some of them right at my desk."

"Nice. Keep it up." These small chats were what Ayanna's last few weeks had been reduced to, but she tried her best to connect with the staff when she could.

"You don't have much time." Chloe handed her a snack bar.

"I could kiss you. You're a lifesaver." Ayanna's stomach clapped in appreciation. She'd been running on espresso, and her hunger pangs intensified.

Chloe pointed to her cheek, and Ayanna smacked a loud "mwah" on her assistant. Chloe handed her a file folder. "They're waiting for you, Dr. Crawford."

"Thanks, Chloe." Ayanna hurried to their staff meeting.

When she arrived at the conference room, she plopped into a chair, between her colleagues Herbert Levy and Henrietta Newton, and opened her file.

"Good morning, everyone," Ayanna said, pinching the hot coral top of her scrubs and fluttering it to fan the layer of perspiration forming on her neck and chest. A few other therapists filed in after her.

"Hey, Ayanna. I've hardly seen you since you got back. You've been so busy." Henrietta leaned over.

"I know. Things are settling down, which is good. I'm thrilled to not be traveling for at least a few weeks."

"Yeah, you're like our own celebrity," said Herbert. His studies had also helped support Ayanna's research. "My calendar is booked with patients since we were mentioned in your research."

"That's what I like to hear." Ayanna and Herbert high-fived. That her findings helped shine a light on their facility and the other PTs made her proud that she helped not only their clients but also her colleagues.

Their head partner, Randall Dane, drew their attention when he entered the room. "Good morning, everyone."

Jumbled responses filled the room.

"I apologize for my tardiness, but we had some last-minute changes. Fran?" Randall motioned to his administrative assistant to ready the videoconferencing and projector equipment.

Randall continued, "We had a call come in late from Europe last night." He looked over at her. "This one might interest you, Ayanna. Our former colleague, Daniel Finnegan, head physician for the Dublin Rovers in Ireland, has an injured player. The client suffered an ACL injury during a game. I have Daniel and team joining us. Once they present the case, then we'll move on to additional partner business, including patient load and scheduled leaves. All dependent on what happens with Daniel and his patient."

Everything stopped as if someone had pressed the pause button at the mention of Daniel's name. He often went through normal referral channels to work with Ayanna, but he always gave her a heads-up. That he hadn't had an opportunity to get in touch prior to the meeting meant he needed to get the ball rolling as soon as possible. Ayanna prayed neither Eoghan nor Pippin had been hurt.

Fran dialed the number, and once it connected, Daniel's image, seated at a round table, popped onto the screen. His usual cheery cheeks sagged, the bags under his eyes were puffed, and stress lined the corners of his eyes. Two empty seats were positioned to his left.

"Greetings, my friends." Daniel's Irish accent filled the room, and he raked his hand through his short gray hair before fumbling with the file folder before him. "We're glad you're able to meet with us today, and I apologize for the short notice, but everything is moving very quickly here." Daniel's attention was drawn elsewhere for several seconds, and his hands waved someone inside. "Yes, please come in. We're connected," he said to the person off screen.

In a moment a redhead in a casual suit filled the screen, and he and another well-dressed man sat at the round table.

"This is Shane MacCallum, team and logistics liaison for the Dublin Rovers, and William Edwards, the surgeon who performed the surgery," Daniel said, gesturing to the men by his side.

It had been weeks since their tiff in Liverpool, yet seeing him again after all these weeks still made Ayanna's chest rise and fall as she took several deep breaths to regain her composure.

"Time matters in our field, so no apologies necessary. You have the floor, Daniel," Randall said. Randall ran through introductions on their side, and they each raised their hand or nodded to identify themselves.

Even on screen, Shane's eyes lingered on her. *Fuck.* Her racing heart wouldn't quit, and she struggled to pay attention to Daniel.

"Do you know that guy?" Henrietta noticed first.

Think fast! "Yes, he attended the Liverpool conference with Daniel," she whispered.

Daniel began his overview. "One of my players got terribly injured, and . . . well, I . . . we need your help. He's a star athlete on the team and an international treasure in soccer. The stakes are high, and I strongly believe Ayanna can assist here."

Please, please, please don't be Eoghan . . . or Pippin. Definitely not Eoghan . . . She drank some water to soothe her cotton mouth and prayed that though her adventures in Ireland had followed her to Liverpool, they wouldn't follow her ass all the way back to New York as well. She summoned every bit of professionalism she could muster and got right into healer mode. Daniel had called her out, but they still needed to address the case as a team. "I'm sorry to hear that, Daniel. You and your colleagues must feel very pressured right now."

Daniel's head bobbed. "It's important we get this right."

"Of course. You've come to the right place. We'll do whatever we can. Tell us more so we can help," Ayanna said.

"He's had surgery and is recovering, but we know that you can have a successful surgery and a destructive recovery," Dr. Edwards explained. "We've seen Dr. Crawford's research and believe that she would be the best fit for this case."

Francine split the conference screen to project the presentation of the player's case. Reconstructive surgery information and images of x-rays lit the screen. Ayanna choked midswallow on her water as she squinted at Eoghan O'Farrell's case file.

"Ayanna? Are you all right?" Henrietta simultaneously patted her back and handed her a tissue from one of the many boxes around the room.

She coughed the excess water from her esophagus. "Yes," she croaked and offered mumbled apologies.

"When was the surgery?" Randall asked.

"Just about a week ago now," Dr. Edwards responded.

"And his therapy is not planned? Is there a reason we're coming in at the eleventh hour?" Herb asked.

"It's a matter of compatibility. We first looked at sending him to Qatar for recovery and rehabilitation, but it's not working out." Shane's clarification didn't quite give them the details they needed.

"The patient is refusing care at this point, and the team owners are livid. The season is at an end, and he won't be able to play in the UEFA tournament, which is disappointing, to say the least, for the organization. Next year, however, is a FIFA World Cup. We've spoken with the coach of the national team, and as you can imagine, without their captain and star player, Ireland's chances at winning the cup would be drastically reduced. They need him back as fast as possible, and we know that his case, in most hands, would require six to twelve months of rehab. I immediately recommended Ayanna from our studies together, as did Shane after learning about her research from the Liverpool conference."

Eoghan was hurt? She hadn't had any further contact with him since their time in Dublin, but what they'd experienced together had been one of her fondest memories of Ireland. She felt for him. She'd seen his passion for football on the field.

"How can I help, Daniel?"

"Instead of having Eoghan in Qatar, where he'd spend months there rehabilitating, we'd send him to New York once he's recovered from surgery. If Dr. Crawford would commit to rehabilitating him." Shane cleared his throat. "As we understand it from her research, a full-time, live-in situation where Dr. Crawford is overseeing everything from nutrition to support services would be ideal."

Daniel nodded. "Since reviewing your work, the organization is adamant about getting you and committing to this unique approach. I understand the timing is challenging, Ayanna. You're in high demand, but we could really use your miracle hands."

"Thank you, Daniel. We have the capabilities to support your cause, but we'll need to review this case as a team and get back to you with our decision," Randall stated. "As you can imagine, we have quite a lot to discuss, since Ayanna would likely have to readjust her work and travel schedule, not to mention her life, for at least six months."

"Yes, of course," Daniel said. "But please, if you can get back to us with a decision as soon as possible, it would be greatly appreciated."

"We'll get back to you within twenty-four hours, likely less. Thank you for entrusting us with such an important case to review."

Francine ended the feed, and the chatter bombarded Ayanna. But her brain focused on analyzing the facts. Eoghan. Badly injured. Needed a physical therapist who specialized in ACL injuries. Live-in rehabilitation stint here in New York. Her mind, on the other hand, swirled with the drama of her reckless European fling come home to roost.

Oh, the Fates.

Chapter Eleven

The cool hardwood floor supported Ayanna's bare feet as she wore a path from her mounted electric fireplace, past her couch, to the bookshelf on the opposite wall. Each step less a curse and more an affirmation of her current disaster. She recounted the wicked joke to an audience of one—Charlotte—who leaned against the wall with a glass of wine she'd helped herself to upon arrival. Ayanna delivered her punch line.

"Eoghan is coming to New York, Shane is accompanying him, and I'll be living with both of them."

"Both of them?" Charlotte shrieked.

Ayanna halted and raised a pair of fingers in the air. "Both of them."

"In the universal cosmic reality, or whatever you call it, this is like a one-in-one-quadrillionth possibility." Charlotte put down her glass of wine and Ayanna picked hers up, the cherry-red vino sloshing in its large bowl.

"Right? It's not just me?" Ayanna pointed to herself with all fingers in an expulsion of nervous energy. "This is straight up some fantasy shit."

"More like karmic betrayal," Charlotte corrected.

"This can't be happening."

"Fess up, Yaya. What the hell did you do in Ireland that you're not telling me to invite the rain of this particular havoc down upon you?"

"Nothing," Ayanna said.

Charlotte tilted her head, pouted her mouth, and scanned Ayanna with lie detector eyes.

"I told you literally everything. You know me. Matter of fact, this is your fault."

"How?" Charlotte chuckled.

"You sent me off alone to skank up Ireland, and look where it's gotten me." Ayanna pointed her accusation. "In the institute's live-in rehabilitation house with both of them. Living, sleeping, eating, breathing—"

"Fucking," Charlotte added.

"You got jokes? At this particular moment. Seriously?"

Charlotte took a zen posture and breathed. "Okay, let's just calm down and look at this as the opportunity it is. Both of your Irish boos followed you all the way home. There is a reason for all this."

Ayanna plopped down next to her. "Like, maybe I was always meant to meet them so that I could help Eoghan?"

"I was thinking more like, the Lord Jesus is telling you that you need to get laid."

"Charlotte. Will you stop? This is not funny."

"It kind of is," Charlotte said, then wiped away her smile and fortified her face with seriousness. "Look, this is not ideal." She paused. "For you."

"If you mention sex again, I swear—"

"Okay, okay. For real, though. You're the consummate professional, and despite this curveball pitched your way, you are going to go in there, claim that space, and turn sour grapes into fine wine."

"I'm glad to see that one of us is optimistic about this catastrophe," Ayanna said.

"Like you said, I know you. You're going to flip the script and create an environment for healing and recovery because that's what Dr. Crawford does with her magic hands. That's what you do, Yaya."

Ayanna massaged the curls at the back of her head and the tightness in her neck. Her friend's confidence in her was admirable, but this was bad. Really bad.

"You have to admit it's kind of funny."

Ayanna grabbed one of the dense couch pillows and whacked Charlotte with it.

"My makeup, Yaya," Charlotte hollered, and Ayanna laughed at the smudge of red lipstick that now drew a thick line from the corner of Charlotte's lips toward her cheek.

"That's what you get for adding way too much levity to a crisis." Oftentimes Ayanna appreciated her friend's humorous perspective, but Charlotte wasn't the one who would have to endure months in a house with Shane and Eoghan.

"Look how you messed up your pillow." Charlotte displayed the lipstick stain on Ayanna's fluffy off-white pillow. "All to get back at me."

"Worth it." Ayanna rolled her eyes.

Charlotte hopped up and stepped over to a mirror. "Maybe I deserved that," she said as she plucked a nearby Kleenex to fix her face. "By the way, Jada texted me."

Ayanna placed her hands on her hips. "My sister texted you and not me? She's so annoying." She'd called and texted her sister several times only to leave messages and get no response. Jada, though twenty, still chose when she wanted to rebel against her.

"She said she'll call you soon. She's studying." Charlotte used air quotes.

"I bet." Ayanna knew Charlotte's point exactly. Her gorgeous sister used her feminine power in ways that Ayanna neither was blessed with nor had been afforded the privilege of freedom to explore, because she'd had to adult up and take care of Jada and her mother. Ayanna's struggle to be all things to her sister had convoluted their relationship. "I should take a drive up there and make my displeasure known."

"Don't do that," Charlotte begged. "You two are a lot when you get together. Like you've always said, you have an order of operations when dealing with Jada. Provider, then mother, then sister, then friend. You don't often get to the last two, and I get it, but at least you have me to run interference."

"You know she's wildin' out over there."

"Yeah, but she's brilliant, pulling a 4.0, and fairly responsible."

"Charlotte?" Ayanna crossed her arms.

"Okay, questionably responsible. I mean, she's supposed to have fun at college. Let her live," Charlotte said.

"She could have at least returned my call." More than annoyed, Ayanna was hurt. She'd sacrificed a lot for Jada, and though her sister was a handful, she wanted to know she was okay.

"How's your mom?"

"Okay, I guess. I spoke to her a couple weeks ago."

"Maybe give her a call," Charlotte suggested.

"She texted you too?"

Charlotte squinted at her. "If I don't ask you the tough questions, who will?"

"I know. Sorry."

Morgan Crawford was still working on getting her life back together. It had been years since she'd pulled herself out of the worst depression Ayanna had ever seen when her father had died. She and Jada had forged a relationship. In fact, her mother had visited Jada at school and paid for her last two semesters' books. Over the past five years, her mother had started hosting Christmas Eve at their childhood home, and though Ayanna attended for Jada's sake, she did what she'd done since her father had passed. Took her sister and spent Christmas Day with Charlotte and her family.

"Jada wants us to be more of a family, but . . ." Ayanna chewed her lip. "I don't know."

Charlotte came over and put her arm around her shoulders and squeezed. "You are family and dysfunctional as fuck, but I have faith you guys will figure it out."

"True." Ayanna laughed.

"Right now, however, you have two fish to fry."

Ayanna groaned. "Don't remind me."

"Look here, no matter how uncomfortable it is being in a house working with your two fantasy football frolics, you have a job to do. They want you. You have the pressure part down pat. All I'm saying is, if it were me? I'd be looking for all the ways to enjoy it."

Ayanna rubbed her hands together, and they didn't feel magical. Charlotte might have been scripting her own version of a romantic comedy, but a seriously injured football player was on his way to New York. This was only the beginning.

The quiet of the institute at night added to the tension building in her as she stared at an irradiated, magnified image of Eoghan's reconstructed ACL. It had been a month since his surgery, and according to his surgeon, his range of motion was nearly equal to the opposite leg's. He'd be here in a week, and their work would begin.

Sweat dampened her armpits, and she clasped her hands over her head. She moved in close to look at the image and then backed up. Fear coursed through her. She yanked off her glasses and rubbed her eyes. She couldn't fuck this up, yet that was what she feared she was about to do. Eoghan's value as a player was twofold, as he played both for a successful local team and at the national level. His type of ACL injury was one of the worst a footballer could have. Both his anterior cruciate and lateral ligaments had been injured, and though the surgery had gone as well as could be expected, he had to rebuild from scratch. It would be as if he'd been reborn with a new, foreign body part. His total-body cardio and conditioning? Gone.

Recovery in a year plus, before returning to performance, was a decent prognosis, but for Ayanna's reputation that wouldn't do. Eoghan had three stages of rehabilitation to get through. The back office would want him sooner.

She rubbed her head.

"Ayanna?" Solomon called to her from the door of her office.

"Oh, hey," she responded with a dry mouth.

"I've been calling you for at least ten seconds. You okay?"

Tears threatened, but they were no match for her. She had a problem and needed solutions. "Am I gonna fuck this up? Maybe they should have sent him to the facility in Qatar. This is bad."

"You've worked with this injury before."

"But their hope is that a nine-month-minimum recovery plan will occur in less time. I can't rush this. He has to be stronger before I can push him. Both his ACL and LCL were torn."

"You're not rushing this. You're using your techniques that have consistently sped up the recovery process."

"What if it doesn't work this time? What if I hurt him or make him worse and he has to have surgery again?" Given her light-headedness, she was sure she was hyperventilating.

"Okay. I can see it's magical-negro time." Solomon sat her down.

"Stop." She smiled at his attempt at humor.

"You are the same woman whose research on this experimental technique has been gobbled up by the bigwigs. You've traveled all over the country and the world delivering talks and case studies. Where is this doubt coming from?"

"I don't know."

Solomon eyed her.

"I know him," she confessed.

"Like, you know of him?" Solomon said.

"No. We met before he got injured when I spent a few days in Dublin. I've seen him play, I've seen how spectacular he is, and I know him . . . personally."

Solomon's eyes widened. "Have you told Randall?"

She shook her head.

"Why not?"

"Because he was insistent that I take the case, and I owed Finnegan, and I wanted to help this person I know who I never thought I'd ever see again, much less now have to live with at Purchase House." The mansion with all the amenities of a facility was for their most high-end clientele who required private rehabilitation. The accessibility allowed both therapist and client to be immersed in the healing process. It had all the bells and whistles and was an elite working environment. She'd have everything and anything she needed. So would Eoghan. And also Shane. She covered her face and breathed audibly into her hands. "This is a disaster."

"Okay, forget all of that. You are a professional with something spectacular that can help a Premier League soccer player like Eoghan get back to preinjury performance. You can do this."

She stared at the x-rays as if in a trance, searching for answers in the film.

"Ayanna!"

She jerked her head up as if he'd pulled her hair.

"Find the solution and get him better. Do what you do best, and you won't fail at this."

She was nodding, but she didn't know what she was nodding for or to. One thing was certain: Solomon was right. She had to be at her best, despite the circumstances, not this doubting version of herself, if she had any hope at all of making Eoghan better.

"And, Ayanna?"

"Yeah."

"Tell Randall. He may take you off Eoghan's case, and he might not, but ethically, it's the right thing to do," Solomon said.

"Thank you, conscience."

He smiled. "You're welcome."

Chapter Twelve

Ayanna and Charlotte arrived at Purchase House and Eoghan's temporary lodgings early Monday morning. The heart of spring should have brought end-of-May flowers, but instead it showered her with dread. She'd spent the past several weeks stressing over the arrival of this day, and now it had finally arrived. Rolling her purple luggage up the brick walkway, Ayanna scanned the expanse of the rehabilitation estate. She'd visited the house a few times but had never had the pleasure of working on one of her clients there. Valued at close to $2 million, the property, bequeathed to the institute by a wealthy donor, definitely hovered at the highest end of impressive real estate. How much space did two people need? Eoghan was here for rehabilitation, not an episode of *Lifestyles of the Rich and Famous.*

"Wow." Charlotte gawked at ninety-six hundred square feet of colonial elegance. "And here I thought *we* were livin' large."

"Large in spirit and friendship," Ayanna teased and scratched her itchy nose at the fragrance of fresh-cut grass. She, too, felt that the location spoke volumes about how Eoghan and his club's management wanted him to be cared for while here in America.

"I'm doing things wrong. Who pays for all this?" Charlotte asked.

"A combination of personal and professional insurance. It's close to the institute in White Plains is what matters." She was sure that though it was close to other resources, the house had much of what

Eoghan needed to rehabilitate in a comfortable setting. After a session with her, he'd need it. "This is just excessive, but it keeps Eoghan safe from anyone eager to meet him. There should be, like, a family of ten living in here."

"Girl, who cares? There's a staff of people here, from the groundskeeper and housekeeper to house manager and all the people they manage. Not to mention security. And guess who's not paying for it? You, bitch." Charlotte had a point, yet on the cusp of something Ayanna didn't know, the mansion seemed little consolation.

"This is an awesome work environment. With the exception of the love-triangle bit." Charlotte adjusted the large purple duffel bag on one shoulder and held her Parker Clay tote in the crook of her other elbow.

Ayanna had told Randall about the conflict of interest, and though he'd frowned upon her connections to Eoghan, he respected her for disclosing the relationship. The case remained hers. "There is neither love nor triangle. Only regret for getting myself into this situation to begin with."

"Yaya? Please miss me with that bullshit. You had a great time in Ireland. You said so yourself. There are no regrets, just some unforeseen consequences and situational irony that'll reveal itself later."

"Oh, shut up. I've had just about enough of you." Ayanna mimicked several of Charlotte's anecdotes before trailing off.

"Just sayin'." Charlotte snickered and helped Ayanna with her bags to the front door. Ayanna adjusted her dusty-pink blouse and smoothed her gray loose-fit slacks. She rang the bell, and they waited.

"Mmm-hmm. I see you." Charlotte side-eyed her. "Glad you didn't wear your scrubs for this reunion."

The large wood door whipped open, and Shane stood before them in a sky-blue V-neck shirt rolled up to his elbows. The vision of him made the already warm spring day that much warmer.

Captivating blue eyes locked with hers, and her already palpitating heart revved further with memories of Shane only inches away and about to lay his lips on hers.

"Hello, Dr. Crawford," he said.

This is what we're doing? "Hello, Mr. MacCallum," she returned. When he didn't look away, she turned to Charlotte. "This is my friend Charlotte. She's helping me move in. Charlotte, Shane MacCallum, team liaison for the Dublin Rovers." She followed his lead.

"A pleasure, Charlotte," Shane greeted with outstretched hand.

Charlotte raised an eyebrow at Ayanna before extending her hand to shake Shane's. "Nice to meet you," she said. "I've heard a lot about you."

"A lot, have you?" Though Shane spoke to Charlotte, he returned his gaze to Ayanna.

"Well, not *a lot* a lot, but Ayanna has mentioned you," Charlotte backpedaled, and Ayanna wasn't sure if she did more harm than good. "Did I mention I love your accent?"

Shane tilted his head. "Thanks?"

"I told her about the day at Aviva," Ayanna said.

"Right." A tight smile followed. "I'll take that for you." Shane slid the handle of Ayanna's luggage from her hand.

"I got it." Ayanna's complaint was weakened by Shane's familiar scent.

"I'd embarrass my ma if I didn't take your bags." He then relieved Charlotte of her bag as well. They followed him inside.

A dramatic marble-tiled foyer with a sweeping stairway welcomed them inside. The sun flooded in and further brightened the neutrals and whites, and the marble shone as if recently polished. Air flowed in from an open door somewhere, enchanting the space. The open plan led to the living area, where a large beige Persian rug was centered on dark hardwood floors. With all the amenities of a rehabilitation facility,

Purchase House remained gorgeously decorated with both traditional and modern elegance that made both her and Charlotte's jaws drop.

"Is this everything?" he asked, interrupting their gawk fest.

"Yeah. I live a couple towns away. I can always go get something if I need it," Ayanna said.

"Sound. I'll take this to the guest wing for you," Shane said. He walked farther inside, giving Ayanna and Charlotte an excellent view of strong legs and an exceptional ass wrapped in dark-blue jeans. Barefoot, he padded onward with her luggage. "You're familiar with the layout of the place, yes?"

"Yes, thanks."

"So the three of you will be living in this house. Together?" Charlotte asked as they followed Shane.

Ayanna elbowed Charlotte's upper arm.

"Ow." Charlotte's soundless complaint carried with it more exaggerated facial expressions than Ayanna had ever seen.

"Cut it out," Ayanna mouthed through clenched teeth.

"Appears so," Shane tossed over his shoulder.

Shane's casual response should have put Ayanna at ease but instead unsettled her enough to make her question herself. Was she the only one stressing this setup? Over three months had passed since Ireland and Liverpool. Her ego suggested that she might still have the affection of both men, but maybe she'd stressed for nothing.

Shane faced them, and the slight flush on his cheeks spoke volumes, yet she wanted to know the details about what he really thought about being here.

"Eoghan is on the patio. We're about to try for lunch. Charlotte, you are invited as well," Shane said.

Try for lunch? What does that mean?

"Great. Thanks." Charlotte's excited response charged the living space.

"You're welcome," Shane said. "There's a washroom, just over there. Join us when you're ready." He left with her bags, but Ayanna caught up to him.

"Mr. MacCallum," she called.

He spun to face her. "You can call me by my given name."

She stood her ground. "Well, you can call me by mine."

His mouth twisted, and she wished he'd just be normal with her, but how could she ask for what she was unable to do? "I was trying to be professional, given the situation."

"I appreciate that. It's just . . ." She hesitated. "It came off kind of cold."

"Not what I was shooting for." He scratched his brow with his thumb. "I know this is an odd setup."

"Tell me about it," she said.

"I'm here to help Eoghan," Shane affirmed.

"Good. We have that in common," she said.

"Good," Shane echoed.

She studied him studying her and then tore herself out of his orbit. "What did you mean when you said 'try for lunch'?"

The mustache part of his beard twitched. "Eoghan isn't the same man you knew in Dublin. He's been in a dark place since the surgery. Maybe having you and your friend Charlotte here will be helpful. I don't know."

Ayanna's frown shadowed her vision. What was she about to walk into? Questions swirled in her head, but her gut told her that she'd have to see for herself what Shane was trying to convey. "Okay. Thanks."

"He needs your help, Ayanna," Shane blurted like a trial witness who'd cracked under cross-examination.

"That's why I'm here." She tried to soothe him with a smile like she would a client's relative, but Shane's tight features were worrisome. Eoghan couldn't have changed that much, could he?

Shane departed for the guest wing, but an eerie feeling stayed in his wake. Ayanna rejoined Charlotte, who dreamily stared at the white board and batten accent over the fireplace in the living room.

"I've gots to get me one of these," Charlotte said.

Ayanna laughed and pulled her friend along to freshen up, welcoming the brief reprieve to synchronize with her bestie.

What Shane called a washroom was a luxurious powder room with a small chair, which Charlotte quickly occupied. "I can't believe your freakin' luck," she said in a hissing whisper. "I've seen a picture of Eoghan online, but you really downplayed Shane. He's *magically delicious.* I mean, redheads scare me a little bit—maybe it's a clown thing—but I'll make an exception."

"Let's reel it in," Ayanna said as she washed her hands in the porcelain basin. "Here's what's going to happen. We're going to have lunch, and you are going to try to enjoy the meal without adding your heavy smatterings of instigative questions and comments."

"You're glad I'm here, aren't you?" Charlotte said, dismissing Ayanna's reprimand.

The warm water melted the muscles up Ayanna's arms, and her shoulders dropped away from her ears. She rolled her shoulders and head. "This is stressful for me, and you're adding to it." Ayanna dried her hands with a plush sea-green towel.

Charlotte pouted.

"But yes. I'm glad you're here."

Charlotte jumped up and smothered her in a hug.

They headed to the patio, and Ayanna readied for the unknown.

Chapter Thirteen

Ayanna and Charlotte navigated their way to a chef's dream kitchen on their way to the patio. At the counter stood a middle-aged woman who looked like the space was designed and equipped just for her.

"Louisa, right?" Ayanna asked the brunette, who wore an apron that read *I think someone kneads a hug* with a smiling loaf of bread at the center.

"Welcome, Dr. Crawford. It's nice to finally meet you." Hired by their logistics team, Louisa Doyle had spent years working as a house manager and cook, making her perfect for the assignment. It didn't hurt that she, too, had Irish ancestry, which Ayanna hoped would help the two men feel more at home.

"It's a pleasure to meet you too." Ayanna shook her hand. "Did everything go well with the nutritionist? We'll be interacting constantly, but do you have everything you need to keep this place running?"

"Yes, thank you for all your help. I was able to be here before they arrived, get things organized and show them around."

"Great. We're a team. No thanks necessary," Ayanna said. She evaluated the beautiful spread of nourishing foods that Louisa had prepared for lunch. "This food looks wonderful, by the way."

As Charlotte introduced herself, Ayanna walked to the sliding glass door leading to the patio. A pool and hot tub, also part of the inviting outdoors, were fenced in by large leafy trees, some of them blooming buds of white, pink, green, and yellow. Decorative bushes for privacy and aesthetics were part of the landscaping design.

Ayanna spotted Shane. At first, she didn't recognize the man he spoke to as Eoghan. He'd grown more than a five-o'clock shadow, and his uncombed hair needed a wash. He sat in a patio chair by the table with his injured leg sprawled out as he chugged a beer. Being out for the season must have been tough for him, but she hadn't expected this. He reached for a pizza box nearby and folded a slice enough to bite off a third.

"What in the . . . ," Charlotte whispered. "Is that? That's not . . ."

"It's him." Ayanna rolled her shoulders before pulling them back. "Ready or not, here we go," she said, unsure who her statement was actually for. She opened the patio doors and made her way to the two men. "Hey, Eoghan," Ayanna greeted and then exchanged glances with Shane, whose face confirmed her concern.

"There she is," Eoghan said with a mouth full of food. "Thought the last time I'd see you would be the morning after our night in Dublin together. Turns out you're some therapy genius."

Ayanna's cheeks flamed. "It's good to see you again, Eoghan. I'm sorry it is under these circumstances, but—"

"Who're you?" Eoghan asked, looking past her shoulder.

"This is my friend Charlotte. She's helping me move in." If he hadn't sounded so pissed and insulting, Ayanna might have said more, but given his rough demeanor, she streamlined her communication. Charlotte, on the other hand, did not.

"Is that you or the pizza?" Charlotte asked, fanning her nose.

"Hey, Charlotte, do you mind asking Louisa if she has any vinegar?" Ayanna asked.

"Vinegar? For what?" Charlotte asked.

"Just . . . please." Ayanna firmed up her tone.

"Okay." Charlotte backed away with her hands up.

Eoghan wiped his mouth with the back of his hand, uninterested in either of them. Her elite athlete had chosen pizza and beer over the nice spread of fresh fruits and vegetables, lean meats, and healthy grains. Everything she'd worked with the nutritionist to make sure was in his diet for ultimate muscle rebuilding and joint mobility was present on the table, yet Eoghan dismissed it as decoration.

"Tell me about the last couple of weeks. I know that being bedridden and then having so many rules regarding movement restrictions as well as the pain had to be an adjustment."

Eoghan grimaced as if remembering the last month or two of just postop healing. "I can't walk properly. What else is there to know?"

"But you can bear weight on it. You may still need the crutches, but—"

"I can't walk," he grumbled.

He could walk, just not well or without support yet, but she opted not to correct him further, given his touchy demeanor. "How are you feeling?" She folded her arms over her chest and looked down at him as he drained his beer, in the hope that he'd pick up on her disapproval.

"Well, um, let's see now. My leg's mangled. I haven't been able to aim my piss properly until a week ago, and my team is in the championship without me. How the fuck do you think I feel?"

"Quit acting the bollocks, eejit," Shane said. "If I were you, I'd be nice to your therapist."

"Wonderful." The sarcastic tone Eoghan used grated louder than the heavy metal chair she dragged across the stone patio until it was in front of Eoghan.

"Your leg should be elevated." Ayanna squatted to lift Eoghan's injured limb.

"Leave it," Eoghan said when she touched him.

She flinched, surprised by his bark, then straightened slower than molasses. She made her five-foot, four-inch figure taller, put her hand on her hip, and waited as she stared down at him.

"It still hurts," Eoghan mumbled. "I'd rather you just let me do it."

"It will feel better once it's elevated. I know that's on your list of dos and don'ts because I sent it over myself in addition to whatever your surgeon's instructions have been." Ayanna sat down next to him.

"I wanted to sit normally for once," he said.

"Well, once we get going, we'll have you feeling better in no time."

"We?"

"Yes. You and me. I can't do this without you, Eoghan. I'm going to give you one hundred percent. I expect you to match that."

He slowed his food inhalation, and even though he wouldn't admit it, something she said penetrated.

"I'll share a secret: beer and pizza won't get you there," she whispered jokingly. "This is a lovely spread you got here. Why not try to enjoy some of it?"

"The cook insisted on making it, even though I told her I was good with this," he said.

"Ms. Doyle is more than a cook. She plays as vital a role as I do in getting your health back. It's so warm today. Fresh fruit and water are good for hydration and, like elevating your leg, will help you have less pain."

Eoghan reached into his pocket and pulled out a pill bottle. "Taken care of." He shook the contents at her.

Hot under the collar, she fanned herself. "It's warm out today."

"I'll pour you some water," Shane said, reaching for a yellow pitcher on the table. He poured glasses for her and Charlotte, who returned with an oil-and-vinegar cruet set.

"Thanks," Ayanna said to Shane, knowing she needed more than water to take the edge off. She readied a plate. "Well, do you mind if we enjoy it?"

Eoghan shrugged.

"Let's eat, guys. We can't let this go to waste." Ayanna encouraged everyone to gather at the table to eat. She wanted to believe that Eoghan's bratty attitude was due to his condition, so she did her best to take it in stride. She spooned and forked food onto her plate. "Charlotte, you love quinoa, don't you?" Ayanna asked.

Perplexed, Charlotte stared blankly at her for a moment, then understood Ayanna's intent. "Oh yeah. It's packed with protein, and it's so good like this."

Shane chuckled and took a helping of salad and grilled chicken. He opted for a whole-grain bun over the quinoa.

Ayanna loaded her plate with salad. "You're sure you don't want any, Eoghan?"

He didn't answer.

"Where'd you find pizza, anyway?" Ayanna asked and then took a bite of her salad.

"Shane bought it," Eoghan said.

"Did he now?" Ayanna wordlessly directed all enabling accusations at Shane.

"What?" Shane cleared his throat. "I ordered it for me."

"Obviously, that worked out well," Ayanna said.

"I didn't expect him to confiscate the whole thing," Shane complained.

"This is a house of healing, so I suggest we all eat well. After all, Eoghan is priority number one." Ayanna shoved another forkful of salad into her mouth and used each crunchy chew to exorcise her annoyance. She swallowed and took a sip of water. "Anything that jeopardizes his rehab will be dealt with."

Charlotte choked on her food. "Oooooh."

"Dealt with?" Shane repeated.

"Dealt with, eliminated, adjusted, whatever." Ayanna didn't even try to be nonchalant.

Shane leaned back in his chair. "That some kind of threat?"

"I don't threaten. I promise and keep my word so we can all keep moving forward together." Ayanna hoped she wouldn't have to deliver on that promise. "Today, I'll get settled in and discuss the schedule with you all. Tomorrow it's all hands on deck, so whatever this is"—Ayanna waved her hand to Eoghan and back to Shane—"please, get it out of your system, because we have real work to do."

Eoghan all but ignored her. She'd give him a short grace period, but if either Shane or Eoghan thought this was how the next few months were going to be, then they were sadly mistaken.

Later that night, Ayanna spent time in her new office attached to the gym on the ground level of the house. The wall-to-wall cherrywood furnishings were a bit oppressive for her taste. She reminded herself that for a long-term temporary work space it would do the job. What she did love was the massive number of books filling the shelves, which housed nearly everything she'd read in grad school along with many other texts on physiatry, biology, anatomy, and various therapies.

She organized the information she needed for the next day and put the routine she planned to implement with Eoghan up front and center. She liked that the office and the gym were next to each other. When she retired for the day, the layout would allow her to make the shift from work to "life," even if she'd share common space with her client and his liaison. That was what they were when she was in this space, and she vowed to never break that rule.

She finished her office work and acquainted herself with the gym. The beige utility carpeting and windows gave an uplifting feel to a place that her client might detest after a few rounds with her. The white-and-black-themed machines, ranging from treadmills and cycles to a reformer and weight-lifting benches, lined the sections. At the far end, a mirrored dance studio, also used for circuit training and aerobics, completed the fully equipped gym.

She opened the massage table and moved it to where Eoghan could watch television if he wanted to or if he needed a distraction from the pain she'd likely inflict. She spread a white sheet on top of the table and placed several towels by the pillow. The first session would test him, and she hoped he didn't faint or throw up with the deep-tissue pressure and leg manipulations she'd use to extend his range of motion and flexibility. She kicked a step stool over for her and for him. In the morning, she'd take another look at his chart and x-rays.

On her way to her room, she stopped in the kitchen, where Louisa was prepping some fruits and vegetables.

"Is that for Eoghan?" Ayanna asked.

Louisa nodded. "And for you too. If you find there's anything that I'm missing that you'd like, let me know, and I'll be sure to get it for you."

"Thank you, I will," Ayanna said. "I'm on my way up. Thought I'd grab a snack."

"Pantry is right over there. It's pretty filled up. I'm sure you'll find something to your liking."

Ayanna eyed the bowl of fruit, plucked two clementine oranges from it, and turned on an electric kettle. "I'll make a little herbal tea to take upstairs with me, but it's nice to know where the hard-core stuff is. I'm sure I'll need it."

"According to everyone who's worked with you, it eventually gets better. I expect not without a few bumps here and there," Louisa said. "I'll do my best to buckle in."

Was that the current chatter about her and her work? She had to admit that if the present lore about her physical therapy carried an edge of fear, she'd accept that. In fact, she liked it. "Good choice, Louisa." She winked and left Louisa to her work.

Ayanna climbed the stairs to her room. As she walked the corridor, she did her best not to spill her filled-to-the-brim cup of scalding-hot chamomile-and-lavender tea, but she dropped one of her clementines in the process. "Shoot!" The fruit rolled past one of the bedrooms. The door opened, and Shane popped out in checkered navy-and-white pajama bottoms and a white T-shirt that looked like he'd hastily stretched into it. His messy, wet, straight-out-of-the-towel hair hung two inches past his shoulders, and he smelled zesty in an aquatic kind of way. She inhaled, unaware that her body leaned toward him until droplets of her tea pelted the light-cream-colored carpet.

"Ayanna?"

She recentered her body. "Yup. That's my name."

"Everything all right?"

"Yeah." She huffed. "I just dropped my snack on the floor." She aimed her nose at the fruit that had stalled its getaway right in the middle of the corridor in front of them.

"Oh," Shane said and then reached down, scooped it up, and tried to hand it to her. Seeing her struggle to manage her lot without both hands, Shane walked with her. "I'll come with you."

"It's okay, no worries. Just stick it in the crook of my elbow, here." She shook her arm and, as it wiggled, realized what a silly suggestion she'd made.

"It's no problem." He walked with her.

She'd have sped up if it weren't for the ceramic mug, whose already hot temperature increased against her knuckles. She balanced the bottom of the mug on the clementine to adjust her fingers around the handle, the heat on the fruit releasing the fragrance of orange essence.

Shane opened the door to her room for her, and the cozy space that Charlotte had worked hard to decorate greeted them both. A turquoise, coral, and yellow rectangular floor pillow, fluffy off-white bedding, pictures of her with Charlotte and her sister, Jada, as kids, and her childhood teddy bear, Mr. Warren, were all strategically placed for comfort.

"Is this the same room from earlier?" Shane asked.

"I know," she groaned. "Charlotte wanted me to get comfortable fast and took it upon herself to grab some of my items from home and express her inner interior designer." Ayanna pointed to a few whimsically placed scarves.

He smiled as he put her Cutie on the nightstand.

She put her mug down. If she held it one more second, her knuckles would be singed to the third degree. "Thanks."

"Cute, you even still sleep with your teddy," he teased, and Ayanna stiffened. Shane noticed. "I was only teasin' ya."

Her face felt pulled and tight as she smiled. "Yeah, I know." She debated saying more. "It was a gift from my father. The last before he passed."

"I didn't mean to bring up a bad memory for you," he said, shoving his hands into his pajama pockets.

"It's not," she said. "Not completely, anyway." When Vance Crawford had died, he'd left Ayanna with his broken wife, who would have been happy to follow him to the grave if she could, even with two daughters to raise. Mr. Warren marked so many things. The end of her childhood, the year she'd had to learn to iron Jada's clothes without burning them. How she'd learned to read maps and navigate the public transit system to get around and pretend she was older so Jada and everyone else would take her authority seriously. She'd turned from a fairly outgoing kid to one who kept to herself to keep the questions at bay. The milestones the bear marked were many.

"It's nice that you have something of his," he said at last, and she wanted to know if it was sentiment or experience that cracked his voice.

"Bittersweet."

Shane shifted from one foot to another. "Looks like you were heading to bed."

"Yeah. Tomorrow will be a tough day."

"Right, then. Good night."

"Good night, Shane."

That night, like always, she took off the gold bracelet she wore every day and stuffed it into the secret pocket on Mr. Warren's tummy, the same way her father had presented her with the gift so many years ago. Instinctively, she slept with the bear in her arms to keep the nightmares away.

Chapter Fourteen

Ayanna waited patiently in the gym for Eoghan. The walls seemed whiter than they had been when she'd looked over Eoghan's case last night and the night before that. He'd missed their session yesterday, and today looked strikingly similar.

A half hour later, Shane entered the gym with grim reaper vibes.

"Where is he?" Ayanna asked when Eoghan didn't follow.

"He claims he's not feeling well—again," Shane responded with the heaviness of a friend who'd been bequeathed the honor of delivering lies.

"That so? Was it the leftover pizza and more beer that made him miss breakfast this morning?" Ayanna asked. She hadn't seen Eoghan eat anything nutritious in the forty-eight hours that she'd been at Purchase House. "Let's go ask him, shall we?"

Shane stopped her. "He won't come down, Ayanna."

"Well, I'm here to work on him, not to cater to a toddler having some kind of tantrum. He's a professional athlete."

"He's just having a bad day."

"Since I got here, apparently." She dropped her shoulders. "He's going to have a lot of bad days, but he has to work through them, the same way he's played through them. The longer he sulks about the injury, the harder it will be to get him back."

"I'm aware." Shane's tone carried the bite of frustration.

"Then help me get him down here so I can work him out. We need to start exercising that leg. My techniques don't work without a subject." Ayanna headed upstairs.

Shane trailed her up to Eoghan's room. She knocked but got no answer. "Eoghan?" Still nothing. She gestured to Shane to enter.

Shane shrugged and opened the door. Ayanna's jaw dropped when she saw Eoghan asleep hugging a bag of Cheez Doodles with one arm and gripping the remote loosely with his other hand. A gambling app played on the screen, displaying Eoghan's losses and winnings. His only saving grace was that he wore his brace and kept his leg elevated.

"Let me guess." Ayanna's hands went to her hips. "This is what 'not feeling well' looks like?"

"Like I said, he's having a bad day," Shane said.

Ayanna had had just about enough of Shane and his disregard for Eoghan's behavior. "Why do you keep making excuses for him?" she asked. She didn't give Shane a chance to answer before she went over to Eoghan and gently shook him awake. "Eoghan?" she called. "Wake up. You're late for your therapy session."

Eoghan groaned, the bag of Cheez Doodles crinkling as he hugged it closer like a pillow and tossed himself away from her.

"Come on, Eoghan. You've had six weeks to sleep, rest, and get your mind ready to work on rehabbing this leg. I need you to get up." She shook him again. This time Eoghan aggressively jerked his arm away.

"Leave," he growled. "I'm not up for it."

"Eating cheesy snacks and gambling? Hmm, seems like you're pretty capable to me," she said. "Where's the star athlete I met in Dublin?"

Eoghan craned his neck, and she was met with a hard mask of anger. "A star athlete with this shit leg?"

"Listen to yourself. You're giving up, and you've not even started yet." Shane tried to sit on the edge of the bed, but Eoghan kicked him off. *Brave man.*

"I don't want your arse on my bed or your pep talk. So go and whistle," Eoghan said.

"Ungrateful gobshite." Shane scratched his head with both hands, and his complexion gave his frustration away. "I know your battle, but there's lots of money invested in you and your treatment. Get on board."

"I'll start when I'm damn well ready."

"Eoghan, I understand."

"No," his voice boomed. "You don't understand." He turned back over.

She swallowed hard. With her clients she tried hard not to say those words because even if she could identify with them, she didn't understand the pain they went through as individuals. She could empathize, but each had their own journey. "You're right. I don't understand everything you're going through." This wasn't her lane. She might be able to motivate and inspire her clients through mental blocks when it came to physical therapy, but she wasn't a mental health professional. "But I can listen if you want to get some things off your chest. Maybe I can explain more about the therapy?"

"Just go," he said.

Ayanna had seen athletes get depressed after an injury and suffer from insecurities about their ability to come back, but Eoghan lacked any motivation to even try. No matter what she said, not even a sliver of his ambition showed up.

"Leave him, Ayanna." Shane touched her upper arm, and she looked up at him. "We can talk with him when he's up and start again."

She nodded, and they left his room. In the hallway, Ayanna paced with hands on her hips. Then she bolted to her office and opened Eoghan's file. She checked to see if he'd had any counseling needs met during his postop period. Shane knocked on her door but hung in the frame.

"He hasn't had any therapy?" she asked Shane.

Shane crossed his arms over his chest, his short-sleeved black shirt tightening around the biceps. "He refused."

"Refused."

"It's optional."

"Yeah, but he's a celebrity player who has a serious injury that could have complications and in the past would have definitely been career ending. Surely he has some insecurities about that. Talking to someone might help."

"He has very strong feelings about it."

"Why?"

"Not my place to say." Shane massaged his forehead.

She closed his file and plopped into her chair and tapped her fingers on the desk. Day two was another bust, and she hated nothing more than wasting valuable time.

"I can see you're frustrated," Shane said.

"I have a job to do, and I'm sitting on my ass because my client is having a bad day. I'm not a fan of idle time, but alas, it's not about me."

"It's better for him to be on his own today," Shane said.

"You keep saying that. I feel like there's something you're not telling me. If it's something that will make things go smoother—"

"If all of a sudden, your hands stopped working, how would you feel?"

"I get it, Shane. I'm well acquainted with loss," Ayanna said and breathed to soothe the ache that often crept in out of nowhere. "I've done that exercise of putting myself in his shoes, but the fact of the matter is that he only has a chance if we do the work. The last thing I'd want to happen is that he doesn't make any progress, gets handed off to another therapist, and never makes it back because he has lost critical beginning-stage rehabilitation."

"Understood. Give him today, and tomorrow we'll try again."

"I don't have much of a choice." She surrendered to the situation. "How are you doing? I'm sure being here wasn't on your list of things you expected to do."

"Me?" He seemed surprised by her pivot and came fully into the office.

"Yeah, you," she confirmed.

He sat on a small love seat by the window. His lengthy body barely fit on the thing. "I'm staying positive that Eoghan will come around. New York is kind of my second home. I've been here often to visit family and the country. It's different being here like this, but Eoghan wanted me here, and he's one of my best mates, so . . ."

He wasn't here for her. Ayanna filled in the blanks and jumped out of her seat, letting any disappointment fall away. "I need to figure out how to get him in that gym and on that table. I mean, what am I going to do the whole day? My schedule has been completely cleared for this."

"You can take a swim or do something else to relax."

"Are you trying to say I'm uptight?" she asked.

Shane raised a brow and smiled. "Uhh, no. I'm just suggesting you take advantage of the house while you're here. Yes, you're here to work, but you can have a little fun too."

"Fun?"

"Yes, fun." Even from his post by the window, his eyes sparkled.

She straightened herself into Dr. Crawford posture. "Do you not realize the intense pressure rehabilitating Eoghan comes with?"

"All the more reason for you to be relaxed. Remember when you attended the match? You had fun then."

"News flash—we're not in Dublin anymore. I'm not an unknown therapist who can let her hair down and let the chips fall where they may. The Rovers' management and the national team are expecting results, and now isn't the time for my reputation and research to take a hit. Eoghan and his recovery are the only important things here. I can relax when this is over."

"Got it," Shane said, and the brightness she liked seeing in his face darkened again. "That's my cue." He stood up and headed for the door.

Several seconds passed before she realized how what she'd said might have sounded to him. She leaped from her seat. "Hey, I didn't mean—"

"I have an appointment in the city."

"Shane," she called to him.

"You haven't said anything I don't already know," Shane said. "I've gotta go."

"Hey, wait." Coming around her desk, she reached for his arm.

"What?" He turned on her. He was close, too close. Her breast grazed the top of his tummy, and she fell into the sensation of his hard body against her livening nipples. His hands were on her shoulders, resting unmoving, and she felt his breath fan the hair on top of her head. *Don't look up.* Her head, confused by what her heart wanted and what practicality demanded, made its choppy tilt upward to see what, if anything, his face revealed.

"Ayanna," he said, his eyes blazing blue.

"Excuse me, I wasn't—" she began, not wanting him to think she'd tried to jump his bones on purpose, but then he gently steered her back away from him.

"I'll leave you to your work." He made a quick exit.

She full-body sighed, then collected herself and blamed what had happened on being familiar with him. "It's only a little attraction. This is nothing new or different." She might not believe it, but it would have to do. She couldn't have another day like this with Eoghan or with Shane. She had to stay focused and get Eoghan on the table. Every small win counted. She'd give him today, but his grace period had officially ended. Whether her housemates knew it or not, things were about to get real.

Chapter Fifteen

Ayanna leaned against the massage table in the gym, staring at the clock. Eoghan had skipped breakfast again, and the day looked similar to the previous ones. She summoned the low tank of patience she had left and waited in the gym for Eoghan to show up.

She heard the slow click of crutches, and soon Eoghan limped inside in yesterday's clothes. It became apparent to Ayanna by his lethargic movements that either he wasn't resting well or something else was up.

"Good morning," she greeted. "How are you?"

He shrugged.

"Our session started ten minutes ago," Ayanna said. She marched through the room like a drill sergeant.

"I'm here, aren't I?"

"Yes. You are." *Even if your attitude stinks.* "Please arrive to your sessions on time so we can maximize our time."

"Or what? You're being paid either way. You give two shits whether I can play again or not."

Ayanna accepted her invitation to Eoghan's pity party and decided she would give him two minutes to get it out of his system before they started. "I care, Eoghan. I want you to get better and play."

"No," he said, pointing at her. "My career is over. My team's playing without me. I'm fucked."

Ayanna kept her voice level and firm. The last thing he needed was to feel as though she were patronizing him. "I think you can get better, but you have to help me help you, Eoghan."

"Fuck you," Eoghan yelled. '

That escalated fast. At the corner of her eye Shane appeared and was about to approach them, but she held up a hand to stop him. Ayanna didn't acknowledge Eoghan's outburst.

"First thing we need to do is warm you up. Let's get you to the table," Ayanna said, but she didn't approach him. Experience had taught her well enough to be prepared for another angry outburst or worse.

Eoghan threw one of his crutches, and she ducked instinctively, like when her baby sister used to have her tantrums and turn her LEGO into weapons, launching them her way.

Motherfucker! Her gut might have told her he hadn't thrown it at her, but an airborne crutch was dangerous all the same.

Shane strode toward them in an instant. "You all right, then?" he asked, glaring at Eoghan.

"Yeah." She frowned and adjusted the gold bangle on her arm. "We're having a conversation. You can get out of here. I got this."

At age eleven Ayanna had become Jada's mother figure, the one she could rely on, the one to raise her and take care of her. Ayanna had also had to learn to step out of her sister shoes and become a disciplinarian, and the skills had never left her. Hell if she didn't need to serve up a buffet tray of super tough love.

Shane seemed reluctant to leave.

"Please. This is between me and him. Go," she said.

"Behave yourself," Shane commanded Eoghan before leaving.

"Fuck this," Eoghan said and tried to leave, but he'd thrown one of his crutches away and still needed both. "Pick it up," he yelled.

Ayanna took deliberate breaths to calm herself, because Eoghan was about to come face to face with the politest bitch he'd ever meet. They didn't know this side of her, but they were about to. With the same level firmness, she replied, "Why? It's obvious that you don't need it very much."

"I need it," Eoghan growled.

"Then maybe you should have thought twice before you threw it. If you want it, you can go pick it up yourself, and then when you are finished with your tantrum, we can start." Ayanna once again folded her arms and waited.

"Fuck you and fuck this place," Eoghan said and hobbled out on one crutch.

She rolled her neck and stretched it from side to side. Eoghan had started a battle, but his amateur bullshit paled in comparison to her PT-warrior skills. She stepped over the crutch to get to her phone, which she'd left on one of the workout benches, and pocketed it.

Shane returned, a strained look of concern on his face. "I saw Eoghan heading out. You okay?"

"I'm fine. He's just going through it. He'll come around on his own," she said. "Or by force."

"Force?"

"That's as long of a leash as he's going to get," Ayanna said.

Shane went to retrieve the crutch.

"Leave it." Ayanna's voice was louder than either she or Shane anticipated. "If he wants it, he will have to come and get it himself."

"Ayanna, he's still getting used to bearing weight on his leg," Shane said.

"Then he should have valued the crutch instead of throwing it," she said.

"I'm not comfortable with this."

She touched his arm. "I know what I'm doing, Shane. Leave it."

"All right," Shane said at length. "Would you like some lunch or a shot of Bushmills?"

She looked at him like she'd done countless times in Dublin when she'd needed a translation.

"Whiskey, love." Shane's face turned the color of Red Hots candy. He looked just as surprised as she felt at the endearment he clearly hadn't intended to use.

"Uhh . . . shot."

By the end of the week at the house, things had gotten ugly. Eoghan hadn't moved since he'd lost his crutch, and he continued to over-medicate, even though he wasn't eating well. Shane, though he hadn't retrieved the crutch, made sure Louisa brought food to Eoghan.

Late in the morning, Ayanna found the house manager in the living area tidying up. The housekeeper who came in twice a week had already gone, leaving behind the scent of pine. Louisa often followed the housekeeper's path to add her own personal touches to the couch pillows or centerpieces and the like on various tables.

"Louisa?" Ayanna called to her.

"Ah, Dr. Crawford. You look lovely in your yellow scrubs."

Ayanna peered down at herself as if she'd forgotten she wore a different color uniform each day to work out with Eoghan. The stylish hems and flowy, breathable material made her look both professional and casual. "Oh, thank you."

"You're welcome," Louisa said. "Did you need me?"

"Yes, I did. At mealtimes for Mr. O'Farrell, can you please make a place setting at the table and serve him there? The dining room preferably, but the patio table is also fine. My point is, *he* comes to the meal. The meal doesn't go to him."

"But he says he can't walk," Louisa said.

"He can if he tries and attends therapy. Let's help him try, okay?"

Louisa chewed on her lip.

"I'm here to help him, Louisa," Ayanna soothed. "He needs to move."

Louisa nodded. "Will do."

At the next mealtime, Louisa set a place setting, and Ayanna braved letting Eoghan know that Louisa had set up his meal on the dining room table. Though he did get up, he struggled to take himself outside by the pool, where Shane had been reading, and commanded Louisa to serve him there.

"I'm over it." Ayanna stood. The time had long passed for Eoghan to snap out of whatever funk had him drowning in a sea of shitty behavior. She marched outside, and the sound of Shane's disapproval grew louder as she approached them.

"You're acting the bollocks," Shane said in an attempt to talk some sense into Eoghan.

Ayanna was done talking. If Eoghan wanted to hurt himself and fail at recovery, he wasn't going to do it on her watch.

"Shane? Can you give me and Eoghan a moment? We need a heart-to-heart," Ayanna said with hands on hips.

"Shane, stay your arse," Eoghan said.

"Your choice." Ayanna had no time to waste on further arguments. Eoghan would be taught a lesson whether Shane stayed or not.

"You know what, Eoghan? Ever since I've arrived, you've been throwing heat at me like a dragon whose lair I entered." She went over to the side of the house and turned on the outdoor pipe. She yanked on the water hose, unwinding it from its reel.

"What ya doing there, Ayanna?" Shane asked, tilting his head.

"I've been patient and understanding, but that has only fanned the flames." She turned the nozzle from spray to jet and aimed the handle at Eoghan and Shane, who was by his side. Neither one of them had time to react as she squeezed the handle and let the jetted streams fly.

"Feck all!" Shane ran away from Eoghan and watched her in shock.

Since Eoghan couldn't move well, he twisted in the lawn chair, sputtering water. His lunch flew about under the forceful streams, and he yelled and cursed.

Cold mist flew back on her, decorating her scrubs with water marks. She might be hot under the collar, but still, goose pimples rose on her skin as spring's temperate evening air blew.

"What the hell are you doing?" Eoghan shouted between breathing attempts.

Barely moving, she briefly released the handle to answer. "Cooling you off."

"Ayanna." Eoghan choked on her name.

She again halted her assault. "Do you want to get better or not, Eoghan? Tell me now."

"You've lost your fucking mind," Eoghan yelled.

"Wrong answer." Ayanna pressed the handle to release the water again. Relentless, she continued to wet Eoghan's already soaked clothes and body.

"Ayanna," Shane called. "That's enough. He—"

Ayanna turned her vicious spray at Shane. "Shut up or go away!"

Shane hopped and skipped away from the sprays, and Ayanna turned the streams back on Eoghan.

Eoghan tried to cover his face. "All right. Stop!"

"Ready to talk to me like your therapist instead of your doormat?" Ayanna asked.

"Yes," Eoghan panted and wiped his face.

Ayanna moved in close to tower over his sitting figure. "It stops, now. There will be no more junk food in your system, no more over-medicating and hurting your body, and no more alcohol." She grabbed the can of beer and threw it into the pool.

"I'm Irish!" Eoghan said, shaking water off his arms.

"Look at my face. Do I look like I give a shit?"

"No," Eoghan mumbled.

"No, I don't. You can survive without drinking for a few weeks." She barreled on. "Keep your leg elevated every time your ass is in a chair, and be nicer to everyone who is here sacrificing their time to help you." She started to take her leave. "Shane can help you change your clothes. Be ready to work out at three." She dropped the nozzle like a mic.

Shane held his hands up. "Jaysus, Ayanna. Remind me never to piss you off."

Both Eoghan and Shane stared at her, wide eyed.

She left them with the taste of Ayanna version 2.0. Louisa giggled behind her hand, but Ayanna wasn't done.

"He eats at the table, or he doesn't eat. Am I clear?" Ayanna said to Louisa.

Louisa straightened. "Yes, Dr. Crawford. Crystal."

Ayanna was turned up, but they all had to understand that she wasn't in Purchase to play house. Every day she hadn't worked on Eoghan had been an opportunity wasted. She plucked a snack bar from a basket and went to her computer to enter in some notes on Eoghan's progress. *Responds to shock therapy*, she typed.

At three that afternoon, Eoghan hobbled down to the training room, retrieved his crutch, and made his way to the massage table.

"I'm ready, Ayanna," Eoghan said.

They'd reached their first milestone. Mutual respect. "Welcome to day one of your road back."

Ayanna completed her session with Eoghan and kept her distance by design. She wanted to keep the mystery alive. She'd had a breakthrough with Eoghan, but they needed to keep moving toward creating a progress mentality. She ate dinner, a bowl of soup and a beer, alone in the garden. Her favorite and most peaceful part of the house.

Shane found her and offered her a beer, which she gladly took. After the day's events, another cold one was just what she needed to take the edge off.

"Thank you," she said.

"Mind if I sit?" He'd changed out of his wet khaki pants and white shirt into gray jogging pants and a black shirt.

Ayanna shrugged.

"You were a pistol today, but you got through to him." Shane's accent mushed the words together.

"Yeah," she said. Shane might be there to support Eoghan, but she considered that he might be doing more harm than good and inadvertently sabotaging her efforts. "Hey, look, I know you want to help Eoghan, but I'm going to need you to stop enabling him. I know you guys are friends, but if he wants to get better quick, he has to do what I say."

"Enable him?"

"Yes. Sharing beers and getting him junk. Talking to him like he's in charge. He's not. I am—at least until he's better."

"You don't have to hold on to everything so tight, Ayanna. Maybe if you relaxed a bit—"

"Relaxed? I'm living with two men instead of teaching classes, running clinics, working with clients who are motivated to do the work, and expanding my research. I have a career, reputation, and future on the line."

"Again, maybe you need to relax," Shane said. "You're not the only one with things on the line."

Ayanna guzzled her beer for about three seconds in an attempt to not spew venom at Shane. She was the financial head of her broken family, taking care of herself and putting her sister, Jada, through college and parenting her and her wild ways from afar. She'd been all but married to her career until recently. The last thing she needed was to be antagonized by someone who had nothing to lose and was vacationing here in the US with his buddy. She rose from her seat to leave.

"Sit down," Shane commanded.

"Did you just command me to sit?" She seethed.

Shane stood up, towering over her. "You're not talking to Eoghan anymore."

She began to storm off toward the house.

"Please," Shane called to her, even if the manners he summoned lacked any politeness.

Tempted as she might be to test him, his usually pleasant disposition had been replaced with brewing annoyance she could feel from every part of his form. She turned, sat down, and stared straight ahead with the most miserable face she could muster.

"Everyone is thankful that you're here. Me more than anyone. I know you think that I'm an enabler, but you have to understand that football and celebrity are all Eoghan has. He wouldn't know what to do if he couldn't play. That fear is making him irrational."

Ayanna tried to read Shane's pensive thoughts, but like her, he'd taken the master class at keeping them a mystery.

"You know this from experience?" she challenged.

"Yes," he said. "I played. Eoghan, Pippin, and I played together."

"You played? Professionally?" she questioned, surprised by her own ignorance.

"Better than Eoghan, he'd tell you."

How had she not seen it before? The hoodie at Aviva. Liam at the bar alluding to him being clobbered, and Shane revealing himself as they went through the stadium like his very image was some sort of currency. Of course he'd played. Why had she never searched him on the internet? Because she'd been too busy with Eoghan, and the less she knew, the easier it was to walk away.

"We grew up wanting to dominate football, and we did for a time until I got hurt. I had a horrible time of it. Lost my girlfriend." He choked on that last bit. "There was no coming back to the game for me. Luckily, the lads and me folks were supportive."

A slight streak of jealousy ran up Ayanna's spine, and she shivered. She reprimanded herself for feeling it while he shared so candidly about so much more, and she shoved it down. "What happened?"

"I broke my ankle. Tore my Achilles. The break was bad, and the surgery didn't go well. I tried to come back, but no matter how hard I pushed, the leg has never been the same."

"And your girlfriend?"

"Eileen." Shane said the name like it was a mouthful. "She was great, so long as I was playing and the fame of dating me had its rewards. She wanted to have fun, not be in love and stick it out with her injured lover. So she moved on to another man."

She reached for his hand and held it a moment before letting it go. "I'm sorry, Shane. That's awful." If he omitted any details, it was his prerogative, and given the painful memories, she couldn't blame him.

"It was a very challenging time for me. I may not have been as bad as Eoghan, but I came pretty close, if you can believe it." He rubbed his head. "So I do know what he's going through, firsthand. Sometimes he just needs to be left with his thoughts."

Ayanna didn't know what else to say, so she said nothing.

"Thought you should know that you're not doing this on your own. I can help you, even if it's not always your way."

She nodded. "Okay, but my rules still stand, Shane."

"They're good rules, but just like you want to help Eoghan, let me help you," he said.

His face held the same tenderness it had when he'd spoken to her in the stands a few months ago, and Ayanna again questioned her feelings for Shane, which kept bubbling below the surface.

Ayanna stood. "Don't ever command me to do anything again."

"Neither you nor I would ever want me to make that promise." His mischievous grin made clear his meaning, and Ayanna's cheeks were hot and flushed.

"Good night, Shane," she said and fled. She headed into the house and grabbed another beer before retiring to her room. She was already feeling the effects of the first and second one, but she wasn't driving. No, she was coping—trying to, anyway. Her emotions were tricky to pinpoint, like an unsteady infrared on a rifle unable to scope its target. Eoghan was so different from the man she'd initially been attracted to in Dublin, and though she knew it was because of his injury, that fact didn't seem to help. Then there was Shane, who seemed to be attracted to her and flirted with her at times but kept a fair distance from her in that department. Could she feel for Eoghan past their match-day surprise and the romantic moments that she'd sworn would stay in Dublin? Did she even want to?

And why the hell did her temperature rise every time she thought about or came in contact with Shane?

Chapter Sixteen

Shane tossed in bed, haunted by another dream of having her. He'd beaten one out of himself in the shower last night in hopes he'd get a restful sleep, but beyond his desire for her lay the tender way she'd listened to him and touched his hand as if his feelings were her own.

"Feck, lass," he groaned into a pillow, squeezing it to him like he'd wanted to do to Ayanna countless times. Why did she have to be a woman both he and Eoghan wanted? Did Eoghan even want her, or had she just been a local convenience? With Eoghan's ego, he couldn't always tell.

Shane scrambled out of bed like his alarm had gone off. Why did he have to be so fucking honorable to the agreement between them? The pact hadn't even been because of anything he'd done other than be a good boyfriend to Eileen. He'd given her his all even while injured, given her his black card to shop for anything that would make her happy, and fucked her as best he could even when he'd come dangerously close to blacking out from the excruciating pain in his leg as he'd tried to heal. Still, Eileen had set her sights on Eoghan.

Had it not been for his stepmother, who'd introduced him to the senior center in the Bronx, he didn't know who he'd be today. Three years ago when his stepmother had brought him there for the first time, he'd been drowning in despair, heartache, and betrayal. He'd needed a trip away from Ireland—in fact, his life had depended on it. Volunteering at the center and taking care of others had taken the focus off himself and allowed him to truly start healing. The residents like Daphne, Martha, and Fred had since become his friends. Now as he stayed at Purchase House, he volunteered there every Thursday, and the change of scenery and sense of giving back helped him check his ego, but he still had a few days until Thursday.

He stripped naked to cool off, yet his mind wandered to how Ayanna would look in nothing at all. When she touched his bare chest, his thighs, would she attack him like she did her workouts or skim her fingers down his muscles like the way she lightly stroked the back of her hair?

Blood pumped through him. "Christ Church Cathedral." He was hard again from his unruly thoughts. If he had any hope of getting back to himself, he had to get out of the house.

The fresh spring air invigorated Shane as soon as it hit him. The tension of the last few weeks had finally started to compress him like the black material of the Under Armour leggings he wore beneath his shorts, just not in a good way. However, as soon as he flipped his gray hoodie and his trainers hit the ground for his run, his lungs opened up and he remembered what it was like to move his body this way. He hadn't been as consistent as he should with his exercise. He planned to change that and take advantage of the healthful environment, aside from living with and wanting a woman he couldn't have, and easy access to the gym.

How'd he get into this situation again? He and Eoghan had promised to never date the same woman again after Eileen, but Shane had no idea how Eoghan felt about Ayanna now, given his sulky mood and ill-treatment of them all since he'd gotten here. Shane wasn't even sure what their pact meant anymore or what he would do even if he did have the all clear to pursue Ayanna. He ran faster until the sharp pain in his ankle seized him. He slowed down and walked the rest of the way. He hadn't taken any painkillers in weeks, but he might need one tonight.

When he returned to the house, he headed for the gym. He obviously needed to focus more on strengthening some of those muscles around his ankle. He heard a voice he didn't recognize. Inside, Ayanna was working out, performing burpees, five by his current count, from a strength-and-conditioning workout via Peloton.

Feeeck! The brutal circuit kept going, and Ayanna looked right fit doing it. He heard her breathing, but she was smiling, enjoying every minute of it. She did a double take when she saw him, gave him a quick wave, and kept going.

"Five more seconds," he heard the instructor say before continuing the countdown. "One and done."

"Whew!" Ayanna huffed, pouring sweat that glistened over her brown skin.

If anyone knew how much he wanted to lick every drop off her, they might think him weird. "You do that every day? That's a proper workout."

She guzzled water. "I do something four, sometimes five days a week. It's good for me to be strong and flexible for my work. I tell my students that all the time. Legs aren't light. Neither is deadweight when someone can't hold themselves up."

He hadn't thought on it. He'd always get worked on before matches and after but hadn't really considered that his therapists were also keeping themselves strong and conditioned for their profession.

"Are you getting ready to work out?" she asked.

"Yeah. Had a run. Getting back into a routine," he said.

"You should try it," she suggested, pointing to the machine.

"Do you mind if I work out while you're here? Or sometimes when you're working on Eoghan?"

"Why would I mind? You're exercising. Eoghan's your friend. Plus, it might be a good thing to keep you accountable and on a schedule too."

"Are you sure? If you want the privacy—"

"You're good. Do your thing." She toweled off and did her stretching while he worked on cardio.

He focused on a thigh machine, which happened to be in view of her yoga mat, and his wandering eyes kept sliding her way. Her flexible legs, balance, and coordination rivaled any athlete's.

"What do you do for core?"

"Mostly floor exercise, crunches, planks, and the like," he answered.

"Try yoga or Pilates."

"Are you trying to get me on your routine, Ayanna?" He hadn't meant to become a part of her workout in any way, but this was the most conversation they'd had in some time, and he remembered how interesting she was and how much he enjoyed talking with her.

"It's good. Look, this is a chair pose." She reached her arms up and sat back on her heels in a bit of a squat. "Try it."

He did, and she came out of the pose and over to him. "Mind if I . . ." She mimed touching him.

"No, no. Go on." He gave his body over to her freely.

She gripped his hips, and he faltered at her gentle, small hands on his waist. "Easy. Try to keep your balance. Stay grounded. Arms up, and tighten your core." She continued to touch him on each area she mentioned, and he held his breath for fear he'd moan or embarrass himself in some other form.

"Breathe," she whispered close to his ear.

Even with the growing intensity of the chair pose, the woman undid him. "Ayanna."

"Hold for a couple more breaths." She ran a hand down his back. "Keep it straight. Strong."

Fuck me. He squeezed his lower abdomen and willed himself not to get hard.

"And stand up. Reach for the sky. Hands to the side. Follow your breath," she instructed. "Good! How did that feel?"

"Fucking amazing."

By the light crimson dusting her cheeks, he already knew that his complexion flared red with the heat she so easily ignited in him.

She busied herself with some arm stretches of her own. "You'd be surprised how great you feel. Especially Yin for stretching your leg."

He bounced in place to shake out the tension in his body. "You just can't help yourself, can you?"

"With what?" she asked, eagerness in her voice.

Turning me on. "Fixing people."

"I don't fix people. I help them fix themselves." She stopped mid-pose. "They just have to want to."

Her words settled on a seat in his heart.

"Oi, finally decided to get back in form?" Eoghan chided him as he strutted in with a "the talent has arrived" vibe.

Shane groaned inside at the interruption. "Soon, I'll be sporting a better figure than yourself."

"Keep dreamin'." Eoghan threw a nearby towel at him.

"Shane says you used to play together," Ayanna said. Her head moved back and forth between them as if deciding where to place her focus.

"The MAKin' crew. With Pippin." Eoghan's eyes lit up, and she got a glimpse of the man she'd initially met. "Best midfielder."

He hated that Eoghan had brought this up. Ayanna knew he'd been hurt playing the game and never come back. "Story done. Case closed."

"He's in pain."

"Will you shut your gob, Eoghan. Don't you have a workout to do yourself?" Shane asked.

"Hmm . . . I could take a look at it," Ayanna suggested.

"Good luck so. He'll not let you near it," Eoghan answered.

"Why not?" she asked him.

"He's a girl about it. No offense," Eoghan said. "He'll tear your head off if you try."

"Offense taken." Ayanna crossed her arms. "And oh, by the way . . . I'm tougher than you and Shane put together."

Shane gave a sly smile at her comeback. He was dead for her.

"I don't doubt it, Ayanna," Eoghan said.

"Don't patronize me. Go do your warm-up exercises," she said. "I'm going to get a shower. I'll be back shortly for our session."

Shane imagined what sharing a shower with her would be like. Streams of water cascading over her luscious skin, trickling down the curve of her back, and dripping off her breasts. He imagined darker nipples that he'd lick and tease as she raked her fingers through his hair and kissed the top of his head. Based on how she worked out, he'd run his palms over the supple skin covering defined abs, down to her center, where his mind's eye flipped back and forth between hair and no hair. How much he wanted to kneel in front of her, lift her leg over his shoulder, and . . .

"Get a good warm-up, Eoghan. It's a tough one," she tossed back on her way out.

Eoghan groaned. "She's going to brutalize me."

"Great. You deserve it." Shane couldn't help himself.

"What's up your arse?" Eoghan asked, clueless as ever.

"Maybe next time, you'll let me speak for myself," Shane said. "Ye dope."

Eoghan dismissed his comments as nonchalantly as always.

Exasperated from overstimulation, Shane returned to his workout.

Ayanna manipulated Eoghan's leg in a stretch. Though her face neared his crotch and they both panted, the completely unsexy torture of rehabilitation echoed through the gym. She'd just had a shower, yet the sweat dampened her forehead and her pits as she worked on Eoghan.

"Push." She exhaled to modulate her fatigue like she would in a workout.

"Agh," Eoghan growled, covered his sweating face, and huffed painful breaths through his fingers.

"A little more." Her shoulder rested in the crook of his knee, and she pressed her body forward, stretching his hamstring with her small but sturdy frame. "Five . . ."

"Fuck, Ayanna."

"Three, two, and one." She released him. "And relax." She massaged his thigh and hamstring and down his leg.

She grabbed the cold-therapy circulator machine from the corner of the gym and took it over to an armchair. "Any aversion to needles?" she asked him.

"No. Why?" His accent shortened his words.

"I'm bringing in an acupuncturist. I think it will help you release that IT band, and your working leg could use the relaxation as well. The last thing I want is for you to get bursitis from overcompensating."

"I've done IMS before for sciatica," Eoghan said.

"Intramuscular stimulation is more . . . intense. That's not what you need." She lugged the machine over to him and readied it for his knee. "The things you guys put your body through. How do you feel?"

"I'm afraid to tell you 'cause you'll just dig your elbow into me." Eoghan gave a nervous laugh.

"I'm not that bad," she said.

"No. Worse." Soft humor rang in his words. He'd made excellent progress since he'd been forced to get on board a month ago, and she couldn't ask for more from her client at this stage.

"Come on, tell me where it hurts and I'll fix you up."

"It's tender here." He pointed to just below his butt.

"Over," she instructed, and Eoghan obliged.

She ran her hand under the roundness of his butt, where the hamstring started. "Let me know when I've hit it." A short month had passed since she'd started working with him, yet his athletic body responded quickly.

"Mmm," he said.

"Is that where you feel it?" She kept her hand there and waited for confirmation.

"No, I just haven't been touched there in a while." He propped himself up on his elbow and glanced back at her. That youthful smile that had gotten her to agree to go to the soccer match with him spread across his face. He horrified her further when he squeezed his butt cheeks a couple of times.

Her skin flushed, and she fumbled to find her words. "You need a shave." That was the best she could come up with? *What the fuck?*

"I'm only teasing ya." Laughter rumbled in his chest, and he lowered back down onto the pillow. "Let me show you." He took hold of her hand and moved it to the exact spot. "There," he added for good measure.

"Got it," was all she could muster, and her elbow followed. Eoghan winced from the unintentional punishment and clenched tight rear muscles. She tempered her massage. If only she could do the same for her speeding heart rate.

A few minutes later they were done. "You're all set." She folded towels and moved weights around, anything to not make eye contact with Eoghan for fear that he'd see the pink in her cheeks or the curiosity in her eyes. He was charming—she'd give him that. Sexy and annoyingly handsome, too, but did he want to pick up where they'd left off in Dublin? Did she?

"You might be sore, but I'll check in with you after dinner to see how you're feeling," she said. She stood by while he got up, a precaution to make sure he didn't fall, but he managed well. "Oh, and I have a surprise for you." She jogged to her office and came back with a blue cane and handed it to him. "You're officially off crutches."

"Great." Eoghan's less-than-enthusiastic response was a downer, but she understood that if he wasn't on the field, not much had changed.

"Test it out," she encouraged him and kept a fair distance.

He hobbled over to an armchair.

"How's that feel?"

"It's progress."

"Well said." She accepted Eoghan's version of a confetti popper and bent to wrap his thigh and knee for the cold compression therapy. "Fifteen minutes," she reminded him.

He gave her a quick salute, settled back in the chair, and closed his eyes.

The lasting effects of their session followed her as she jetted to the kitchen. She needed to get away from him and fast until she could sort out if what had happened between her and Eoghan had been his attempt to renew their tryst in Ireland or just the fun provocation of a player.

She'd worked as hard as Eoghan during their session, and the way he'd unsettled her with his boyish flirtation called for calories both to nourish and to treat. If anyone heard the loud grumbling of her stomach, they'd think that if she didn't get food in her soon, she'd waste away. Nothing that some potatoes couldn't handle. She didn't care if they were sweet, Idaho, russet, purple, new, or baby. She just wanted them cooked up and in her belly. Maybe mashed or boiled with a little mayo-ketchup combo.

She stopped when she saw Shane rummaging through the back of a low cabinet. "That where you keeping your stash these days?" she asked.

Startled, Shane hit his head on the top of the cabinet.

"Oops. Sorry about that," she said as he rubbed the spot.

"Shh," he said with a finger over his flushed, full lips. "Eoghan can't know where they are."

"Silly," she giggled, yet she strained her neck to see what he pulled out.

"Want some?" he asked, presenting her with a bag of Kettle chips.

"We just worked out this morning. I'm about to make some potatoes. Maybe air fry some chicken and have some of Louisa's salad."

"You're sure?" He shook the bag, taunting her.

"Oh, all right." She waved away her willpower. "You can't eat too many potatoes, right?" She knew the complete foolishness of her statement.

Shane hurried to pour some in a bowl for them to share, resealed the bag, and hid it again.

"The lengths we have to go to keep him on his nutrition plan." Ayanna shook her head and shoved two chips in her mouth. "I'm starving."

"Me too. Want to share your meal with me?"

"Hmm." She tapped her chin. "Okay, but only because you gave me chips."

"Fair enough. Thanks." His soft gaze locked with hers, and she could have sworn he turned up the blue in his eyes.

She broke unwillingly from his spell. "I'll get started," she said and grabbed a handful of chips and supported the overflow with her other hand. "And I'm taking more of these." She toddled to the refrigerator.

He crossed his arms tight like he was cold and stepped back away from her, leaning in to hear her. She'd seen him do this before and might have thought that he was just cold, save the fact that the patio doors were open and warm air flowed in.

"You cold or something?" she asked.

"No. Why?"

"It's just you look cold. You know, tight," she said and mimicked his closed arms. She wanted to keep it light in case she was personally causing him to react that way.

"No, no. I'm not cold," he said without offering any further explanation.

"Oh," she said, regressing to her teenage years, when she'd been trying to figure out boys for the first time.

Maybe she smelled from working with Eoghan. She low-key sniffed her underarm. *Nothing wild there.* She quit obsessing and started a pot to boil.

"Can I help?" he asked.

"Yup," she said. "You can get the salad out of the fridge. No one wants ice-cold salad."

"Umm . . ." He raised his hand.

"Whatever," she rushed on. "While I get the chicken started, do you want to scrub those potatoes? We want nice, clean skins."

He laughed. "Gotcha."

Eoghan limped in then, crutch-free. *Shit!* She'd almost forgotten about him while she and Shane were settling into domestic life.

"Look at you, testing out the new strength." She applauded over-zealously given that she'd just seen him fifteen minutes ago.

"It's coming on." Eoghan hadn't completely gotten on board, but his mood had improved. "What you chattin' about?"

"Dinner." Shane eyed her, and she commanded her body temperature to stay low key. How would she explain blushing for no apparent reason?

"Where is it, then?" Eoghan scanned the room, then touched Shane's elbow.

"What?" Ayanna asked, confused.

"There's something in here Shane's trying not to touch. He only closes up like that when he's trying to stay away from something. Probably crisps or stout," Eoghan said. "Whatever it is, he's probably been staring at it."

Ayanna swallowed hard when she realized that Shane had been staring at her for the past few minutes. Their eyes met, and he didn't back down. Eoghan, thankfully, was fascinated by the bowl of chips on the counter and didn't notice.

"Hey! That's not on the approved list," she reprimanded him.

"Come, Ayanna. Give us a break." Eoghan sulked like a child who'd just had his lollipop taken away. "I've been doing great."

Ayanna had to agree that he had been doing great in therapy and taking care of his nutrition, but she didn't want him going on a bender. "Okay, but don't overdo it," she said. "I'm making potatoes."

Eoghan smiled and stuffed a handful of chips into his mouth. "Sure."

She would have preferred to continue her conversation with Shane, but Eoghan's desire to socialize was a good sign. She wanted to keep that train heading in the right direction, even if she speculated about why Shane wanted to touch her.

Chapter Seventeen

In the gym, Ayanna glanced over at Shane, who growled at the soccer match on the television as he lifted weights. They'd been consistently working out for the past several weeks now, and she'd come to enjoy his company and not feel self-conscious about gasping for air when she pushed herself to go harder.

She'd quickly realized that it didn't matter what match was on from what country: Shane ran with the men on the field and shouted coaching plays at them like he was there.

"Be careful!" she both yelled in alarm and laughed when he nearly dropped a weight on himself, recovering just in time before getting hurt. "Look at you, losing it over the game. Maybe do one or the other. Watch the game or lift weights."

"It's a simple play." He rattled off something that she didn't understand, and she ignored most of what he said until he got to the end. "That's the play they should have made," he finished.

"Have you ever thought about coaching?" she inquired. His work as team liaison kept him busy and close to the game, but his passion for analyzing games and none too gently suggesting that the coaches make better plays had been obvious to her.

"I think about coaching these shite teams all the time." He wiped sweat from his brow.

"No, I mean, in real life, boo."

He parked himself in front of her machine and arched a brow. "Boo, is it?"

His clean, masculine scent was offensive and unfair given how hard he worked out, especially since she was sure her pungent odor reeked ten minutes into her workout. She snapped a towel at him. "I'm serious. Has it never even crossed your mind?"

"Dunno? Maybe," he said and slyly increased the difficulty on her machine.

"Shane," she groaned. "Not funny."

"You push me, I push you."

"Yeah, but this shit is already on triathlon mode. No need, but thanks," she said. "You can stop avoiding my suggestion now. You're," she huffed, "good. At. Coaching." She went from a sitting ride to standing. "You're good . . . at it."

"How do you know? All you've seen me do is holler at the eejits on the telly."

"No, you taught me at the game in Dublin."

"I was teaching you the game."

"Boy, could I go for those fries right now."

"Focus," he said.

"What I'm saying is that you do it all the time and naturally. Why not give yourself a chance? You're here. Don't you have any friends on the MLS teams? Network, reconnect with friends, and at least get some information on how getting into it works. You're famous, right? Surely someone would love to have you."

His eyes went a little far off.

"Are you with me, dude?" she asked.

"Yeah." He swallowed and went to get some water and guzzled down a bunch.

"You okay?" she dared to ask.

"Yeah, yeah," he said.

"So will you at least think about it?" She wiped her forehead with her towel.

"Can't hurt."

She clapped above her head. "Sweet! I'm done with this machine." She hopped off the cycle with wobbly legs and shook them out. Before she knew it, Shane was by her side.

"All right?" he asked.

"Yeah. No thanks to you."

"You'll thank me when those gorgeous legs are even more sexy," he said. She looked up at him only to watch his fair skin slowly turn from splotchy red from his workout to beet red.

"Holy shit, you are so red."

"I don't know why I said that."

Between his arms steadying her and his filterless compliment, she almost fell to the floor, and it had nothing to do with her overworked legs. "It's cool. Just don't explode, okay?" She moved away from him because her own heat flared in Fahrenheit.

Her phone vibrated loudly in the cup holder where it rested, interrupting her and Shane. She groaned when she saw her mother's number.

"I gotta take this," she said to him, then picked up the phone. "Hi, Mom. How are you?" Ayanna couldn't keep the natural enmity out of her voice.

"I'm good. I have Jada on," her mother said quickly.

Ayanna again looked at the time. "Shouldn't you be in class?"

"Hi, sis, nice to finally hear your voice. How are you doing?" Jada's sarcasm dripped through the phone.

"I'd ask you that if you answered my text or returned my calls," Ayanna noted.

"I told Charlotte," Jada said as if it were the most reasonable answer she could give.

"I'm busy. What's up?" Ayanna wanted to hear from her sister, but she already knew what this call was for.

"Well, you know I just started to get the house in order, and I'm a little low on funds, and Jada needs a pretty expensive book for one of her labs," Morgan said.

She looked around. Shane was giving her space but hovered just a bit.

"How much?" Ayanna asked.

"Four hundred." Jada casually mic dropped her request.

"Four hundred bills for a book?" Ayanna stiffened.

"It's summer session, too, and I don't get paid from work until next week. The extra would help," Jada said, sounding younger than her twenty years.

Ayanna let out a loud, exasperated noise that drew Shane's attention.

"Fine, I'll send it when I get off the phone." She just wanted this call to be over already, even though she was happy to hear her sister's voice. "Go to class."

"Love you, sis."

"You love my bank account," Ayanna grumbled.

"I love you more, though," Jada clarified. She left the call, leaving Ayanna and her mother.

"Thanks, Yaya. I know it's a pain, but I appreciate it," her mother said.

"No worries. It's nothing I haven't done before." Ayanna bit her tongue. She might not have the most respect for her mother, but she didn't want to get into old family drama either.

"What's that supposed to mean?" Morgan asked.

"It's nothing." Her response definitely sounded like something.

"I'm trying, Ayanna. I have been doing my best."

"I know, Mom." Ayanna closed her eyes. "Look, I can't do this right now. I have to go."

"Busy, huh?" Her mother repeated the status Ayanna always used to get off the phone. Whether it was true or not.

"Like I said when I picked up. I gotta go. Talk soon," Ayanna said, knowing that the proverbial *soon* lay somewhere undesignated in the future.

"Everything okay?" Shane asked.

"Yeah, just my sister. I'm putting her through school, so she needs money."

"Your mam doesn't handle that?" he asked.

"My mother hasn't handled anything for me and Jada in a long time." Ayanna sighed.

He continued to hover. "You want to talk about it?"

She shook her head. "Those kinds of calls take a lot out of me. The last thing I want to do is talk about it."

"Fair enough, but if you ever do, I'm your man." Shane beeted up again. "I mean, I'm here."

"Thanks."

"I'm gonna go. Eoghan wanted to go into town before his session with you," he said. "Later, then." Shane jogged out of the gym, barely waiting for her reply.

"Later."

◆ ◆ ◆

Shane rubbed his nose the moment he entered the flower shop in the Westchester mall. Too many different fragrances meshed together and triggered allergies he hadn't even known he had. The central air and filters helped a bit, but the clock on his tolerance of the place ticked quickly.

"Do you want to tell me again why we're here?" he asked Eoghan, who perused the store, on the hunt for what, Shane wasn't sure.

"I'm picking up something for Ayanna," Eoghan said and fluttered his brows.

Shane groaned even though he laughed at his friend. "No, man. Flowers? Really?"

"Yeah. I think she's on me again," Eoghan said and picked up a vase and angled it in the light.

"And what makes you think that?" Despite Eoghan's foolery, Shane's curiosity won out.

"She touched my bum. Made me want to ride her right then and there," Eoghan said.

"You do realize that she's your rehabilitation therapist. Even the physios in Ireland dig into those muscles. Why do you think it means something?"

"It was the way she touched my bum," his friend said, his tone exaggerated.

"Ugh," was all Shane could come up with. "Best you give her flowers to apologize for the gobshite things you said when you first arrived."

"I need to show her I'm still romantic," Eoghan said and rubbed his clean-shaven face.

"Which part of you?" Shane shoved him.

"The part that took her to the Shelbourne and to Kilkenny," Eoghan replied.

"Shelbourne was my idea, and Kilkenny was because she only had a day left and wanted to sightsee. You forgot all the running your mouth did at the bar that time?"

"But Aviva really got her ready," Eoghan said.

"Please." Shane held up a hand. "The vile things you're talkin'."

"Help me out, mate. You're much better at this than I am."

Why he should help Eoghan came down to a simple word. *Friendship.* One that he valued despite Eoghan's shortcomings. He had a good heart that had been ill influenced by his overbearing father, but still, despite Eileen, he was mostly a good mate.

"How about these?" Eoghan showed him a bouquet with teddy bears and such.

"Tone it down a bit, hot stuff. She's a lady of class." Shane put on his best impression of manners for the invisible gentry.

"Shut your bake and just help me pick something out."

"These ones," Shane said when he saw a bouquet that reminded him of the wildflowers in the garden at the house and thought Ayanna might like that.

"You think they're big enough?"

Shane rolled his eyes to the ceiling. "Bigger isn't always better."

"Speak for yourself," Eoghan sniggered.

"Jaysus, let me out of this nightmare," Shane said. "Trust me. She'll like them."

Eoghan shrugged, and after they left the florist, they returned to Purchase House with a little time to spare before Eoghan's session. Ayanna sat in the living room, looking at a diagram of a body that she used to note Eoghan's improvement.

"Hey, guys, how was town?" she asked, looking cute as hell in her scrubs. He liked how she changed the colors, each one bringing out her skin tone and accentuating every part of her body he liked. The whole thing.

"Good. Not as busy."

She ran her hand over the back of her short hair, which had grown just a bit since they'd arrived in New York. The move he'd seen her do often and daily. "How was it walking without the cane, Eoghan? Or did you keep it close by?" she asked.

"Hands-free," Eoghan said. "I think I'm ready to start running."

Ayanna clapped. "Bravo. We'll test it out, but we won't rush it. That you're walking well, unassisted, over a fair distance and the leg's stable is huge."

Eoghan bowed, and Shane was going to hurl into the sink.

"Did you have fun, Shane?" she asked.

"Huh?" he asked, and then her question registered. "It was all right."

She frowned at his abrupt response, and he wanted to kick himself. What had possessed him today? He'd said things to her that he'd never say without thinking, and now he was doing the opposite, giving her abrupt, short replies.

"These are for you." Eoghan handed her the vase of flowers.

Shane pursed his lips.

"Thanks, Eoghan. That's sweet." Wide eyed, Ayanna admired the flowers, and Shane knew he'd chosen right.

"See, mate. I'm sweet." Eoghan nudged him in the ribs.

Shane didn't think Ayanna would fall for Eoghan's antics, but the smile on her face showed she did appreciate the flowers after all.

"What's the occasion?" she asked.

"Just for being you," Eoghan said.

Shane wanted to smack his forehead but turned his head and rolled his eyes for what felt like the hundredth time in the past few hours.

"Aww. Thank you. I'll leave them here so we can all enjoy them. Flowers like this need to be seen."

He'd indulged Eoghan and helped him woo Ayanna. What in the hell had he been thinking?

Chapter Eighteen

The weather in New York hadn't yet reached "hella hot" on the ther-mometer but was well on its way. Ayanna couldn't believe that Fourth of July weekend had passed already. The time just flew by. She was enjoying the cross breeze from the open doors and sipping a cool bowl of gazpacho on the couch as she read over her notes when two delicious Irishmen runwayed into the living room. She nearly spilled her savory tomato soup into her lap.

The men were dressed for a much-needed excursion away from the house. Eoghan wore a cream-colored shirt and layered rust-colored vest with tailored brown plaid pants that tapered at the ankle. He modeled his white-sneakers-clad feet to give her the full effect. However, she couldn't take her eyes off Shane, who was delicious enough to eat in a white short-sleeved shirt and black pants and loafers. They looked like money—casual money, but money nonetheless.

"You think I'll wow all the city folk in this, Ayanna?" Eoghan asked.

"I don't know, but if I had a pocketful of ones, I might make it rain in here," she said. "You guys look so nice."

"Thanks," both men said. By the pep in their steps, dressing up worked wonders for their well-being.

"Where're you headed?"

Eoghan twirled a pair of sunglasses in his hand. "We're going to do a little sightseeing, grab a couple pints—"

"But—"

"—within reason, and dinner. I've been cooped up for a long time. If I'm here in New York, I might as well enjoy it a little bit."

"True. Are you guys taking the train?" she asked.

"Shane's driving."

"Glad you took my advice and waited until after the Fourth weekend to hang out. The city would have been dead, because everyone would be away in the Hamptons or getting their grill on."

"Thanks for that. You're sure you won't come with us?" Shane asked.

She looked at the two handsome men, and though it was tempting, she'd been up since the crack of dawn, had a videoconference call regarding Eoghan on Ireland time, and planned on meeting up with Charlotte for a quick girls' night before heading to bed. Plus, Randall would frown even more if she went out on the town with her client.

"Thanks, but you guys have fun. The city awaits you."

"Remember, Louisa and the staff have the night off, so enjoy the peace and quiet," Shane said.

"I will, thanks."

"Seems we're all doing a bit of living today, eh?" Eoghan put an arm around her shoulder. It was innocent enough, but when she saw Shane bristle, she shrugged him off.

"Just don't live too loudly today. You are still in recovery."

"Don't worry, Ayanna." Eoghan reached down and tapped her chin. "Like you said, we're a team."

She sucked in her breath, surprised at Eoghan's forward caress. He'd done the same thing at the Shelbourne before they'd gone back to his place. Was that why she didn't reject his touch? She sobered as Shane, having witnessed the intimate move, scrutinized her every reaction.

"You guys get out of here and be safe," she said, getting up and waving them toward the exit.

Before the door closed behind them, both Eoghan and Shane glanced back at her, one looking like he'd just found his baby rattle, the other like he'd lost his.

◆ ◆ ◆

New York City was alive with summer fever. Shane was happy for the change of scenery from the woods of Purchase to something a little less remote. In addition, Eoghan was due for a night out. The city's sauna-like temperatures and the sweating bodies sitting at patio bars and outdoor dining were exactly what they both needed. He missed home but not as much as he had in the past. Times like these, out with his friend, it didn't matter where they were—they'd always been able to have a good time together.

They had taken the Dark Side of the High Line Tour, walking the length of the elevated old subway line turned gardens and learning about the eccentrics of New York. Though it was interesting, they'd quickly descended and headed to the energetic streets. As they drove, the streets and avenues changed from numbers to names like Lafayette, Bleecker, and Thompson. He and Eoghan parked and walked toward the bars and restaurants of Bowery. They found the sushi place they'd made reservations at, and Shane couldn't wait to fill his belly. Working out with Ayanna was great, but the more in shape he got, the hungrier he felt most of the time.

They ordered a boat of sushi, and given how amazing the soups and salads were on the all-you-can-eat menu, they ordered those as well as one entrée of noodles.

Shane opted for the natural wine over the sake that Eoghan drank. He'd keep Eoghan honest, given his recovery, but he wouldn't babysit him too much. He needed a way to celebrate his accomplishments that was familiar. Sláinte, over a pint, was in order.

Shane popped a yellowtail sashimi roll in his mouth, the combination with the cucumber and avocado bursting with flavor. He liked to make a little sauce with the wasabi paste, ginger, and soy sauce for dipping. The last time he'd had sushi was when he'd visited the US about two years ago. "Mmm, you have to try this," Shane said as he chewed the marinated fresh raw salmon and pointed to the chef's specialty sushi. "It's fucking amazing."

Eoghan dived into the boat with his chopsticks, loading his plate with a few more pieces of sushi, including the one Shane had recommended.

Shane plucked an eel roll from the row, adding it to the spicy tuna, naruto, and rainbow rolls decorating his plate. They hadn't even gotten into the salad and noodles.

"So glad we ordered this over the hibachi," Eoghan said with a mouthful of food.

Shane nodded. He'd been thinking about bringing up coaching. Working with Ayanna had given them some time to build on the small getting-to-know-you conversations, and when he'd spoken to her about his interest, she hadn't laughed at him, shut him down, told him to stick to what he knew, or flat-out ignored him. In fact, she'd told him he owed it to himself to at least look into it.

He cleared his throat of soy sauce and spice. "How are you feeling about your work with Ayanna?"

Eoghan nodded. "It's coming on. I'm fucking ready to get on the pitch with the lads for proper training. The smell of the green. Even Lance and his Mr. Celebrity bit." Eoghan shook his head.

"No way you miss Lance," Shane said. Eoghan himself was a bit of a bird of paradise on display, showing off all his colors. That Eoghan missed Lance, who could stand to learn that there wasn't a *me, myself,* or *I* in *team,* revealed that his friend might have come to appreciate his place in the dressing rooms.

"It's sick, but there you have it."

"It's not a problem to set up more calls with the team."

"It's the off-season." Eoghan often had difficulty with idle time, during the off-season especially, because he was called to do his father's bidding. The man pushed and pushed until Eoghan did too much press, committed to too many endorsements, or overtrained. Now, as he recovered, the disappointment in his voice was magnified by missing the complex comradery with the team to balance out the pressure.

"Not for long. Training will be up soon."

"Don't remind me. They'll all be startin' without me."

"Your evaluation isn't too far off. What's it? Two, three months? If you clear it, you won't be able to play matches, but you'll be back in Ireland and able to start to train. Not bad," Shane encouraged.

Eoghan shrugged. "If I clear it."

Shane didn't want to give Eoghan false hope. After assurances that he could come back after his own injury, Shane had been crushed when it was clear he'd never return to football. As a result, he stayed truthfully positive with Eoghan. "You're already much stronger than you were when you got here. Keep at it."

"Yeah, yeah," Eoghan said.

"Things with you and Ayanna have improved substantially, no?" Shane asked.

"She's tough as nails, and when she's stretching me out, I literally want to tear her head off, but she's got this quiet fire that burns me, and I like it."

"That so?" Eoghan didn't have to tell him about Ayanna's fire. Shane knew it firsthand from when they spoke and worked out, when that quiet fire drew him closer before licking him with a few burns. Yet no matter his own sense of danger or whatever Eoghan said, he still needed to feel the softness of Ayanna's lips and her body pressed against his.

"I was shit to her, but she can't resist my charms for long," Eoghan mused. "Did you see the way she looked at me when we were leaving today?"

"You mean when you touched her without her consent?" Shane asked, sipping his wine from a stemless glass.

"Blow a hole, man," Eoghan said. "She wants me."

"And what if she doesn't?"

"She does."

Shane shook his head. "Speaking of training, I've been thinking about how I could be more involved with the game. The liaison position is fine, but I've been thinking about helping out more on the coaching side."

Eoghan nodded. "Well, there's no use thinking about it now. You're here in America. I'd say between working remotely and helping out here, you've got enough on your plate, no?"

The shutdown bugged him, but what had he expected? Eoghan might have talked about Lance, but he still expected to be the center of attention. Nothing new there. Shane hadn't told anyone, not even Ayanna or his friends at the senior center, about the meetings he'd booked to talk with some of the head coaches in Major League Soccer. He wanted to get a feel for the interest in him here before he even thought about possibly pursuing a spot in the Irish or other European leagues.

"Right." Shane abandoned the effort to talk to Eoghan about his coaching aspirations. If he was going to pursue it at all, he'd need positive support and confidence. Eoghan needed to focus on himself to get back to the league. Now wasn't the time to introduce a new career that would change things for both of them.

"I need to get a ride. It's been months. I can't keep tearin' the handle off myself."

"Relatable." Shane could identify with his friend's desires given the fact that he'd been going to town on himself thinking about Ayanna.

"Would it surprise you to hear that Channing has been recurring inspiration?"

Shane grunted his disapproval. "You were just spouting sonnets about Ayanna."

"Yeah, but the things Channing could do with her mouth . . ." Eoghan's eyes glazed over.

"Please. Spare me," Shane said. "Do you even know what you want?"

"I want it all."

"You sound like your da," Shane said.

Darkness shrouded his friend's face. "Fuck you for bringing him up. It's bad enough he'll be coming here for Maeve's wedding."

"Just making sure you're not acting out, pet," Shane teased. Donal O'Farrell, Eoghan's father, was the rhythm beneath Eoghan's beat. The two were as alike as they were different, and Shane hoped his friend would one day break away from the sometimes brutal influence and make his own decisions. Had it not been for Shane's and Dr. Finnegan's interference, Donal would have shipped Eoghan off to Qatar, because that was where "great players" rehabilitated, instead of what was truly best for Eoghan.

"Dick." The anger that flashed across his face left just as quickly. "Speaking of . . . Maeve's planning her wedding, and you have more freedom than me. None of her bridesmaids you've met at rehearsal tickle your fancy?"

"Besides my three cousins, two are married, and the single one isn't my type," Shane said, but really, only one woman occupied his thoughts on a regular basis, ever since he'd been forced to take her to the football match in Dublin.

"And your point?"

Shane frowned.

"I'm taking the piss." Eoghan chuckled.

"You're sure about that?" Shane narrowed one eye at his friend.

Eoghan flicked his brows in that noncommittal way that bugged Shane at times. "Let's settle the bill and get into the nightlife. I'm sure there's opportunity for some fun all throughout these streets." He winked.

Shane rolled his eyes. "One-track mind."

The next few hours they toured the city. As night fell, they settled on a bar on Bleecker. In the dimly lit, packed bar, Eoghan, on the hunt, chatted up a few ladies, moving quickly from flirting to snogging, and all Shane could think, despite his friendship with Eoghan, was that Ayanna deserved so much better. The display inspired the slumbering spirit of competition in him. How could he honor his pact with Eoghan if his friend continued to flip what he wanted?

Several women had tried to get Shane interested in more than the drinks he'd kindly offered, but his interest was low. He liked being out and about and enjoying the city, but somehow, he knew he'd have a better time at girls' night with Ayanna and her friend Charlotte.

His stomach did a weird flip that caught his attention, and thick saliva coated his mouth as nausea began to creep over him. He sipped his beer, and that made him feel a bit better for the moment, but then a few minutes later the feeling returned.

Something wasn't right.

"So you want to get out of here?" the woman chatting with him asked, twirling her auburn locks and pressing her breasts against his arm. He'd only known her for twenty minutes, and though he did want to get out of there, it wasn't because he wanted anything other than a bottle of Tums, ginger ale, or both.

"Hey, you don't look so good," the woman said and backed up a bit.

"I'm not feeling too great all of a sudden," he responded.

"I'm going to see if my friend needs anything," the woman said and made a quick exit.

Shane sipped his pint again and then released a rancid belch. He needed to find Eoghan. He made his way through the crowd and saw Eoghan speeding toward the jacks. So it wasn't just him—definitely something they'd either eaten or drunk was making them feel ill.

In the bathroom, Shane thanked God that no one else occupied the stalls.

"I feel shite," Eoghan said, splashing his face with water.

"I think we need to go," Shane said.

Eoghan shook his head. "I don't know if I'll make it."

"Do we have a choice?"

They left the bar, and Shane prayed they would make it back to Purchase House without incident.

Chapter Nineteen

Ayanna returned to the house after drinks and a movie with Charlotte. She'd even stopped by her apartment to swap out some clothes and check on things. Exhaustion tightened her muscles, and all she wanted was a shower and her bed, but as she walked up the staircase, her nose twitched and her stomach turned.

"Oh my God," Ayanna whispered. A foul smell hit her nose. She walked down the hall and peered in at Eoghan's open door. His discarded pants lay on the floor. Groans floated toward her from the en suite.

"Eoghan?" she called.

More groans. She passed his pants, and the odor grew stronger.

"What the . . . Eoghan! Eoghan, are you all right?"

"Ayanna? What are you—don't come in here! I'm in the jacks."

Too late. She'd already passed the point of no return. "It reeks in here. What's going on?"

"I don't know," he whimpered. "My stomach. We came back from the city, and—" Eoghan grunted, and Ayanna couldn't unhear the sounds that followed.

"Are you . . . what did you eat?"

"Sushi. Lots of sushi."

"Oh damn. Did you get a recommendation for the place?"

"How the fuck should I know."

Food poisoning was bad enough, but bad-fish food poisoning took the effect to a whole other level.

More of Eoghan's bathroom playlist echoed through the door. Ayanna rubbed her face before smearing her skin downward. "Let me get you some water." She jogged to the kitchen and grabbed some trash bags and a few water bottles. She rounded the corridor leading to the staircase and pulled her brakes.

"Shane." She ran to his room. His door was slightly ajar, and she knocked softly. "Shane?" She didn't wait for him to answer and pushed the door open. Shane lay in the fetal position on the bed, shirtless, and with a sheet around his waist. He was squeezing his eyes shut so tight she only saw his long lashes against his cheeks. She dropped the items she was carrying into a chair nearby. She called his name again, and as she got closer to him, the all-too-familiar aroma clenched her stomach.

Light from a small lamp glistened against his muscular arms and the dark-red hair on his chest. His pillow and sheets were soaked with sweat.

"Shane?" She stroked his forehead. His breath was shallow, and his skin felt clammy to the touch.

Ayanna looked around the room for signs of what else might have taken place. His discarded clothes lay on the bathroom floor.

She dry heaved a little bit. "What a nightmare."

Shane opened his eyes and stared at her for a long while before his glazed eyes darted around.

"Easy," she said when he tried to get up, and she settled him against the bed. "Shane? Do you know who I am?"

"Ayanna," he managed to get out.

She tried not to inhale too deeply, because even when she pulled her shirt over her nose, the stench was potent. *Mental note? Grab a mask.*

"Did you have sushi too?"

He nodded too slowly.

"It sounds like you and Eoghan have food poisoning. It feels like you also have a bit of a fever."

Shane winced and collapsed into a fetal position again, and she rubbed her hand along his arm.

"I'll be back in a few minutes. I need to get these to Eoghan. Can I get you anything?"

"A new pair of pants." He tried to chuckle, then winced in pain and pointed to the dresser.

Her shirt slid off her nose as she moved to the dresser. "The good news is, your symptoms should only last a day or two. The bad news is that your symptoms may last for a day or two." She ran her finger over his clothes. Tucked under the top two items in the drawer were a pair of black sweatpants. She retrieved them and placed the folded garment on the bed.

"Here's some water for now. Do you need anything else?"

"I need the jacks."

"Jacks. Toilet. Okay. Can you get out of bed?"

He shook his head.

"Are you in too much pain?"

His whole body, though pale, flamed with red splotches, and he put an arm over his face.

"Shane?"

"My sheets," he growled.

"No," Ayanna gasped, and her hands smushed and slid down her face.

"Yes," Shane bit out.

"You guys are killing me." Ayanna puffed air from her nose.

"I'm sorry, Ayanna—"

"It's not your fault." *Yes, it is.* "You guys are sick." *So the fuck what.* It wasn't in her job description to clean up like this after not one but two grown men. With Louisa and the staff enjoying their night off, though, Ayanna didn't have a choice. She thought of calling Charlotte for help, but her friend would most certainly have a laugh and wish her luck. "Let's get you up."

"But—" He pulled the sheets closer.

"It's okay, c'mon."

"I don't want you to judge me."

"I'm one hundred percent judging you." She smiled.

He moaned again, and she wasn't sure if it was in pain or embarrassment.

"Don't worry." She met the concern in his blue eyes. "It's okay. You need your jacks."

"To see me like this . . . like a child . . ."

"I've seen worse," she lied. This was the worst.

"Ayanna!" Eoghan yelled her name from down the hall.

"Coming," she yelled back.

"Go to him. He needs you."

"You both do. I'll go to him once I get you to the bathroom."

"Please. Go." He tried to push her away, but he was so weak he had to decide between pushing her away, staying upright, or letting his shitty sheets fall to the floor.

"Come on." She inched with him to the bathroom and sat him on the toilet seat, sheets and all. She went back to the room for a bottle of water and handed it to him. "Drink as much as you can. You might struggle to keep it down if you're nauseous. Your body is in elimination mode, so bear down and take it. I'll be back."

Ayanna hurried back to Eoghan. She felt like she was in that episode of *Brady Bunch* she'd seen online, where all six kids were sick.

Eoghan's pants were still where he'd left them, and she used the trash bag to collect them. Steam had filled the room, which didn't help the stifling odors. Eoghan came out with a towel around his waist. Even in this situation, he was a vision of athleticism.

"What took you so long?"

She scowled. "Did you forget that you didn't go to dinner alone?"

"Shite. Shane's got a bad dose of it, too, then?" He groaned. "Brutal."

"Do you feel any better?" she asked.

"A bit." By the way he winced, he likely was still experiencing cramps.

She handed him two bottles of water and gave him the same instructions she'd given Shane.

"What's that?" Eoghan regarded the trash bag hanging by her side.

"Your clothes. Are there more in there?" She jutted her head toward the bathroom.

Eoghan nodded, guzzling water.

She turned her head to look and then rolled her eyes. "Jesus!"

From his shirt to his shoes, everything had gotten hit. She'd give her third-born child up for a mask. Instead she pulled her shirt over her nose, stuffed everything into the trash bag, and ran back out.

"Those are Gucci loafers."

"Eoghan, look at my fucking face."

He groaned.

"You want to clean them?" she asked.

"No." He winced.

"I'll be back."

She rummaged through the kitchen supplies until she found a few pairs of gloves, a mask, and a bucket of cleaning supplies. She pulled out her phone and dialed the supermarket for delivery.

"Hi there. I have a bit of an emergency here at the house. Do you think you can get me an order here as soon as possible?"

"Sure, what can I get you, Dr. Crawford?"

"A couple cases of Pedialyte."

"Any particular flavor? We've got strawberry, tropical fruit, grape, plain, berry frost, and bubble gum."

I don't give a fuck. "Umm . . . you know what? Give me one of each. Also bananas, rice, apples, and bread. Oh, and a papaya. Please."

"You have a few favorites here. Would you like me to stick to the brands the household has on the list?"

"Sure." She hung up and opened a bottle of 1800 tequila. After she poured a shot, she slung it back. Then she slogged herself to Eoghan's room and finished up the task at hand.

Ayanna wasn't about that laundry life for the soiled piles. Everything went into the trash, from Eoghan's shoes and favorite pair of jeans to Shane's belt, socks, and button-down shirt. She cleaned Eoghan's room first, while he slept, praying she didn't kill him with bleach.

When the store delivery order arrived, she added cases of Pedialyte to the water bottles on their bedside tables as well as a tiny dip bowl of papaya seeds from the fruit she'd cut with a teaspoon.

She checked on Shane, who was weakly trying to clean up, pulling the remaining bedding off the mattress and into a pile.

"What are you doing?"

"You shouldn't have to clean this up, Ayanna."

"I appreciate the effort, Shane, but you're in no shape to be doing this."

"No, I can—"

"Oh, sit down," she snapped and peeled off the remaining sheet. She nearly genuflected when she saw the clean, dry surface and found fresh linens in the closet. She maneuvered the fitted sheet.

"Let me help you," he offered.

"Shh. Drink your electrolytes." She quickly made up the bed, but Shane persisted.

"Ayanna?"

She tossed a pillowcase at him and walked a pillow over to him. "Happy now?"

"Yes." He flashed her that half smile that made her heart palpitate.

She shook her head, but a smile twitched at the corner of her lips. If cleaning up shit with Shane made her smile, she was in deep doo-doo.

"How's Eoghan?" he asked.

"He's sleeping."

"Is it strange that I'm hungry? And nauseous?"

"Seeing as you literally eliminated everything, no. Drink," she commanded and finished up the bed. "You can get in now."

"Thank you."

"You're welcome," she said and went downstairs for what felt like the hundredth time.

Ayanna was exhausted. She'd been up since five thirty, and it was nearing the twenty-four-hour mark. Between caring for Shane and Eoghan, the stress, and the strength she'd used to clean up, she was the walking dead. She'd put some bananas and toast in Shane's and Eoghan's rooms, and if they felt up to it, some broth and rice were staying warm on the kitchen stove, but given the hour and the fact that their sleep was being interrupted with bathroom breaks, she'd save it for the next day.

She stumbled into Shane's room. He was still awake, drinking tropical-fruit-punch electrolytes and nibbling on a banana.

"You look wrecked," he said and put the banana down.

Her entire face tightened. "No thanks to you." She wanted to check his fever, but he had the wicker trash can on that side. He might have upchucked in the plastic bag that lined it, or he might not have, but she was tired of cleaning for the foreseeable future and avoided his side of the bed altogether. She climbed onto the mattress.

Shane startled and whipped his head toward her but quickly got over his surprise, helping her with his noodle arms.

"I'm just checking your fever." She placed a hand on his head, his eyes on her the entire time. "Thermometer." She pointed to his bedside, and Shane put it in his mouth. Once it beeped, she read it. "It's normalizing. The last thing we need on top of this night is to have to take you to the hospital." She leaned back against the pillow.

"What a holy show." Shane angled his body toward her. "You must be knackered."

"Mmmm. Are you feeling better? I see you're trying to eat something."

"Don't want to overdo it."

"Is your stomach still cramping?" she asked him.

"Not as much."

"I can get you some hot herbal tea. That might help." She went to move, but he gently pressed her back down and patted her thigh as if soothing her.

"There's no rush."

"Chew and swallow the papaya seeds. They'll help kill any bad bugs in your stomach. It'll light you up like wasabi, so go easy," she mumbled.

"Er . . . okay."

"I'm just going to rest my head for a second, okay?" She nestled the side of her head into the pillows, facing him, and clasped her hands between her thighs to keep them warm.

"Fine with me." His soft tone lulled her further.

"I'm right here. Promise you'll tell me if you need me."

"I definitely will," he said. "Sleep, love." His words swathed her and allowed her to settle from the past few hours.

"No, don't let me fall asleep. I believe in you," she mumbled, fighting against her rising melatonin levels.

Humor resonated deep within his chest. "*Geall dom*," was the last thing she heard.

Chapter Twenty

Ayanna stretched into something warm and hard yet welcoming, with the aroma of lemon hinting at a fresh spring day. "Mmm," she moaned and opened her eyes. Clarity settled on her, and the memories of yesterday's nightmare came flooding back. She gently tilted her head up to see Shane sleeping soundly. Her body faced his, and her head was buried under his arm.

Fuck! She'd fallen asleep in his bed. This wasn't early-morning sun that flooded into the room. Ayanna couldn't remember a time when she'd slept past six, but apparently, she'd become a downright rebel against her own rules. She stared at the long-lashed, red-freckled bad influence, memorizing the peacefulness on his face. What was he dreaming of? She wanted to be the answer. Despite her efforts to run away from him, she kept landing closer.

She gingerly tossed away from him and eased herself to sit on the edge of the bed. She rolled her stiff neck and shoulders.

"Sneakin' away, are ya?" Shane's gentle question functioned like a heating pad on her shoulders. She should be freaking out from waking up in his room, but his soothing tone had the opposite effect.

She twisted to see him eyeing her from his recumbent position. "You should have woken me up."

"You looked as soft and peaceful as a flower. I couldn't bring myself to wake you."

Her stomach flipped, and his comment hit her in the heart like a dart finding its bull's-eye. "How do you feel?" she stuttered.

"Praying the worst part is over," he said. "I owe you for last night. We both do."

"Yeah, you do." She smiled. "I'm going to check on Eoghan. I doubt he's up for his session today, so you both might want to take it easy and stay close to the jacks."

"Thanks again, Ayanna. Truly," he said.

"You're welcome."

Ayanna was blasted by Charlotte and Louisa when she relayed the story to each of them. Charlotte couldn't stop laughing and, true to her nature, was happy she hadn't been Ayanna's emergency contact for that particular situation. Louisa was kind when Ayanna explained why the house still smelled when she returned, and she stressed that Ayanna should have called her, but by the relief on her face, she was glad she'd dodged that bullet.

The following day, the men's food poisoning symptoms subsided. Shane and Eoghan tiptoed around the house, both of them struggling to meet her eye. By the evening, she'd had enough. She'd never be able to use it against either of them, at an opportune moment in the future, if they never got over it.

"Okay, guys. I'm going to need you to get over our shit-tastic night together. Quick. Now that Eoghan is feeling better, we're starting drills, and I'm going to need both of you on your A game. So forget about the other night. You're feeling better, and that's all that matters."

"You're an angel for what you did," Eoghan said.

"Don't I know it."

Louisa snickered behind her hand.

"Okay, then," Shane said.

"It seems you guys weren't the only ones who got sick. I called the restaurant, and the owner is looking into the matter. They'd been trying to call patrons, but apparently the number on your credit card is your Ireland number. It's pretty bad for business to have sick customers."

"Next time we'll ask for a recommendation," Shane suggested.

"Good on you." She used one of the many sayings that had grown on her.

Shane's phone buzzed. As he read the text, his brows lifted.

"Everything cool?" Ayanna asked.

"Everything's fine," Shane said. He jutted his head toward Eoghan. "Our parents confirmed their flight for the wedding."

"Wedding?" both Ayanna and Louisa said simultaneously.

"They're coming to New York for Shane's cousin Maeve's wedding. They'll be staying here with us for a short visit," Eoghan explained.

"Did we not say?" Shane questioned. "She's my first cousin, very big event."

Ayanna frowned, and Louisa put her hand on her hips. The two men had every right to have guests over whenever they wanted, but since they'd been in the house together, it had never come up. However, with her living in the house, it was just courteous to let her and the house manager know so that everyone would have a smooth stay.

"No, you didn't say," Ayanna said. "What? Did it just slip your mind that we'd be hosting your parents?"

"I didn't think anything of it, really," Shane said. "Before Eoghan got hurt, it was tentative whether we'd both even make the wedding. Now that we're both in New York, we assumed we'd be going with our parents. I think that's why we didn't think twice on it."

"Sure, I'd like to be prepared for your folks, as would the rest of the staff." Louisa's accent was layered with parental admonishment.

"Sorry 'bout that. We'll do the work. Well, mostly Shane, since I'm recovering and all," Eoghan said.

"When will they be here?" Louisa asked.

Shane peered down at his phone. "Last weekend in August."

"Oh, we have plenty of time. Near a month." Louisa's shoulders relaxed.

Ayanna bit her tongue. It was too soon to give Eoghan hope of getting a date set for his evaluation, but based on his progress, she had tentatively suggested the middle of September. He'd still have another month or two with her afterward, but they would be transition weeks for him to start training.

"Ayanna?" Shane called to her, pulling her from further analysis.

"Yeah?"

"That going to be okay?" he asked.

"Absolutely." She meant it.

"If it's a problem, we can make other arrangements." Worry lines creased Shane's forehead. She'd heard a bit about Eoghan's father but little about the other parents.

"Huh? What are you talking about? They're your parents, and this is your home while you're here. We just want to know so we can be prepared to accommodate them and Eoghan's rehabilitation schedule. Now we know. Right, Louisa?" Ayanna asked her ally.

"Right for sure," Louisa said. "It'll be nice to see who you two come from."

"Because we're so wonderful, darlin'," Eoghan cooed at Louisa.

"Definitely," Louisa teased and waved him off.

Shane moseyed over to her while the spunk fest between Louisa and Eoghan continued.

"Are you excited about seeing your folks?" she asked.

He nodded. "They're a fun pair."

She thought of Morgan and Vance Crawford, who had been the happiest couple in the whole world, and their family, though not perfect, had been loving and joyful. Her father had been a vital man, and when he'd gotten ripped away from them, their family had crumpled. She was curious to see how Shane and Eoghan were with their families and hoped their dynamic was better than that of her own.

"Something on your mind?" Shane asked.

"Always." She smiled, then clapped to rally the troops. "Playtime's over. Let's get after it." She focused on work again—anything to get her mind out of the past.

◆ ◆ ◆

Three weeks had passed since Eoghan and Shane had started working on drills, and Ayanna wasn't happy. She'd expressed her concern to Shane about his technique, but still, nothing had changed, and she'd reached her threshold for understanding.

"You're going soft on him," Ayanna said at last after studying the men on the grounds outside Purchase House.

"I'm not," Shane complained.

"Yes, you are. Either that or he's anticipating you."

"Well, we have played together since we were kids." Shane's tanned and freckled outstretched hands showed his frustration.

"You don't have to pummel him with the ball, but you have to give him drills that test his instincts and his explosiveness from a set position. You're not playing catch. Make him run."

"She's worse than any gaffer we've had," Shane said.

"This isn't working," Ayanna said. "I have to call in a favor."

"You're just going to chuck me, then," Shane said, sweat on his brow and shirt slightly clinging to his torso.

"I'm not chucking you. I think you're too close to this situation, and even though I think you can be helpful later, you're not right now. The fact is . . ." She considered her words. Shane was tough, but she'd seen his tenderness, no matter how hard he tried to hide it.

"What?" he asked.

"Maybe you're afraid to hurt him, and that's okay." She held up a hand to stop the interruption those full lips readied. "You've been injured in the game, and here your friend is trying to work himself back. I get it. So we'll get someone else to do it for now."

"Right." Shane flipped the ball onto the grass and left for inside.

"Shane," she called to his departing figure.

"Leave him, Ayanna." Eoghan tapped his toes behind him to stay warmed up.

"What did I say?" she asked. She had expected Shane to maybe bristle a little at her suggestion but not flat-out abandon ship.

"He's hurting," Eoghan said. "He'll never admit it, but on days like this, his ankle gives him a run."

She hated that she hadn't seen it sooner. She watched him walk into the house, his uneven gait as clear as day. "Why didn't he just say something?"

"Pride. He'll be sorted in short order."

"Cool down with a stretch, and I'll take your measurements in the gym. I want to compare your ROM stats," she said, focusing on Eoghan's leaps in improved range of motion to distract her from the fact that she'd upset Shane.

"Weight training next. Hop to it," she said.

While Eoghan worked out, Ayanna left the gym and traipsed to her office. She hadn't meant to make Shane feel bad. She only wanted to make sure they did Eoghan's exercises right. She came down pretty hard on herself but also understood that when it came to his injury, Shane's sensitivity went through the roof.

Ayanna dialed her former client. Oni Moore had believed that her childhood dream of playing at the top level in soccer had been crushed. When they'd met, Oni's hopelessness had been gut wrenching, but Ayanna had been hopeful about the injury and even more so about Oni's recovery. With Ayanna's experimental treatments, Oni had returned to the game she loved and now pursued her professional career full steam ahead.

Oni had sent Ayanna an email to arrange dinner, but with her client in Purchase and Oni's tight schedule while in New York, they hadn't yet settled on a time.

"Hey, Ayanna," Oni said when she picked up the phone. "I'd planned to give you another call, since I'll be leaving next week, to see if we could squeeze in a meetup."

"So soon? Wow, you are really busy."

"Not as busy as you are, but I'm getting there." Oni had that raspy laugh that Ayanna often associated with outside sports.

"So I was thinking that if you weren't too busy, we could kill two birds with one stone. I have this client who is coming back from an ACL injury and needs a bit of a push. Think you want to ruffle his feathers a little bit?"

"Be glad to."

"How's this weekend looking for you?" Ayanna asked.

"Let me take a look." Oni hummed for a bit. "I can make it work for the morning and lunch, but I have to be back in the city that evening," she said.

"That sounds great. I'll send you the train information and driving directions."

"Awesome."

"Then we can do lunch by the pool and catch up. How does that sound?" Ayanna asked.

"Sounds divine."

They settled on a time, and Ayanna felt better. Eoghan needed a push, and Shane needed a break. Thanks to Oni, they'd all get what they wanted, at least for one day.

Inside the house, Shane paced by the window in view of the backyard, where he and Eoghan had been tossing the ball around. Ayanna's words rattled in his head. He hated when he couldn't give his all. He'd been working out and getting stronger, yet still his damn ankle caused him problems. What he hated most of all was how short he'd been with Ayanna when all she was trying to do was help Eoghan push his limits.

He heard the padding of her soft footfalls, her short steps now a familiar sound in the house.

"So are you just going to stew the rest of the day in here or go back out there?"

"Done for the day," he said simply.

She crossed her arms over her chest, slightly squishing her boobs through her purple tank, a detour from the normal scrub top she wore when she worked out with Eoghan. "Listen, I didn't mean anything by what I said. I needed to be honest if that exercise was going to work."

"I know. I shouldn't have lost my temper." He adjusted his shorts.

"Agreed," she said. "You want to tell me what's up?"

He didn't, but that didn't stop his brain from instructing his mouth to speak up. "I . . . um . . . sometimes my ankle's a bit tender." He watched her brows lift. "What?" he asked.

"Eoghan thought you might be hurting but said you'd never admit it."

"Seems to not be the only rule I've been breaking."

"I can relate," she mumbled, and he wondered what she was referring to. "I notice you walk with a bit of a limp sometimes." Ayanna spoke as if she'd cannonballed right into the deep end. "You could have residual scar tissue that's causing you pain. I know quite a few specialists and could take a look at it if you want—"

"No, but thanks." He'd been down this familiar path. First came hope, then disappointment, and he'd had his fill.

"Why not? You allergic to feeling better?" she asked.

He chuckled, something she made him do easily. "The pain is good."

She evaluated his nonchalance, and he could see more questions bubbling in her mind. "Why do I get the feeling that you've heard this before?"

"Because I have." He strolled with her into the kitchen.

"And you're not even the slightest bit curious about the possibility of getting better?"

He'd been more than curious—he'd been downright obsessive in the early period of his injury, but now, he didn't see the point. "Not sure for what."

"What does that even mean?" she asked, narrowing her eyes at him.

He distracted himself with a water bottle he flipped in his hand before opening. "I don't need to know."

"Why?" she pushed. "Don't you want an improved quality of life?"

Of course she didn't understand why he wouldn't explore that, but she hadn't been through the torture of rehabilitating an injury only to have to give up the sport he loved.

She continued on the roll she'd been on. "What if—"

"Because I don't want to know if my injury wasn't really career ending. If I gave up my soccer dream of playing for a World Cup and lost the woman I loved because medicine hadn't yet improved enough to help me like it is helping Eoghan. I don't need to know that losing everything never had to happen if I'd had you."

Fuck! Now he'd done it. He'd said too much, lost it, shed his skin, and slit his heart open, because with her it was too damn easy.

"Shane, I—" She swallowed hard, making her muscles visible.

"I-I shouldn't have . . . I didn't mean to say . . ." He cursed under his breath. What had possessed him to unload all of that on her?

"How did you lose her? The woman you loved?" she asked so softly.

He studied her face in search of judgment, but there was none. "She chose someone else."

"Was it someone close to you?" she asked.

He wished she hadn't asked him that, because he wanted to tell her. "Eoghan."

She winced, and her mouth twisted with questions he could only imagine she wanted to bombard him with, but instead, she listened.

"She wanted to make her way through popular players for fun, but we had both fallen for her. It wasn't pretty."

"I'm sorry. We don't have to talk about this if you don't want."

He didn't, but it felt okay sharing this with her. "Ever since then, Eoghan and I promised never to date the same woman."

"What does that even mean? You could date the same woman at different times. It's doubtful that you would actively be dating the same woman. I mean, what if you both just liked the same woman and decided to . . . I don't know. It seems like . . ." She stopped herself.

"No, say it."

"If Charlotte was dating someone, like in-a-relationship-type for-real dating, I'd never pursue her man. I get that on extremely rare occasions, things happen even though no one wants to hurt anyone. At least, I've seen that in movies. But if that guy was decent and Charlotte no longer dated him or had any interest in him, he's fair game." She eyed him. In her one example, she'd said a lot about Eoghan and, whether she knew it or not, a lot about Shane and his feelings for her.

"I see what you're saying, but you must know that in real life, it may not work out that smoothly."

"Yeah." She dreamily tapped her lips. "Is that why you didn't kiss me in Liverpool, Shane?"

Oxygen hitched in his throat.

"Don't answer that. I have no right—"

"Yes." He couldn't remember walking toward her or her walking toward him, but now they were inches apart.

"Do you still want to?" The breath of her whisper touched his lips.

"Ayanna." He breathed her in. "You know I do."

She moved even closer, her lips close enough to touch his. Anticipation infused his body at the idea of even coming close to realizing the multiple dreams he'd had of kissing her.

"Not today, Sam. I need to organize the washing and get the evening meal go—" Louisa barked into the phone, then stopped abruptly as both he and Ayanna pulled away from each other.

Louisa spun in a full circle, pocketing her phone and likely hanging up on whoever she'd been rowing with, and her cheeks stained with the embarrassment of walking in on two lovers. "I didn't realize. I—"

"It's okay, Louisa," Ayanna soothed, her face as flushed as his and Louisa's. "We were just having a conversation."

"No worries. I'll come back later." Louisa didn't wait for a response and fled the kitchen.

"Listen," Ayanna said to him, barely meeting his eye. "I know opening yourself up to hope about your ankle is difficult, Shane, and you don't have to make any decisions about it now, but think about letting me look at your ankle and talk to some people for you. Now instead of being hijacked with disappointment, you can go in with realistic expectations and your eyes wide open."

He nodded. She'd pivoted, and he couldn't blame her. The intensity between them teetered on explosion, and if he didn't keep it in check, he could have easily taken her on the kitchen counter. However, he experienced something altogether new for the first time in a conversation about his ankle. Trust.

"I have to run into the city," he said, not wanting to leave her.

Curiosity narrowed her beautiful brown eyes. "Where do you go when you jet out of here every Thursday? I know you're still working for the Rovers as team liaison, but what do you do?"

"I'm not working for the Rovers today," he stated.

"That doesn't quite answer the question."

"Want to come see? You're done with Eoghan for the day." He wanted more time with her, alone. She'd started him on a sharing wheel, and he didn't want to get off.

Her mouth twisted, and her eyes slid back and forth as she thought on it. "Why not?"

Chapter Twenty-One

Shane walked side by side with Ayanna to the senior center in the Riverdale section of the Bronx. He'd never taken anyone there before but didn't dwell too much on the fact that he wanted to share it with her. He just hoped he'd made the right choice.

"You teach a class?" she asked him.

"Yeah. They really appreciate learning about technology. I take it slow for them, and they do well." He showed her to a seat between Martha, a lovely gray-haired Jewish woman, and Daphne, a dark-skinned Jamaican beauty, and immediately regretted it when his two favorite students started to speak.

"Are you Shane's girlfriend? We are always trying to set him up, but he's been holding out on us this whole time," Martha said and looked up disapprovingly at him.

"What's your name, dahlin'?" Daphne asked, her accent sweeter than normal.

"Ayanna. I work with Shane. I'm a physical therapist, helping his friend rehabilitate his injury."

"Oh, you're the one living in the house? Shane never told us how lovely you were," Daphne said. "Did he, Martha?"

"No," Martha confirmed.

More disapproving looks flew his way, and Ayanna stifled a laugh.

"Now you've done it, bringing her here," Fred, Martha's husband, said. His mostly bald head with a crown of thin hair was grayer than his wife's. "It'll be all they talk about."

"Hush now, Freddy," Martha snapped.

"You're from the islands?" Daphne asked.

"Yes. My father is from Sint Maarten," Ayanna said. "How did you know?"

"All children raised by parents from the islands have a little bit in the way they pronounce some words," Daphne said in her Queen's English.

"Daphne is Jamaican," Shane said.

"Oh," Ayanna said. "My father only raised me for a short time. He passed away when I was younger."

"I didn't know he was from Sint Maarten," Shane said. He'd been with Ayanna for months and hadn't asked her about her family.

"It never came up," she said simply.

Both Daphne and Martha looked on with interest.

"They're all after him, you know," Martha said, quite abruptly. "Lauren from Zumba and Pria, the yoga instructor, all have their eye on him. Even the dance instructor. He's always trying to get Shane to waltz, but Shane bounces on out of here quicker than a tiny rubber ball."

"They're always asking us questions about Shane," Daphne chimed in. "Where's he from? Is he married? What's he like?"

"Really?" Ayanna eyed him, stifling her laughter.

"Look at him. Redder than a Flamin' Hot Cheeto, but still a handsome devil," Martha said.

He had let them go on for much longer than he should. "Okay, everyone, let's settle down. Today we are going to explore the dos and don'ts of the World Wide Web and how to stay safe while we look for what we want," he said.

"What do you mean?" Fred asked, his voice booming, which meant either his hearing aids were turned down too low or the battery was dying.

"Well, there are scams out there," Shane explained. "Unfortunately many of them prey on you young ladies and gentlemen, but if you follow a few of my tips, you'll be right as rain."

Shane went into internet security, unsecure websites, and pop-ups. "You can also help keep your computer safe by telling it in the computer preferences where it is allowed to go."

"Oh. A dat me wan fi know. Me dahta did tell me about virus and all kind a tings. Me nah know nothing 'bout it." Daphne let her patois fly.

"That's why we are going to take it one step at a time." Shane readied the presentation for the class. As he went through his lesson and practice started, Ayanna helped Daphne and other members in the class by repeating his steps.

"You gonna teach us the next step or keep staring at her?" Fred asked with a mischievous smile and flicker of his brows.

He felt hot again, and Fred shook his head, laughing.

Shane continued until the end of class, when he thanked his students for their time. "I'll see you all next week."

Ayanna hugged Daphne and Martha goodbye, and his stomach dropped at her kindness to his favorite ladies at the center.

"You should join us again. Shane is a wonderful teacher. He can teach you as well," Martha said.

"Thank you. I would love that," came Ayanna's gracious reply.

Two woman instructors passed. They smiled at him but gave Ayanna the cold shoulder.

Martha elbowed her. "Lauren and Pria," she said, in a whisper that was louder than her normal speech.

"Is it chilly in here, or is it just me?" Ayanna asked, humor in her voice.

"A dat me a tell you," Daphne said, flinging her hand toward the women. "They're infatuated with him."

"We should go." Shane smooshed his face in his hands. "You guys are going to get me in trouble."

Ayanna laughed. "Thank you for letting me crash your class."

"Be well, dear," Martha said before they left.

"That was fun," Ayanna said on their drive back to Purchase House.

"Worst idea ever." He pressed his cheeks with a cool hand.

"It wasn't that bad." She turned in her seat to fully face him. "They care about you. I love Martha and Daphne. They are hands down my favorites."

"I'm not supposed to have favorites, but they're mine too," he said, stealing glances at her.

"Why'd you hide this?"

"I didn't. I'm just not doing it for anyone but the students in the class. It's important for them to feel useful and a part of this fast-paced world." He felt her staring at him, evaluating him. "What?"

"You're a good guy, Shane," she stated. "Thanks for letting me be a part of that. It was really special."

"I'm glad you had a good time," was all he could muster.

A few minutes of comfortable silence sat between them. "Are you hungry? I sometimes stop in the Bronx and pick up a beef patty and cocoa bread at Daphne's daughter's Jamaican bakery."

"I love those." She giggled.

"What's funny?"

"I find it funny that a white Irishman is taking me to get Jamaican food when I'm the one with the Caribbean heritage."

"The Caribbean neighborhoods are not far away from the Irish neighborhoods where some of my family lives. I've wandered through here and there."

"That's true."

"Bottom line: I like good food."

They picked up their takeout and ate it in the car on the drive home, gushing over how hot, spicy, and delicious the food tasted. Shane chose a veggie patty for Eoghan and sweet bread for everyone in the house to enjoy. When he and Ayanna got back to Purchase, they found Eoghan playing a video game on the couch.

"I'll put this stuff in the kitchen," she said, taking the bag away from Shane. "Enjoy the rest of the evening, guys. I highly suggest you both get a couple good nights' rest. This weekend we have a special guest coming to give us some help."

Ayanna retired to her room, but her cryptic warning settled on him and Eoghan.

"Who do you think it is?" Eoghan asked him. "Did she say anything to you while she helped you with your volunteer thing?"

"Not a word," Shane said.

Eoghan gave him a quick up-and-down. "Anything interesting happen with your oul folks at the center?"

"Nothing interesting at all," Shane stated. Except for the fact that he'd had the best day with Ayanna Crawford.

Ayanna jogged through the backyard on a hot Saturday morning and hugged Oni Moore when they were finally in reach of each other.

"I didn't know you were here already," Ayanna said.

"Louisa said to tell you she let me in," Oni said. Her medium-brown skin, tanned from outdoor training, glistened in the sun.

"You look great. Healthy and ready to take on the league," Ayanna said. Her friend and client was wearing a lime-green-and-gray tracksuit with matching athletic shoes.

"Thank you." Oni did a quick curtsy. "This is a nice spot. I'd ask why we didn't have therapy here, but I'm not a men's Premier League footballer."

"I'm really glad you're here, and I can't wait to catch up. Come meet the guys."

Both Shane and Eoghan moved toward them.

"I'd like you both to meet—"

"Oni Moore," Shane said.

"NCAA phenom." Eoghan sort of stared, his foot resting on the soccer ball.

Ayanna watched both men spaz out a little. "Surprise," she said, excited that maybe being a little starstruck might push Eoghan a bit more.

"I'm here to help Doc Crawford out. I hear you got injured," Oni said to Eoghan.

"ACL," he responded.

"Bummer. You're good," Oni said to Eoghan and then turned to Shane. "I've seen you play in the national league. I loved watching you break up defenses. Bananas. I learned watching you. Wish you were still playing."

Ayanna watched Oni work her magic. Her energetic, athletic body ready for play.

"Were you hurt?" Eoghan asked Oni.

"Yeah, but Ayanna put me back together, so if you listen to her, you can get back to preinjury form. Once you have surgery and the surgeon starts fiddling around with an already perfect system, things in other places are affected. I don't know all those things, do you?"

"No," Eoghan responded.

"Ayanna does, so if she tells you to do something, no matter how trivial or stupid or waste of time you think it is, do it. She's doing it for a reason. She's got your back."

"So Olympics, huh?" Eoghan asked.

"Yeah," Oni said. "Maybe I'll see you there."

Eoghan folded his arms over his chest. "Oh, we're country challenging?"

"Maybe." Oni mimicked his move.

"Okay." Eoghan nodded but couldn't conceal his humor.

"Well, there's this thing called the trials. We both gotta get there first," Oni said and kicked the ball resting under Eoghan's foot. "Let's see what you got. Ready for a couple drills with me? That is, if you think you can handle it."

Ayanna saw the glimmer of competitiveness in Eoghan's eyes. *Yes! That's it.*

Shane arched a brow. "You might have unleashed the beast, Oni."

"Talk is cheap. Let's see what he does on the pitch."

Ayanna and Shane looked on. "Brilliant," he whispered.

"She is," Ayanna said of Oni.

"I wasn't talking about her. I was talking about you," Shane said. "I haven't seen that look in Eoghan's eyes in some time. He enjoys a bit of competition, and you gave that to him."

"Cool." She fumbled the compliment because he'd taken her off guard. She pushed his shoulder. "Are you going to get out there, or what?"

"Maybe."

"Well, I'm going to go inside and see what time lunch will be ready for Oni. Do you think you can coach the kids for a bit while I'm gone?" she asked.

"Sure."

After Ayanna got an ETA on lunch, she looked out the window at the footballers playing. Oni and Eoghan darted around the backyard, and Shane appeared official as coach. She hoped he'd taken her seriously when she'd suggested he follow his aspirations as part of the back office in football. One thing was certain as she watched them in the summer sun: they were all doing what they loved.

Chapter Twenty-Two

The meeting for Eoghan had been going on for an hour, but there was still much to discuss, from his progress to the timeline leading up to his evaluation and some of the media they wanted Eoghan to start doing at the behest of his father and some additional sponsors.

"For my portion I just want to make sure the Purchase House remains a sanctuary of healing for Eoghan. If the press wants access to him, they can accomplish that elsewhere," she said to the participants on the conference call.

"Fair enough, Dr. Crawford," Eoghan's agent, Ronin Kelly, said. She'd seen Eoghan chatting with him pretty regularly, and he'd become more present on the last two calls. She was grateful Ronin respected her boundaries and stayed in touch with his client, who needed the support.

"Please, Ayanna, let's have that new imaging for his leg in the next week," Dr. Finnegan said.

"Not a problem," she said to Daniel.

They concluded the call soon afterward, and Ayanna added new notes and schedule entries on the desktop computer. She was about to head into the gym to get things ready for Eoghan for the next day when Louisa called her name.

"Dr. Crawford? Visitor."

"Visitor? Who's visiting me?" Ayanna peered down at her watch. "And at this hour. It's nighttime," she said, even though the sun was still out. She walked into the foyer and rounded the staircase that obstructed her view, and when she saw her sister standing there, she screeched to a halt.

"What are you doing here?" Ayanna asked, snapping her neck with her hand on her hips and summoning every layer of Black-mama attitude she could gather.

Her sister, Jada, stood there, swinging her long hair like she didn't have a care in the world. "Is this any way to greet your baby sis?"

Ayanna was pissed off beyond all words, as the last person she'd expected to show up at the front door of Purchase House now stood in the foyer with the weekender bag she'd given her for her birthday two years ago.

Ayanna stormed over to Jada. "I asked, What the hell are you doing here, Jada? You're supposed to be at school."

"Hello? It's August. My summer session is almost over and I took a few days off work. I'll be back in plenty of time for finals," Jada explained.

Ayanna's sister had already begun her flirtation with her male targets by simply existing in her super short floral mini and blue tank top. Her black bone-straight weave swung down to her rear. Even without it, Jada would have made Ayanna appear small and insignificant with her height, which was a foot taller than Ayanna in her heels.

Shane evaluated Jada with interest, and Ayanna rolled her eyes.

Jada pulled her into a hug. "Mom told me you got this gig up here, and since I decided to come home, I thought I'd spend a day or two with you."

"This is not my house, Jada. I'm working. You would have known those details if you'd returned my calls or texts." Ayanna leaned toward her sister and spoke under her breath. "You shouldn't have come without at least calling first."

"Are you her client?" Jada sauntered over to Shane.

Ayanna yanked her sister back to her. Jada had a problem. She couldn't stop herself from flirting, but it wasn't okay, and definitely not with Shane.

"Uh, no." Amusement spread across his face.

"I just want to hang out with you," Jada said.

"What part of 'I'm working' don't you understand? This is not a hotel for young coeds," Ayanna said.

"We can make an exception." Eoghan, who had been doing some exercises in the pool, entered the foyer in a white pullover, a yellow towel around his waist, and shower shoes. "Any friend or family member of Ayanna is welcome here. Plus, we have plenty of rooms for you to choose from." Eoghan made his way closer to greet Jada. He took her hand and gazed into her eyes. "Eoghan O'Farrell."

"Jada Crawford." Her sister smiled in that come-hither way that made Ayanna want to give her a time-out like she had when they were younger.

"You can stay as long as you like," Eoghan said. "Right, Shane?"

Shane cleared his throat. "I'm fine with it, but this seems like a family affair. It's Ayanna's decision."

Decision? What decision? Jada was her sister, her priority, her responsibility.

"You're fine with it, aren't you, Yaya? We have so much catching up to do. I promise only a night or two."

"What do you say, Ayanna?" Eoghan's accent carried with it a slight rasp, likely from his activity in the pool.

Ayanna looked from Eoghan to Jada and from Jada to Shane. The men didn't know Jada like she did. Having Jada around changed her. She needed to work with Eoghan, but Jada had been her priority for years and still was. Coupled with being in a house with two attractive men? This was the worst of bad ideas, but it had been the two of them for so long, and Ayanna would never send her away.

"Two nights, and then it's back to school."

"Of course." Jada smiled. "Now, which one of you two tasty snacks is going to show me to my room? How about you, Ginger Snap?" Jada sauntered over to Shane.

"Jada." Ayanna threatened her sister with a look.

"Sure," Shane said. "You can head to bed, Ayanna. I'll get your sister settled."

Ayanna continued to protest. "You don't have to. I—"

"I insist." Shane took Jada's bag from her. "Follow me."

"Why don't you wear your hair like that, Ayanna?" Eoghan asked.

The comparisons between her and her sister that she was used to hearing hadn't taken long to commence.

"Because I have better things to spend money on than hair when what I have suits me fine," Ayanna bit out. "Go to bed. You need your rest for tomorrow."

"Yes, Drill Sergeant," Eoghan said and hopped up to his room.

Ayanna heard Jada giggling and the rumble of Shane's laughter, and misery clung to her like plastic wrap. Why was Jada here? Did she need money? Was she lying about the summer session and her job? Ayanna didn't know, but she'd get to the bottom of it and fast, because with Jada in the house no one was safe from her shenanigans.

When Ayanna arrived downstairs the next morning, Jada was cooking breakfast, and both Shane and Eoghan cozily sat at the high dining island, enthralled by a story her sister was recounting.

"And then he hauled me right out of the water," Jada said, excitedly delivering the punch line to her story.

Eoghan seemed captivated by the tale, and Shane smiled politely.

Ayanna's grumpy mood had started upon wake-up but now grew exponentially at the vision of Jada entertaining the Irish dudes. Not even the bright-yellow floral sundress she wore lifted her spirits.

"Morning, sis. You look pretty." Jada handed her an empty plate. "I made breakfast."

"Thanks." Ayanna took the plate and searched the room and beyond for the house helper. "Where's Louisa?"

"Laundry," Shane said. "Why don't you have a seat and eat something?"

Ayanna didn't have an appetite, but causing another scene wasn't going to help.

"This is good, Jada," Eoghan said.

"Thanks. Yaya taught me," Jada said as she slid an omelet out of the pan and onto Ayanna's plate. Jada fed herself last when she cooked for a crowd—something she had also learned from Ayanna when they'd tried to act like normal kids when people had come by to check on them.

Shane nudged her, and Ayanna peered up at him. "Eat."

Ayanna took a bite. Given her lack of appetite, the food might as well have been sandpaper. With Jada in school, Ayanna'd had a break from being responsible for her. Ayanna had been able to at least help her mother to rely less on her over the years, but Jada showing up like this threw her back into the role of parent.

"What are you up to today, J?" Ayanna gripped and released her fork.

"I don't have much to do, so I'm going to lie out by the pool." Jada unbuttoned her tight-fitting shirt to reveal a pink polka-dot bikini top.

Eoghan straightened in his chair, and Ayanna was certain his dick had responded in kind.

Ayanna shrank in her seat and stared at her plate. She feared to see what Shane thought of her sister's swimwear.

"Anyone want to join me?" Jada asked and unbuttoned her shorts.

"Jada," she warned. "Do that outside by the pool."

"It's a bathing suit, Yaya," Jada scoffed. "Stop being so bossy. Maybe a swim might help you relax."

"I wish everyone would stop telling me to relax." Ayanna addressed Eoghan. "Ready to get started?" When Eoghan didn't respond, Ayanna knocked her knuckles on the granite countertop to get his attention and repeated her question.

"Sure thing. Let me just get Jada set up by the pool." Eoghan, worse than an unneutered dog chasing tail, trailed behind Jada and her perfect ass.

Shane clinked his fork against her plate, drawing Ayanna's attention. "Eat some more."

"I'm not hungry." A lump formed in Ayanna's throat. She hated this role. She loved Jada, but her sister's presence always upped the stress level.

"Few more bites. You need it to work with Eoghan," Shane said. "Especially after your workout this morning."

Ayanna had gotten up earlier than usual and worked out. She needed the conditioning to keep up with the physical demands of physical therapy, but she'd also needed to let off some steam. She tried to get more food down, but if she continued, it would come back up on her. "I'm done." She dropped her fork and pushed her plate away. "Are you going to hang out by the pool too?"

Shane dragged his eyes up to meet hers. "Are you asking me or accusing me?"

"Sorry." Ayanna shifted in her seat. "I just get a little nervous with Jada around."

"Why?" Shane asked through a cheekful of pancakes.

"She's a big flirt, and it sometimes gets her into trouble." Like the one time it had landed two guys in jail after they'd gotten into a bar fight over who had the right to buy Jada a drink first.

"Flirt? Her? No way."

Ayanna met Shane's teasing brows. She barely felt her mouth move from the smile she tried to deliver. It was sheepish at best.

"She's an adult," Shane said at length.

"That's what you call an adult?"

"Take the training wheels off, Ayanna, and maybe she'll steer her own bicycle," he said.

What Shane said made sense, but Ayanna knew her sister better than anyone, and letting Jada steer her own bicycle wasn't so easy, especially when she was always crashing the damn thing.

"Tell Eoghan I'm in the training room," Ayanna said.

Shane's hand shot out, halting her departure. "Whatever it is that's troubling you. It'll be fine."

"Yeah," Ayanna said as she watched Eoghan slather Jada's back with sunblock. She wished Shane's words were true.

Eoghan skipped into the gym a half hour later, and as Ayanna stretched him, he questioned her about Jada.

"How old is she?" Eoghan asked.

"Barely legal," Ayanna said.

"Come on, Ayanna, I'm just asking."

"Twenty."

"What does she study?"

"This year?" Ayanna questioned. "Physics."

Jada was smart, which made her even more threatening.

"What does she want to do?" Eoghan asked.

"I don't know. Last year she was interested in engineering, and a few months ago she was interested in biological diseases. You'll have to ask her." Ayanna straightened Eoghan's leg and stretched it toward his head.

"You and your sister are very similar."

Ayanna sucked her teeth. "We're nothing alike."

"Sure you are. You're both extremely smart, beautiful, sexy, and funny."

"Compliments will get you nowhere."

"Says you." He sat up, and his hand stroked her brow. "But really, Ayanna. I'm serious."

She stopped working on his leg and looked into seductive eyes. "Eoghan." Within seconds his mouth moved toward hers. "No." She pulled away. "That's not what I want."

"You're right. That was presumptuous of me. I'm sorry." His blush might have been adorable if he hadn't made the moment so awkward. "I know when I got here, I was different, but you've brought me back to life, Ayanna."

Still shocked that he'd attempted to kiss her, she just stood there. There was a time when Eoghan's kiss and touch had made her feel excitement and desire. He remained the handsome footballer who made her laugh, but when he'd almost kissed her, she hadn't felt any of those butterflies that had once fluttered. "I'm glad you're doing so well, Eoghan, but . . ." She trailed off and focused back on their work. "We're not in Dublin anymore, and things have changed. I'm your therapist, and getting you better is the relationship we have now."

"Ayanna," Eoghan groaned and reached for her hands.

She slid out of his grip. "I think you should start your circuit. Alternate the weighted leg lifts with the foam roller."

"I'm sorry, Ayanna," Eoghan said, and she left for her office.

Between Jada's arrival and Eoghan's overstepping, she needed a moment to collect herself. She checked her watch. It wasn't even noon.

Later in the day, Ayanna had to run some errands in town and pick up a reformer from the institute for Eoghan. Shane had gone into the city to take a few meetings and would be back later. Ayanna tried to get Jada to come with her, but her sister insisted on reading a physics book by the pool and decided not to go with her.

"We'll catch up when you get back," Jada said. "I need to study."

"You're sure? You can give me the whole story about what you're really doing here while we're in the car," Ayanna suggested.

"It's cool, sis. Do what you gotta do. I know this is work for you."

Ayanna eventually accepted her sister's decision and left for the institute. She hoped she wouldn't regret leaving Jada behind.

Chapter Twenty-Three

Ayanna drove up to the institute in White Plains. She hadn't realized how much she missed the place until she parked in her regular spot and went inside. The training rooms were busy and energetic, and a few of the staff waved to her. The house with Eoghan and Shane was fine and luxurious, but even with all the bells and whistles, she missed her people.

"Ayanna," Chloe hollered and hugged her. She smelled like a combination of baby lotion and formula. "It's so good to see you in real life. Talking to you online isn't the same," her assistant said.

Solomon came out of his office and hugged her. "Hey, you. How's it going?"

Which part? The part where I tried to kiss Shane or the move Eoghan pulled on me? Or the fact that my sister is at the house without me? "Well, we're finally making some progress now that my client has become more invested." She thought back to a few short months ago, when Eoghan's despair had swallowed him whole. "He's guarding his nutrition and sticking with the routine and his workouts. He could push a little harder during our manipulations sessions, but I can't complain."

"I never doubted that you'd get him there," Solomon said. "And I heard you pulled out the Oni card. Nice one."

"You know, you have to keep one trick in the bag," Ayanna said, desperate for comradery, especially after the morning she'd had. "You guys should come by the house for a lunch meeting or something. Maybe we can schedule that over the next few weeks."

"Maybe then we can officially celebrate your award," Chloe exclaimed.

Solomon clapped. "Congratulations, my friend. The KPTA—truly an honor." Ayanna had been awarded the Kellinger Physical Therapy Award in teaching and research excellence, but with her busy live-in client and her sister showing up, she'd had little time to let the receipt of the honor settle in. Her colleagues, on the other hand, made sure to celebrate her.

"Nothing gets by you guys, does it?" Ayanna teased. "Thank you."

"We really do miss you," Chloe said.

"I miss you guys too. Now that Eoghan is stronger, I might have him come here on occasion. The socialization with other athletes might be helpful."

"Have you started thinking about back-to-sport evaluations?" Solomon asked.

She nodded. "We're looking at mid-September. He's been kicking the ball around a bit, and I've been pushing him, but he still has a ways to go. He still favors the leg, but I think it's lack of confidence, because the x-rays and MRIs look great."

"You'll get him through," Chloe said.

"How has it been here?" she asked. "Baseball and tennis are in season."

"And here I thought you were getting rusty. It only took you"— Solomon looked at his watch—"five minutes."

She waved him off. "I am going to see if Randall has a minute and then get the reformer."

"You know it's not set up and weighs close to two hundred pounds."

"Yeah, I figured I'd get it to the house since I was here. I can at least get it started."

"Ayanna, there is a limit to your jack-of-all-tradesmanship," Solomon said.

"Agreed." Chloe looked horrified at the thought of Ayanna transporting a reformer on her own.

"Don't worry. I got it. Plus, I have help at home to bring it in."

"Be careful not to hurt yourself. We need you."

"I won't." She gave them last hugs and went to see Randall.

When Ayanna got to Randall's office, both he and his assistant had already gone for the day. She wrote him a quick note to tell him she'd stopped by and that they'd connect to start discussions about return to sport for Eoghan. She was disappointed to have missed him, but she thought it best to get back to the house. She wanted to run a few drills with Eoghan before the acupuncturist arrived. A few of the staff helped her get the 150 pounds of equipment into her car, and soon she was on her way back up to the house.

Ayanna pulled into the driveway and successfully got the heavy box to the front door. She might not have thought through her plan on how to get it to the gym. She had thrown practicality out the window, or else she would have just waited for the professionals to bring it and put it together. Time for reinforcements. Ayanna couldn't find anyone in the house. She looked at her watch. It was midafternoon, and Louisa often ran errands around this time. The groundskeeper was off today, and the housekeeper wouldn't be here until tomorrow. Shane was in the city, but she thought he might be back by now.

"Jada," she called when she opened the door. "Come help me." Ayanna sounded like when she'd had Jada help her bring the groceries in from the supermarket when they were growing up.

No response. In fact, the house was eerily quiet for a weekday afternoon. She called Jada again. Not a peep. Frustrated, Ayanna did what she always did. She lugged the equipment in on her own. It was heavy and uncomfortable, and the corners scratched her legs through the thin material of her workout pants, but she had been parentless and manless for years, and as head of her household there were many times she'd taken on whatever role necessary to get the job done. This was no different.

Shane showed up as she was dragging the box through the living room and down to the gym and came to her aid.

"I got it," Ayanna snapped when he tried to take the equipment from her. She wiped her perspiring brow and pulled at the heavy steel.

Shane watched her struggle for a moment. "Ayanna."

Ayanna ignored him and continued.

"Stop!" He yanked her away from the equipment and held her at a distance with one arm. "Let me do it."

"I can handle—"

Shane glared at her for a long time, silencing her.

He lifted the equipment. "Jaysus," Shane said when he realized how heavy it was and how far she had already moved it. His frown intensified. He carried the equipment to the training room. "Is this everything?"

"Yes."

"Why didn't you get someone to help you or wait till I got back?"

"I was taking care of it." The shaky words vibrated in her throat.

"So hurting yourself was a better option," he said and gestured at her torn pants and scratched legs.

"I'm fine," she said.

Shane took her by the hand and pulled her to a workout bench to sit. He left her and returned quickly with a first aid kit.

"Take off your pants," he instructed.

"That ain't happening," Ayanna complained.

"It's so I can tend to your marks," he growled. "Should I take them off for you?"

When she didn't move, Shane attempted to make good on his threat.

"Okay," she said and eased out of her spandex pants. The scratches were bleeding slightly, but other than that, no real damage was done.

Shane treated the scratches with disinfectant. The cool, burning sensation spread through the area surrounding the grille-like scratches just above her knee. She winced and hit his arm.

"Big baby." He smiled and blew on her wounds. It reminded her of something her father would do when she was younger. Shane spread antibacterial ointment on the scratches, his soothing touch rippling over her skin, and put Band-Aids over the deeper wounds.

Ayanna watched him work with care and tenderness, and the tight control she had held on to started to melt.

"Thank you for helping me," she said, and tears stung her eyes. She blinked them back. She had to always be the strong one. Letting her guard down had often been a nonoption, but Shane seemed to want to take that burden from her. To let her be vulnerable and dependent on him.

He stroked her cheek. "If you need help, you ask for it," he said. "Ask me."

She swallowed the lump in her throat and nodded, because if she tried to speak, she'd be a weak mess.

"What is it, love?"

His question challenged her habit of stuffing down the emotions, and through the pure distress of opening up and allowing him to see the deep scars she carried, she released what surfaced.

"'Be strong,'" Ayanna whispered, the hot tears burning her cheeks. "That's what they said to me when my father died. It was like I had five minutes to mourn the man that meant everything to me."

Shane consoled her, his hands moving to her thighs and rubbing before they settled.

"While my mom drowned in grief, someone needed to take care of Jada. So they told me to be strong for my mom and my sister." Ayanna sniffled, and her shoulders crept up to her neck.

Shane breathed, as if giving her space to continue. "How old were you?"

"Eleven. Jada was five."

"How did he die?" he asked, his voice barely above a whisper.

"Car accident, during a pretty bad storm on his way home from work. He was a science teacher and in school to get his master's in engineering. I think that's why Jada flips back and forth between her majors."

A half smile tugged on his lips.

"I just remember hearing the thunder and watching the rain whip around. I'd never thought he wouldn't come home, you know?" she stated more than asked. "I think that's why thunder frightens me."

He nodded and listened.

"When he died, my mother lost the love of her life and was devastated. I didn't recognize her. So I made sure Jada played and was tucked in at night—that she and my mom were clean and fed. I did well in school because I wasn't sure how long I'd be there and I wanted to make sure I was smart enough to get a job to support the family."

"You were a child. That wasn't your job." An intense frown formed on Shane's face. "Who took care of *you*, Ayanna? Who made sure you were fed? Played with you? Tucked you in at night?"

Ayanna scoured her brain for an answer, searching for another grown-up who would have helped her family. After the repast, neighbors had continued to deliver their casseroles, cakes, and juice boxes, which Ayanna used to feed her family. But with her father's relatives in Sint Maarten and her mother estranged from most of her small family, there was only Ayanna.

"I did." She wiped her tears. "When Charlotte found out what was happening, she helped me keep CPS at bay."

"CPS?" Shane asked.

"Child protective services. If they knew what was going on in our house, they would have taken me and Jada. Possibly even split us up."

"I see." Shane breathed audibly through his nose. "Did your mom ever come round?"

She swallowed. "Years later, when Jada was a rambunctious preteen. My mother tried to parent her and build a relationship with us. Jada was more open to it, even through her puberty party, but me? I had it handled. I had successfully stayed away from drugs, avoided pregnancy, and got a full scholarship to school. Soon, I was off to college. I'd come home to visit, but I never lived with them again."

His hands became soothingly active again on her thighs, but his jaw muscles clenched. "You don't always have to handle everything on your own. Asking for help can be strong too."

Ayanna was glad that he didn't pity her or shower her with apologies. He just gave her the space she needed to share her feelings so they didn't eat at her soul. "I don't know why I'm telling you all of this."

"Maybe you just needed to get it off your chest. No matter what, I'll always listen." He stood up, and his slacks tickled her knees. "Okay?" He wiped the tears that dripped from her chin.

"Okay." Ayanna couldn't help but think that Shane was going to wrinkle quicker than he aged if he kept frowning the way he did. His brows softened, and his face moved toward hers. His lips were so close that Ayanna licked hers in anticipation of his touch. He was going to kiss her, and she wanted him to more than she'd ever wanted anything. She could feel the heat of his exhale vaporize the moisture on her wet lips, and just when she was ready to surrender to him, he retreated so quickly that she wasn't even sure the moment had happened.

"Shane." She didn't mean to grab hold of him or tell him how much she wanted him to kiss her, but she did.

"If I start kissing you, Ayanna, I won't stop. Not with you so soft and vulnerable and looking at me like that. It's not what you need."

"It's what I want." Her brazenness surprised her, and she was more exposed from the words she shared than the arousal that threatened to overcome her any minute.

"I can't." Shane fumbled with the first aid kit and focused on getting the items back in and discarding what he'd used for her legs. "I won't."

"Because of some pact you made with Eoghan?" Rejection diminished her vocal cords.

"Eoghan," he began, then stopped and appeared to use his bionic ears to listen for movement in the house. A scowl creased his face. "Where's your sister?"

His question was the pin that popped the lust bubble that had surrounded them. "I called her, but she didn't answer. Sometimes she wears her earbuds and . . ." Ayanna stood and picked up her pants, fully aware that she was in front of Shane in pink cotton underwear. His question sat heavy in the air and coated her with implications. "A better question is, Where's Eoghan?"

Chapter Twenty-Four

Shane tailed Ayanna as she ran up the stairs, her small figure taking two steps at a time. She jetted to her room and threw on a skirt to accommodate her bandaged scratches before she started scouring the house for her sister. He'd had to get himself together quick, because if he'd had even a few more seconds with Ayanna half-dressed, confiding in him and telling him she wanted his kisses, he'd have been done for.

"Anything?" Ayanna asked Shane.

"Nothing yet," Shane said, but he hadn't really been looking, since he knew where they'd likely find Jada and Eoghan.

"Jada," Ayanna called upstairs where the other bedrooms were. Shane knocked on Eoghan's door, and when no one answered, he opened the door gently. True to form, Eoghan pulled on a shirt, and Jada smoothed her clothing. Ayanna pushed past Shane to see the holy show.

"Are you serious right now?" Ayanna growled.

"It's cool, sis," Jada said nonchalantly.

Ayanna dived at her sister with murderous intentions, but Shane grabbed her by the waist and hoisted her out of the room.

"Come on." He dragged her out of the house and to the garden. "I know you like it out here, so do what ye need to get it out of your system."

Ayanna paced, huffing and puffing and flinging her hands about. "This is her MO. I'm so tired of this."

"Are you mad that she pulled someone? Or that it was Eoghan?"

Ayanna stopped in her tracks. "Both! She just got here yesterday, and she's in his bed? He's injured. Apparently, he can't keep his dick in his pants when a tight twenty-year-old is walking around."

"Right. I get you're upset, but we have a strict no-violence policy in this house," Shane said.

"Look, I appreciate you trying to deescalate this situation, but I have to get my sister."

"Not until you calm down."

"Shane, this is not a game."

"No, it's not," he said. "But you'll be miserable if things get worse between yourself and herself. More if you two have a row over Eoghan. Calm down, and then you can handle your business with her."

Ayanna was livid. "Why do you care, anyway?"

"Because while you're running around trying to control things and take care of everyone and everything, you won't let anyone take care of you. I'll volunteer."

Any wind that was in her sails deflated, and her shoulders slumped. "I don't need anyone to take care of me."

"Yeah, you do," he said. His defenses had deteriorated, and his filters were useless.

"I have to go get my sister," Ayanna repeated, but he blocked her with his body.

"I'm not done," he said. There was a real possibility of her directing some of her anger at him, and though that wouldn't be enjoyable, he would rather she have fewer regrets from anything that happened between her and Jada.

She crossed her arms and waited.

"You're dealing with a lot, but remember—these are two consenting adults. The sooner you deal with that, the better off you'll be."

"You know nothing about what I've had to deal with. She's not just my sister."

Ayanna pushed him out of her way, but he held on to her.

He hooked his arm around her waist, locking her to him, her middle warm against his skin. After one weak attempt to release herself, she softened against him and rested the back of her head against his chest. "I'm tired."

He closed his eyes, squeezing her gently. "I know." He could only imagine the burden she'd carried all these years.

He could stay like this with her forever, if she'd let him.

"Now I'm done talking," he whispered softly against her ear. Her fresh summer scent intoxicated him further. He freed her, and she sped off without looking back.

He found Eoghan in the kitchen chomping on an apple.

"What the fuck were you thinking? Rather you get rat arsed with her. Do you fancy her, then?"

"She's fit as fuck, and I haven't had a ride in months. I wasn't thinking. Nothing happened. We just snogged a bit."

"But with her sister?" Shane asked. "I thought you fancied Ayanna."

"I did. I do. I don't know."

"You're impossible to keep up with," Shane said and forced himself to face his own demons. He'd be a fool not to see how dangerous this was for him and Ayanna. She'd shared so much with him, and he'd wanted to wash the pain away. She'd lost a parent. His had left him, and the betrayal had stuck with him. When Eileen had left him for Eoghan, it had just confirmed what he feared. He wasn't worth it. Somehow, things felt different with Ayanna, but was he ready to take that chance?

◆ ◆ ◆

Ayanna marched inside with a calmer temper to deal with her promiscuous sister. She found Jada sitting under the open multicolored umbrella at the patio table by the pool with a bottle of wine and two glasses.

"I'm young and horny, Yaya. What can I say?" Jada poured a glass and slid it toward Ayanna.

"And you wonder why you stress me out?"

"We just made out. I swear, that's all," Jada said. "I really did come to see you, but you treated me like shit when I got here."

"So hooking up with my client was some kind of revenge?"

Jada shrugged. "I guess I decided to get back at you and do what you expected me to do."

"That's real mature," Ayanna said.

"I'm twenty," Jada reminded her. "You need to let me make my mistakes and stop treating me like I'm still your five-year-old baby sister. It was embarrassing the way you greeted me in front of the Irishes."

Ayanna evaluated her sister. She'd never thought Jada cared about what she thought. Whenever she saw Jada, she led with all her assumptions based on her sister's past. "Can you blame me?"

"Not really, but you didn't give me a chance either. You were just mean to me," Jada said with tears in her eyes as she drank her wine.

Ayanna let her sister experience her emotion instead of trying to comfort her right away.

"I miss you, Yaya. You never seem like you want to see me anymore. You just check to make sure I'm in class and not off with someone. I know I haven't always been easy to put up with, but you're my sis, and I love you." Jada sniffled.

"I'm sorry," Ayanna said, blinking back her own tears. "I didn't mean to make you feel like that, J. I just want you to be responsible and take care of yourself so that I don't have to. You can't keep sleeping around with every guy you think is cute. I mean, you can, but . . . whatever. I want you to have fun and experience all the things I didn't, but you have to start letting your brain be the organ you stimulate most of the time instead of every dude's pecker."

Jada laughed as she wiped tears from her eyes.

"That was bad." Ayanna laughed with her, then got up and wrapped her arms around her sister.

"I stayed away from Ginger Snap. Alas, he has no eyes for me. But you? I know you like him too," Jada whispered in her ear.

Ayanna released her enough to see Jada's amused expression.

"Don't act like you don't, sis. You almost whupped me when you saw me flirting with him."

"Keep your voice down," Ayanna hissed.

Jada giggled. "See? You got it bad."

Soon Eoghan and Shane made their way outside.

"Good?" Shane asked Ayanna.

"Good." Ayanna had had enough of this day. "Excuse me."

"Ayanna?" Eoghan called, but the last thing she wanted to do was have a conversation with him. He'd almost kissed her that very morning, and by that evening he'd hooked up with her sister. Any trust she'd had for him turned to ash as she fumed. Eoghan was vastly different from the man she had spent the day with in Dublin, and she wasn't sure she wanted to even know him anymore.

Chapter Twenty-Five

The next day, Jada slept in while Shane took off to the city and Ayanna worked with Eoghan.

"Hey there," Eoghan said when he arrived at the training room.

"Let's start with the usual stretching. Next week I think I'm going to have you start running outdoors. It's more unpredictable than a treadmill, and your stability is good but not where I want it to be. Shane's been running, so joining him is preferred. We have to start pushing your leg so we know where to increase your strength as well."

"Okay." He moved over to the table and hopped up. "We should talk about what happened with your sister."

"That's shockingly mature, Eoghan, but there's nothing to talk about. You and my sister are grown-ups," Ayanna said, disbelieving her own words of maturity. "Mostly, anyway," she muttered. She moved his leg over her shoulder and pushed it toward him to stretch his thigh, moving it in circular motions to target his hip and hamstrings. "You can do whatever you want."

"Do you care, Ayanna?" Eoghan asked. "I mean, ever since we reunited here in the States, you've treated me like your patient instead of someone you fancied when we met in Dub—ow!" Ayanna's elbow rolled into the muscle for a deep-tissue massage.

"Sorry," Ayanna said as she eased up on the movement, noting the tender spot.

Eoghan stopped her hands from moving. "You didn't answer. Do you care?"

Ayanna saw the genuine desire for her response. "What do you want me to say, Eoghan?"

"That you're crazy with jealousy and that you want me and you to finish what we started that night at my apartment," he said as he held her by the shoulders.

Ayanna was so distracted by what he was saying that she didn't see Shane walk into the training room and witness the exchange.

Shane's fists were clenched at his sides. "Sorry to interrupt," Shane said through tight lips. "I just wanted to see how things were going?"

"We're fine, mate. Give us a minute," Eoghan said to Shane without looking at him.

Shane's eyes lingered on her before he strode out of the training room.

"Ayanna?"

"You've been different from the man I met in Dublin," she confessed. Maybe the truth was that Eoghan was the same man but in the current environment they just didn't click. "Everything's different."

"I know, but I still think about you, Ayanna," Eoghan said.

Ayanna wondered if Eoghan had any idea how he sounded to her. He had been a pain-in-the-ass patient for weeks, had been intimate with her sister, and now he assumed that because he said he thought about her, she would just go with the flow? She wasn't even flattered this time—she was flabbergasted by his ego.

"I'm your therapist, Eoghan. Let's focus on getting you better and back to your team."

"So you're not going to give me a chance to make up for it?"

"There's nothing to make up." Ayanna attempted to finish her stretch-and-massage session with Eoghan, and he allowed her to continue.

"I'll show you, Ayanna. I'll do whatever it takes to make it better." Eoghan lurched to kiss her, and she turned her head. Her hand came up as extra protection, and he ended up kissing her palm.

"Please don't," she said.

"Okay, it's too soon," Eoghan said.

"No. Our time has passed."

There was no coming back from the past twenty-four hours, but he was a competitor and not about to give up. His confidence had returned—in all areas, apparently—but the expiration date on their romance had long since passed. She wanted to chuck it out to keep it from souring their growing friendship, but Eoghan didn't know when to quit.

Once the training session ended, Ayanna found her sister collecting and packing her things to leave.

"Hey," Ayanna said. "You all ready to go?"

"Yup," Jada said.

Ayanna sat on the bed while Jada finished up. "Are you still a physics major?" she asked.

"Sure am. If I don't change my major again, I will graduate next year," Jada said. "You have to be there."

"Do you know what you want to do?" Ayanna asked.

"Not sure yet, but I'll figure it out," Jada said.

"I trust you will," Ayanna said. "Umm . . . give Mom a hug from me." Maybe she was feeling generous, or maybe the love for her sister had a gentling effect, but she extended a smidge of that to her mother.

"Does this mean we can try for a meal together soon?" Jada asked excitedly.

Ayanna didn't want to get Jada's hopes up. Family gatherings felt strange to her and weren't on her list of top priorities. "Maybe."

"She'll like that." Jada paced like she had something on her mind. "I'll make you proud, Yaya." They embraced before Ayanna let her go.

"You're a smart cookie, J. You already make me proud."

Ayanna walked her sister to the door, and both Shane and Eoghan said their goodbyes.

"It's been a pleasure, Ginger Snap," Jada said to Shane, then turned to Eoghan. "I have your number. I'll call you."

Ayanna stared at Eoghan. For all his promises, he'd given his sister his number, surely for another hookup while he was in the States.

"Love you, sis," Jada said.

"Love you too."

And just like that, the Jada storm passed as quickly as it had rolled in. However, the heavy tension that existed among the remaining trio continued to swell, and she wondered not how but when it would burst like frozen water pipes.

Shane and Eoghan watched a replay of the match. "Smash it," Shane yelled as if he were coaching. The match got interrupted by Gob Chat conference.

"Aww, come on," Eoghan groaned and pointed the remote to answer the call. Pippin's model visage popped onto the screen.

"Hiya."

"Oi, Pip-Pip." Shane raised an arm up like his name had been called for attendance.

"Shane, man. How goes it?"

"Good, and yerself?"

"Passing the time till I'm off to Nigeria for a few weeks. Then training ramps up again in September," he said. "What are you shitheads doing?"

"Watchin' the United match."

"American football? It's shite, isn't it?"

"Not great, but not as shite as I thought," Shane said.

"How's the leg, pet?" Pippin asked Eoghan.

"It's coming on, Mam," Eoghan teased back.

"We're here at the bar, and the lads wanted to say hello." Pippin turned his phone, and the camera spanned the group at the bar, who waved and called out greetings.

Seeing his friend lifted Shane's spirits, and with the three of them together again, Shane kept his annoyance with Eoghan to the usual. He didn't know if Ayanna still thought of Eoghan as more than her client. He knew she was attracted to him, but Eileen had been attracted to both him and Eoghan and had acted on her feelings as well. Was he setting himself up for that drama all over again? He refused to be caught in the middle of another love triangle, yet here he was, longing for a woman whose feelings were divided.

Ayanna entered the living room in her white pants and light-blue top, a similar outfit to the one she usually wore when she worked with Eoghan, but she'd mixed and matched her colors this time around. They'd had a session earlier, but she hadn't yet changed.

"Hiya, Ayanna," Pippin said.

Surprised to hear her name coming out of the telly, she snapped her head to the greeting. "Oh! Hi, Pippin. Nice to see you again." Ayanna waved at the camera.

"You're lookin' the vision." He laid the compliment on thick.

"Thank you. Are you well?" she asked.

"Yep. Thanks for askin'. Eoghan says his leg is coming on."

"It is. Maybe he'll give you a show-and-tell, and you can see what he can do now that he couldn't when he first got here." She winked at Eoghan and gave Pippin a set of thumbs up.

"Right on."

"Well, I have to work, but enjoy your playdate," she said.

"Playdate? What's that?" Eoghan asked.

Ayanna laughed. "Have fun, guys."

"So Ayanna still looks fit and ready for a ride," Pippin said, and even through the screen he purposely aimed his dig at Shane.

"I'm torn, lads. Ayanna's lovely, but her sister easily snared me in her web." Eoghan sank farther into the couch, and his pelvis pushed forward as if he was remembering his closeness with Jada.

"Your friend here has been actin' a bollocks." Shane shook his head and recounted the drama for Pippin.

"Madness," Pippin said. "Sounds like you have your fair share of excitement being in that house together."

"Not a dull moment yet," Shane said.

"So are you ready for the arrival of the oul folks?" Pippin asked.

"As ready as you can be for receiving your parents," Eoghan said. "Maybe Da'll get lost?"

"Sure that only applies to luggage. It's only for a short time. You'll manage. You always do," Pippin offered.

The struggle between Eoghan and his father for control over his career was constant and well known. Shane had been surprised that Donal O'Farrell hadn't shown up unannounced when they'd first arrived.

"We'll keep him busy," Shane assured his friend. Neither Ayanna nor Louisa had any idea of the sheer mayhem that was about to descend on the house with the arrival of the MacCallums and O'Farrells. Their parents would be here in two weeks for his cousin Maeve's wedding and to visit with family.

"Well, good luck with it, and we'll talk to you soon."

"Let's order in tonight. Greek is pretty good. Think Ayanna would approve."

"I'll ask her, plus she might want something." Shane stood. He'd give any excuse to be alone with Ayanna even if only for a minute or two to get her food order. What had he turned into?

Ayanna had avoided talking to her mother for two weeks. After what had happened with Jada, she'd decided that she'd check in more often just to keep the surprises at bay, so this time when her mother, Morgan Crawford, called her cell, Ayanna picked up.

"How are you? It's been a long time since I've caught you without having to leave a message."

"It's been really busy."

"Jada did say that you had a lot riding on this client."

Fucking Jada. Her mother didn't have to know all the details about her life. When it came to her mother, sharing about her career and accomplishments was akin to talking about her sex life or her salary with any random Joe. Ayanna might wish things were different, but this was the status of her relationship with Morgan Crawford.

"Congratulations on your award."

Ayanna hadn't told anyone about the award, and only her colleagues knew of the accolade she'd received. "You know about that?" Ayanna asked.

"I follow everything about you, Yaya. I may not have been a big part of why you're successful, but I'm proud of you. You're my daughter, and I love you," her mother said as if to remind them both of their blood connection.

"Thanks." Ayanna had lessened the frequency of her digs about her mother's parenting here and there and resorted to keeping her mother at a fair distance, mostly for Jada's sake. Nonetheless, Morgan had called twice a month consistently for the past few years, even if Ayanna didn't always pick up.

"I'd really like to see you, Yaya."

"I'm really busy, Mom. Maybe when things settle down or when Jada's back at the end of the summer session."

"You always say after the next thing or the thing after that," her mother sighed.

Ayanna had used all her avoidance techniques, and her mother had noticed the repetition. "I'm just being honest. It's not a good time."

"All right. I'll look forward to when you have a little time," her mother said with hope in her disappointed tone. "We'll set something up then."

"Okay." One thing Ayanna respected was her mother's persistence. Whether she was curled up in bed, refusing to eat, bathe, or face the world in her grief for her husband's passing, or pursuing a relationship with her eldest daughter, Morgan Crawford gave it her all.

"Good luck with your client."

"Thanks."

They hung up, and Ayanna took a big breath while rolling her neck. Being standoffish with her mom took more energy than giving in and letting her get close again, but Ayanna needed to keep herself safe from the one person who should have protected her the most.

She went back to work. There were a few things on the schedule that she needed to address, including taking care of her own personal bills. She had to check on her apartment at some point and send back an RSVP for her awards ceremony. It was a formal event in the fall, requiring a speech. She created a schedule and list of to-dos to keep it on her radar. She had a few consulting emails that she read through, evaluated, and replied to. She completed and sent progress reports on Eoghan, copying the team here in New York and in Ireland.

It had been almost three months, and Eoghan already showed great progress. The length of his workouts and his conditioning had improved, and the swimming pool routine she'd incorporated improved his circulation and flexibility and strengthened his muscles without the joint stress. He even looked healthier. Whatever her personal feelings for him, he not only proved her research worked but was well on his way to passing his evaluation next month should all continue to go well.

Her phone buzzed, and she glanced at Charlotte's name. Ayanna was in a groove and thought it better to call her back once she finished up. But Charlotte called twice more, and Ayanna gave in. "Girl, I'm working. Let me call you—"

Charlotte cut her off and rambled mostly undecipherable information. Ayanna listened harder to make her out through the chaos in the background and Charlotte's fast delivery. Before Charlotte even finished, Ayanna reached for her bag.

Shane walked into the office. "Ayanna? We're going to order in tonight for dinner and wondered if you wanted anything from the menu."

She held up her hand to quiet him, but her mind raced, heightened, taking in information. "Okay," she kept saying over and over for no reason. Her tense body ached, and her heart pounded in her throat. "I'll be there as soon as possible."

"Are you okay?" Shane asked and hurried to her. His hand palmed her shoulder. His blue shirt highlighted the concern in his eyes. "Nothing's happened, no?"

She shook with fear, and Shane squeezed her hand.

"Tell me what's happened."

"It's Charlotte."

Chapter Twenty-Six

Ayanna couldn't sit still in the passenger seat as Shane sped to the Harlem police precinct to get Charlotte.

"Are you cool enough?" he asked as he maneuvered the vehicle through the busy New York City streets. If it had been her, she'd have been speeding through and likely would have landed herself in a fender bender or gotten a ticket.

"Yeah, I'm fine," she said. "Thanks for offering to come and for driving."

"Sounds serious. I didn't want you to be on your own," he said, his eyes focused on the road.

"I hate not knowing what's happening." Ayanna ran her hands through her curls, which had gotten longer over the past few months.

"And she told you nothing, just to come to the police station to pick her up?" Shane asked.

"She tried, but I couldn't understand most of what she said because it was either too loud or she was going too fast." She resisted the urge to pluck her eyelashes out one at a time. The fact that she only had that sliver of a detail to go on and the address of the station tortured her. "I don't even know if she's still there. I mean, if something happened to her, she could be in the hospital by now. Did she hurt someone? Kill someone? Did she get arrested?" She closed her eyes and took a couple of breaths. "Okay. I won't know until we get there. I'll figure this out."

"You don't have to figure it out on your own. I don't know everything about law enforcement here, but I'll be with you."

"There." Ayanna pointed as Shane drove through the streets of Harlem.

"You go in. I'll park the car."

"Okay. Thanks." She hopped out and jetted through the green double doors of the station.

A police station on a Friday night was not the place she wanted to be. Even though she was there to find Charlotte, she felt like the discolored white walls with army-green trim jailed her in with a guilty verdict. The line of plastic black seating, melded together by its steel frame, screamed order. She'd always hated those chairs, even in school.

Ayanna went to the front desk to let the officer in a dark-blue uniform know who she was and why she was there. "Good evening, Officer. My name is Ayanna Crawford, and I'm here to pick up my friend Charlotte Bowman."

"ID, please," the officer said. He was big and brown with a "don't mess with me, I'm an hour away from being off duty" kind of attitude. The man reviewed some information on the computer screen and then gave her a clipboard so she could sign in.

"Do I go back, or does she come out?" Ayanna asked.

"Hold on a second. I'm checking."

Ayanna waited, the officer's silence killing her slowly. Her need to see Charlotte and make sure she had all her fingers and toes mounted. She was about to jump over the barrier and look the information up on the computer herself. "She called me only about an hour ago."

"Oh yeah," the officer said. "She's a bit shaken up after what happened. We offered to drive her home, but she preferred to phone a friend."

"What happened exactly?" Ayanna asked.

"I'm not permitted to say, but Miss Bowman can explain the details of her case when she comes out."

Details of her case? "So you can't tell me anything? Not even the tiniest thing?" Ayanna felt like she was in a crime-series episode.

"Like I said, confidentiality. Have a seat," the officer said. "She should be out in a few."

"Thank you," Ayanna said. She tried to sit but ended up pacing a path on the worn tiled floor. Behind the glass the officers appeared cooler than she was in the stuffy, warm waiting area she occupied.

The station doors flew open, and Shane rushed in and came to her. "Parking's shite at this hour."

"Can I help you?" The officer gave Shane's white shorts and blue fitted short-sleeved shirt an up-and-down evaluation.

"I'm with her," Shane said.

The officer shrugged and went back to his duties.

"What's the word?" Shane asked.

"The officer said she'll be out soon. I still don't know what happened, and because of privacy, he won't tell me." She pointed her accusation at the officer.

"Okay, well . . . do you want to sit?"

She shook her head, the lack of circulation inside and the lingering smell of perspiring bodies and the ink from triplicate forms stifling her. "I tried that."

"Then we'll stand together," he said.

She gave him a weak smile. "I'm just worried about her, you know? She's the love of my life."

"I know how much she means to you. She'll be out soon to explain things herself," Shane said.

"Are you suggesting I be patient?"

"Better than me suggesting you relax. You hate that." Shane winked.

"I don't hate it. It just implies that I walk around not relaxed."

Shane pursed his lips, and his eyes traveled everywhere but to hers. She scoffed. "I heard that."

"I literally said nothing."

"You said it with your eyes." She pointed two fingers at him.

"At least it got a smile outa ya," he said. "This is stressful, Ayanna, but the good thing is, she's here and will be out soon."

She nodded. "Yes, you're right."

They waited a few more moments before Ayanna heard Charlotte's voice.

Charlotte sped over to them and hugged Ayanna, her body shaking. She didn't appear hurt, but that didn't mean she was all right.

"Hey," Ayanna said. "What happened? Why are you here?"

"I got mugged," Charlotte confessed.

"Hiya, Charlotte. You all right?"

"Hey, Big Red. Been better," Charlotte replied.

Ayanna squeezed Charlotte down the arms, checking for broken bones and wounds. "Are you okay? Did you get roughed up?"

"No. I'll be fine."

It had been a long time since Ayanna had seen the light in Charlotte's eyes so muted. "What are you not telling me?"

"It's nothing," Charlotte dodged, but Ayanna could tell that not answering had an impact on her friend.

Another officer jogged over from the doors Charlotte had come through earlier. She carried Charlotte's bag. "Miss Bowman. You left your bag."

"Oh my gosh." Charlotte smacked her forehead. "Thank you, Officer Soares."

"Is this the friend you were waiting on?"

"Yes," Charlotte said.

Officer Soares turned to Ayanna and Shane. "Take care of her. She's a lucky woman. Getting robbed at gunpoint can be pretty traumatic," the officer said.

"What?" Ayanna's voice boomed in the now fairly quiet station, and she immediately checked Charlotte for bullet holes. A few other officers snapped to attention. Ayanna would have tried to lower her voice, but she had nothing else to say, as fear held her words hostage.

"When you get home, try to relax. We'll be in touch if we hear anything, or you can check back to see if there are any updates." Officer Soares dropped her bomb, then left.

"Yaya, stop fussing," Charlotte said and pushed her hand away. "That's why I didn't tell you anything until you got here."

"Do you have everything you need, Charlotte?" Shane asked as he put a hand on each of their shoulders.

"Yeah, thanks," Charlotte said. "Let's get out of here, please."

But all Ayanna could think about was Charlotte with a gun pointed at her and every worst-case scenario available.

"You all right?" Shane asked close to her ear. Shane's calm demeanor helped her regain a sense of equilibrium after the chaos of the past few hours, but Ayanna was anything but all right. "I think I'm going to be sick."

The seriousness of the police station, here in America, had made Shane uneasy. What made him even more uneasy was the way Ayanna forced herself to be practical under her stress, though her hands continued to shake. This wasn't his country, and he had a basic understanding of how things worked. Break the law, and get arrested. However, Ayanna seemed even more nervous.

"Charlotte's getting a bath," Ayanna said but sounded far away.

"I made tea for you and Charlotte. I thought it might be calming," he offered. "If there's something else you think she'd like, I can make it or find it." He felt compelled to do whatever he could to brighten a dim situation.

"That's very kind."

"How is she doing?" he asked. He'd been shocked at the quiet in the car until they'd neared Charlotte's apartment, when Ayanna, having bottled her questions, had bombarded Charlotte with a slew of inquiries that even he couldn't keep up with.

"Being Charlotte—talking a lot, making me laugh, trying to make sure I'm okay when she's the one that was at the police station." She shifted her weight and seemed not to know what to do with her hands.

"Maybe that's a good thing," he suggested. "Her way to cope."

"Yeah," she said. "We're going to head to bed soon. We're pretty wiped. I know you didn't plan for this. I'm sure you want to head back, so take my car. I'll get a car or take the train. Eoghan is probably wondering what's up."

"I texted him," he said. "If it's okay with you and Charlotte, I'd like to stay." He didn't know if he'd overstepped, but he needed to be here for her, near her. "I'd feel better not leaving you alone."

"No, it's fine. I'm sure she'd appreciate you being here too." Her shoulders lowered slightly, and her face relaxed. Charlotte had been through an ordeal, and Ayanna had been anxious ever since she'd gotten the call.

She stepped closer to him. "Thank you, Shane." She choked on her words like she was struggling to hold on to her slipping emotions. "I don't know what I would have done if something really bad had happened to her."

He could only imagine the scenarios she'd gone through in her mind. He held her by the shoulders and sat her on the couch. "Come, sit down."

Before her butt hit the cushion, she'd buried her face in his chest. He held his breath, his heart racing and aching for her. He cradled her against him and stroked her arms. "She's fine, Ayanna." He held her tighter. "It's all right, love. She's okay." Before he could stop himself, he pressed kisses on her head and temple. She looked up at him, her watery eyes a knife bleeding him.

"Shane."

"I shouldn't have—"

"Don't apologize," she whispered, her mouth centimeters from his, silently tugging him closer. He tested her request and leaned forward. She was vulnerable, raw, and he needed to be sure she wanted his mouth as much as he wanted hers.

Her lips parted, and she tilted her head in reply. With the coarseness of his beard in mind, he connected slowly. All his nerves gathered at his lips, and with trepidation his tongue savored her. She moaned, and the sound hit him like a boulder to the chest. In his mind flashed the first time he'd seen her and her laughing, screaming, and jumping as they'd watched the football match together. How much he'd wanted to kiss her in the stands afterward was still a fresh feeling. Now, his tongue played with hers with the goal of soothing her, but this was so much more than a kiss, so much more than this moment.

His hand moved to her neck, caressing the curved skin there. He stroked her cheek with a shaky thumb, his palm ablaze from her heat. "Is this okay, Ayanna?"

She nodded, trembling like him, deepening the kiss and wrapping her arms around his middle.

He tasted the salt of her tears. Part of him wanted to ravish her right here on Charlotte's leather couch, to strip naked with her and intertwine in a lovers' embrace until he slid inside her and gave her all of him. The other part would do anything to assure her that everything would be okay. Since they'd been at Purchase House together, he'd done his best to stifle his feelings, but all things caged sought freedom.

He inhaled her scent mixed with the distinct fragrance of dried florals and woodsy cedar of Charlotte's apartment. Blood rushed to his lower abdomen, and his hardness pulled against his shorts. He wanted nothing more than to keep going, to please her and make her feel good inside and out, but the reality of their situation, of Eoghan, and the uncertainty crept in like a drop of ink, tainting the purity of the moment. Those circumstances would be the same when the fog of this supernatural attraction between them lifted.

Separating from her was one of the hardest things he'd ever done, and he prayed she didn't think for a second that he didn't want her. He stroked the wetness their kiss left behind on her swollen lips. He stared into confused eyes clouded with hunger. "I think Charlotte is done with her bath." He tried to smile.

Pink dusted her cheeks. She licked her lips, her tongue calling him back. "Yes. I think she is," she said, rubbing her eyes. Her hand slid down his chest before she set herself upright and patted her cheeks dry. "I-I'll go check on her." She stood up slowly and started toward the back of the apartment. She spun on her heels. "Thanks again, Shane. Good night."

"Good night, Ayanna."

He thought he'd never catch his breath again.

The next morning, Shane stretched stiff muscles from his position on Charlotte's couch. He lay there for a moment, recalling the adrenaline-infused night. Then he heard the shuffling of slippers against the hard-wood floor.

"Boy, you better get your long-ass feet off my side table. That's Marie Burgos."

He didn't know who that was, but it was obviously important to Charlotte. "Sorry, I'm long, so there's kind of nowhere else for my legs to go." He stretched and rubbed his face before sitting up.

She plopped down next to him in her orange pajama bottoms and light-blue robe. Whether he was ready to get up or not, Charlotte was ready to reclaim her couch.

"Thanks for being with Yaya last night."

"She was very worried. How are you doing?"

"Nothing like getting mugged to fuck up your weekend." She led with a joke, but then she breathed deeply. "I'm okay. It doesn't happen every day, so I'm trying not to let it freak me out and make me afraid of my own neighborhood."

"Do you think they'll catch the guy?" he asked.

"I really hope so," she said, but her voice lacked hopefulness.

"Me too."

"After my horrible ordeal last night, it's got me thinking about life." Charlotte looked up at the ceiling at that moment, collecting her thoughts.

"Yeah? That sounds big."

"Uh-huh. Especially how short it is and how one incident can end it."

"That's a bit morbid, isn't it?" he asked.

She swatted his comment away. "Are you going to stay on the bench or get in play?"

"Sorry?"

"With Yaya. I have to ask. You've been living with Yaya for months now. Don't play dumb. I know you like her."

"I—"

"Look, Yaya's a tough nut to crack. Like walnut . . . no, macadamia-shell tough. Seriously. Working hard and keeping dudes at a distance is her Achilles' heel. Even worse? She does them both exceptionally well."

"I'm aware." He looked out toward the bedroom for Ayanna. He couldn't believe that he was indulging Charlotte or himself in this line of conversation, but seeing Ayanna last night and being unable to guarantee her Charlotte's safety had killed him. He'd wanted to console her, and when they'd kissed, he knew he'd been ruined, even if there was little he could do about it. She needed to obsess over Charlotte's care and not let her out of her sight. He didn't initially intend to take any of Charlotte's suggestions, because he had his own Achilles' heel to manage, both physically and metaphorically. But being away from Purchase

House and with Charlotte breathing down his neck, he dared to take her advice. "What do you suggest?"

"Don't believe the hype. She likes you, I know it, but if you just want to be like your buddy and be a blip on the screen, keep playing on the sidelines. I googled you. You used to be fire on the field. You need to connect with that. You're a good guy, Shane, but if you're in this to win Yaya, you've gotta come harder."

Shane raised a brow. "Uhh . . ."

"That wasn't the pun I intended." Charlotte's mouth twisted slightly.

"No, of course not." He smiled.

Charlotte continued, "She deserves far more than another bone 'n' bounce. She needs a long-hauler. A ride-or-die like me, but in you form. You know?"

"I think so."

"There. I've said my piece. I'm going to get dressed. Yaya will be up soon. That bitch can't sleep past seven, no matter what."

Ayanna had, once, sleeping next to him. He got up and went into the kitchen.

"And, Shane—there's a little bakery just across the street that's open. Yaya really likes their apricot-and-almond galette, and I'm sure by now you know how she takes her tea in the morning."

"She doesn't have tea in the morning." He frowned. "She has herbal tea before bed and espresso in the morning."

Charlotte nodded with a knowing smirk.

He'd fallen right into that one. "I see what you did there."

"I'll take a raspberry-ginger muffin, please."

"Got it." He saluted.

He laced up his trainers, smoothed yesterday's outfit, retied his hair, and headed out to get them coffee and breakfast.

Chapter Twenty-Seven

She shouldn't have given in to kissing Shane. It had been two weeks since that night at Charlotte's place, and Ayanna still marveled at his easy smile when he'd plated her favorite pastry and handed it to her during breakfast. The earthquake of a kiss they'd shared the night before had been calming and cozy. She'd needed comfort. She'd needed *his* comfort. Since then, and once she'd come back to the reality of the situation, she'd given herself several good talking-tos about the road to devastation she was certain to travel if she let her feelings continue on this path.

"But I can't control it," she said, close to tears and tired of thinking on it after yet another restless night's sleep. Dodging him hadn't helped because he catered to her every need, from setting a towel out on her cycle to readily handing her electrolytes when she was done. And how could she forget his having the absolute gall to make her bedtime mug of herbal tea. She couldn't even complain because he did all these things the same way he'd watch matches with Eoghan or tease Louisa. Naturally.

Their parents would be here next week, and they'd be so busy with family that she'd likely not see them for the entire time. She'd take that time to put to bed this . . . whatever this was with Shane.

"Come on, Yaya. You can be natural too," she said, pumping herself up. She had good news to share with Eoghan, and when she found him and Shane outside staring up at a tree, she marched over to them only slightly slowed by the humid August heat, with the mission of delivering said good news.

The two barely noticed her arrival. "What are you two doing?"

"There are some funky-looking birds up in this tree," Eoghan stated.

"It sounds like a flute," Shane added.

Ayanna listened, waiting for the birdsong. "It sounds like a wood thrush, which is kind of funky looking. Brown. Cute. You know, there are quite a few apps to help you figure that out, as well as bird-watching sites."

"We're not bird-watching. We're trying to figure out what kind of bird it is," Eoghan assured her.

"You mean, watching the birds?" She couldn't contain her sarcasm.

Shane's low chuckle made her step closer to him. "I guess we are bird-watching," he said.

"There are binoculars inside. It's peaceful and exciting to do. You'll be out here for hours not bird-watching if I hand you the pair," she added. "Anyway, I have news."

"What?" Both men, coolly attired in shorts and T-shirts, turned more fully to her.

"The team and I have been shooting around proposed dates for your evaluation. If all goes well, it'll likely be the second week of September, two weeks after your cousin's wedding, Shane," she said.

"No," Eoghan gasped.

"Yes." Ayanna smiled.

"That's only about a month." Eoghan's eyes were wide, and his relaxed bird-watching body became more animated with each passing second.

"You've been doing extremely well, and . . . whoa!" She yelped as her feet left the grass when Eoghan lifted her, spinning her. Startled by how easily he threw her up in the air, she clung to him for dear life. "Ground. Now. Please."

He softly placed her back down. "Best news, Ayanna. Thank you," Eoghan said. The rims of his eyes reddened, and she could only imagine how much this meant to him.

"I'll have the exact date by our next meeting on Wednesday, but you might get a personal call from your coach," Ayanna said.

"Mate?" Eoghan went for Shane next and squatted to bear-hug Shane's stiff body before raising him off the ground.

Shane slapped his friend's back as he hugged him back. "Good news indeed. Now put me down before you injure yourself, eejit."

"This calls for celebration," Eoghan said.

"You two go celebrate. I have some emails to send." After sprinkling her fairy dust of happiness, she fled to her office. *Way to take charge, Ayanna.*

Ayanna had never seen Shane and Eoghan this nervous. August had sneaked up on all of them, and she almost hit the floor when she saw the two of them going around the house making sure things were tidy for their parents, who were an airport ride away. Even Louisa checked them both for hot heads. Not that they were untidy the rest of the time, but their excitement bubbled for their parents' visit, and her curiosity about the family relations grew.

Eoghan's form had significantly improved, and just in time to receive their visitors. She kept their sessions professional, but faced with Eoghan's charm and humor every day, it was hard not to lean toward forgiving him for his transgressions, even if he had a permanent spot on her shit list somewhere in the ether. He and Shane had made her aware that they had a wedding to attend in the Bronx by the marina and that both their parents and a slew of relatives would be in town for the event.

Though their parents had their own accommodations, they were on their way to visit Shane and Eoghan and have a long-overdue family dinner and stay a night or two with their sons. Since Charlotte had a hot date that night, Ayanna decided that she would go to a movie alone to give the family time to reacquaint.

When the parents arrived, Louisa welcomed them inside. The volume of their chatter further elevated the energy in the room from that of nervous kids to a family reunion. Both Shane and Eoghan took turns hugging and kissing both sets of parents.

Ayanna tentatively approached. As a person in the house, she thought it rude to just disappear. Resemblances were starkly obvious for Eoghan's parents but not as clear with Shane's folks.

Eoghan began the introductions. "Ayanna, these are my folks. Grace and Donal O'Farrell."

"Hello. It's a pleasure to meet you," she said, shaking their hands.

"You're the lovely woman taking care of my son?" Grace asked. Her brown hair had the same curls as Eoghan's, and her brown eyes shone like his as well. She hugged Eoghan around his waist and appeared half his size.

Ayanna had to really listen to her words to understand. "Yes. I'm his rehabilitation specialist."

"He's on the mend and'll be booted up and back to winning matches in no time," Donal boasted, his short dark-brown, almost black hair the color of Eoghan's. Donal might not be as tall as Eoghan, but he had a posture that commanded attention. "My son's a winner. No foolish injury'll keep him down. Now that I'm here, we'll get you back on track, son."

Foolish injury? Ayanna studied Eoghan, who displayed doubt that she hadn't seen in months. "He is certainly on his way," Ayanna said and exchanged glances with Shane, who then turned to his parents.

"This is my mam, Nadine, and my father, Conor," Shane said, his waist still in his mother's embrace.

The first thing that Ayanna noticed was the warmth emanating toward her from both of Shane's parents before they even spoke a word. The second thing she noticed was that she couldn't attribute Shane's red hair to either parent, though Shane carried his father's height and alluring blue eyes.

Nadine said something in Gaeilge, and Shane turned a bright shade of red. Grace and Donal seemed to share Nadine's sentiment, and Ayanna waited for someone to translate for her.

Shane clarified. "They hadn't known how pretty you'd be."

"The boys have spoken often of you. They just never described ya," Conor said, his cheery voice an octave or two higher than Shane's.

"Oh." Ayanna fumbled with what to say to such a sweet compliment. "Thank you. I guess my skill mattered more to them than what I looked like."

Nadine took both Ayanna's hands. "It really is very good to meet you. Shane speaks highly of you, Ayanna."

The tightness in Ayanna's shoulders thawed at Nadine's warm greeting.

"It's nice to meet you too," Ayanna said and glanced at Shane, who smiled at their interaction.

"We're dying to eat out, but the boys haven't had an Irish meal in months, so we're cookin' up something for them tonight," Grace said.

"But—" Ayanna was about to mention that Louisa had made them a few Irish-influenced meals, but both Shane and Eoghan quickly silenced her with desperate, voiceless pleas.

"Can't wait, Mam," Eoghan quickly filled in.

"Surely you'll join us, Ayanna," Conor said.

"Course she will," Donal said, brushing his hair with long fingers. The mannerism was scarily identical to Eoghan's.

"Um . . . I really don't want to intrude on a family meal—" Ayanna began.

"If you'd like to have dinner with us, Ayanna, we'd love to have you," Nadine said.

Ayanna looked over at Shane, who occupied himself with the tag on one of the luggage pieces but was sneaking peeks up at her. She felt like she was being asked to stay for dinner after studying with her crush. "Yes," Ayanna said despite the intimidation of feeling like the only third wheel in the world. "I'd like that."

"Good." Shane grinned at her and gathered the rest of his parents' luggage. "Let me show you to your rooms," he said to his parents.

"Where do you all sleep?" Donal inquired with a raised eyebrow similar to one she'd seen on Eoghan occasionally.

"Upstairs, but there are bedrooms on every floor," Eoghan said.

Ayanna helped Shane with the luggage, grabbing Eoghan's parents' bags.

"No, dear. The men'll take care of that. Let's have a spot of something before we get to the cookin'," Nadine said and hooked her arm through Ayanna's.

Grace took Ayanna's other arm. "Show us the way to the kitchen."

"She doesn't stand a chance," Ayanna heard Donal mutter, and she looked back to see the O'Farrell and MacCallum men laughing as they departed.

Ayanna couldn't remember the last time she'd been doubled over in fits. Her abdominals ached like she'd worked out and her jaw was fatigued from smiling while she listened to the women tell stories, many of which she didn't fully understand, due to their heavy accents, until they reached the punch lines.

"Can you imagine, Ayanna? Shane without his knickers and Eoghan with his hair singed clear off," Nadine laughed.

"Oh, it was a sight," Grace added. "The two of them often got into some mischief, but ever since then, the Legend of McKnickers lives on."

"If they ever knew we told you this story, Ayanna, they'd die," Nadine said.

"They know us well enough to know that you can't keep a good oul tale tucked away," Grace said.

Ayanna cut potatoes, Grace chopped up a few onions, and Nadine browned sausage in fat from the bacon she'd crisped minutes before. The coddle they were in the middle of making had a bit of time left to it, but with all ingredients mise en place, the women moved quickly.

The house smelled delicious already, and with one bottle of wine already done and chased by a round of beers, the laughs kept on coming.

"I hope the boys haven't displayed barnyard manners." Grace sprinkled flour to make a roux and then emptied a bottle of Guinness stout to deglaze the dutch oven. "They're raised better'n that," she said, stirring the contents together.

Ayanna's stomach growled as she imagined the flavors in that pot dancing in her mouth. "They've been fine. It's not like we're here on our own—there are teams of great people helping us out, from cooks and cleaners to people from the institute and other health professionals. They've done all right." Ayanna kept the boys in a good light even though they'd had their mishaps here and there.

"Good, good," Grace said. "When d'you think Eoghan'll be ready to go back to Ireland?"

Ayanna couldn't say. Yes, Eoghan had already shown great progress, but giving any false hope or date for Eoghan's mother to latch on to could potentially result in career suicide if things unraveled. "He's making progress, but it's still too early to tell. The body is healing. Once my part is done, he'll be ready for training. My part is still in progress," she said honestly.

"His father'll bombard you when he gets the chance, so you'll have to do better'n that," Grace said. "He wants to see Eoghan on the field come September."

"That's unrealistic." Ayanna's professional self stepped forward. "Not to mention dangerous for Eoghan. There's a time to push and a time to rehabilitate. Sometimes they're one and the same, sometimes not. It's up to someone like me to keep him progressing and not reinjuring himself. I'd be happy to invite Donal into a conversation about it and clarify the expectation."

"Ballsy, girl. I like it," Grace said and winked. "Now I see how you've been holdin' your own with the boys so well all this time."

Nadine laughed. "And we were worried."

Ayanna sipped her beer.

"Has Shane been a help to ya, Ayanna?" Nadine asked, though not a bit of concern showed on her face. Nadine tossed in the other half of the ingredients and followed it up with cups of ham broth, then transferred the pot to the oven. Ayanna salivated at the porked-out dish.

"He's been great," Ayanna said excitedly before her brain could turn the enthusiasm down. She gave a more measured response. "He's been supportive of Eoghan and his therapy while still working for the Rovers. His insight has been invaluable."

"Sounds like Shane, for sure," Grace said to Nadine.

Shane continued to surprise Ayanna with every day that passed, and hearing his mom talk about him only intensified her growing admiration for him. "Do you know he volunteers at a senior center?" She focused on Nadine. "They love him."

"Oh yes. I took him there a few years ago after he hurt his ankle."

"Poor thing had been hopeless. D'you remember, Nadine?"

"Hard to forget." Sadness covered Nadine's features, and Ayanna knew the woman had conjured up the memory of her son in a poor state. "He'd lost the things he'd loved."

Ayanna filled in the blanks. Soccer. Eileen. By the quick glance between Grace and Nadine, they, too, knew all the things Shane had lost and to whom.

"An old school friend of mine used to run the program," Nadine continued. "I used to love to volunteer and help her out once or twice during our vacations. Now, when Shane comes to the States, he continues to go. A lovely community to keep seniors happy and active," Nadine explained with pride in her voice. Ayanna clung to an old memory from before her father had died, when they used to donate clothes and food to shelters, especially during the holidays, but the vision blurred, and she wondered if she had the details right.

"He's a good boy," Grace said. "You raised him like your own, and he loves you right back."

Ayanna straightened. She had assumed that Shane's ginger hair had been bequeathed by a grandparent, since Nadine's fair features and Conor's darker hair weren't reflected in their son. She dared to ask, "So you're not Shane's biological mother?"

Nadine shook her head. "Shane looks a lot like her. She decided she didn't want to be a mother. Left when he was four."

Ayanna's insides twisted for four-year-old Shane. If losing her father at eleven had impacted her the way it had, she could only imagine what scars being abandoned by his biological mother had caused.

"Have they ever met since?" Ayanna asked, and Grace and Nadine looked at each other. "I don't mean to pry."

Nadine waved off her worries. "Once. It was pleasant but very . . . hands off for a boy who'd built up the reunion in his head."

Ayanna fought the urge to go find Shane and hug him close. "How old was he?"

"Conor and I had been married a year, so he was about seven or eight at the time. I tried to foster a relationship, but Shane didn't fit into her new life." Sadness with notes of anger settled on Nadine's features. "But Conor and I did all right. Shane also had lovely friends, like Eoghan and Pippin, and poured himself into football. He's a good man, my Shane."

"He is," Ayanna said. Her voice sounded far away even to her.

"And all the girls know it. They fall over themselves for Eoghan, but Shane has many admirers, even if he barely notices." Grace laughed.

"You've noticed, haven't you, Ayanna?" Nadine asked.

"Course she has. I'm surprised there isn't a gang of fans outside the house for 'em."

"Yes, I've noticed." Ayanna felt her cheeks warm as she shared a glance with Nadine, confirming that the two of them were talking about something altogether different from Grace.

"Well, girls, our work here for the time being is done. The coddle'll take about two hours, so we'll set out some aperitifs for the boys and go freshen up for dinner."

Ayanna was standing up to help put out crudités of cheese, fruit, veggies, crackers, olives, and fresh bread when she felt the drinks she'd swilled carrying on with Nadine and Grace fly straight up to her head.

"All right, dear? We still have predinner drinks and drinks with dinner ahead."

"How many drinks?" Ayanna asked.

Grace and Nadine cackled and flanked her on each side. "Don't worry about that. Just have fun. Ye've earned it."

The dining room in Purchase House felt more like a home, overflowing with loud voices telling stories from full mouths and drinks being poured plentifully in celebration. For a moment, Shane forgot that they weren't in their family home in Limerick.

"And Mrs. Doyle sends her regards," Grace said to Eoghan. "Her daughter is still available and awaiting your return."

"Mam," Eoghan said and blushed. "What am I going to do with a lass nearly three hours away in Sligo?"

"She's not as pretty as Ayanna here, but she's Irish," Eoghan's mother said. "I'm just saying you have choices."

Ayanna sported a quizzical look as if trying to figure out how her name had gotten into Eoghan's mother's statement.

"She can't wait to marry me off," Eoghan said. "She thinks we're foolin' around." Eoghan fluttered his eyebrows, and Shane wanted to box the expression off his face.

"I'm his physical therapist," Ayanna said, but her announcement landed on deaf ears.

"Well, you're a catch. Any woman who doesn't snap you up . . . well, it's her loss," Grace said and glanced over at her. "Wouldn't you agree, Ayanna?"

"Mmm-hmm."

Shane couldn't help but analyze every tilt of her head, focus of her eyes, movement of her shoulders, and twist of her mouth.

"Maybe while I'm here, we can do some training. Get you back on track," Donal said.

Eoghan looked like he'd just bit into lemon rinds.

"Not unless I'm supervising it, but you're welcome to watch Shane and I work him out," she said, referencing him. It was his turn to pay attention to how his name came up in conversation.

Donal puffed his feathers like a wild turkey. "I've been coaching my son since he could walk. Sure I know him better'n yourself."

"Da," Eoghan interjected, but his father silenced him with a glance, a look Shane himself had gotten plenty of times.

"I'm speaking to the lady," Donal said, and Shane didn't like the tone he carried.

"Of course you know him better than I do, but surely we can agree that I know more about healing injuries, or Eoghan wouldn't have come to America," Ayanna said.

Donal reddened. "You're a smart one, then?"

"Forget your manners, have ye, gaff?" Grace said.

"I'm doing my best with him. The injury is complicated. The last thing either of us wants is Eoghan reinjuring himself, because then he'll have no chance of coming back this season."

"Work out with us, and I'll give you a run, oul fella," Shane said in an effort to end the argument, because if Donal attempted another shot at Ayanna, he wouldn't respond as kindly.

"All right, then." Donal folded, and Shane's eyes slid to Ayanna.

"Thank you," she mouthed, and he wanted to leap over the table and devour her.

Dinner ended on a highlight reel of stories. Ayanna retired to bed, as did most of the house, but his mother enjoyed an after-dinner walk, and Shane was happy to escort her. They strolled arm in arm through the garden. It had become Ayanna's favorite place and by default his, a perfect spot to calm down. Dinner had felt a bit like being back in Ireland, but Donal and Grace as usual had bulldozed Eoghan and made suggestive comments that weren't their place. Ayanna had held her own, but he couldn't just sit there and let anything be said or implied. Also, who wanted to argue with their client's parents by choice?

"The garden is beautiful," his mother said as they followed the narrow path.

"You must be tired, Mam. The long flight, the cook. Don't you want to rest?"

"I want to see more of you," she said and patted his arm. He hadn't seen her in months and had missed her and the love for him in her eyes. He leaned into her.

"Ayanna seems lovely," she said.

"She's been great with Eoghan," he said simply.

"Anyone who can shut Donal down in a hurry gets a check in my book," she said. "Tell me. Are there feelings there?"

He knew he'd gone all scarlet again when his mother's musical laugh teased him.

"You're prying."

"I can't help it. You look at her in a way that reminds me of Conor and me when we first met. His eyes were only for me."

"They still are."

"Come now, tell me truthfully."

"Is it obvious?" he questioned, praying he wasn't giving himself away that easily.

"Only to me." She smiled. "So you like her, then?"

"But she's not Irish," Shane said, impersonating Grace.

"Grace and Donal haven't changed at all," Nadine said.

"Do you care about such things?"

"Course not. You know me and your dad better'n that," she said. "It would be different. People might talk or be insensitive, but that's their problem. I haven't a care so long as you're happy, pet," Nadine said. "Maybe grandchildren or pet children at the least?"

The thought of making love to Ayanna cantered across his mind several times daily, but the thought of seeing her belly full and round with a MacCallum inspired new feelings in him.

"Ye've gone too far, Mam. No words have been spoken between us, and there's . . . things are complicated." His feelings for Ayanna had been growing since the day he'd met her, but his pact with Eoghan and the fear of betrayal if he gave in to his feelings forbade him to act.

"How complicated?" Nadine questioned. "Is she with another?"

He gave his mother a quick, high-level synopsis of how both he and Eoghan had come to meet Ayanna.

"Fate is pulling your leg, isn't it?" His mother snickered.

"Eoghan and I have an understanding about women."

"One woman turned you boys upside down, and now you have an 'understanding about women'? Eileen never deserved either of you, and Eoghan . . . well, I'll not start on his part in the whole thing. What is this understandin'?"

"We don't date the same women. Ever."

"I've never heard of such foolishness, but seeing as what's happened, I understand your understanding," his mother said. "The thing is, neither of you are dating Ayanna."

Nadine had a knack for splitting hairs, but in this instance she was right. Eoghan wasn't dating Ayanna, and neither was he.

"Think on it," she said, knowing full well she'd already started that machine rolling like the handloom that stitched his family's tartan. What he really wanted to know was who had her heart.

Chapter Twenty-Eight

The next day Ayanna slipped quietly into the living room to grab the notebook she'd left there earlier when she'd scribbled some notes down about her thoughts on Eoghan's upcoming evaluation the second week of September. She'd worked on Eoghan and worked him out with Shane and Donal under her close supervision. She'd made sure everyone knew her boundaries, which she'd delivered in kinder bitch mode. That Eoghan had come out of the session sweaty and injury-free was a win.

The lively conversation the families were having about the weekend wedding in the Bronx continued to get louder.

"Ayanna, you should come to the wedding," Nadine said.

"I should do what, now?" Ayanna said, picking up her notebook and hugging it close to the floral top she wore.

"The wedding we're here for. It's on Saturday. We've taken the liberty of inquiring with the family, and it's agreed that you should come," Grace said.

Ayanna slow blinked as her mind rushed to catch up with Grace. "Thank you, but I wasn't invited. It's a wedding. I'd hate to impose on the happy day that is clearly meant for family and close friends."

"It'll be fine. It's my niece, Shane's cousin. They are quite close, and she'd love to have ya. All we have to do is give a call to confirm," Conor said.

Ayanna looked at Shane for help. Shane's and Eoghan's families were here to spend time with them. The last thing she wanted to do was get in the way.

"My father's right. You'd be welcome," Shane said.

"You'll come to the wedding with us, and that's the end of it." Shane's father, Conor, pretended to put his foot down, but since she'd met him, he'd been the most laid back of the group.

Ayanna stroked the tiny curls at the nape of her neck. She couldn't remember the last time she'd been parented, since she was the one both her mother and sister relied on. Did this man realize that she was (1) a grown woman and (2) not his child?

"Dear, she hasn't agreed." Nadine shook her head at her husband. "Would you like to go, Ayanna?"

"Why not. Sure. I'll go." She surrendered to the charming lot.

"Perfect," Nadine said.

"Are you sure it's not a problem?" Ayanna never wanted to be where she wasn't welcome.

"It'll be grand," Grace said.

Shane inched over to her. "And that's the end of it," he said, mimicking his father.

Ayanna pursed her lips to refrain from laughing.

Later that week, Ayanna slipped out after her session with Eoghan to meet Charlotte at one of their favorite downtown Manhattan boutiques to shop for a dress for Maeve's wedding.

"I can't believe that I'm just hearing about this," Charlotte said when Ayanna told her about Jada's visit a few weeks ago and all its trimmings.

"You forget you had a run-in with the law?" She'd wanted Charlotte to go to the range out in New Jersey, just to get familiar with guns so that she wasn't afraid of them anymore, but Charlotte wasn't ready. "How are you doing with that?" Ayanna asked.

"Well, my therapist and I are talking it through. I'm sleeping better, too, since they caught the guy."

"Amateur." Ayanna winked at her.

"Thank God, right?" Charlotte's chest collapsed as she blew out her anxiety.

"Yes." Ayanna's prayers had been answered when she'd gotten the call from Charlotte that they'd caught her assailant. Knowing he was in custody gave Charlotte a clear path to fully regain her confidence walking through her neighborhood.

"Anyway, I don't know how you didn't throttle Jada." Charlotte pivoted back to Jada's visit. "I love her, too, but she is so messy sometimes," she said. "I'm glad you two had something of a heart-to-heart, though."

"Yeah, it was overdue."

"So are you happy that she sucked face with Eoghan and not Shane, or are you heartbroken about what happened?"

"I'm not heartbroken." Ayanna left it at that. "Eoghan and I are ill suited for each other, but I think he is hell bent on trying to prove otherwise. I've helped him. He's grateful. We had a little abroad encounter, but he's not the one for me, and I'm not the one for him. He needs someone to whip him into emotional shape, someone like him but not. Someone . . ." Ayanna evaluated Charlotte. "Like you."

"Oh no."

"Not you per se, but someone like you." Ayanna hurried to qualify her statement.

"Dafuk outa here with that mess," Charlotte said.

Ayanna giggled at Charlotte's rejection of the mention of her and Eoghan's names in the same sentence.

"That man is forever ruined in my eyes. Did Shane appear affected by Jada's feminine wiles?" Charlotte asked.

"I don't know. Shane is hard to read sometimes." Ayanna knew that Shane cared about her, but like her, he carried the weight of the past. Even with the occasional breaches in their determination to keep a fair distance, she assumed his unfair agreement with Eoghan was the root cause. "I really just need to do my job before this becomes any more dramatic."

"Well, just remember that you are a dime and that it would be a blessing for either of those men to have you. You're the prize, boo."

Charlotte always had a way of lifting her spirits, and it was only after Ayanna heard the words that she realized she'd needed the boost. Ayanna smiled. "Thanks, girl."

Charlotte chose a dress off the rack.

"No bad and bougie for the Irish wedding, please," Ayanna said when she saw Charlotte eyeing a very provocative dress that would go better with high-heeled leather calf boots for the club than heels for a formal occasion.

"This is for me. I know how we have to represent for the race everywhere we go. You might be the only one or one of a few of us there." Charlotte rubbed her finger over the brown skin on the back of her hand. "This is hot, right?"

"For you, yes," Ayanna said, eyeing the skimpy black piece.

"And for you. Shane might like this," Charlotte threw out, and Ayanna scanned the store for Shane or anyone who might know any of them in a dress shop in New York City.

"Stop being ridiculous," Ayanna said, patting her hot face with the back of her cool hand.

Charlotte sniggered. "You got it so bad."

"Nothing is going on, so quit the soap opera narrative, please."

"Mmm-hmm." Charlotte shuffled through dress after dress and stopped. "Talk to me after he sees you in this." She whipped out a pink chiffon ensemble that was flirty, sexy, and formal enough for a summer wedding.

"Oh." Ayanna gravitated over to Charlotte with "gimme" hands.

"You have to try it on."

"You don't think the hem difference is too much?" Ayanna asked, stretching the material out to get a better look at it.

"Nope."

"But my arms—"

"You're competing with Michelle Obama's bicep definition with your arms, girl."

"My stomach." Ayanna puffed her midsection.

"Fit as a fiddle and nothing that Spanx can't fix if you want to overobsess about it."

"You are going to see a lot of leg—"

"That are gorgeous and will be the envy of the whole wedding party."

Charlotte sang the lyrics from J. Cole's song "The Storm" to her with all the hand movements and bobbing she could muster, while highlighting the beauty of Ayanna's eyes, skin, and thighs.

"I ain't no Nina, though." Ayanna held up her palm.

"No, girl, you got your own funds," Charlotte assured her.

The cashier looked their way. "You ladies need any help?"

"My friend here is going to try these on." Charlotte handed the woman the dresses.

"Okay," the salesperson said and took the items off Charlotte's hands.

"Really, though. Is it okay for a wedding?" Ayanna asked in vain.

"If you want me to say no, you're talking to the wrong one," Charlotte said. "It's not upstaging the bride, just everybody else. Shane is going to love it."

"Stop," Ayanna said, but secretly she hoped Shane would.

"Matter of fact, Eoghan is going to be beside his disastrous self that he couldn't get it together and do the right thing." Charlotte winked at her.

Ayanna didn't really care much what Eoghan thought.

"Just try it." Charlotte turned her toward the fitting rooms.

Soon afterward, Ayanna found herself at the cash register, sliding her card into the chip reader to make the purchase.

"You really look amazing in that dress," the energetic salesperson said. "You should follow us on"—she listed the top three social media sites—"for an extra twenty percent on your next purchase and post a picture of yourself in that dress at the wedding."

"Thank you so much for your help." Ayanna walked out of the store with the prettily packaged dress.

The wedding grew in importance with every second that passed. Ayanna had never really experienced a prom, since she'd had to come home after an hour at her high school one because Jada had come down with strep. Her sister's fever had spiked and had her feeling horrible. Dateless, Ayanna had convinced herself that she wasn't missing much and sped home to care for her ailing sister. Now as she carried her dress home, she hoped she'd enjoy the wedding as much as she thought she would.

Chapter Twenty-Nine

Ayanna click-clacked into the living room in her heels, the soft material of her sleeveless, V-neck, pink chiffon dress brushing against her thighs. She slowed her steps, and the fabric brushed against the backs of her ankles. Her flowy dress, long in the back and cut at the knees in the front, moved poetically around her with even the slightest hint of breeze. She'd fallen in love with the dress as soon as she'd seen it, despite her complaints to Charlotte. Her seventy-studded, strappy, three-inch tan Christian Louboutin So Me stilettos complimented the decorative gold embellishment around the Athena waistline and her jewelry.

When she sauntered into the living space, she found Shane and his mother already there. Shane had donned a traditional kilt with a black jacket and a green pleated plaid skirt. Kilt pins sealed the tartan, and a sporran decorated his waist. Shane was one of those beautiful men you googled or searched for on Pinterest under *sexy Irish redheads*, but having him so attired and gorgeous in real life was another story. Her steps felt like those of a toddler shuffling along in too-big heels.

Nadine, in a pale-yellow dress, fixed his green bow tie and adjusted the collar of his white shirt with the care and intimacy of a mother. She pulled Shane down for a kiss on one of his cheeks.

"*A stór*," Nadine said. When she smiled and pinched his other cheek, Ayanna thought she'd just about cry at witnessing their tender moment.

Nadine saw her first.

"Ayanna. There you are. Why, you look the vision, dear." Nadine looked over at Shane. "Doesn't she?"

Shane's eyes found hers and then slid up and down her body, and Ayanna had to refrain from fanning herself.

Shane left his mother's side and approached her. "You're absolutely exquisite, Ayanna."

Ayanna's breath caught in her throat, but she managed to speak nonetheless. "Thanks."

"What've I done now?" Shane asked.

"Huh?" Ayanna was confused by his question because she'd been on conversation autopilot since Nadine had called her name.

"I just gave you a compliment." He analyzed her like a scrambled puzzle.

"I know." She waited for further explanation from him, inhaling for clarity only to whiff his scent. The woodsy notes in his fragrance most times relaxed her, but today, along with the image, they invigorated her like smelling salts.

"Then why are you scowling at me?" He raised a brow.

"I am?" Ayanna felt the knit eyebrows on her expression and immediately relaxed her face. "You haven't done anything wrong. It's just that you look—"

"Foolish in me skirts," he said. He played with his accent and looked down at his white hose and garter tie flashes.

Ayanna was about to admonish his self-deprecation until she saw the teasing glint in his eyes.

She shook her head. "You look very handsome." They were the most understated words she'd ever spoken. People of all genders, ages, races, and cultures wouldn't be able to deny how sexy Shane was in his traditional clothes.

"You think I'm a looker, do ya?" He tapped her chin and smiled mischievously.

Ayanna swallowed to keep the arousal at bay, especially with his mother mere feet away. "Is this your family tartan?"

"Aye. MacCallum." She should be used to Shane teasing her by now. It was the only way she had been able to manage her growing feelings for him.

"Umm, where are the O'Farrells? Are they not coming with us?" She looked past Shane for Eoghan and his family.

"They're actually attending with Grace's cousin Tady. She and Donal'll meet us there," Nadine said as she gathered her purse and bridal gift in her arms.

"I've got it, Mam." Shane took the gift from his mother.

"Ayanna, if you'd like to throw your card in the bag here, we can present the gift as one from the family," Nadine suggested.

"Great." Ayanna dropped the card into the bag Shane now carried.

"See there? You're part of the family," Shane whispered.

What is wrong with him? Now that he was in Irish regalia, his boldness was something she wasn't handling well at all.

Conor came rushing in looking fresh out of a kilt catalog. "I'm ready. How do I look?" he asked his wife.

"Very handsome, *mo ghrá*," Nadine said and took the arm Conor offered her. Shane did the same, and Ayanna felt like she'd been thrown into a period piece. Moments later, they were navigating the parkways and streets to Yonkers.

If Ayanna had forgotten that Eoghan was a full-on celebrity, she was rudely reminded when they arrived at the Saint Paul church in Yonkers to find him surrounded by a gang of paparazzi, who snapped wildly to get photos of him. Reporter after reporter bombarded him with questions.

"Eoghan, how's the leg?"

"Eoghan, when are you back to Ireland?"

"Eoghan, are you in contract negotiations with the Rovers?"

"Eoghan, will you be back to compete for a World Cup spot?"

On they went, and Ayanna was glad she hadn't come with Eoghan, or else she might have been the one fielding those questions. This wasn't an official press conference, and in all honesty, her work was all that mattered, not satiating a ravenous crowd that was trying to capture sound bites they could manipulate to their own advantage.

Eoghan handled it well and quickly gave a line or two before ducking inside the church. Plus, she could imagine that the August heat along with the inquiries about his health had made him hot under the collar.

When it was their turn to walk in, the photographs started again, this time for Shane, who she'd come to realize was similarly famous as an almost martyr for the game.

"Shane, how's Eoghan doing?"

"Shane, are you here to make sure that Eoghan recovers?"

"Shane, are you reliving your second chance through Eoghan?"

Knowing Shane's battle, that question hurt her for his sake more than any of the others.

"Shane, how are tensions between you and Eoghan?"

What the fuck? Ayanna had thought the questions they'd shouted to Eoghan were bad, but with Shane, they really dug into his emotions.

As one of only a few grains of pepper in a sea of salt, her spot in the family came into question.

"Pink dress, who are you?"

Ayanna immediately felt Shane grow bigger as he all but shielded her with his body.

"Shane, who's your date?" the press continued.

In protection mode, Ayanna loaded a few choice words she readily aimed at the nosy media.

"Come on, pet," Nadine said and tugged Shane along, who then tugged her along.

Inside the church they found their seats, and as part of the wedding party, Shane and Eoghan disappeared for pictures and to set up for the wedding procession.

"I'll translate for you what I can, Ayanna, without disturbing the ceremony," Nadine offered, and Ayanna appreciated her thoughtfulness.

Shortly after they settled in their seats, attention was called, and the wedding procession began. Both Shane and Eoghan walked in with bridesmaids dressed in simple teal sleeveless chiffon dresses.

As the bridesmaids and groomsmen separated on each side, Ayanna had endless time to gawk at the handsome wedding party, yet her eyes gravitated to Shane, who pointed her out to Eoghan, since he hadn't yet seen or spoken to her. Eoghan said something to Shane, and they both smiled and nodded. She wished she were a bow tie around either of their necks to hear their whispers.

Eoghan's green, black, and tan tartan differed from Shane's green, black, and azure. She wished she knew more about the history and the colors, but as she ogled them, she enjoyed how striking they both were.

The wedding march began, and as everyone stood, she had to pull her eyes away from Shane to focus on the bride walking the aisle. Maeve, with a bun of black hair, sparkling tiara, and veil, stared at her sweating groom, a slightly thicker man with brown curls. Without knowing them, Ayanna felt the love emanating from the pair.

Ayanna tried to focus on the words by the priest, but her eyes kept returning to Shane and to Eoghan—but mostly Shane, given his eyes never left her. The heat building in the already warm church, even with the AC blasting, kept her pulse revving and her temperature hot.

"'A day lasts until it's chased away, but love lasts until the grave.' Meaning true and deep love lasts forever and overcomes all," Nadine whispered to her.

"What?" Ayanna whispered with a dry mouth. These men were trying to destroy her, weren't they?

"The Gaeilge translations," Nadine reminded her.

"Oh yes."

Nadine did the same when the groom recited his phrases. "'Two never kindled a fire, but it lit between them.' Which means love and attraction come naturally to those meant to be together."

The beautiful words hit her deeply, and as she looked back at the wedding party, she locked eyes with Shane. His gaze spoke volumes to her with understanding that almost had her running out of the church. When had she lost hold of her feelings? When had Shane become this important, and when had the unspoken pronouncement readied itself on the tip of her tongue like a swimmer on the edge of a diving board?

"Love," the priest said, and she blinked like she'd been outed, "joins these two in holy matrimony."

She fanned herself with a booklet in the pew.

"Are you all right, Ayanna?" Nadine asked.

"Yes. Just a little warm."

Thankfully the bride and groom were pronounced husband and wife and shared a sweet, tender kiss. The cheering nearly blew the roof off the arches, and Ayanna clapped in a daze as all the implications of her feelings weighed on her.

"The wedding party will meet us at the reception," Conor said. "Shall we?"

Ayanna had never fled from a church more quickly than she did at that moment.

The Long Island Sound at dusk created a magical backdrop for the wedding reception. August's muggy mood didn't even dampen the energy from the family and friends who attended. Ayanna had been grateful that she didn't have to drive over to the reception with Shane—or Eoghan, for that matter—because the ceremony had provided fodder for love-inspiring poems and happily ever afters.

She'd slow-walked the boardwalk with Nadine and Conor before experiencing the elaborate entrance to the catering hall, where a large centered fountain sat upon marble flooring and a grand chandelier sparkled overhead. It had dawned on Ayanna that she'd experienced more places with grand entrances in the last few months than she had in all her life.

Into the cocktail hour they went. Ayanna met many of the relatives, some whose names she actually remembered before her memory card got overloaded. She smiled and nodded but made zero effort to store any more names of cousins and uncles on so-and-so's father's side, twice removed and remarried.

After a while, however, anticipation built for the wedding party's intro. Those who gathered wanted to see the bride and groom, but she could only think of Shane. An hour later, after two glasses of wine, a shot forced on her by one of Grace's relations, and appetizers and various small-plates, she was full and a little buzzed.

An MC got the attention of the attendees, and the intro started. Ayanna stretched her neck to see Shane, and relief poured over her when her eyes got their fill. He'd quickly become some sort of vitamin supplement she needed. The full house of family and friends clapped and cheered the new married couple. After the first dance and parent dances, when everyone was on the floor, someone asked her to dance, and she swayed with him on the dance floor.

"Cutting in, Declan," a voice said, interrupting her and her partner.

Shane stepped easily into Declan's spot, grasped her hand with one hand, and held her by the waist with the other. "Having a good time?" Shane asked.

"Yes." She nodded frantically, then cleared her throat at how much bigger and more handsome he'd gotten during their short separation.

He gave her a full study. "You all right, then?"

"Wine. Shot." She kept it basic.

His chuckle vibrated against her chest. "There's much more to come. Best to pace yourself." He pulled her close until the heat of his neck was on her forehead, and she silently thanked her heels for the height boost.

"Did you enjoy the ceremony?" He pulled back just enough to see her face.

"It was the thing of dreams. Emotional and beautiful," she answered honestly, leaving out her revelations.

"You're beautiful, Ayanna." She met his gaze, which lacked humor and demolished her sensibilities.

"Is that why I've been called *fleá* multiple times?" she teased. She'd come to find out the word meant "feast or banquet." Apparently she was a tasty treat.

Shane laughed then. "You're a right fleá. Eoghan and I said the same thing while at the altar. Sinful."

"No, you're fleá."

"Why, thank you, lass," he said.

"Ayanna?" His hand rested on the curve of her lower back, and her breathing stopped.

"Yes," she said.

Eoghan came into view then and cut in on Shane. "Do you mind, mate? I've not had a second with this woman yet."

Her head ping-ponged between the two men. *Oh boy.*

Shane's chest inflated, but he acquiesced and left them to pull his mother into an embrace and drag her to the dance floor. The sound of her laughter mixed with the music and whirring chatter.

"I thought of you during the wedding," Eoghan said.

"What?" She pulled her eyes and longing from Shane.

"I hoped you'd understand some of the poetry and sayings in Irish."

"Oh." She regained herself. "Nadine did a good job translating for me, thank you. It was a very sweet ceremony. Did you enjoy it? I'm sure from your view it was very special."

"It was, but I've stood in so many weddings. They do become similar. It was a bit long."

"Yes, but you only get married once."

"With any luck." He smiled.

"True." Ayanna lightly laughed at his truthful perspective. It was a characteristic she liked about him, but for a wedding where love was in the air, she would have expected him to be a little more affected by the romantic bug biting many of the attendees.

The music turned fast, and she danced with Eoghan for half a song before the groom called for the groomsmen and all sorts of wild dancing and chants played out on the dance floor. Ayanna enjoyed the spectacle but steered clear.

Both Shane and Eoghan were seated at the wedding party's table for dinner, and Ayanna could have sworn the universe was playing a cruel joke on her. All she wanted was to have Shane close to her. When the waiter came by and asked her if she wanted chicken, beef, or fish, she wished that her redhead were a fourth option.

Chapter Thirty

The dancing continued, the spirits flowed, and Ayanna refused to be one of the shoeless women dancing around their pumps and stilettos. She walked outside, happy for the cool and windy air from the sound. She found a small group of men and women playing instruments around a rock firepit. What sounded like a Gaeilge hymn of pretty notes being strung together floated around them. Shane sat with the group, and she lingered. The song sounded familiar and absolutely beautiful. The participants were a mix of people she'd already met and some she hadn't. When Shane spotted her, he waved her closer. The faint smell of candle wax from additional lanterns on the tables nearby mixed with the scent of spilled ale and humidity.

"Smaointe," by Enya, Ayanna almost blurted out, like a contestant on Name That Tune or a similar song-guessing show. She only remembered because she'd looked up the translation once and it had brought her to tears, like it almost did now. The female soprano who sang the song smiled at her, and those seated on a small bench made space for Ayanna to sit. Since the performance was in progress, no introductions were made, just smiles and nods to her presence. Ayanna sat across from Shane, who was speaking to one of his cousins, Ron, who she'd met earlier at the ceremony.

And Ayanna learned firsthand why his friends and family called Shane "McKnickers."

Her cheeks flushed from heat, and her eyes were glued to the dim yet clear silhouette of Shane's cock under his skirt. She twisted in an attempt to dislodge the visual connection from the soft definition of the tip of his member directed toward her, but she couldn't because it was truly the prettiest specimen of male genitals she had ever seen. She wondered if anyone else could see it. Due to where she sat and how his knees, though comfortably spread, were angled, Ayanna quickly realized she was the only blessed soul to have such a view. Half-mesmerized by his resting size and half-shocked by the fact that she wanted to see it grow to its full potential, she stared, barely allowing herself to blink.

Her body must have commanded his attention, because at that moment Shane witnessed her ogling his dick. Ayanna's eyes dragged from his member to his desirous gaze, and the intensity, coupled with her embarrassment, pinned her to her seat.

Shane adjusted his clothing as he spoke to his cousin, yet his eyes were squarely on her, his breathing visible and in sync with her own. She was so wet that she was about to slide off the seat. She had to get out of there, but she didn't want to interrupt the singer. Still, she would not soon forget this memory of Shane's model cock using the shadowy space between his thighs as its runway.

When the song ended, Ayanna excused herself and fled, nearly running, indoors to the cool air-conditioning, which did little to lower her temperature. She could feel the dress floating behind her as she rounded the corner to an exit leading to one of the many vistas of the marina. As she got close, she could see the water of the marina, and it was the solitude she sought after what had just happened.

Ayanna was inches away from the door when she felt hands on her upper arms that stopped her, whirled her around, and pinned her in a dark corner. She didn't need to see his face. She could feel his skirt and hardening cock through the tartan wool. She could see people coming in and going out of the exit, but they couldn't see her and Shane in the shadows. The light coming from the marina through the small glass window on the exit door allowed her to see Shane's face.

"Where are you going, Ayanna?" His voice was as soft as a whisper, and Ayanna felt the heat of his breath against her lips. She didn't struggle, because no matter how hard she tried to professional her way out of her growing feelings for him, she wanted him close. Closer.

"I-I'm . . ." Ayanna tried to ignore the hardness poking at her hip and the warmth of his arms framing her body on either side, but with Shane this close, she didn't stand a chance. "I can't believe I saw you."

"Saw what?" Shane's lips curled into a half smile.

"Your . . . you-know-what." Ayanna knew what it was called. She'd said it to other men outside of and during sex. However, the intense longing coursing through her veins had her tongue-tied.

"My you-know-what? You mean my mickey?"

"If that's what you call it." If Ayanna hadn't been so heated, she might have laughed. "That was embarrassing. Where are your underpants?"

"I don't wear them when I'm in clan attire." Shane chuckled, yet his pelvis pressed against her. He nuzzled his cheek against hers and spoke in her ear. "Didn't you want to see me?"

"Shane." Ayanna sighed and arched to meet the pressure of his body on hers.

"Tell me you wanted to see me, Ayanna." He took her hand and brought it under his skirt. "And touch me."

Without the wall holding her up, she'd be laid out on the floor from weak-knee syndrome at the feel of Shane's hard cock in her hands. "Y-yes. I wanted to see." She swallowed hard. "And feel you." She gripped her fingers firmly around him and stroked up and down.

"Jaysus, Ayanna," he hissed, and within seconds his mouth devoured hers. His tongue slid inside her open mouth, and Ayanna tasted the warm remnants of ale.

His mustache and beard scratched her in the most delightful way as Ayanna drank him with wild passion. Passion that had been growing since the first time she'd experienced Shane at Aviva, admiration of how he cared and sacrificed for his friends, and desire that she knew she could no longer turn away from.

Shane's hand easily slid under the short hem at the front of her dress, and Ayanna's instincts had her opening her legs to make room for his seeking touch. Shane's heart thumped against her breast, and when his fingers found her dripping-wet center, he stopped kissing her.

"I've wanted to touch you like this for so long," he said as he slid his fingers inside her.

She trembled with fear and desire. Was this what it was like for her mother with her father? To lose herself so completely in a man? Her heart beat faster, and her entire being whimpered at his skilled caress. She felt his fingers pulling out, and her hips called them back, but she melted in delight when his slick fingers rubbed her clit.

"I've wanted this too." She shamelessly continued to massage him, hardening him further. Their mutual pleasure sandwiched between their trembling bodies, and their mouths again collided in hunger. Shane sucked at and bit her lower lip, and her tongue pleased him with wanton licks. Ayanna wanted nothing more than to let go and give herself to him.

"I'm not going to come, Ayanna," he breathed against her lips as he kissed her. "And I'm not going to make you come either. Not here."

"Shane," she almost screamed.

Ayanna felt his fingers withdrawing, and she nearly cried. "Don't leave me, Shane." She choked on the words and tugged his member toward her, doing her best not to draw attention to their make-out session. "Please."

He stroked her cheek with shaky hands. "I won't share your heart. Forgive me, Ayanna." Shane breathed heavily, the heat of his mouth calling to hers.

"Share?" Ayanna tried to sober despite her aching insides.

"Eoghan." His Adam's apple moved, cutting off his words.

"I'm going to try not to wring your neck for bringing him up at this particular moment," Ayanna said and separated from him to get some good, fresh, thinking air.

"I know he has . . . that you two . . . slept together," Shane delivered through tight lips.

"Did he tell you that?"

"Yes. You'd met him first, and he and I'd made that stupid pact when all—"

"Why do you care?" She'd dodged having to explain herself to Shane because who she slept with, even if it was his friend, was really none of his business. She did, however, care for him and wanted whatever this was to be honest if nothing else.

"It doesn't change how much I want you. You've undone me, Ayanna. To lose you . . ." Shane trailed off and reached for her, but she grabbed and held on to his hand.

Ayanna smoothed and straightened her clothing with her free hand and prayed there weren't any wet spots on her dress or legs from either her or Shane. "Come here." She pulled him out the exit of the marina.

"I can't." Shane looked down at his stiff cock poking at the kilt.

Ayanna followed his gaze and smiled. "Serves you right. We could have been blissfully satisfied, but instead we're playing these games."

"It's not a game, Ayanna." He stopped her. "I'm going crazy, but I won't have you until I know you're mine."

She wanted to continue to protest, but his strained brow carried with it the soft touch of sadness. "Okay," she said. "Umm . . . I'll help you hide it."

There were many people enjoying the night air on the boardwalk, and Ayanna positioned herself to hide Shane's arousal.

"What exactly did Eoghan tell you?"

"That night after the match at Aviva, he took you about, and after you both got sloshed at the Shelbourne, he took you to his place and . . ." Shane didn't continue.

"Wow. This is really hard for you to say," she noted.

"Then why do you keep making me say it?" he said with clenched fists.

"Because I want to understand if Eoghan lied or if you just misinterpreted his meaning."

"I don't follow." Shane arched an eyebrow.

"Did he say we had sex or that we slept together?"

"He said he slept with you. What's the difference?"

"First of all, I have too much respect for the Shelbourne to ever get sloshed there. Secondly, the difference you asked about is that Eoghan and I did sleep together, but we didn't have sex. Eoghan, on the other hand, got pretty happy. I mean, he wasn't drunk, but he was a little more than nice. Anyway, he suffered from what we call whiskey dick."

"Whiskey dick?"

"Right. Irish," she said, using one of Shane's sayings. "He couldn't get it up."

Shane didn't speak for a moment. "So you and he didn't . . ."

Ayanna shook her head. "No, we didn't."

"He lied," Shane said.

"Not really, but perhaps when he was kissing and telling, his ego allowed you to believe we did have sex that night," Ayanna said. "He's not a bad guy, and I was attracted to him when I met him—"

"I don't want to hear this, Ayanna—about how you felt about another man. Even if he's my mate," Shane said.

"But," she continued despite his objections, "when I remember that day at Aviva, I remember my time with you the most."

They heard the muffled microphone voice of the MC.

Shane groaned. "I have to give a toast for my cousin," he said and ushered her toward the door.

Ayanna was in love with Shane, and there was no turning back.

Chapter Thirty-One

Ayanna wandered through the big house alone. For the past few days a tropical storm alert had been swirling all over maps on the local and major stations. She hated storms, and this one was freaking her the fuck out. She had sent the staff home to shelter in place. In the previous days they'd helped secure the exterior of the house and stocked up on flashlights and candles. Regardless of all their efforts, she felt unprepared for the unpredictable storm outside . . . as well as the one swirling inside of her.

Shane had been avoiding her, and Ayanna hadn't seen much of him since the wedding over a week ago. He hadn't worked out with her all week, and if he wasn't jetting off to the nursing home, he was working with his team in Dublin online. Training had begun again in Ireland, and she understood more than anyone that duty called. But he'd somehow managed to take a sledgehammer to the lock on the box holding all her secrets, reservations, fears, desires, and literally every emotion she allegedly had well guarded and protected. Now, after scarcely seeing him the past few days, she missed him. Had this always been his schedule? After what they'd shared at the wedding, he'd all but abandoned her for work. She'd been no better. Her stomach fluttered every time she heard his voice, and she clumsily turned to her own duties.

She kept going over what had happened between them. Like a dream, those details got sketchier the harder she tried to remember them. Did he really feel for her? Maybe she'd made the whole thing up. Wouldn't that have been better? What did she want, a moment that couldn't last? She was tired of her own thoughts and kicked rocks through the house until she reached the office.

She sighed as she plopped into her desk chair. Perhaps if she worked, she'd divert her brain resources to something more productive. Fitting her noise-canceling headphones over her ears, she navigated her mouse on the desktop to Spotify and listened to a chill playlist.

There were a few extensive forms and presentations she needed to work on for Eoghan, so she had a lot to keep her busy. Eoghan, in preparation for his upcoming evaluation, had been required to meet with the press. To keep the sanctuary of his healing at Purchase House, a car had taken him to the city. With the parents still in town, Eoghan had a scheduled dinner with his folks and a few of their family members in Yonkers, where he'd planned to stay the night. She had overheard Shane say that he'd be returning to the house, but his plans could easily have changed.

Suddenly, the lights went out.

Ayanna sat in darkness with nothing but the faint backlight glow of her monitor, which soon faded to black. She checked the time, and it was nearing nine, but the storm clouds made what was usually still sunset appear black as night. She steeled herself for the clattering of hurricane winds lashing at everything in their path.

The thing Ayanna hated most about tropical storms was that when they hit, the results often included downed trees and power lines. The current rager outside was bound to cause some serious damage. The farther north of the city she went, the worse the storms seemed to get, hence her current lights-out situation. She heard movement upstairs and then quiet again. Had Shane come back? The prospect that she might be alone all night wiped clean the state of chill from the last few hours.

Given how long she'd been in the house, the layout should have been second nature to her, even during a blackout, but the fact that she hated thunderstorms serrated her nerves. Noise creaked again from upstairs. Her creativity on steroids suggested that maybe an animal had gotten inside. An opossum, a raccoon, something bigger?

You're being ridiculous. She knocked into things that should have been familiar. She needed help.

"Shane," she called with trepidation as she tentatively stepped through darkness. No answer. She'd been submitting her notes on Eoghan's final clearance on the office desktop when the lights had gone out. Her laptop probably still held a charge, but she'd left it with her phone on her bed upstairs. She made her way to the closest window, but she couldn't see anything but the shadowy figures of the trees as they swayed wildly in the wind. The rain poured down, and a snapped limb hung from one of the trees. The lack of streetlights wasn't new, but the landscaping lights that often glowed on the property were out as well.

"This is bad," she said, in search of anything that would give her a little light. She was petrified of storms, so when the thunder rumbled, she jumped in her skin and screamed. She walked forward, bumping into more things. Lightning followed, and though it illuminated the house for a quick second, the curtained windows didn't do much to give her a clear idea as to where she was.

"Shane," she yelled again, desperate for him and not the animal to answer her call. Her heart raced, and she tried to rely on intelligence and memory, but she was too frazzled by fear to think straight. Thunder rumbled, and Ayanna clung to the wall. She didn't know how much shit she'd knocked over, but the noise in the quiet house made her even more anxious. A shadow of light glowed around the corner of a corridor, and soon she came face to face with bright white light pointed in her direction.

"Ayanna?" Shane's voice called. "Why are you just standing there?"

She couldn't make out his face with the light shining in hers. "I can't see."

"You all right?" he asked and touched her arm. She almost leaped out of her skin. "You're shaking."

"I don't like storms," she said, squinting to make him out. "I was calling you."

"I'm sorry, love. Rain like this puts me right to sleep."

"Can you get that light—" She swatted the flashlight beams.

He lowered the light. "Come." He found her hand and moved it to his waist. "Hold on and follow me."

Though he'd told her to hold on, he never took his hand off hers.

A thunderous clap sounded again, and Ayanna screamed and jumped.

"You're okay," Shane soothed.

In an instant, she was hugging Shane tightly around his torso. She almost let him go when her hands touched smooth skin and a six-pack of abs that she counted. "Are you naked?"

Laughter vibrated through his belly and back muscles. "No. Just no shirt." One hand stroked her arm while the other guided their path with light. He led her upstairs. "Know where you are now?" he asked when they stopped at his room.

"Yes."

"Your room's that way," he said, straddling the threshold to his room.

Her feet pedaled in place with indecision.

"D'you want to come in, Ayanna?" he asked. "I know you don't like storms, ever since, well . . . I don't think you should be alone."

"Is that the only reason you're asking me inside?" Even now she needed confirmation that what had happened between them wasn't some figment of her imagination.

"No." The silence hung, speaking volumes. He waited in the doorway. "So?"

"Yes," she said as her body slid against his on her way in. "I want to come in."

Shane steered her through the space, his scent all around her.

"I'll be back," he said and soon returned with a few candles she recognized from the mantel over the fireplace in the living room. He lit two, and it was enough to see Shane in nothing but formfitting boxer briefs.

Ayanna was in immediate trouble when her eyes absorbed the softly lit contours of his body. His hair was out of its ponytail. She hadn't seen it loose since the first day she'd arrived, when he'd helped her retrieve her clementine. It was longer now, the ends sweeping lightly over the curves of his collarbones, and it fit him so well. Too well.

She sat on the bed, her mouth dry, and she tried to find words to fit the moment, but she came up empty. Speaking was the last thing she wanted to do. She wanted to reconnect her lips with his, to feel him and taste him as his tongue moved with hers.

Shane checked on her, only to catch her devouring him with her eyes. Though he hesitated, he was breathing heavily, and desire was clearly present across his beautiful features.

Thunder clapped again, and Ayanna pounced backward on the bed. Shane's agile body made it to the bed in two strides, and instead of sitting down next to her, he curled up behind her. Her chest rose and fell in anticipation, and when his hands encircled her waist and pulled her to lie close to him, she didn't resist.

"It only took a storm and a heart full of fear to get you into my bed?" he said against her ear.

"Doesn't hurt that the storm raging outside has me all discombobulated," she said.

The low rumble of his laugh vibrated the bed and echoed hauntingly in the electricity-free house. "I should thank the elements, then," he said.

She rolled over to face him, the vision of him stretched out on the bed one she'd gladly stare at all night. Yet much had been on her mind over the last week, as she'd been left only with her own doubting thoughts, without him to contradict them. "I haven't seen much of you since the wedding," she said.

He traced the outline of her face with his fingertips, sending a chain reaction down her spine. "I didn't want you to feel pressured to do anything you didn't want to do. Weddings have a way of making things feel more possible that might not otherwise exist."

She wiggled her body closer to his until their legs touched and their feet rubbed together in a game of footsie. "And you think I feel that way?"

"No, but I did," he sighed. "There's been lots to consider, Ayanna. I've wrestled with this for some time now because ever since I met you, I've realized it might be time for this pact I have with Eoghan to expire."

"What you and Eoghan have been through is a big deal. I honor your friendship, I really do. The way you've supported him reminds me of me and Charlotte, but after learning about this pact, I've felt . . ." She paused. "I'll just come right out and say it. It's unfair, Shane, especially to you."

"It took me a long while to see that what I feel can't be determined by an agreement I should have never made."

"Shane—"

"Hear me, love." His hand rested on her chin.

"Okay." She quieted all the impulsive responses building in her throat.

"I figured we'd talk eventually, but I didn't want to see the regret in your eyes if for any reason . . ." He trailed off, and she knew his next words were too important for him to swallow this time.

She propped herself on one elbow. "Say it. I'm listening, Shane." She stroked the soft hair that framed the candle-highlighted contours of his face.

"If for any reason you changed your mind and didn't want me," he said.

He ripped her heart right out of her rib cage, and her throat constricted with emotion. "I do want you, Shane. I've always wanted you." She'd broken her own rules for him, and on a much deeper level, no matter how hard she tried to negotiate with her feelings, they had other plans.

He wore his struggle between the loyal friend and the lover on his face. She should stop this to save him from this dilemma, regardless of what she thought about it, but all the discipline she'd acquired over the years was completely useless against his intense blue eyes.

"It's not easy for me, Ayanna, but . . ." He sighed. "But with you . . ."

She slid her hand down his arm and gripped his hand to put it on her waist. Her hand cupped his cheek and caressed his beard, scratching her fingers through the hair and smoothing over it. He closed his eyes and leaned into her touch. He hauled her to him, enveloping her in a bear hug, and she wrapped her arms tightly around him. She hoped she made him feel at least half as safe as she felt in his arms.

"Love and attraction come naturally to people who are meant to be together," he whispered in her ear.

"That's from the wedding ceremony." Her heart pounded.

"This feels natural, you, me, Ayanna. It always has."

"For me too, Shane." She never wanted that feeling to end.

He joined his mouth with hers, matching her desperation for the ultimate closeness. The rough hair of his beard bruised her lips as he licked into her mouth and then soothed her skin with traveling kisses. All the while his large hand explored the length of her body before settling on the soft flesh of her breasts.

"And maybe," he said between kisses, "I can give you a reason to like storms a little bit more."

She moaned, trying to perform the impossible task of pressing her body even closer to his. The feel of him had become her own personal drug that both calmed and invigorated her. He scared her shitless, yet there was no safer place for her than in his arms.

He twirled her into his body, and the length of her back hit the wall of his muscled torso. He cupped her breast from behind, squeezing and kneading, his thumb teasing her nipple through her thin summer dress. He wrapped his legs around her like he'd never let her go, and she felt the imprint of his hardening shaft on the crack of her ass.

"Is this okay, Ayanna?"

"More than okay." She reached for his roaming hand and clamshelled it at her center. The truth was she'd wanted to give herself to him for months, but he'd been an expensive gamble that could cost her everything, from the life she knew to her sanity. Now, here with him, she bet it all.

"Jesus, Ayanna. I want to do everything to you, with you," he said, fondling her through her cotton underwear.

His words sent her soaring.

"You're soft and perfect like I knew you'd be." He pulled his fingers out of her death grip, and his fingers crept into the top side of her panties. Ayanna opened so wide that her leg rested on Shane's thigh, brazenly exposing herself to the room as she hooked the top of her foot over his calf. He rubbed the soft skin of her pussy, and her hips moved in strained small circles as her hunger for him spread through her.

"I need you, Shane." She was hot and eager, and she puppeted his hand to slip inside her slit with hers.

Shane kissed and bit her neck as two of his fingers and one of hers stretched her canal. She welcomed the growing intensity. Even in bed they worked together.

"Your gash is soaking wet, Ayanna," Shane said, and without another word, he removed his hand and flipped her on her stomach. He pushed feverishly at her panties, as did she, to get them off. Kneeling behind her, Shane gripped her hips. He propped her ass up, and his teeth teased with gentle bites over the thickest parts of her. She stretched and arched, calling him to what felt good and where she wished he'd go. He spread her legs before burying his head between her thighs. Her dress gathered around her breasts.

"Oh fuck, Shane. Yes." She clutched the pillows and squealed into them as he ate her out from behind. As he lapped at her love juices, he caressed her from her lower back, down her ass, and to the backs of her legs.

"I'm going to drink all of you," he moaned, his words vibrating against her clit. "Every fucking drop."

Her knees dug into the mattress as her hips quivered at the feel of his tongue against her heat. Each gentle caress he graced her with strummed at her heartstrings, and in these moments, she let him into her very being, where she'd hold him forever no matter what happened.

He slid his fingers into her. It was more than two. The combination of the pressure on her G-spot and his flickering tongue and mouth on her lips and clit sent her soaring. The throb of her approaching orgasm ached as his other hand squeezed. "Shane," she called, and she was undone. "I'm gonna come. Don't stop."

He obliged her with quickening speed, and Ayanna's arrival burst through her body as she rocked back and forth like a jockey on a horse. The air in the room was warm from their body heat, and the sound of rain whipping against the windows was as tumultuous as the orgasm spasming through her body. Shane held her to his mouth and bathed her with tender, intimate touches until she screamed at his relentless sucking, and she trembled as the sensation of release fluttered throughout her lower belly. She had enjoyed sex before, but this? Never like this. Never with Shane. Was this what it felt like to truly give all of herself to love?

Shane pulled her up enough to lift her dress over her head and tossed it aside. With her back to him, she couldn't see him and craned her neck to get a dim glance at the intense desire on his face. "Was that nice, flower?" he asked.

"Yes." She gave him her mouth. She didn't know when he removed his briefs, but the full measure of his engorged cock poked against her ass. She wanted every inch inside her. Even more than that—she needed it.

"You're beautiful, Shane." She ran her hand over his defined arms and over his muscled chest and abs.

Kissing him, Ayanna maneuvered herself around to face him. His lips made love to her in a kiss so soft she felt a sob building in her chest.

"The way you kiss me," she mumbled against him. She breathed and groaned, this tenderness drugging her, arousing her. She tasted him and herself the deeper his tongue dived into her mouth. "No one has ever kissed me like this. Ever."

"The way *you* kiss me," he teased, and his arm hooked around her waist to steady them both. "I never want you to stop."

She didn't know how much time had passed, but their mouth play continued, each lick, suck, and nibble feeling as good as the last.

"You're the music in my heart, flower. You must know that," he breathed against her lips, filling her heart with a joy she couldn't describe. He didn't need to touch her anyplace else, and if they went on this way, she'd surely come just from this intimate moment with him.

"You mean everything to me, Shane," she gushed. Ending the earthshaking connection of their kiss nearly broke her heart, but she needed to pleasure him. She rocked her hips to leverage her legs back and pressed loving kisses on his stomach. Her caress progressed all the way down to his pelvis until she positioned herself on her hands and knees before him. His hand glided through her hair as she looked up at him, his hair veiling his face.

"Can I kiss you here?" she asked, knowingly, teasingly.

He raked his other hand through his strawberry-colored strands, revealing his anticipation. "Yes. I'd like that." His chest heaved, and the tempo of his caress urged her to keep going. "Fuck, I want that more than anything, Ayanna."

She nuzzled her face into the curls around his stiff cock and to the soft balls below. He smelled and tasted of cedar wood and floral greens from the soap he used. His fragrance further enticed her to action. Her hand gripped him, and she slid him into her mouth, sucking him in with appreciation.

"Fucking hell," he hissed, and he slid down to the bed. "Take it all, love."

Ayanna loved his size, even if she needed to expand the limits of her reflexes. Knowing she made him feel a fraction of how good he made her feel gave her all the motivation she needed. She felt his large hands glide down her back, and she arched, sending her ass into the air. As she lapped him from base to tip, he traced the split of her ass. His hand disappeared momentarily, and she peeked to witness him wetting his fingers. His hand returned to her ass, sliding into her crack and finding her hole. She arched farther.

"Mm-hmm," she affirmed, wiggling her hips in anticipation. She trusted him more than she'd trusted any other man with her body and knew that he'd never physically hurt her. "Please, Shane. I trust you. Please don't stop."

Inside he went, slowly, gently. She groaned and lurched against the loving touch. Deeper he caressed. She'd seen his large hand do many things over the past few months. Aid a friend in practice, make her coffee, hold her hand, type an email, and massage his beard, but this particular skill of his finger trumped them all. She envisioned what they must look like. Her perpendicular to him with his dick in her mouth and him bent over her back with his finger in her asshole. A fresh stream of wetness slicked her pussy, and she reached to please herself.

Ayanna was elated to please him this way. Shane palmed her rear, squeezing her flesh with one hand while steadying himself with the other. He entangled his fingers in her curls, her hand followed, and together they pressed gently on the back of her head. She did her best to accommodate his massive size in her mouth and throat. Her aching pussy wanted him, but not until she had satisfied him. Not until she made love to him the way he'd made love to her.

"What you doin' there?" he huffed and gently stroked her arm as she rubbed her fingers on her clit.

She released his cock with smacking lips. "Your hands are full," she said. She licked the tip of his cock, and he groaned.

"Do that again," he commanded.

She did as she was told, lingering, playing.

He caressed her cheek. "I'll come if you continue."

"Sounds very good to me."

"You're a beautiful little devil." His soft laugh wrapped her snug and tight like a steamed dumpling.

She went to take him in her mouth again, but when he hoisted her up and flipped her on her back, it was clear he had other plans.

She yelped, grabbing onto him. He pressed her gently back and hurried off the bed. She heard the familiar sound of a plastic wrapper as he tore it open, and she watched him fit himself with latex. He climbed between her legs, and she accommodated his body.

He lined himself up for entry. "I need you now, flower," he said, hovering over her. He was strong and powerful between her thighs, and when he dived deep into her, she wasn't prepared for the way his cock filled her. "Shane," she hollered.

He stilled and retreated, but she clutched his hips, shaking her head. "Don't pull out," she groaned.

"I'm sorry, I-I didn't realize . . ." Stress covered his face.

Ayanna tried to iron out the lines on his face with her fingertips. "That's the same dick I just had in my mouth, right?" she teased.

"Same one." Breathless, Shane tried to smile, but she could see his worry. "I've gone and hurt you, love."

"No." She pecked his lips several times. "I just wasn't expecting . . . you're larger . . ." She had a hard time explaining herself. "I wasn't ready."

"Do you want me to stop?" Shane said. "Fuck, I don't want to, but I will."

"No." She held his face. "You make me feel good, Shane. I don't want you to ever stop making me feel like this."

His lips made love to hers so tenderly it hurt. Kissing, soothing, and asking for forgiveness. "I want to see your face when you come this time, Ayanna. Let me see how good I make you feel."

She moved against him slowly to allow her body to acclimate to the new entry. "Please, baby, make me feel good." She smiled.

"Straightaway." He glided in and out, and she relished the feel of every blood-rich vein and ridge of his cock. "You're so good and tight, Ayanna."

Her hand smoothed over tense muscles, and his reddening skin glistened with perspiration. He went deeper with each glorious push.

"Come on, baby," she said, heaving, unable to look away from the blue eyes that locked on her as they moved together.

His thrusts sped up while he stole breathless kisses. "Fuck!" he shouted into her mouth, crushing her with his forearms.

She received every spasm, feeling the heat of his seed as he jerked into the latex shield.

Ayanna was so wet and close to orgasm. She held Shane's face, kissed him and caressed him with love in every touch. She felt his hands slide between her legs until his fingers found her clit. Even as he rode the wave of his own pleasure, he continued to massage every drop of her pleasure out of her. "Come for me, Ayanna. Let me hear you. I need . . ." He grunted and rubbed her pussy until she writhed underneath him.

"Sh—fu . . . oh fuck, Shane!" Her arrival exploded from every part of her, fracturing her into delicate, sensitive pieces. She rode the crest of each wave washing over her. She fastened her legs around him and dug her fingernails into him. Her body bucked, and she squeezed her thighs as the shock waves reverberated through her from her toes to the crown of her head.

When her body finally settled, Shane was lying on his side facing her, and he pulled her in close. He intertwined his legs with hers and cradled her in his arms.

"I love you, Ayanna."

"Shane," she began, but he silenced her with a kiss that curled her toes.

"I have ever since I saw you with the old man before I met you for the match at Aviva," he said.

Ayanna placed her chin on his chest. "What?" She didn't want to tell him he sounded delirious, so she listened.

"That day when I met you at the pub. Before I even knew who you were, I saw this beautiful Black woman in rival colors." Shane touched her nose. "You're small, Ayanna, but you think you're big. I saw you guard the old man, on your own, in a sea of people, as if you were a seven-foot-tall gladiator. I loved your heart and the kindness you showed to a stranger. It was only a matter of time before I fell in love with you."

Ayanna smiled and squeezed him tighter, but she was speechless. Her head swirled, and her heart swelled. She wanted to tell him she felt the same, that he was all she'd ever dreamed of and wanted, that she loved him so much that she lost herself completely in him, and that was exactly why she had to let him go.

"You don't have to speak your feelings, but . . ." He paused. "I hope one day you will."

What was wrong with her? The way he'd treated her and made love to her and what they'd shared meant more to her than anything. Why couldn't she just bury the past and love him without the anticipation of doom and gloom? Why couldn't she tell him how the fear of anything happening to him, of him leaving whether he wanted to or not, would do its best to kill her?

"But," she stuttered. "What if I never do? What if I can't, Shane?"

"Shh . . . don't think on it any further. Rest now." His fingertips massaged her head. "Because this'll wake in a moment, and you'll wish you had." He tilted his hips and smiled down at her.

"I better get to it, then." She cuddled up against him, but her heart ached. She said a silent prayer that when the time came, she'd be able to let Shane go.

Chapter Thirty-Two

The next morning Ayanna awakened at the sound of chatter in the house. She heard Shane's name and hers.

Eoghan.

Ayanna sprang to a sitting position and pulled a sheet up over her naked body.

"Don't go." Shane's gentle hand on her back accompanied his sleepy request. She didn't know if he'd heard Eoghan in the house, but if he had, he made no attempt to spring into action.

She craned her neck at him. Wide-awake deep-blue eyes stared up at her. "It's Eoghan," she said.

"I'm aware."

Without a mirror, she knew she looked well ravished and felt every mark and memory of Shane all over her body. "This is not the most professional position to find your rehabilitation therapist in," she said. "I mean . . . this is a visual he can't unsee. I don't want to upset him." Ayanna didn't know how Eoghan would take the news about her and Shane, but seeing her in bed with him wasn't going to ease that conversation.

"Why d'you think you'll upset him?" Shane's stiff muscles rippled under his skin.

She shrugged. "I don't know. Pride?'"

"He'll have to find out one way or the other."

"Yeah, but not like this," she said. "Please, Shane."

She felt his growing agitation and ran her fingertips over his jaw. She might not want to hurt Eoghan, but Shane's feelings were exponentially more important to her, even if voicing her own feelings to him stuck like peanut butter on the roof of her mouth. It tasted good but was complicated to get out.

"Tell me what you want me to do, love, and I'll do it."

She bent down and pecked those irresistible lips—a bad move, because she lost time until she heard the thud of footsteps on the staircase. She pulled herself away. "Get dressed, man." She jumped out of bed and dived for her dress.

Eoghan knocked on the door and didn't wait for Shane to answer before he entered.

"Wait." Shane leaped to his feet, cupping his dick and racing to her side, but his directive quickly drowned in the chaos that followed.

"Shane! You up, man? The town is tossed after the storm—" Eoghan stopped short just as Ayanna was in the middle of pulling the dress over her naked body. Her underwear lay right near Eoghan's feet.

Eoghan's eyes scanned them and the room, and his fists were clenched at his sides. "Get a ride in, did you, then?"

"Behave yourself." Shane pulled on a pair of jogging pants, but that was as far as he got before Eoghan grabbed Shane in some complicated hold around his head and neck and shoved him against the wall. That was the only advantage he got, as Shane wrestled him to the ground before restraining him.

"Stop, you fool," Shane yelled at Eoghan.

"Let me go, you fuck," Eoghan said.

Shane did, and Ayanna wasn't sure that was a good idea.

"Are you getting back at me for sleeping with your sister?" Eoghan accused her.

"What?" She looked from Eoghan to Shane and back again. "Uh, no."

"Then why'd you sleep with Shane?"

Ayanna thought of words that would help soothe and maybe not sound harsh, but only one thing came to mind. "There was a storm, and it was dark," she rambled.

"Right," Eoghan said. "You fancy her, then?" he asked Shane.

"It's more than that."

"What d'you mean, more?"

"I love her."

"Bullshit. When did that happen?"

"Neither of us wanted to upset you, least of all Shane." She took a breath.

Eoghan shifted his stance. "Is that why you took on my case? Because you wanted to be with Shane?"

Ayanna was surprised and offended that Eoghan would think that she would put his career in her hands just to be with Shane.

"No, Eoghan. Of course not. And I don't think that you truly believe that." She reached for him, and he stepped back. It was too soon for touch or reconciliation. "I took your case in the service of two friends. You and Dr. Finnegan."

Eoghan looked conflicted about what to say and turned on his heel and limped away.

Ayanna rushed to him. "You're limping? Did you hurt yourself?"

He turned on her. "Leave me the fuck alone."

"Come." Shane pulled her back.

"But he's limping."

"Give him a bit."

She picked up her underwear and paced. "This is a disaster. What have I done?"

Chapter Thirty-Three

Shane rolled his jaw, and the taste of blood, metallic and bitter, coated his tongue. The jujitsu hold Eoghan had gotten him into had been unexpected and hammered into his jaw. It was likely bruised, but he'd gotten in a few licks himself and bested his best friend in the row.

"How's your face?" she asked.

"Fine." He chewed to loosen the stiffening cheek muscles.

Ayanna went to the freezer and pulled out a bag of edamame. She rolled it to separate the bits inside and handed it to him. "Here, put this on it. It should feel better and keep the swelling down."

"Thanks."

Ayanna jabbed herself into a sweater. "We have to find him."

"Why?" he asked quite honestly. "He needs to cool off. We all do."

"Didn't you see him limping? He's made so much progress, and fighting with you may have reinjured him. Aren't you the least bit worried about him?"

Shane had looked after Eoghan most of his life, motivating him to do better at training. He'd even shown him how to best tie his boots when they had laces and needed to be tightened. He'd even forgiven him for Eileen. Now, when he'd finally followed his heart, again Eoghan fought him. "I'm sure he's fine. I've known him a long time. He's probably blowing off some steam."

Ayanna looked at the door and rolled her car keys in her hand. "How does he blow off steam?"

"Sex, drink, fight. He already fought, so he's probably seeking one of the other two."

"That's okay with you?"

"He's a grown man," he snapped. "You're very concerned about him."

"He's my client."

"Right."

"Spare me the jealous bullshit, please." Her exasperated smile made him feel petty as fuck. "Are you going to help me or not?"

He'd heard once that when someone's lover was in danger, they'd help them at all costs. Ayanna dropping everything to scour New York to find Eoghan was more than he could bear. He wanted nothing more than to let that tosser get himself together. Experience had taught him that Eoghan would show up pissed drunk or hungover, reeking of hours-old sex, get some rest, and then approach them with a clearer head, even if he was still a bit cranky. However, watching Ayanna worry unsettled him to the point that he found himself by the door, pulling on his trainers. "Okay, we can try a few spots we've been to together to see if we find him, but it's only to make sure he hasn't fucked himself."

Ayanna nodded. "Deal."

They buckled up and headed into White Plains. When they didn't find him at the first few spots, they drove south to the row of bars on McLean Avenue. He couldn't forget the last time he'd been here. He'd been with Ayanna and his parents at Saint Paul for his cousin's wedding. He'd finally given in to his feelings for her and touched her the way he'd wanted, the way she'd begged him to, and confessed his feelings to her.

"Shane?" She interrupted his thoughts.

"Sorry?"

"Where'd you go just now?"

"Thought of Maeve's wedding and the time we had." His mouth obviously had a mind of its own, because it didn't even give his brain a chance to make the decision. She drove in silence for the next quarter of a mile. "It was a great time, Shane," she said softly.

He struggled with the undertone of sadness in the statement. Did she regret what had happened between them at the wedding reception? Even worse, did she regret last night, even after the things they'd said and done to one another?

"I asked if you think he's at Molly's," Ayanna finally spoke again.

"In the city?"

"Yeah."

"Maybe," he huffed and adjusted himself in his seat, the passenger side suddenly becoming too small. "Do you mind the drive?"

She gave him a smug glance.

"Course not. We need to find your client."

"And my friend. We are all friends, aren't we, Shane?"

The classification stabbed him in the gut. "Do you fuck all your friends?" He regretted the words as soon as they came out and hated how he'd let his jealousy and fear rule him.

Ayanna stared ahead, her face as cold as stone. The steering wheel creaked under the pressure of her hands.

"I'm shit, Ayanna. I—"

"Don't." Her throat moved as if she'd swallowed a frog-size ball of emotion.

He needed her to know that he regretted his words, that he was sorry, but the moisture in her eyes reflected the Henry Hudson Parkway lights. He'd never expected to be the one to make her cry.

◆ ◆ ◆

Ayanna parked her car, leaving it to idle with Shane inside, and hurried toward Molly's. The cooler night had been a brief reprieve from the last week of humid August air and was now a welcome change from the stifling car ride with Shane. She was losing herself in him, wanting what he wanted, needing him around, and wanting him to choose her, like she'd chosen him in her heart. What had that desire gotten her? Her insides splintered, tumbling to the floor, and no matter how hard she tried, she couldn't scoop herself back together. Not without Shane. This was what she'd tried to avoid, and now Shane had insulted her, insulted what she'd thought they had by making her out to be some sort of random piece of ass making her way through him and his friend, even though he knew damn well she hadn't slept with Eoghan. She knew his past, but that didn't give him the right to assume she'd play him and Eoghan like Eileen. What was wrong with him?

She pulled open the door to the bar, hit by the fragrance of beer, and gave a silent prayer that she'd find Eoghan inside. Goose pimples blanketed her skin from the cool, air-conditioned air. The last thing she wanted was to continue scouring the city for him like he was some seven-year-old who'd decided it was time to pack up and run away from home. Besides, with Shane behaving like she'd cheated on him, her annoyance grew every second and was bound to come to a head.

Ayanna searched the bar and expelled a sigh of relief when she spotted Eoghan straddling a barstool. He clenched and released his fist as if stretching it from the altercation with Shane. However, he'd lost that fight, and Ayanna focused squarely on his leg. She made her way over to him, and he turned his head at her approaching figure. Realizing she'd found him, he shook his head.

"Hi, Eoghan."

"I'm not interested in anything you have to say, Ayanna."

"The only thing I want is to make sure your leg is okay. You were limping when you left." She stood next to him.

"So you're not even going to give me a story about you and Shane and how it was the worst mistake you ever made."

She searched her heart. She'd wanted to be with Shane, to share her body and soul with him. Even with his creative assumptions, she wouldn't take it back. "No."

"Why not?" he asked.

She pulled up a barstool and sat down. "Because it wouldn't be true."

He shifted his body to face her. "No regrets at all, Ayanna?"

"Only that it upset you and that you chose to fight your best friend." The revelation shocked her too. "Now you're here getting drunk—"

"I'm not drunk. I just needed to cool off and be among my clan." He drank some of the golden liquid in his pint glass. "A bit of home."

It hadn't occurred to her that a falling-out with Shane would cause him to feel homesick, maybe even alone.

"I care about you, Eoghan. We're friends." The last time she'd made that statement, Shane had tossed a whopper her way that just hung between them like weighted balls.

"Fuck all! I didn't know you felt for Shane. That you'd choose him."

"Why?"

"Because I like you, Ayanna."

"Yeah, but if we have mind-blowing sex—mind blowing on your part, I might add—do you want to move here and stay in a long-term relationship with me?"

"Fuck no!"

"Wow," she said. "I feel like I should be offended by that."

"Sorry. It's . . . I don't know. Maybe?"

"Exactly." She wasn't at all offended. "So you'll make up with Shane?"

"I will in me bollocks," he said and gulped his beer.

"But he's your friend who's been here the whole time with you, helping you get back to the game."

"Don't give a bollocks," he grumbled.

"If you use *bollocks* one more time, Eoghan, I swear—"

He gave a little chuckle.

"Do the right thing. That's all I'm going to say about that," she said. "But I do want to get you back to the house so that I can evaluate that leg."

"I'm fine."

"Did *you* go to seven years of school for physical therapy and work on world-renowned research?"

"You're taking the piss." He finished his beer.

"Obviously. So you comin' with us or what?"

"Us?"

She could have kicked herself for using the pronoun. In her opinion, she had him halfway out the door. "Shane is in the car waiting for us, but we just had our big-boy talk, and you're not going to get all bullish, are you?"

"I'll find my own way home."

"Come on. You don't even really want to be here, or else you'd be smashed." She lightly punched his arm.

"You think you have something with Shane?" He scoffed. "Good luck."

She rubbernecked and felt the scowl forming on her face. "Why do you say that?"

"Shane'll never leave Ireland or the Rovers."

"Oh." She didn't know what to say. The conversation wasn't supposed to trot down a path to Shane and whether he'd move to America for her. Nor was she asking him to. Had she even had the idea of asking Shane to leave his job? She hadn't thought about any of it because she'd been so wrapped up in her love for him. She'd even thought about how to continue her research away from the institute. Eoghan seemed to think that even the smallest hope of Shane wanting something more with her was ridiculous.

Eoghan's silence offered her a turn to probe.

"Do you love me, Eoghan?"

Eoghan rubbernecked. "I like you a lot, Ayanna. I guess I missed my chance."

"Eoghan—"

"I didn't romance you the way you deserved. Instead I was broken and trying to get back to who I was. Then when you first arrived to help me, I wasn't my best. Then I snogged your sister." Eoghan rubbed his face. "Shane's like my brother, Ayanna. He tells me everything."

"But he didn't tell you about this." She nodded and respected the place of hurt from which he spoke. "Eoghan, I think you're great, and I have always thought of you as a friend. That is, after that night in Dublin. You gave me a once-in-a-lifetime experience. Twice. Once at Aviva and a second time when you agreed to come here and let me help you get back to soccer. I am very fond of you."

"You and Shane." He tilted his head. "How'd I not see that one coming?"

"Look, what matters is that you're okay and that you haven't hurt yourself for your evaluation. If you do well enough, you can start your training in a month or two. It might still be a few months before you're back on the pitch, but this is it, Eoghan. Do or die."

"We're not in some film like your *Rocky*."

"No, we're not. This is real fucking life. Are you ready to stop fucking about and show them what you got, or are you going to keep sulking like a toddler over the fact that you didn't get what you wanted?"

"Brutal." He recovered quickly and stood up. "All right, but keep yer nose out of it with me and Shane. We'll sort it."

"Deal." Little had Ayanna suspected that she'd be wheeling and dealing to get Eoghan back home injury-free. "Come here."

She hugged his hard body and smiled, knowing that she'd been a part of helping him strengthen, heal, and condition those muscles. She separated from him and saw Shane standing by the door.

Chapter Thirty-Four

Ayanna's guilt had her shoulders slumped so low that her knuckles might as well have been dragging on the floor. She cared about Eoghan, but she was in love with Shane, and the two were fighting about her.

She didn't know how else to resolve the situation. She wanted to crawl back into Shane's bed and the warmth of his arms, but the house was in unrest and she thought it best to stay in her room and try to go on with business as usual. However, Eoghan's evaluation loomed. After the fight, she'd made sure he was physically okay, but he needed to be motivated to stick with it. In the morning, she'd give him a few words of inspiration to get his mind right, but what they all needed at the moment was a little distance.

A knock sounded on her door. She had half a mind to ignore it, whether it was Shane or Eoghan.

"Come in," she called.

Shane appeared in her doorframe and wouldn't meet her eyes. "Hey."

"Um . . . hi." Even out of sync, Ayanna's body gravitated toward him.

"I know you wanted to be alone, but I have someone here for you," he said, and Charlotte appeared.

"Charlotte." Ayanna gathered Charlotte in her arms. Seeing her friend was like a breath of fresh air. "It's so good to see you."

"I have literally been blowing up your phone to see how you made out with the storm, and when I didn't hear back from you, I was like, *Eff it. I'll just stop by.* Are you okay?"

"Yeah. We made it through okay." Ayanna looked at Shane, whose strained expression re-upped her stress levels. "Shane helped."

"I'm headed to the city. I'll probably stay there tonight," he said. The unspoken reference to Eoghan was clear.

"Okay," Ayanna responded.

She didn't want to see him go, and she didn't want him staying in the city tonight, but he'd made his disappointment and assumptions clear.

"Nice seeing you again, Charlotte," Shane said and turned to leave.

"That was intense," Charlotte said when Shane was finally out of earshot. "What's going on? It's like a morgue in this house."

Ayanna filled Charlotte in on what had happened, from the misunderstanding revealed to her at the wedding to the events of last night and this morning.

"Damn, girl. I told you to have fun, not create a romantic drama."

"Trust me, it wasn't intended." Ayanna exhaled with her whole body.

"To fall in love with Shane?"

"No," she sputtered. "I-I'm not."

"Yeah, you are," Charlotte stated too simply not to grate on her nerves. "Do you think Eoghan will get over it? I mean, if he was fighting with his buddy, then perhaps he really does have feelings for you."

Ayanna frowned. "I think he likes me as a person, but I think any objection he has to me and Shane is about his ego and winning."

"Well, you're in love with Shane. There is only one choice."

"They've been friends for years. You know that whole 'bros before hos' thing," Ayanna said. "It doesn't feel right."

"First of all"—Charlotte held up a finger at her—"not a ho. Second of all, I'm sure it didn't feel right when he was sucking face with Jada either. Remember that," Charlotte reminded her. "You deserve someone with dick restraint, Yaya."

Though there was truth to Charlotte's words, she still hated that Shane and Eoghan's friendship from childhood was strained over a woman again, and that this time, she was said woman. "I'm just going to try to handle business as usual."

"Business as usual? What are you going to do about Shane?" Charlotte asked. "I mean, you're in love with him."

"Stop, Charlotte. You sound like a parrot." The reality of the situation started to settle in. "He lives in Ireland, has work there. A life. I'm a workaholic who lives in the States."

"Here we go," Charlotte mumbled.

"I can't possibly have a real relationship with him. I let my desire override practicality."

"About damn time," Charlotte noted.

"He's going to leave, and I'm going to get hurt." Ayanna sank to the bed.

"There it is."

"There what is?"

"Yaya, Shane is not your dad. I was there when you lost him, Yaya. The fear of loving someone that hard, losing that love, and being so devastated like your mom has always held you back. At some point you have to take a worthwhile risk."

"This is ridiculous." Ayanna flapped her arms.

"C'mon, girl. Be positive. If you really want it to work, it can."

"How?"

"If I knew that, I'd be a rich woman. That's for you and the sexy ginger stick to figure out."

Ayanna huffed out an audible breath.

"Let's go out for some food."

"Hey, wanna stay over? With Eoghan angry at me and Shane in the city, it's going to get pretty lonely."

"You got it, sistah."

While Ayanna reviewed a few papers for Eoghan's evaluation, Charlotte used her laptop, and they both worked by the pool. The weather was changing, and the bit of brisk near-fall air mixed with that of the warm setting summer sun.

Eoghan appeared at the pool entrance. He didn't offer any greetings. "Can I talk to you, Ayanna?"

Ayanna glanced over at Charlotte. "Sure."

"Alone, please."

"Of course." Ayanna rose and followed Eoghan inside.

"I want to thank you for getting me this far. I know this evaluation will allow me to at least start training, even if it may take me months to be cleared for performance."

"You've been pushing hard these last few weeks. You're in a good position to show them you're ready. It wasn't an easy road, but I'm proud of you. So are we cool?" Ayanna asked.

"Cool."

"Will you be cool with Shane too?"

"We'll be fine. We just needed to let the steam out of the pot," Eoghan said. "Was she always this cute?" he inquired about Charlotte, who was still working by the pool.

"I see you're shooting for strikeout number three. She'll eat you alive, Eoghan. Even someone like you can't handle Charlotte."

"Really?"

"That wasn't a challenge. It was a true warning. Proceed with caution."

"I got it, Ayanna," he said. "I'm going to work out."

"Make me proud."

"Just as soon as I say hello to Charlotte," he said, gathering up his familiar swag and making his way to the pool.

Ayanna tsked. "Don't say I didn't warn you." She watched Eoghan approach Charlotte, whose irritation at being disturbed was visible from her spot several yards away. "Poor man."

She leaned on the counter and thought about Shane, dreaming about how things could work if she ever let herself truly love him without fear. Was she ready to give up the life she'd worked so hard for? Could she leave Jada, Charlotte, her mom, her team?

Tension squeezed her shoulders. She pulled out her phone and texted Shane.

Ayanna: Hey. Can we talk when you get back tonight?

Her phone buzzed a few minutes later.

Big Red: Won't be back tonight. Meet up at Eoghan's evaluation in the morn.

◆ ◆ ◆

The night tortured Shane with thoughts of Ayanna's body intertwined with his and the softness on her face as she surrendered to her desire. The things she'd said had him tossing and turning. Her haunting smell smothered him, aroused him, and made him miserable all at the same time. It had been bad enough that during the day his mind had drifted constantly to her sweet lips, her almost whimsical laugh, and how she never let him off the hook, challenging him to be better, healthier, happier. She should be in his bed with her head on his chest. Instead he lay on the couch in his cousin's empty apartment, the unfamiliar surroundings only adding to his distress.

Tomorrow was Eoghan's evaluation, and Shane had no doubt his friend would do well. He and Eoghan might be a bit on the outs, but it didn't even cross his mind not to attend the evaluation. He'd given his assessment, but his wasn't the one that mattered for Eoghan to return to the sport and eventually to Ireland, training, and performance. His friend still had a stretch to go but was well on his way. Shane's time, on the other hand, was up. With the friction in the house and his usefulness at an end, it was time to go.

He sat up as nausea gripped him at the thought of leaving Ayanna. He drank some water from a glass on the side table. He thought he'd won her and hoped that what he felt for her was returned, but her concern for Eoghan and the way she'd embraced him cracked his fragile confidence, and every insecurity and fear about being discarded again took the driver's seat.

His phone buzzed.

Yaya: Hey. Can we talk when you get back tonight?

Shane: Won't be back tonight. Meet up at Eoghan's evaluation in the morn.

She wanted to talk. *About what?* he wondered. To settle any doubt that despite what had happened between them, they were only friends? Maybe to ask him a professional question or set new boundaries in the house? Either way, he'd already made the decision. He opened his phone and navigated to the Aer Lingus website.

Chapter Thirty-Five

Ayanna's tense muscles wrapped her in stress like plastic wrap as she smiled and shook hands with Eoghan's coach; two trainers, one from the Rovers and the other from the national team; the team physiatrist, Daniel Finnegan; and Randall, their institute's lead physiatrist. All hands were on deck and had come to see Eoghan in action. With her other soccer clients she had never had this many eyes, and Eoghan's evaluation was for his return to the sport for training, not for performance.

"How're you feeling?" she asked him while he stretched.

"Hashtag blessed," Eoghan teased.

She relaxed a bit, because his boyish mischief was beginning to return after the incident with Shane. "Good."

"You all right, then?" he asked.

"Yeah, of course," she lied. She was so nervous for him that she might puke a frog, which was unusual for her. She'd been on stages giving talks, teaching, and working with clients for years. For the first time she realized just how personally invested she had become in Eoghan's recovery. Not just for her job but for his success, she wanted him to do well.

They were going to start in fifteen minutes, and Shane had not yet appeared. He'd said he would, and Ayanna prayed he hadn't changed his mind.

"Dr. Finnegan," Eoghan said, which jolted her back to the present.

"Looking well, Eoghan," Daniel said, then turned to her.

Shane arrived and spent a few minutes greeting the team, some with hugs, others with handshakes. Ayanna could almost feel Eoghan relax, and she knew it must mean a lot for Shane to be here when he could have opted out after being tackled by his friend.

Shane carried a ball in his hand, and as he approached their group, Ayanna recognized it as a ball from the house that had been signed by Eoghan, Oni, and Shane. There were only three in existence, one for each of the players.

"This is my one now." Shane tossed the ball to Eoghan, who caught it. "Ready, then?" Shane asked.

Eoghan nodded with a sly smile on his face. "I'm holding it now, sure."

Ayanna nearly clutched her chest at the tender moment between the two friends.

Shane nodded a greeting to her.

"Hi—"

"Daniel, a pleasure," Shane said, cutting her off to greet the team doctor.

She stared at him, but he wouldn't meet her eye. *Well, that's not very nice.* She'd give him the benefit of the doubt given the high stress of the evaluation, but he'd promised her a talk, and she'd be cashing in that promise later.

"Good to see you, Shane." Daniel shook Shane's hand excitedly. "Looking forward to your return to Ireland. The players are lost without you. Both of you."

What? Return to Ireland? When? Ayanna had always known that both men would be heading home when the time came, but was that soon?

"Sounds about right," Shane said, and Eoghan agreed.

Ayanna stopped her spin cycle and joined the conversation. "Looks like we're ready to start." She nodded to the team.

"Good luck, Eoghan," Daniel said.

Ayanna moved to Eoghan for a final pep talk. "Remember what I told you. Trust your body. You got this."

They gathered, and when the whistle blew to signal the start of play, Ayanna held her breath.

◆ ◆ ◆

Ayanna jumped out of a dead sleep when she felt something shaking her. "What the fuck?"

Strong hands steadied her, and her eyes focused on Shane.

"It's me." His accent was a thick whisper. He rubbed her shoulders.

Clarity arrived, even though her pulse still raced. She caressed his growing beard. "Are you okay? Is everything all right?"

He returned a strained smile and offered her his hand. "Will you come with me?"

She nodded. She tugged on her robe and stepped into her slippers. "Where are we going?"

Shane led her outside to the garden, where he always took her to relax. The air was warmer than the AC in the house. Nerves started to grip her, and her hands fisted.

"Sit with me, Ayanna," Shane said and offered her a seat and then sat next to her. "I'm sorry to wake you, but this couldn't wait. We have to talk about what's happened between us."

Nothing good could come of the seriousness in his voice.

"What's wrong?" she asked.

"I'm leaving for Ireland. Now that Eoghan is on the mend and his evaluation marks were good, there's no need for me to be here."

She stared at him for a long time until the words stopped rattling around in her head.

"Ayanna?"

She finally blinked. "Oh. When?"

"Tomorrow night. I'll be at my cousin's till then."

"That soon, huh? I thought you two would go back together." She was saying everything except what she wanted to say.

"I came at Eoghan's request, and . . . well, um, things have changed. Work calls me back." He tucked a wayward hair behind his ear.

"Which is it? Things have changed with Eoghan, or work calls you back?"

"Does it matter?" he snapped.

"It matters to me." Her voice got smaller with each word.

"Look," he said. "My departure will give everyone the space they need. Maybe I need the space too."

"Will you come back?" She swallowed the thick saliva building in her mouth and breathed. "I mean, won't you miss your family, your friends, Eoghan?" *Me?* she screamed inside, but what did she have to offer him?

"I'll only miss one thing about being here, and it's the one thing I can't have."

"Shane." She wanted to tell him she loved him, that they could be happy together, that she wasn't scared anymore, but she couldn't get any of those past the inner jail she'd crammed her thoughts and feelings into. Shane waited. The hope in his eyes tortured her like some diabolical device.

"Right. Well. I just thought you should know. I leave in the morning, so. Take care of yourself, Ayanna." He gave her a rigid hug and left.

What just happened?

Chapter Thirty-Six

Shane had been back in his apartment in Ireland a week, and his nights remained sleepless. Twice he'd fallen asleep only to wake up anxious, which he'd never wish on even his mortal enemy. Ayanna haunted his every thought, something he'd hoped would dissipate, but his longing for her only intensified with each passing day. The one thing that made being back the slightest bit bearable was the lush greenery and sun-bright day of fall in Ireland.

Training had been underway for a few weeks for the season starting in September, and he'd had to reacquaint himself with life back in the league as team liaison.

"Would you get out of that garden! Shane, man." Pippin ran to him and jumped into his arms as if he were scoring the last goal to win a cup trophy, wrapping Shane with strong limbs.

Though Shane could only imagine what he and Pippin looked like in the team dressing rooms, he'd missed his friend, and despite Shane's fuck-all attitude, he needed a hug. He slapped Pippin's back before tugging him away, and the man jumped off as quickly as he'd jumped on.

"How are ya, mate?" Pippin asked.

"Glad to be back in Ireland," Shane lied. Though he loved his country and had missed seeing the players and the people he cared about, being back savored less of home.

"Why'd you not say you'd be back? I thought you and Eoghan would return together. They don't tell us shite what's going on. Last news I got was gob chattin' with you canaries online." Pippin's excitement subsided by a hair.

"It was time to go," Shane said.

Pippin studied him, then put his hands on his hips, a reprimand building up from his yellow Nike boots to his head. "Make a bollocks of it, have you?" Pippin said at last.

Shane struggled. After a week of festering on his own, he needed to vent. He started to rattle off some details.

"Bah-bah-bah. We have training now. I'm going to need refreshments to hear of this holy show. Meet up later?"

"Craic on, then."

Shane went back to his job of scanning emails and texts for player requests. With Ayanna, he'd let his dreams and ambition soar to where he'd actually believed that he'd be a good gaffer one day. However, as he ended the day with a list of logistical tasks, he felt trapped.

Shane watched some of the training session to see the new lads and the old players feeling each other out. Every year the game changed, with less teamwork and more individual celebrities, but that was where a good gaffer came in. Win or lose, the players did it as a team.

"So I hear you've been inquiring after a few coaching positions in America," Boyle, their head coach, said, interrupting his thoughts.

"Gaff?" Shane asked, not sure he'd heard the words correctly.

"Thinking of coaching in America, are you?" Boyle asked.

"And where'd you hear that?" Shane thought it best to be cautious to learn what Boyle was after.

"Coaches around the globe talk. Just like the players," the coach said. "You could have come to me if you were interested."

"It wasn't a thing. Just asking about."

"The Rovers would hate to lose you as team liaison, but honestly, it's about time to try your hand at coaching a team of your own."

"What?" Shane craned his neck to see the coach's mocking expression but found sincerity instead.

"Everyone knows it, Shane, except you. That is, until the reference inquiries started. Your record and reputation as a coaching player and a leader are well documented."

Shane blinked his shock away. Apparently, he'd been an open book and hadn't even known it. All the times the players looked to him for leadership. Their wanting him to come out only to talk plays and strategies, even with Eoghan, their team captain, present. The time he'd wasted pretending that just being around the Rovers was enough.

"We don't have an opening until next year, when Rollie heads to the UK, but there are openings with some of the local clubs if you want to stay in Ireland. And as I'm sure you know, there is a spot on the national team's coaching staff available in the new year. That's a tough one, but prove yourself and you've a shot. Loads of people would put in a good word for you."

"You really believe all that?" Shane asked.

"Course. You've had a rough time of it since your injury. Trying to find where you fit in the game and all. I think this could be really good for you. So are you interested?"

"I'm interested, sure," Shane said.

"Good man." Boyle patted his shoulder. "And, Shane—to be a good gaffer, you have to take chances. So get comfortable with that, yeah?"

"Appreciate it." Shane shook his hand. "Thanks."

Shane headed to his office with a bit more spring in his step, even though the thought of working on logistics didn't tickle his balls. He had real prospects, not just inquiries made in America—now the Rovers' coach not only had him in mind for coaching jobs but was willing to put his reputation on the line and put in a good word for him. His excitement was short lived, as his mind drifted, as it often did, to Ayanna. She'd be happy to know about this new development, which was in no small part because of her. He wished he could tell her, not on the phone or in a text, but gather her in his arms, lift and spin her in happiness, and tell her how much he appreciated what she'd done for him. That he couldn't do any of those things gutted him. He sat with the feeling, his punishment for taking the easy way out, and dived into his liaison list of to-dos.

In the middle of updating the press schedule to make sure there weren't any conflicts with training sessions and press appointments, a knock sounded on Shane's office door. He looked up to see Dr. Finnegan's bright smile.

They exchanged greetings.

"When did you get back?" Shane asked.

"Few days ago. While I was there, I took some meetings at the institute and with Ayanna."

Shane wanted to bombard Daniel with questions. How was she? Did she get her meals in (because sometimes, when she was busy, she'd forget)? Did she still smell like rose petals and coconut? Did she know how much he missed her?

"How's the team?" Shane asked at last.

"Good. Since Eoghan's evaluation, his progress has accelerated, even as compared to the last three months. He's even starting some very light training. Ayanna and her magic hands strike again," Daniel said.

"Yeah."

Daniel eyed him. "You left for home in a hurry. Everything all right here? No emergencies, no?"

"All's well," Shane said.

"You three made a great team over there. I'm sure Eoghan and Ayanna feel your absence," Daniel said.

Shane wasn't sure. All he knew was, he'd folded his cards before seeing everyone else's hand. "No doubt they're getting on fine without me."

Daniel tilted his head. "Seems you're cocking a lot in the chamber. Anything you want to unload?"

He wasn't about to explain to Daniel his sordid tale of love and woe. He'd made his decision, and no matter how hard the mattress was, he'd suffer the aches and turmoil of lying in the bed he'd made.

"There's nothing to tell."

"Funny, that's the same thing Ayanna said." Daniel arched a brow, and when Shane harnessed all his energy to focus on the completed schedule, the physician hoisted himself out of his seat. "Bah! Probably just a coincidence. Well, I'm off to check on Santana's sprain. Always a pleasure."

Shane shook Daniel's outstretched hand. "Same, Daniel. Good evening to you."

The powers that be sure played him like a harp, and his emotions stayed on high alert, waiting for the next blast of news to shoot him in some unexpected direction. Best to be on his guard.

Later that night, Shane met Pippin at the Paddy Bath with some other players.

"Here's himself," Pippin sang.

"Lads," Shane said. His spirit had continued to tank, especially after he'd gotten the small kernel of information from Dr. Finnegan.

"Step into my office, deary." Pippin's khaki, orange, burgundy, and green plaid tracksuit pulled against his athletic build as he ushered Shane to a chair next to him. "Lance! Liquids for my patient. Stat!" Pippin said, patting the seat.

"No need to shout," Shane said. No sooner had he plopped into the chair than two pint glasses were placed in front of him from behind. He turned to see Fitz and Andreas from the Rovers cheesing at him. "What is it?"

"Smithwick's, of course, Your Grace," Fitz said, with a stiff upper lip.

"Go and whistle," Shane responded and took a long sip of his beer. He took a break to breathe, but Pippin gently pushed the glass back up to his mouth. "Forcing drinks down my throat's your plan, then?" Shane asked.

"You only truly start singin' after two pints, so we'll get you there in a hurry."

Lance arrived with a shot of something and another pint of something else. "Glad to see you, Shane. These"—he placed the drinks down—"are on the house. Heard you're up to your neck in it."

Shane reached for Pippin, who ducked him. "Telling tales?"

"We need all hands," Pippin explained.

"Fuck off," Shane mumbled but continued drinking.

One of the barkeepers came around with shots for them all.

"You didn't think we'd let you drink alone," Andreas said with his thick Spanish accent.

"According to Eoghan, you're an arse not worth a bollocks," Pippin said. "Still, he assured me things have cooled off some."

"I only saw you a short while ago. When did you talk to Eoghan?" Shane asked.

"I asked himself about this little love triangle not long after training. Grumbled quite a bit about me calling at an odd hour, but I needed to be prepared for this little meeting," Pippin said.

Shane should have known that Pippin, with his "look at things from all sides" mentality, would gather evidence.

"Well?"

"No judgment, mate. I'm all for listening to the juicy bits." Pippin winked.

It wasn't long after the drinks tainted his bloodstream that Shane blurted out the story that had been looping in his mind since he'd left. He rubbed his eyes, which were likely bloodshot by now.

"Crazy love," Andreas yelled.

"Pipe down. Can't you see I'm in session?" Pippin said and then returned his attention to Shane. "Eoghan's in America, your folks are in America, the girl you love is in America, and you're here getting rat arsed with me? That summarizes it, then."

Shane's attempt at smiling barely made a dent in his face.

"Feck all, I'm going to America," Pippin groaned. "And this girl built you up and encouraged you to go after coaching, as well?"

"You heard what I said, didn't you," Shane grumbled.

"What do you need, man? An invitation to your own life?" Pippin went to whack him in the head, but it was Shane's turn to hunker. "You're one of my best friends, mate, and Eoghan's the other, but from the start, Ayanna was never for Eoghan."

"What do you mean by that?" Shane asked. "He'd met her first, sure. I'd been getting in the way from the start."

"No. You've been running away like the spooked cat at Byrne's Farm. So." Pippin evaluated him. "You did your duty—or, as the Americans say, your dirty—and left before you got left this time. Now you have a heart broken. A lone bird."

"You after fixing the problem, now?"

Pippin shook his head. "That's your pickle to brine, Shaney, but seems to me you've some unfinished business to tend to. If it were me and I'd fallen, I wouldn't wait to get up."

Shane half smiled. "Okay, oul wisest."

"But whatever you do, I'm the wall behind ya."

He'd needed to hear that and appreciated the support. He'd never wanted to admit how lonely he'd been without Ayanna, even surrounded by Pippin, his colleagues, and the lads on the team. Pippin had lifted the mirror and shown him his sad state, though it wasn't like he hadn't a clue how he stood in front of misery. Nothing could replace her, and he might not have fought hard enough for her. The question was, What was he going to do now?

Chapter Thirty-Seven

Jada resembled her mother so much, not only in features but in mannerisms as well. It had been two years since Ayanna had actually seen her mother, Morgan, choosing mostly to stay connected when necessary by phone. Her mother had tried to build a relationship, but Ayanna had done the bulk of Jada's rearing as a child, as well as feeding, bathing, and clothing her mother. If it hadn't been for Charlotte and Charlotte's mom, Ayanna might have had a different life. So now, as she sat at the table with both Jada and her mother on the other side, it was clear not much had changed. Ayanna sat at the head of the table, the parent, meeting her twenty-one-year-old and fifty-five-year-old children for brunch.

"This is nice." Jada beamed. "How long has it been since we've sat together like this?"

"Never," Ayanna said.

"That's not true," her mother said. "We did it a few years ago when Jada graduated high school. Remember?"

"Sure." Ayanna mixed mayo and ketchup to have with her fries, and her mother watched her intently. "What?" she asked.

"Your father used to do the same thing. In fact, I think you picked that up from him. You've always wanted to be so much like him."

"Yeah, well . . ." What else could she say to that? She'd been eleven when she'd lost him, and though she remembered a lot, so many of her memories had faded to the point that she wasn't sure they were real. Given the distance she kept from her mother, who else did she have to go down memory lane with?

Her mother evaluated her. "You're a lot like him and favor him in so many ways, Ayanna."

"Since when do we spend our time together talking about Dad?"

"Yaya?" Jada used her own tone against her.

"Since I've been able to build up the courage to talk about him with you. I appreciate everything you did when . . ." Her mother straightened as if to summon the courage she'd mentioned. "When I was drowning. I lost myself and didn't know how to get help because people didn't know. Because you took care of us."

"So it's my fault that people didn't know because I kept counselors away?" Ayanna rocked in her seat as if dodging the anger trying to inflame her.

"No, Ayanna," her mother said. "We don't have to do this now."

Ayanna surveyed the light brunch crowd. "Why not? There's no time like the present to listen to you judge me for anything that happened back then." This was exactly why Ayanna kept her distance and restricted her conversations with her mother to surface topics that at max scratched her the wrong way but didn't inflict deeper wounds.

"All right." Morgan Crawford didn't cower at the challenge. "You were my brave girl, and like your father, you took care of everyone and everything, including yourself."

"Yeah, I did."

"But that wasn't your job, sweetheart. It was mine, and I failed you," her mother said. "Both of you."

"Yeah, you did." Ayanna folded her arms. Jada cut her another look, and Ayanna ignored her. "So what? Do you want me to just forget over a decade of pain and abandonment and bonus ten years of trying to reconcile these feelings in me?"

Her mother shook her head. "No. I'm still working on it too. I had to forgive your father for leaving us. I know it sounds strange."

It didn't sound so strange to Ayanna at all. Her grief and anger often swirled together to the point that they were indistinguishable from one another. Now, her mother voiced her own feelings, taking much of the steam out of her pot.

"I just want you girls to know that I'm sorry. I know I've said it countless times, but you girls turned out so well despite me."

"Thanks, Mom," Jada offered.

"Your father would be as proud of you as I am. More. I'd like to be more present in your lives, if you'll let me."

Jada reached for her mother's hand and then Ayanna's. "What do you say, Yaya?"

"I can try," Ayanna said.

"Come to the house—I'd like to show you the garden. It has all our favorite flowers."

Ayanna counted to ten. Instead of reacting to her mother's requests with short-tempered irritation, she listened to the voice she'd smothered within that cried for what it truly wanted. "I'd like that," Ayanna said. All wasn't forgiven, and she knew that any relationship she'd forge with her mom going forward would take effort on both their parts. Right now, this wasn't a bad start.

Ayanna listened to "Slow Burn" by Kacey Musgraves with a party-size bag of peanut M&M's on her lap. Her eyes, swollen and sore, burned with each blink. Brunch had tipped the scale on the emotions she'd been balancing since Shane's departure. She didn't bawl like she wished she would just to get it over with. No, the pain of Shane's leaving required more and more tears that failed to release her from her agony and kept the embers of loss smoldering. The song only helped snowball her emotions with the buried fits she'd suppressed for years and years.

One minute, she mourned for her father and for not understanding her mother more. The next, her anger boiled at her father for leaving, even though it wasn't his fault. Her guilt gripped her for not giving her mother the chance to truly be in her life. Ayanna had been too hard on Jada, the sister she loved as if she'd birthed her herself. Ayanna cried for her lost childhood because she had assumed the role of adult during middle school, when her hormones and growing pains were already changing her. She wiped her runny nose with the back of one hand. In an instant Shane's blue eyes shone at her like they did when she made him laugh. She'd learned two things about love early on in life. One, that great love existed, and two, that losing that great love was devastating.

She hadn't been born to help people. She'd been forced to, and that was all she knew. Thankfully, she had a knack for it, and because of that she was able to combine her love of science with repairing people's bodies.

Her door opened without her permission. "I don't want to talk—"

"I'm going to need you to kill the country. Great song, but you're taking it to a bleak address on the map." Charlotte turned off her Sonos portable speaker.

"I'm serious, Charlotte. I don't want to talk about it." Ayanna's body shook with an emotion she couldn't pinpoint.

"Okay." Charlotte's sad features reflected the mess she must have presented. Charlotte held her gently by the shoulders.

"He left." Ayanna shrugged. "He left me."

"It's okay, Yaya. It's okay." Charlotte pulled her into her arms. "Sounds like things got a little too crowded, and yeah, he's a punk for going back to Ireland, but did you tell him how you felt about him? What you wanted from him? Or were you thinking about your folks?" Charlotte inquired.

"What do you mean?"

"You said you didn't want to talk about it," Charlotte said.

Ayanna glared hard at her.

"Okay, Queen," Charlotte said. "It's just that you always push dudes away. Nowadays it's like we need to be crystal clear about what we want and who we want. Were you clear?"

"I don't know."

"Was he?"

"He told me he loved me."

Charlotte froze like she'd just been lowered into a cryotherapy chamber. "You know what? That is an extremely important piece of information to have. It's only because you're a weeping mess that I haven't cursed your ass out. Well, did you tell him how you feel?"

"I never said the words to him. I just . . . I wanted to, but I couldn't." Surely Shane knew that she had feelings for him. Didn't he?

"Yaya." The disappointment in Charlotte's tone tore her up even more. "Do you need a special card with checkboxes, *I love him, I love him not*, to prompt you to action?"

"I said something about us all being friends, and I guess maybe he took it wrong."

"That'd throw me off too. Just sayin'."

"Now he's gone."

Charlotte stood quiet for a long time. "So?"

"So what?"

More animated than usual, Charlotte paced the room. "So what the fuck are you going to do about it?"

◆ ◆ ◆

In her room, Ayanna stood over her bed and obsessed about the number of socks and underwear she had lined up on the bed. She'd been in a funk ever since Shane had left, and nothing that Eoghan or Charlotte did could pull her out. Not even her work and research helped. The time had long passed for her to regain the reins of her life. Even the gentle breeze from the window blowing against the fresh lavender she'd gotten from the farmers' market did little to calm her down. Was she really going to do this? She felt cliché, thirsty, and completely out of control.

A knock sounded on her door, and outside, the muffled chatter and whispers of what she could only assume was another intervention grew louder.

"Come in," she called.

Eoghan pushed the door open to reveal Grace in orange, Donal and Nadine in white, and Conor in green behind them. Ayanna wondered if the two couples realized that they wore their country's colors. "Hi," she greeted. "You all look very"—Ayanna paused with a smile—"patriotic."

Confusion showed on their faces until they looked at themselves. "Quite right, Ayanna. You know your flags," Donal said.

Eoghan shook his head. "The meddle crew has come to your aid."

"What?" Ayanna looked up from the outfits she'd organized and stacked.

Shane's mother came forward. "I've fallen in love with you, Ayanna. You've been so good to the boys. Hasn't she?" Nadine looked to the rest of her crew for affirmation. She wore her "old mum" fragrance of lily of the valley, rose, and iris.

"Yes, you have. I may not agree with Eoghan being here when he's got a great team of therapists and trainers in Ireland and—"

Grace quieted Donal with a wet-sounding shush. "We would have loved for him to be closer than America, but he's done so well so fast. We owe you a debt of gratitude."

"Thank you, but this is what I do, and Eoghan has been a great client." *When he wasn't cursing me out, eating shitty, drinking loads, and flaking on his sessions.* She shared a knowing smile with him.

He served her uneven brows. "I was a complete arse, Ayanna, but I cleared my evaluation thanks to you. You didn't give up on me," Eoghan said. "I owe you big. I also owe you the truth."

"What does that mean?" Ayanna asked.

Eoghan was quiet. "Listen, Ayanna. I wasn't exactly truthful when I said that Shane would never leave Ireland or the Rovers. I wasn't my best that day, but if Shane loves you, you're as lucky a woman as he is a man."

Ayanna frowned. If Eoghan started crying, she'd be beside herself. She latched on to his previous statement. "What truth?"

"Shane'll do anything for the people he loves. He'd do anything for you, Ayanna."

Ayanna felt her brows stretch up.

"Did you know, darlin', that he took two interviews for coaching positions right here in America? One in New York and another in . . . where was the place, Conor?" Nadine asked, seeking help from her husband.

"Washington, DC," Conor responded.

"He finally did it, huh?" Ayanna asked excitedly. "I thought he'd seek coaching positions in Ireland." Had Shane actually considered moving to America to coach as well? Her body had already been firing with nerves, but Nadine's reveal infused her with even more hope that she was making the right decision.

"Shane wants to coach? Football?" Eoghan asked. "Since when?"

"Since he truly accepted that he wouldn't be able to play again," Ayanna said.

"He mentioned it, but why did he not tell me he was serious about it?"

"You should ask him."

Ayanna felt a pinch of sadness for Eoghan that he hadn't known the extent of Shane's desire to coach, but Eoghan had been focused on recovering, and Shane had snuffed his own desires to support his friend. In more ways than one.

"See, Ayanna? My son loves you," Nadine announced.

"Even though she's not Irish." Donal tarnished the moment as he'd done on previous occasions. *At least he's consistent.*

"You two need to make it up," Shane's father said.

Ayanna lifted her phone to show them that she'd already bought a ticket to go to Ireland.

"You're going to Ireland? Might've told us that before we poured our guts out to ya," Eoghan grumbled.

"It was sweet. You all were." Ayanna laughed. "I feel like a fool about to make a big mistake."

"Not a fool's errand if you feel for Shane," Nadine said.

Tears welled in her eyes. "Soon he'll go back to his life, and I'll go back to mine."

"Really?" Eoghan watched her.

"Isn't it obvious?"

"Well, if you think that, then you don't know Shane."

"Let's all go to Ireland," Conor suggested. "We're heading back—all we need to do is get Eoghan a ticket. Surely since he passed his evaluation, he can have a small reward."

"We'll be on different flights, but we'll wait for you at the airport," Donal said. "You'll stay at our Dublin flat in case Shane puts you out into a driving rain."

"Da?" Eoghan's shoulders slumped like all his hard work had been destroyed.

"Encouraging," Ayanna mumbled.

"Pay no attention to me oul fella," Grace said.

"What do you say, gaffer?" Eoghan asked her.

"You have to be back for your last few weeks, but"—Ayanna tapped her chin—"I think it might be what we all need."

Chapter Thirty-Eight

Shane stepped into a soft day out of the national team's headquarters, feeling good about his interview and prospects. He'd been shocked at the reception he'd received when he'd shown up to discuss why he'd make a good coach for the team. His confidence had returned, but as he walked to his car, he realized none of this would have been possible without his time in America. Without Ayanna.

What good was a coaching position anywhere if he'd be miserable without her? He had to try to win her back. He had to make her see that they belonged together, that he wasn't afraid to trust her and believe unconditionally in their love. That she meant everything to him and nothing would ever feel complete without having her with him and making her happy. He'd been afraid to lose her, and even though he'd preempted what he thought would be the outcome, his worst fears had come true: he wasn't with the woman he loved.

The metro beat of Dublin had only been slightly dulled by the passing rain, and as he maneuvered through the streets without a destination in mind, he was only half-surprised when he found himself at Aviva Stadium and heading for the stands. He looked out at the freshly cut pitch, listening to the droplets of rain patter on the seating and the overhead partial dome. He'd been incomplete since he'd left America.

Ayanna had helped him get physically and mentally stronger without ever wanting anything in return. She'd let him go, and he replayed their time together and the way she'd smiled at him, the way she'd kissed him and loved on him. Love. Ayanna was in love with him just as much as he was with her, even if she'd been scared to say the words.

"Eejit!" he berated himself. Only a fool could only now see that Ayanna had been in love with him. She'd shown him her love, and maybe she was scared, but he was too. Maybe all she'd needed was time, and he hadn't given her that. Instead he'd pouted and fled the country.

"Balls up, O'Farrell." He took out his phone and booked a flight from Dublin to the White Plains airport. He didn't care if it took him five layovers—he'd see Ayanna as soon as possible. His chest filled with air like he'd been suffocating for the past few weeks. He loved his spot in the stadium, but the time for thinking had long passed, and it was time for him to crawl on his belly back to the woman he loved and beg her to forgive him and give him—no, give them—a chance.

He bolted out of his seat. He had some packing to do. The next sound he heard stopped him in his tracks.

◆ ◆ ◆

"Shane," she yelled. He moved so quickly through the stands that Ayanna had no idea if he heard her. She called him again as loudly as she could, because if she lost him in the stadium, she wasn't sure when she'd find him again. He finally turned, spotted her wild waving, and shaded his lids as if to focus on who screamed for him.

She made her way to him. Even with her excellent conditioning routine, she still had a challenge running up to the top level.

"Ayanna?" he yelled, his voice cracking slightly, when she got close enough for him to recognize her.

"Yes," she hollered back, continuing her climb, but he descended at lightning speed, which her lungs appreciated. He was close enough to touch now, but she hesitated. He hadn't expected her, and she didn't know where his feelings stood at this point with everything that had happened. But she needed him to know that she loved him and wanted to be with him. That was why she'd come all this way. She couldn't chicken out now, but her body stilled even as she panted, as if a force field surrounded him that she feared to penetrate. "I-I came to Ireland," she said.

Shane scooped her up in his arms and fell back with her on the steps. She lay on top of him, kissing him with abandon with no one but the birds watching them. "I love you, flower. I was a fool to leave. I'm sorry. I'm so very sorry."

"No. I'm sorry for not making it clear how important you are to me."

"I didn't want to push you. I know the possibility of losing someone is gut wrenching for you. I never should have left you. With everything happening, I only ever wanted to give you space and do the right thing for you, love. Please know that."

"I do, Shane. I needed to decide for myself to take the leap."

"I can't be without you, Ayanna. If you don't want to be with me, can we find a way for me to be in your life? Because I can't be this far away from you and be okay."

He was so good, and so good to her. "That's why I'm here, Shane. You're worth taking this chance for." He was it for her. "I know we don't know how to do this with you being based here and me in New York, but we can try, can't we, Shane?"

"Yes, baby. Whether we're here or in the States or both, we'll figure it out. So long as we have each other."

The passion in his promise tattooed her heart. She nuzzled her face against his red fur, and her tears wet his cheek. "I was afraid, and when you left"—she swallowed hard—"it felt like I was losing everything all over again."

"I'm in love with you, flower. *Tá mé i ngrá leat.* I'll never leave you again. I promise. *Tá mo chroí istigh ionat.* My heart is here." He pressed a hand on her chest. "I need you, Ayanna. I need you." He kissed her eyelids and cheeks and buried his face in the curve of her neck, breathing her in and pressing his lips against her skin.

"I love you so much, Shane." She squeezed him with all her might as if to leave the imprint of her body on his forever. "I'm yours."

Having him in her arms again finally allowed her to put to rest the haunting bones of her past and take a chance on love with Shane. She didn't have everything perfectly settled and resolved, but who did? She didn't, and neither did Shane, but they were stronger in love, together, than they'd ever be apart.

He helped her up, towering over her in the protective way that she'd come to love, and sat her down, his arms refusing to let her go.

"Look there," she said and pointed to Eoghan, his parents, and Shane's parents.

Shane waved, his laughter massaging her through her jacket. She wiggled her finger in his beard, one of her favorite caresses to share with him besides kissing his delicious lips.

"Your mom told me about you trying out for coaching positions with MLS. Why didn't you tell me?"

"Thought it best not to share in case no one took me seriously. Your encouragement when we talked made me feel like I could do anything." He pressed his forehead to hers.

She smiled. "Of course you can." She fought past their clothes and the seat to hug his middle. "I believe in you, and I know others do too."

They nestled into their new space, keeping each other warm and blissfully accepting each other for the vital piece they were to one another.

"Where were you jetting off to when I called you?" she asked at length.

"To DUB," he cooed, his nose tracing incongruent circles on her cheek.

She held his face enough to look into love-hazy eyes that made her insides bloom. "The airport? Why?"

He showed her his e-ticket to New York for a few hours from now.

"You were going back?" she asked.

"I was coming for you, Ayanna. I refused to spend one more day without you." He scratched his head. "Seems you beat me to it."

She laughed. "That's me. One step ahead of you slowpokes." She wrapped her arms around his waist, and he stroked her back. She looked up into his blue eyes, which shone just for her.

"Where are you staying? With the McKinleys again?"

"Your parents' Dublin flat," she said. "They're great in climactic situations."

"Speaking of climactic situations." He kissed her neck, his scruff tickling a laugh out of her.

"Shane," she called, but her hands encouraged his playfulness.

"Okay, we'll stop by there on the way to my place." He stopped and pulled her to her feet.

"Why?" she asked, still stuck on climactic situations.

"To get your things. Now that I have you, I'm not letting you out of my sight for a long while."

"I like the sound of that," she said, and just as the wonky weather of Ireland turned from misty rain to bright sunshine, so too had she and Shane made it through the storm, and their future together had never looked brighter.

Epilogue

Damn if this man doesn't know how to wear a fucking suit.

Ayanna held Shane's hand as they entered the ballroom, which was decorated in gold and white for the KPTA ceremony and dinner, but the grand space wasn't what held her attention. She stared up at him with heart eyes. He intertwined his fingers with hers, his thumb a constant caress on the back of her hand. She was overjoyed to have him with her, but nerves bubbled in her chest.

"All right?" he asked.

"Why?"

"Your hand's gone all sweaty." He jiggled their hand connection but didn't let her go.

"It's just that everyone is going to be here."

"Like you wanted."

"I know."

Everyone was there: Eoghan, Jada, Charlotte, her mother, Solomon, and others from the team. As the guest of honor she'd negotiated an entire table for her people. As she watched the full table, she reflected that she'd never imagined this moment in all her life. She had so many things to be grateful for.

"Are you nervous for me to meet your ma?"

"I didn't think I would be, but I guess so."

She'd decided to be a better daughter and give more of herself. After finding Shane, she felt like she understood how intense her mother's love for her father was, and she couldn't blame her for grieving, especially when Ayanna herself had fallen into despair when Shane had left. If it killed her, she'd be a more understanding daughter and hopefully be able to be closer with her mother.

Shane blew on her palm and then kissed her hand several times. "There's nothing to worry about. I'm here. Okay?"

She nodded.

"Have I told you you're a fleá tonight?" he teased.

She laughed and pulled him down for a kiss. "Love you."

"Love you more, flower," he said.

Shane had offers from both US and Irish teams wanting him to coach, and she'd agreed with the institute that if he settled on Ireland, they'd manage a way for her to be with him, even if that meant part-time travel to and from the US. Shane had also made plans to leave after the season and join her in the US if he chose to coach for MLS.

They were making it work, and she knew it was only because they respected and loved each other enough to do whatever they could to be happy and still be successful. She felt his eyes evaluating her and looked up into those dreamy blue eyes that made her panties drop without his even asking.

"There they are." Charlotte leaped out of her seat when she saw her and Shane. She hugged Ayanna.

"You okay? You're mad tense," Ayanna asked, concerned.

"I'm good," Charlotte assured her.

Ayanna looked at the table and saw a similar expression on Eoghan's face and wondered what had happened in the short time that they'd been there. The other quagmire was that she didn't know if what was happening was good or bad.

"You're sure?" Ayanna asked.

"Yeah. You look the fiercest tonight. Thanks for inviting me to this shindig. You know how I like nice things," Charlotte said.

"You know you were first on the list."

"I thought *I* was," Jada said, stunning in a red dress, and Ayanna knew without even asking that her sister would have after-gala plans.

"You both are," Ayanna said.

Her mother tentatively approached in a blue short-sleeve A-line dress. Her thin but older frame still looked amazing. "Is this him?" Morgan asked.

"Yes. This is Shane."

"Pleasure to meet you, young man. I hope we get a chance to know each other. You must be something special if my daughter chose you."

"She's the one that's special," Shane said with admiration that only he knew how to shower her with.

"I like him," Morgan said before sitting back down.

"Thank you all for coming. You don't know how happy it makes me to have you all here to celebrate this moment. I wouldn't be here if it wasn't for each and every one of you, and that's the truth." She choked on her words.

"You ready for this?" Shane asked.

She knew he was talking about receiving her award and her speech, but she was ready for so much more. "I'm ready for all of it."

The ceremony began, and when her award was announced, the room clapped for her. The table that sat the people she loved, in particular, cheered louder than the rest.

"Go get your award, baby," Shane said and kissed her lips with the tender love that she'd never tire of. She'd already won her award . . . and so much more.

ACKNOWLEDGMENTS

First and foremost, I thank God for his gifts and blessings.

A heartfelt and hearty thank-you goes to my magnificent and absolutely amazing agent, Sarah E. Younger. Thank you, Maria Gomez, for seeing my vision, hearing my voice, and working with me to share my stories. A special thank-you to my editor, Andrea Hurst, and the extraordinary Montlake editing and marketing teams for all your support throughout the process. Lastly, to Keisha Mennefee and the team at Honey Magnolia for all your hard work, thank you!

To my family and friends, thank you for your understanding, love, and support, as well as for helping me find balance through *all* the challenges so I could enjoy this journey. You guys are rock and roll.

Last but not least, to the readers and fans, thank you for escaping in these stories with me. I hope, whether in real life or through my books, you are surrounded by love.

ABOUT THE AUTHOR

JN Welsh is a native New Yorker. She writes entertaining, provocative, and often humorous tales about strong, career-driven heroines of color thriving and finding love in unexpected places. Her punchy, flowing dialogue and big-city stories warm the heart and stick to your ribs. She is passionate about practicing mindfulness for body and spirit through a holistic approach to self-care, routines, and rituals. When she's not writing, she can be found dancing, wining, rooting for her favorite baseball team, or indulging in one of countless guilty pleasures. Connect with her at www.jnwelsh.com.